EMBER IN SHADOW

Book Three of The Dragons of Mother Stone

MELISSA MCSHANE

Night Harbor Publishing

Cover Design by MiblArt

Night Harbor Publishing

www.nightharborpublishing.com

For Cordelia,
enthusiastic supporter of my writing and the model for Lamprophyre in
this book

AUTHOR'S NOTE: ABOUT DRAGONS

Dragons have six fingers on each hand, and the number twelve has a semi-religious importance to them. They measure the passage of time in twelvedays as well as seasons and years, and frequently count by dozens as well as more conventional base ten numbers (thanks to having ten toes on their feet).

Dragons measure time of day by the position of the sun: dawn, morning, mid-morning, noon, mid-afternoon, late afternoon, dusk/sunset. Time of night is measured by relation to midnight: dusk/sunset, evening, late evening, midnight, the dreaming hours, pre-dawn, dawn.

Dragons take approximately thirty years to reach adolescence and are considered adults at age fifty-five, though it can take another ten to fifteen years for a dragon to achieve her full adult size.

Dragon time and distance measurements are inexact and based on the average dragon body. The basic unit of time is the heartbeat, or beat. A dragon's resting heart rate is about twenty-five beats per minute, so a single beat is the equivalent of two and a half seconds, a hundred beats is a little over four minutes, and a thousand beats is almost forty-two minutes.

An adult dragon is approximately the same length and height (not including wingspan) as a double-decker bus, but slimmer. Their basic unit of distance is the dragonlength, which is somewhere between twenty-five and thirty feet long (counting from tip of the nose to tip of the tail). For smaller distances, they use the handspan, which is approximately twelve inches long. For long distances, they are more likely to measure by the length of time it takes to fly somewhere rather than how far it is in dragonlengths. A dragon standing erect is sixteen to twenty feet tall.

Adult dragons weigh between 4000-5000 pounds. An active dragon will eat, on average, 250-300 pounds of meat per day, plus a quantity of stone equaling another 8-10 pounds (sometimes less depending on the "richness" of the stone). Dragons generally eat twice a day, though in lean times a dragon will gorge herself on available food and then not eat again for several days.

An adult dragon can fly up to 120 miles per hour.

CHAPTER ONE

Lamprophyre perched atop the highest tower in the city of Tanajital and surveyed the landscape below. The last rays of the sun tinted the stone and plaster of the buildings orange, warming the city despite the coolness in the air. Winter was coming, creeping over the lowlands so slowly she hadn't realized the weather was changing until it already had.

She gazed past the city wall, built of pinkish granite blocks even a dragon would have trouble lifting. The fields that had been golden with crops last spring and then turned verdant green with the rains of summer were dry and bare now, waiting for humans to lay in new crops. To the west, the Green River ran slow and shallow, its name even less appropriate than usual as winter drew near.

She'd rather be home in the mountains for winter, her favorite time of year. Snow covered the bare crags, softening their lines and giving the dragons something to roll around in. When storms raged, the flight took shelter in the many caves dotting the peaks, some of them natural, some hollowed out by dragons over centuries. The females heated stones with their fire and made the caves cozy and comfortable, and the dragons entertained each other with poetry recitation or drawing on the walls. Sometimes the oldest dragons told stories of what they remembered, taking the flight's imagination back in time almost to the Great Cataclysm. Lamprophyre always remembered her father Aegirine at this time, how he'd buried her laughing in snowdrifts when she was small and flung snowballs at her when she grew too large to be buried. She looked forward to winter every year.

This year, she wasn't so sure. She hadn't seen any of the signs of winter she was accustomed to, just changes that might have meant anything. First, the constant rains of summer had lessened and then disappeared, drying the air slightly. Then the sun had gradually shifted its position southward, and the brutal heat had diminished with it. Now, only three twelvedays from the shortest day of the year, the sun no longer beat down with such punishing heat, and the nights actually verged on chilly.

Even so, chilly wasn't the same as cold, and there was no way snow would fall on Tanajital. Lamprophyre looked at all the landmarks she was now so familiar with. The palace with its dozen gilded roofs, tawny in the light of the setting sun, surrounded by a rich green parkland of trees and grass. The stone mountain of the city guard headquarters, a symmetrical pyramid of square segments that might have been cut from the granite by dragon claws, and the great plaza in front of it. The Archprelate's palace, low and squat except for the spire piercing its center, reaching for heaven. And, just north of where she clung, the dragon embassy, with its blue roof and matching painted decorations. She was too distant to smell supper cooking, but she imagined it anyway.

She let go of the tower and fell about a dragonlength before snapping her wings open to soar over the streets and houses of the human capital. Flying was wonderful no matter where she did it, but it was especially fun to listen to the excited thoughts of the humans below, just within range of her mental hearing. It had been months—she prided herself on finally understanding human measurements of days and time—since dragons had come to Tanajital, and almost all the humans were used to them by now. Lamprophyre rarely heard fear from them anymore.

She coasted above the wide street that ended at the embassy, which had once been a customs house for human trade, and landed neatly on the roof ridge beam to look down into the courtyard. There were more humans than usual, beggars come for a free meal, but Lamprophyre never knew why some days were busier than others. So long as the embassy had enough soup, it didn't matter.

She climbed down the rear of the embassy and entered the dining pavilion near the kitchen. Depik looked up when she loomed over him. "Five minutes, my lady," he said.

"It smells done now," Lamprophyre said, drawing in a big whiff of hot cooked cow, her favorite meal.

"It has to finish cooking outside the oven, you know I've told you that, my lady," Depik said with a smile.

Lamprophyre scowled, but half-heartedly. Depik's genius needed to be obeyed. "I know. I just hoped for once it would magically cook faster."

"I'm sure magic can't do better than me." Depik chuckled. "I'll bring it to you soon."

Lamprophyre proceeded to the main area of the dining pavilion and sat heavily in her accustomed place. Outside, Bhakriya was ladling soup into bowls, aided by young Rassika. "Good evening, my lady," Bhakriya said over her shoulder. "It's been a lovely day."

"If I were home, I'd be playing in the snow," Lamprophyre said. "It's so different here."

"What's snow?" Rassika asked.

"It's what happens when rain freezes. It's light and very cold, like frozen feathers."

Rassika's puzzlement deepened. "What's freezes?"

"It's hard to explain. It never gets cold enough in Tanajital for anything to freeze."

Rassika shrugged and picked up another wooden bowl. She'd changed so thoroughly since she and her baby sister Kavari had come to live with Lamprophyre it was hard to reconcile the clean, alert, helpful young woman with the dirty, frightened girl she'd once been.

Lamprophyre took a look around the courtyard. She didn't see any of her regulars, most of whom stood out in one way or another. Like Sumaan, the one-legged young man who'd been coming less often recently. Lamprophyre wasn't sure whether to worry about him or not.

Maybe it meant he'd found work and didn't need a free meal so often. Darsha, the Sister of the Red prostitute who spied on Lamprophyre for Crown Princess Tekentriya, wasn't here either. But Lamprophyre didn't worry about her at all. Darsha was clever and capable and was almost certainly busy with a client.

The idea of paying someone to have sex with you was still utterly foreign to Lamprophyre, and not just because dragons didn't use coin. She tried not to judge humans by dragon behavior. It seemed wrong and unfair to expect humans to do everything the way dragons did. But sex for dragons was tied so closely to mental communication, to the intimacy of knowing another's thoughts, Lamprophyre had trouble not being judgmental. She reminded herself again that her best friend Rokshan had had sex without being married and it didn't make him a bad person.

The thought of Rokshan made her wonder where he was. He'd left last night saying only that today was reserved for family matters, but she'd thought he meant the daylight hours and that he'd join her for supper as he usually did. Lamprophyre sat up straighter as the creak of trolley wheels signaled Depik's approach with her cow. It wasn't as if she wouldn't see him tomorrow. She'd just gotten used to eating with him in the evenings.

She tore into her cow with more alacrity than usual. Hot juices ran down her chin, and she licked up what she could manage and mopped the rest with a clean cloth Depik provided. He was more concerned about her dining manners than she was, saying frequently that ambassadors needed to set a good example. Lamprophyre had grumbled about her manners being perfectly acceptable among dragons, but she'd understood his point. So she used the cloth and pretended she was a dainty human eating soup in the palace dining hall.

She'd never actually seen the palace dining hall. It was deep within the palace, which wasn't built to accommodate dragons. But Rokshan had described it, filled with candles so it was lit bright as day regardless of the hour, the tables set in a U with the king and his family sitting at the base of the U and the guests spread out along the two long sides. The open space between was for entertainment, dancers or musicians or performing animals. Lamprophyre never wished she could be human

—the very thought made her scales tingle with disgust—but she did wish she could see the entertainments.

"Rokshan didn't send word he wasn't coming, did he?" she asked between mouthfuls.

"No, and we haven't seen him, my lady," Bhakriya said.

Lamprophyre grumbled to herself. Rokshan was a prince and the youngest of five royal children. His family had many duties associated with ruling Gonjiri. He might be her diplomatic liaison, but that didn't mean he could ignore all his other responsibilities. Even so, she looked forward to seeing him every day and it made her irritable when she didn't.

She tore off a somewhat larger mouthful of cow and chewed vigorously. "I suppose this ceremony has him preoccupied," she said when her mouth was mostly empty. "This pair-bonding thing...what did you call it?"

"The royal wedding," Bhakriya said. She released the ladle with a small splash and turned to face Lamprophyre. "It's so romantic. Princess Anchala and her betrothed from Sachetan...it's like a storybook romance, the way he swept her off her feet."

Rassika scowled. "I think it's silly. All that mush."

"You'll think differently when you're older, sweetheart," Bhakriya said fondly. Rassika scowled more deeply. "Falling in love is the most wonderful thing in the world."

Lamprophyre heard Depik's thoughts sharpen and realized he was listening carefully to this. She considered half a dozen leading questions before deciding there was no good way to approach what she wanted to know, which was whether Bhakriya's feelings for Depik were as deep as his for her. "For dragons too," she said instead. "My parents loved each other very much. I hope I fall in love like that someday."

"Aren't you in love with Porphyry?" Rassika asked. "He's here all the time."

"No, Porphyry and I are just good friends and clutchmates," Lamprophyre said. "I don't feel that way about any of the clutch." She listened to Bhakriya's thoughts, but heard nothing that might indicate she was thinking of Depik when she thought of love. Disappointed, she added, "But there are lots of dragons near my age. I'm sure someday one will be right for me."

"You just have to be patient," Bhakriya said. "I...it's not important. But love is sweeter when it comes slowly."

Asking Bhakriya to elaborate was probably a bad idea, given that her former husband had beaten her and tormented her, so whatever love they'd originally felt for each other hadn't lasted. Lamprophyre blocked out Depik's painfully clear thoughts and wondered, as she often did, whether it wasn't cruel to let him live in such close proximity to Bhakriya, if he loved her and she didn't feel the same. But it wasn't as if she could kick either of them out.

"I'll remember that," she said, and took a last bite of cow. "Rassika, would you fetch me a slab of mica? The courtyard is too full for me to safely cross."

Rassika nodded and darted away. Lamprophyre cracked a bone and sucked out the delicious marrow. Rokshan's absence aside, this was a beautiful evening.

She accepted the mica from Rassika and chewed the brittle, easily fractured mineral happily. It crunched like tiny bird bones in her teeth, but without the tickling sensation of feathers. Depik took the remains of the carcass away without comment and without looking at Bhakriya. Lamprophyre felt so bad for him. She'd been so sure Bhakriya would see Depik's wonderful qualities and fall in love with him. But now it seemed Bhakriya wasn't interested in falling in love with anyone. Lamprophyre wished she could pummel Bhakriya's former husband for hurting her so badly, emotionally as well as physically.

Movement at the mouth of the street caught her attention, and she sat up straight. "Rokshan!"

"Sorry about that," Rokshan said as he approached. "Lots of ceremonies today, all of them centered on the families meeting. It's important everyone receive attention according to their status, which means negotiations and politeness and I thought I might actually die of boredom."

"I thought your family outranked Lord Torannum's. Doesn't that make it easy?"

Rokshan lowered himself to sit beside her, his legs crossed under him. "You would think so, yes? But a woman who isn't heir to a title takes her husband's rank, and there's always dispute over when exactly that transfer of rank takes place. And Torannum, Jiwanyil bless him, has a very status-conscious mother and a father who defers to his wife in everything. So Lady Risha makes every ceremony longer with her 'are you sure that's how it should be' and her 'of course I don't know how you do it in Gonjiri, but in Sachetan...' and the way she clears her throat."

Lamprophyre settled back, amused, and took another bite of mica. "I didn't think there was more than one way to clear one's throat."

Rokshan rolled his eyes. "God's breath, Lamprophyre, the woman has turned throat-clearing into an art form." He stiffened his spine and put two fingers delicately over his mouth, and said, "A-*hem*," blurring the syllables so the word was barely intelligible. Lamprophyre laughed and wiped crumbs of mica from her lips.

"But Torannum is nice?" she asked.

"Very nice. He dotes on Anchala, but not in a servile way, and I think I like him best of all my brothers-in-law."

"I thought there was only one. Tekentriya's husband what's-his-name."

"Zekran, and you're not the only one who forgets about him. He's not a bad sort, just kind of a nonentity."

"I can easily understand how Tekentriya would overshadow anyone she's married to." Tekentriya, Crown Princess, was smart, powerful, domineering, and suspicious. It had been a surprise to learn she was pair-bonded at all, let alone that she had three children.

"Anyway, yes, he's the only living one. Manishi's husband Vorshan died of an illness years ago, and I disliked him intensely, if I can be allowed to speak ill of the dead—"

"You know that's not a dragon custom. Speak away."

"He was a braggart, and he and Manishi fought constantly, making everyone around them uncomfortable. They, of course, loved the fighting and didn't care what anyone else thought. I didn't wish Vorshan ill, naturally, but it was such a relief to have an end to the fighting."

Lamprophyre nodded. "I'm glad Torannum is a good man. I like Anchala."

Rokshan leaned against her flank. "And Dharan escapes his doom. Though just between us, I think Anchala was only interested in Dharan because he was a challenge. Torannum is a much better match for her."

"Will the...what did you call it? Will the wedding party come to the races tomorrow?"

"That's the plan, yes. Lady Risha demonstrated the first genuine emotion I've seen from her when my father told her about it. It seems she's fascinated by dragons. You might want to stay away from her, because she's the sort of person who would ask for a ride and not understand a refusal."

Lamprophyre shuddered. She swept the mica crumbs into a pile and pinched them into her mouth. "Thanks for the warning. What about Khadar? Will he deign to grace us with his presence?"

Rokshan tilted his head back. "He and the other High Ecclesiasts are performing purification rituals with the Archprelate, readying the training grounds to be a suitable location for a royal wedding. Though he did say the Archprelate was sorry to miss the races. She's fond of dragons, too."

Lamprophyre nodded. Shevaan, the new Archprelate, was only in her mid-thirties and much more active than her predecessor, who'd been very old when Lamprophyre had known him. Lamprophyre had met the new Archprelate a few days after the woman's appointment, if you could call being touched by Jiwanyil's light an appointment, and hadn't known what to expect. But the new Archprelate had a winning smile and a friendly, open demeanor, and had said, "Gonjiri is blessed indeed to receive such wonderful creatures. I hope you will feel welcome here." Lamprophyre, still smarting over several twelvedays' worth of insults and casual cruelties by ecclesiasts who'd felt themselves justified on religious grounds, smiled and bowed and said nothing. It wasn't this Archprelate's fault the former Third Ecclesiast had been corrupted by an evil entity into lying about prophecy, and Lamprophyre felt she could be generous.

"And Khadar's change of heart has lasted longer than I expected,"

Rokshan went on. "He and I had a civil conversation this morning, and he never took a single opportunity to lecture me on the evils of consorting with dragons."

"I thought all that was over."

"Over as far as official doctrine goes. There are still plenty of ecclesiasts who believe dragons should worship Katayan. And the truth is, that makes sense from a certain perspective. The Lonely God Katayan has dragons to worship him for the first time in nearly a millennium, so I can see how some humans might think the fact that dragons don't would be a problem."

"Just so they don't nag me, or threaten my friends again, they can think whatever they want."

Rokshan nodded. "Are you racing tomorrow?"

"Maybe once or twice. I'm out of practice. And no one's figured out a racing harness yet." Lamprophyre settled herself more comfortably, putting out a hand to keep from knocking Rokshan over. "Though none of us are sure we're comfortable with the idea. It's not as if we need riders when we race."

"I admit my interest is purely selfish. I like the idea of racing with you. I just don't want to worry about being thrown off." Rokshan yawned. "But I understand it might be undignified."

Lamprophyre laughed. "We're all too young to worry about our dignity. Except Chrysoprase, who is awfully stodgy for someone only twenty-seven years older than my clutch."

"I didn't know she was here. Will she race, too?"

"She and Massicot came down this morning to help build the obstacle course. It's going to be so much fun! Even if Chrysoprase is likely to win all the speed challenges."

Rokshan yawned again. "I should get back. I didn't realize how sleepy I was."

"You could sleep here," Lamprophyre pointed out.

"No, the ceremonies start at dawn. Much as I'd prefer to stay." He got heavily to his feet. "Give me a ride?"

"You must be tired if you're that lazy."

Rokshan made a perfunctory rude gesture in Lamprophyre's direction. "If you were in my place, you'd realize how exhausting all this social activity is."

Lamprophyre moved slowly into the courtyard, giving the remaining beggars time to get out of her way, and crouched to give Rokshan a leg up. It was almost full dark, and Depik had lit the lanterns illuminating the courtyard, but despite the dimness there were still plenty of men and women loitering. Lamprophyre flapped her wings a few times, hoping the humans would take the hint, then leaped into the sky, prompting a cry of exultation from Rokshan.

It had been a surprise to discover how much more she liked flying when she had a companion. It wasn't as if she were suddenly a more competent flyer, and as she'd said, dragons didn't need human direction to stay on course. But having someone to talk to was invigorating, and Rokshan loved flying so much it felt as if she'd discovered it all over again.

She dipped low over the palace, made a wide circle around the parkland as she descended, and alit neatly in front of the great front doors, closed now but still guarded by soldiers with halberds. Rokshan hopped down and said, "I'll see you tomorrow, all right? And let the others know Torannum and his family would like to meet them. I'll see if I can't impress upon Lady Risha the impropriety of asking to ride a dragon."

"We'll be all right," Lamprophyre said.

She watched until the great doors shut behind Rokshan before taking to the skies once more. With the light of the half-moon silvering the towers and rooftops, night flying wasn't very dangerous, not the way it was in the big open spaces between here and the mountains, but it still wasn't something Lamprophyre felt comfortable doing. And not because she felt unsafe; she had promised Hyaloclast, the dragon queen, that she wouldn't do it anymore, and keeping that promise felt important. Lamprophyre was sure that feeling didn't arise from her desire to please her mother, but instead came from a sense that the thrill of risking herself was...childish, perhaps?

In any case, she hurried back to the embassy and settled herself in the hall. The courtyard had cleared during her short flight, and no one moved throughout the embassy grounds. Lamprophyre closed her eyes and listened to the thoughts of her household. Depik and Bhakriya were in the kitchen, washing up. Rassika was behind the embassy where the servants' houses lay, putting Bhakriya's son Abhit and Rassika's sister Kavari to bed. They were just like a little family, and if only Bhakriya...but it was wrong to lay all of Lamprophyre's wishes on Bhakriya. If she didn't love Depik, that's all there was to it. And they'd all still care for each other regardless.

Lamprophyre sighed and lay down with her head pillowed on her arms. Time for her to stop wishing for the world to run her way and to accept the way it was.

She listened to the quiet sounds of washing and the idle thoughts of Bhakriya and Depik, both of whom weren't thinking anything more personal than how weary they were, but in a good way, the kind of weariness that comes from honest exertion and accomplishment. The courtyard dimmed further as the lights in the dining pavilion went out, and further still when Depik extinguished the lanterns flanking the embassy doorway. Then the night was still, with nothing but the distant hum of the living city to disturb the quiet.

Lamprophyre closed her eyes and made one last mental check of her human friends. Ever since the night, months ago, she'd been poisoned by someone who'd sneaked into the embassy grounds and tainted her food, she'd had worries about something like that happening again. Only her fears weren't for herself, but for the others in her household. So every night, she listened to their thoughts to assure herself they were well. The children were asleep. Depik was thinking of Bhakriya. Bhakriya was thinking of her daughter Preyanka, a young ecclesiast living in the Archprelate's palace while she learned to control her prophetic powers. Everything was fine. She let herself relax until she gradually drifted off to sleep.

She woke abruptly, disturbed by a sound she couldn't remember, something that in her dream had been two hands clapping once. Pitchy darkness surrounded her, far darker than night ever was, and she blinked as if that might clear her vision. In her confusion, she could tell only that she was surrounded by people—humans, they had to be humans because so many dragons wouldn't fit—whose wordless thoughts were sharp and intent on moving silently. "What—" she began.

Something grabbed her and *twisted,* making her scream in agony. All her bones grated against each other, muscles tore, and she tried to draw breath for another scream and found her lungs unresponsive. A high, keening whistle filled her ears, a shrill sound that felt like a needle drilling through her ears into her skull.

She felt as if she were falling, but the sensation went on and on without pause. Disoriented, she flung out her arms, desperate for balance. Her hands smacked the hard earth floor of the embassy. It felt strange, the surface grainier and rougher than before, and the smell of the dirt was distant, like the memory of a smell.

The hands wrung her again, and she smelled blood, faint as the smell of earth. She became aware that she was crouched on her hands and knees, and the floor still felt strange, as if she were suddenly aware of every particle on the clean-swept surface digging into her scales. The humans' thoughts intensified, and she heard *stop her screaming* and *wake the others* just as giant hands, far larger than any dragon's, took hold of her again. Someone shoved a large wad of cloth into her mouth, and when she reached up to remove it, those giant hands grabbed her wrists and hauled her to her feet.

She felt weak, so weak her legs wouldn't support her, and as off-balance as if her wings were frozen numb and unresponsive. She tried to break free of the giant, but then something struck her hard across the side of her head, and she saw sparks. *My eyes work fine,* she thought crazily, and then something smooth and cold touched the center of her forehead, and despite everything, she fell helplessly into sleep.

CHAPTER TWO

S he woke slowly, her dream fading into memory. Faceless shadows grabbing her, immobilizing her, and pain—

That brought her fully awake. One never felt pain in dreams. That had been real. She blinked, and saw only darkness, the velvety blackness that meant she was indoors rather than the shadowy dimness of a moonless night. Or...had she gone blind? She pushed herself onto one elbow, waved a hand in front of her face, felt the movement of air, but saw nothing. Panic gripped her, and she drew in a deep breath to mingle air with the fiery contents of her second stomach and let a gout of flame explode out of her.

But nothing happened. She didn't even taste the unique flavor of the burning liquid, hot and sweet and ashy all at once. Dismayed, she concentrated again, focusing all her attention on her stomach and willing it to expel matter or even just produce a hot burp. Nothing. It was as if her second stomach wasn't there.

She tried to sit up, but her arms shook so badly she went back to lying on the floor. It felt grainy and slightly warm, like her own embassy floor, but the smells were all wrong: musty and dank like large animals, horse or cow or ox or something like that. Faint, too, as if whatever animal had made them had been gone a long time.

The air was very still, another clue that she was indoors somewhere. Somehow, impossibly, humans had captured her and brought her to this place; it was the only explanation. They'd had an artifact to incapacitate her, probably a sapphire if history was anything to go by, and another to put her to sleep. There must have been many of them to carry her off. But why? Once she recovered from the effects of the artifacts, once her stomachs had settled, she would tear through this place and burn the humans who'd dared attack her.

Then she remembered the rest of her captors' thoughts, and fear for her human friends struck her. If they'd killed Depik and the others to prevent them intervening...they could do whatever they liked to her, but hurt her friends and she would see them all painfully dead.

She tried sitting up again and this time managed to make it to hands and knees, where she paused, trembling with pain and exhaustion. Her muscles and joints still ached from the artifact's attack, and she felt lightheaded—no, light and dizzy all over, as if she might float away if she weren't careful.

Finally, she pushed herself into a kneeling position—and nearly fell over backward when her tail didn't catch her. Confused, she felt around behind her and found nothing but empty space. Empty space... the panic that had subsided returned full force.

She ran a hand down her spine and let out a scream when her hand touched, not scales, but something smooth and warm that ended in round curves. Her tail was gone. Her scales were gone. She screamed again and found herself on her feet, teetering for balance. She flung out her wings to steady herself and felt nothing, just a shifting of muscles near her shoulder blades.

She ran her hands over her body, her legs and stomach and unnaturally large chest. She was *squishy* and smooth and her skin gave unpleasantly when she pinched it. Every nerve felt exposed, sensitive in ways she'd never experienced. She groped at her face, which was flat and bumpy, screamed again when she found hair straggling over her shoulders, and lost her balance and fell to the floor, banging her knees and scraping her outthrust palms. It was impossible, but it had to be true. Her captors had turned her human.

A line of light appeared, then another, and a door in the unseen wall eased open, sliding sideways to let in light from a lantern. Lampro-phyre closed her nictitating eyelids and let out a whimper when it turned out she didn't have any. She flung up an arm to protect her eyes and saw a dark human silhouette in the doorway, impossibly tall—but no, it was she who'd shrunk. The human brought the lantern forward, and light illuminated his face. He had shaggy black hair and a thick black beard obscuring his features, and his eyes surveyed her as if she bored him.

"Here," he said in a gruff voice, and tossed a bundle of cloth at her. It struck her chest and rebounded to hit the floor. "And food's by this door. Better get it before I take the light."

"What have you done to me?" Lamprophyre shouted. Her voice sounded unnaturally high and shrill, and speaking made her throat ache.

The man stepped backward, out of the doorway. "You got one minute, and then I shut the door," he said.

Lamprophyre rose to her feet and took a few tottering, unbalanced steps toward the man. "You dare lock me up," she said. "Treat me like an animal—let me go or I'll make you suffer."

A smile cracked the man's impassive demeanor. It wasn't a nice smile. "Like to see you try, girl," he said. "You want the food, better take it now."

Lamprophyre took two more steps and overbalanced, crying out in pain as she hit the floor. From there, she could see a battered metal tray bearing a flat round of bread and a tin mug of stale-smelling water. Hating the man with every step, she crawled the rest of the way and gulped down the water. Her mouth was an unfamiliar shape, and she spilled most of the liquid down her front. It was cold against her bare skin—skin, not scales!—but she got enough of it into her that it soothed her throat. She snatched the bread aside, picked up the tray, and swung it at the man's knees.

The man grunted in pain as the edge of the tray struck him. "Nice try, girl," he said, wrenching the tray from her hands as easily as if she'd been a newborn dragonet. Then he kicked her in the stomach, sending air whooshing out of her lungs. She curled in on herself, desperately sucking in air. The man nudged the bread with his foot until it rested against her face. Then, without another word, he closed the door, leaving her in darkness.

Lamprophyre lay curled on the floor until her breathing settled to only a little faster than normal. She took hold of the bread and sniffed it. It smelled of yeast and flour and, like everything else she'd smelled in this place, the scent was very far away even when she pressed her nubbin of a nose to it. Her stomach rumbled as the scent roused her hunger. Impossible. Bread was inedible to dragons. She breathed in the smell again, then tore off a small piece and put it on her tongue. The taste was incredible, cool and dry and doughy all at once, and before she knew it, she'd chewed the morsel and swallowed it down.

She clutched the flat, floppy bread to her chest and shuddered. She'd eaten bread and liked it. Her tail was gone and so were her wings. Her skin was smooth and sensitive and she was soft rather than hard. She pressed her fingers to her face again. Human. How was that even possible?

No wonder they'd been able to take her prisoner so easily. Humans were fragile and small, and human females—if she was female—were even more so than the males. They'd transformed her, put her to sleep, and carried her off to Stones knew where. She was lost and helpless and had no idea what to do next.

She bit off the next mouthful of bread and nearly choked on it when it turned out to be too large. Chewing more slowly, she managed to sit upright and take stock of her surroundings. An interior room, with no windows and presumably only one door—that was something she could investigate when she'd eaten. The smell of large animals still faintly permeated the room, so it might be a barn or a stable; she didn't know enough about animals to be able to guess more than that. She didn't know how long her magical sleep had lasted, or she might be able to figure out if she was still in Tanajital. As it was, she might not even be in *Gonjiri* any longer.

She was able to eat half the bread before her stomach protested at being over-full. She tucked the bread under one arm, reluctant to set it down when she might not find it again in the darkness. That reminded her of the bundle of cloth the man had thrown at her. She crawled into the open space, sweeping one hand before her in search of the cloth, but felt nothing but rough earth. Finally, she bumped her head against the wall. It was of rough, splintery wood that smelled dry and dusty. She ran her newly-sensitive fingertips along it, rising on teetering feet and reaching as high as she could manage, but found nothing useful, no closed windows, no loose boards she might break through.

Down on her knees again, she followed the wall, bumping against it with her shoulder occasionally to keep herself oriented. Before long, she came to a corner, where she repeated the process of standing and fumbling along the wooden wall. Still nothing. When she continued along this new wall, however, she almost immediately came to a third wall. This one vibrated when she ran head-first into it, as if it were thinner than the others. Confused, she trailed along beside it until she came to empty air. Why build a wall that led nowhere?

She sniffed. The smell of animals was stronger here. Stronger, like they had been kept in this place longer than the rest of the building. A memory occurred to her, an image of the abattoir when she occasionally went to get her food on days when Depik's illness overcame him. Humans built wooden partitions to contain animals. She hadn't paid attention to what they were called and didn't remember, stops or stands or—no, stalls. This was a stall. There were probably more of them. What good that would do her, she didn't know, but in dangerous situations, more knowledge was always better.

She explored the other stalls—there were four in all—before finding the heavier wooden barrier she guessed was the outer wall. Following that one led her, finally, to a door. Two doors, actually, with iron handles. She tugged hard on one handle, making the door shake slightly, but it didn't open. She thought back to the human who'd opened the door, and turned sideways and leaned away from it with all her weight. It barely shifted. Screaming, she hurled herself against it. Pain shot through her shoulder and arm and hip as they slammed into the door. The door didn't so much as budge.

Cursing her weak, frail human body, she leaned against the wall next to the door and set the half-eaten bread down. The door was a landmark, not a very good one, but enough that she would be able to find the bread again. Finding the cloth...what could it be? She was reluctant to give up anything that might give her an advantage.

She thought back to where she'd been before the door opened. Near the center of the room, she thought, and facing the door. She oriented herself as best she could and struck out again for the emptiness that was the rest of the room. Feeling about her, with her palms and knees abraded by the floor, she felt despair try to overtake her and ruthlessly pushed it away. She might be stuck in this awful human body, but she was still a dragon, and dragons didn't give up under any circumstances. But it was hard to remember that, especially when she realized her heart rate was faster in this form than in her dragon body and she couldn't even keep track of time by beats.

She didn't know how long it took—she tried to guess at how many human heartbeats corresponded to a dragon's—but it felt like forever before her seeking hand brushed against something soft. Snatching it up, she sniffed it all over, but smelled only dry fabric that didn't even smell of soap. The bundle was tied with a rope Lamprophyre tried to cut with her claws—the ones she didn't have anymore. Swearing at the inadequacies of this form, she picked at the knot until it came undone. The cloth came free of its bundle and cascaded over her hands and her lower body where she knelt on the floor. It felt like linen. She turned it blindly in her hands. It might be a blanket—no, it had gaps here and there. It must be a shirt or tunic or something.

She struggled to get it over her head, then struggled further putting her arms through the sleeve holes. Her flesh jiggled unpleasantly as she raised her arms. Breasts. Darsha had taught her the names for all sorts of human body parts. She was female, at least.

The tunic, or shirt, had sleeves that came past her elbows and a hem that went to the middle of her thighs. Another wad of fabric turned out to be too-large trousers with a string threaded through the waistband. She pulled on the string and found it cinched up the fabric around her waist so the trousers wouldn't fall down. Why her captors wanted her dressed instead of naked, which would make her even more vulnerable, she didn't know. What she did know was that humans felt more confident when they were clothed, and she would take every advantage she could get.

Wearing clothing felt so strange. Her human skin was much more sensitive than dragon scales, and the constant touch of fabric against that skin made her want to strip the fabric off again. She told herself she could endure anything her captors might throw at her, even how the linen shirt rubbed against her breasts, which were more sensitive than the rest of her. She squeezed one experimentally; it was heavy and squishy and shifted unpleasantly whenever she moved. She didn't know how human females put up with them.

She made her way back to the door and leaned against the wall. Anyone entering the room wouldn't see her immediately, and maybe she could scramble past the person and reach freedom, even if only for a few beats. Minutes. Seconds. Her grasp of human timekeeping had deserted her in this dark, timeless, horrible room.

She twisted the rope that had tied the bundle and then measured it out. Her hand was too small to serve as a handspan measure, but she used her forearm, which was slightly shorter than a handspan, and counted off lengths. The rope was perhaps five handspans long, which made it about five feet in human measurement. If she could tie the rope to the sides of the door, she might trip whoever came through... but there was nothing to tie it to, no convenient protrusions. Maybe she could tackle the person and use the rope to bind his feet or his hands. It was a slim possibility, but she refused to give in and be a victim.

She went back to exploring the room, walking slowly around its perimeter, testing her tailless balance, until she reached the door again. It was surprisingly large—though why surprising, she didn't know, because she had no idea what the size of the room meant to her captors. Maybe it was just the only suitable room available. The thought angered her, that she could think so civilly about the humans who'd taken her. If only she were herself...but of course, if she were herself, none of this would have happened. She settled herself next to the door, gripped the rope in both hands, and waited.

Time passed. Lamprophyre listened for thoughts, to see if there were humans nearby, but heard nothing but the thrumming of her blood in her ears. It occurred to her that she hadn't heard thoughts from the man who'd brought the food. Had she tried to hear them? She couldn't remember. She'd been so disoriented, maybe she just hadn't been listening. On the other hand, if she didn't have a dragon body anymore, would she even be able to hear thoughts? The idea brought the despair back full force, and this time she couldn't dispel it. Not hearing thoughts…that was almost worse than the loss of her body.

She heard the sound of metal rasping against metal, and the door began to open. Swiftly, Lamprophyre crouched, holding the rope wrapped around both fists with a length between them she snapped taut. A human stepped into the room, bringing a lantern with him. Lamprophyre pounced, wrapping the rope around his ankles and pulling tight. The human exclaimed, and the light swung wildly as he waved his arms for balance. Lamprophyre set her shoulder against his calf and shoved. With another cry, the man went down. The lantern hit the ground and shattered. The light went out. And Lamprophyre dropped the rope and darted past the fallen man, heading for freedom.

Cool air brushing her face told her she was outdoors, as did the welcome starry sky. No moon, so she hadn't been asleep for days, and the line of pale gold along the horizon meant it might still be the same night. Tall buildings rose up around her, some of them lit by lanterns affixed to their door frames. It felt like being at the bottom of a canyon, towered over by cliffs. But the buildings were spaced widely apart, too widely for this to be Tanajital, and Lamprophyre had to remind her panicking self that they only looked tall because she was so very short now.

Behind her, someone shouted, and then other voices took up the cry. Underneath the shouts, Lamprophyre heard anger and anxiety, and for a moment she felt relieved, because she hadn't lost everything in the transformation. But hearing her captors' thoughts was no benefit right now. Lamprophyre cast about for salvation. She couldn't enter any of these buildings, because she would certainly be trapping herself. She was shorter than the humans she'd seen and probably couldn't outrun them. That meant she needed to hide, but where?

Doors opened ahead of her, and men and women spilled out of the buildings to left and right. They caught sight of Lamprophyre and headed her way, their thoughts full of determination to catch her. Lamprophyre turned and ran to her right, where the fewest buildings were. There was a narrow passage between two of them, narrow enough that she almost shied away from it before remembering her current size. She bolted for it, hugging the annoying breasts close so they wouldn't jiggle, and dove for the alley just as her first pursuers reached her.

As she'd hoped, they didn't follow her. She didn't waste time looking back to see what they were doing, just ran, wincing when the ground tore at the soles of her bare feet. She burst from the passage, too late hearing the human waiting for her—and hands grabbed her, lifted her into the air and shook her until her teeth rattled.

"Fast little minx," the man said. He was unshaven and his breath smelled of stale onion. He was one of those whose thoughts mirrored exactly his words, and Lamprophyre could hear no indication of what he intended to do with her. She struggled to free herself, but he hoisted her over his shoulder and carried her away, ignoring how she beat at his shoulders with her tiny fists and the sound of her angry screams.

He carried her, not back to the animal building, but up three steps and through the door of what Lamprophyre thought was a house. She'd never been inside a house before, but she had seen chairs and couches and tables, and there were a lot of those in this place. The stinky man swung her off his shoulder in a dizzying arc and let her fall to the floor. She cried out in pain as she struck the wooden surface. It was smoother than the animal building wall, not at all splintery, but every bit as hard.

She sat, breathing heavily, for a few beats before pushing herself to her feet and heading for the door. She pulled up short before she reached it, seeing the stinky man and a hard-looking woman standing in front of it. "Let me go," she demanded. "Let me go, and I won't destroy you."

The hard-looking woman smirked. The stinky man laughed like she'd made a hilarious joke. Neither of them spoke, but the stinky man was still thinking *fast little minx* and the woman's thoughts were all *can't believe she was a dragon* and *not so big now*. Lamprophyre assessed her chances against them and knew they were impossible odds.

"How interesting, that you feel you still have power," a voice from behind her said. "You dragons are so arrogant—but then, you have no natural enemies, correct? So maybe it's not arrogance so much as conviction."

Lamprophyre turned around. There were stairs at the far side of the room, leading up, and descending them was the thinnest human Lamprophyre had ever seen. He looked like flesh stretched over bone, like someone who might snap if you breathed on him the wrong way. His bald brown head gleamed in the lamplight, sharp-edged with cheekbones like knife blades and deep-set black eyes dark enough that the pupils weren't distinguishable from the irises. He wasn't smiling, and despite the condescension in his tone, Lamprophyre felt he didn't actually care whether she was dragon or human.

She listened hard for his thoughts and heard the background hum of a human wearing a chlorite artifact to blur his thoughts. Fear struck her, fear that he knew her secret power and could defend against it. But no, she was certain that was a secret the dragons had successfully kept, and this was just coincidence. In desperation, Lamprophyre ran at the man, grabbing his wrist in the mad hope that he was thin and brittle enough that she could hurt him. She twisted, but his bones might have been dragon's bones for all they moved.

The skeletal man looked down at where her hand wrapped around his wrist. "I don't believe I gave you permission to touch me," he said, and tore her fingers free with his other hand. "Now, if you'll sit, we can talk like civilized people—something I hear you dragons pride yourselves on being." He turned away from her and crossed the room to sit on one of the low chairs.

Lamprophyre stared at him, her mind numb. She couldn't hurt him. She couldn't hear his thoughts. She really was helpless.

"Sit," the man invited, gesturing to a chair opposite his. Slowly, feeling like a sleepwalker, Lamprophyre walked toward him and sat.

"Why did you do this to me?" she asked.

"Ah, so we're not going to waste time with pleasantries. Good," the man said. "What makes you believe I'm the one who did it?"

"Because you don't act like someone who trusts his inferiors," Lamprophyre replied. She didn't know what prompted that response, had no idea whether or not she was right, but deep within her, she felt it was true.

The man's eyes widened. "Interesting," he said again. "I think you're guessing."

"Am I?" Lamprophyre said. "You used two artifacts on me. One of them put me to sleep. The other...did this." She swept a hand down herself. "It's no guess to know you want something from me. So what was the point of this transformation?" She felt dizzy again, swept along on a tide of words spilling out of herself that made her sound confident and in control. It was a lie.

The skeletal man tapped a finger against his lips, a gesture Lamprophyre had seen her friend Dharan make countless times. "Very well," he said. "I want something from you. Something simple. But as everyone knows, dragons are invulnerable to almost everything, and keeping a dragon captured is virtually impossible. So...this transformation, as you put it, was necessary to compel your cooperation. Give me what I want, and I'll turn you back."

Lamprophyre clasped her hands together to control their furious trembling, not wanting him to interpret it as fear. "And what is it you want?"

The man leaned forward. "I want your dragon hoard," he said.

CHAPTER THREE

Lamprophyre's mouth fell open. "You...what?"

"I need money to fund my magical experiments," the man said. "I know dragons are wealthy. Give me your hoard, and I'll turn you back—once me and mine are safely away, of course."

"But...who told you about dragon hoards?"

The man shrugged. "Irrelevant. Now, do we have a deal? Or should I return you to the stables until you become more compliant?"

Lamprophyre shook her head. The urge to scream warred with the urge to laugh. "I'm sorry," she said, "but you've been misinformed. Dragons don't have hoards."

The skeletal man's eyes narrowed. "You do realize your fate is in my hands," he said. "No one knows where you are. In that body, you're vulnerable to pain, injury, and death. Defying me is a very bad idea."

"I know very well I'm at your mercy," Lamprophyre said. "It's still true. Dragon hoards are just a story humans made up—"

"*Do not lie to me*," the man shouted, erupting from his seat and making Lamprophyre cringe involuntarily. "I know from an impeccable source that dragons have access to gold, gems, valuable magical minerals. You *will* give me your hoard or you will suffer!"

Lamprophyre made herself sit up straight and gaze fearlessly at him, though she was painfully aware of how much taller he was and how mad he looked. Such a man might do anything. "I cannot give you what I do not have," she said, enunciating precisely, "and you are wrong to try to coerce me. Why can't you earn money the way everyone else does? If you're an adept, you need stone—you could trade with us for that. You don't need to kidnap me."

The door opened, drawing both their attention. A woman shorter than the hard-looking woman at the door stepped through. "Master Evart," she said, "the dragons are on the move."

Lamprophyre's heart leaped. Evart walked away from her a few steps. "Are they headed this way?" he asked.

The woman shook her head. "They're circling over the city." Her thoughts weren't fearful, just alert, as if she were capable of fighting dragons as an equal. Lamprophyre longed to have her body back so she could teach the woman a lesson about fighting dragons.

"We should move out anyway. We've been here too long." Evart turned back to look at Lamprophyre. "Time to choose, ambassador. Give up your hoard, or give up your freedom."

Lamprophyre glared at him in silence.

Evart shrugged. "Bind her, and put her in the wagon," he said. "We'll head west at dawn."

Lamprophyre rose and backed away as the stinky man came toward her with his hand outstretched. "Don't do it," she warned. "Once I'm free, I will make you suffer."

The stinky man smiled. To her surprise, it was a friendly smile, as if she'd just offered him a treat rather than a threat. "You're a real spit-fire," he said.

Lamprophyre gasped as he grabbed her wrist and spun her around, securing first one, then the other hand behind her back. Rough, ticklish rope went around her wrists, and then he hoisted her once more like a sack of grain over his shoulder and went through the door held open by the hard-looking woman.

The line of light along the horizon had brightened, but lanterns were still needed to illuminate the buildings. Now that she wasn't running for her life, she could look at her surroundings more closely. Lamprophyre knew what farms were, and she guessed this was one, either abandoned or the property of someone who agreed with Evart. Or maybe it belonged to Evart himself. If he wanted money, he could sell this place instead of abducting dragons for ridiculous reasons.

Lamprophyre, bouncing along over the stinky man's shoulder, wished she had some means of attacking him. Biting his ear or his neck, maybe—she tried twisting around, but couldn't bring her head in range of his. His thoughts were unexpectedly friendly, and it made her furious.

The stinky man swung her off his shoulder and laid her, almost gently, in the bed of a wagon. Barrels and sacks that smelled of grain filled the back half of it, and Lamprophyre used her feet to scoot herself against them so she could sit up. As she did so, a huge dark shape settled over her, and she felt canvas press against her head. Why they needed to protect the cargo when there was no rain on the horizon anywhere, she didn't know...or was it she who needed protecting, say, from the keen eyes of dragons searching for her?

She scooted down a little so her hair didn't rub so uncomfortably against the canvas. The space beneath the canvas was dark, but light coming through an opening at the foot of the wagon made it less oppressive than the animal building had been. Her wrists were sore and her shoulders ached from having her hands tied behind her back, but she ignored the pains and examined her surroundings more closely, looking for a way out. The barrels didn't smell of anything, even water, so maybe they were empty. She wasn't sure she could do anything with that fact. The smell of grain dust filled the air, and if she had her second stomach she could make it blaze bright. She grimaced. Time to stop thinking about what she didn't have.

She heard people running around, and low-voiced conversations as if they were afraid someone might overhear them. Lamprophyre strained to listen, but heard only murmurs, and their thoughts were incoherent, the sound of dozens of people in close proximity. Despite her resolve, fear crept over her. Her friends would have no reason to suspect she'd been transformed into a human, unless Depik or Bhakriya had seen something—but she couldn't count on these people having left her human friends alive. Better assume no one knew her current form. And for all the dragons knew, Lamprophyre might have gone off on a night flight, or a gleaning trip. They might not start worrying until it was race time and she didn't show up.

But no, the woman had said the dragons were moving. It was too early for the clutch to start racing, or even to get ready for racing. If they were moving over Tanajital, it had to be because they were searching for her. But they would be searching for a dragon, not a human woman. That would take them so far astray it was impossible they would ever find her. She needed to figure out how to free herself.

She began working at the ropes tying her wrists, but couldn't find the knots to untie them. Grumbling to herself, she looked around for some sharp protrusion, a nail or a sharp piece of metal. The interior of the wagon was clean and well-kept, and it smelled of varnish, which suggested it was new; no chance of finding anything out of place. Finally, after wriggling over the entire wagon, she lay back on a grain sack and sighed. If she wanted to escape, she would have to wait until they moved her out of the wagon.

The light coming into the wagon was almost bright enough for her to see the wagon's contents. She wiggled into a more upright position just as the wagon lurched, then moved forward, bumping her painfully into one of the barrels. She wedged herself against it and spread her legs to brace herself further. Wherever they were going, she hoped they reached it quickly.

The wagon jostled her along for longer than she could keep count, either in dragon or human measurements. Despite the movement, she drifted into a hazy sleep, semiconscious and imagining that she was flying through a warm, dry, dust-smelling storm that shook her with turbulent winds. Rokshan was there, but silent, and she'd begun to worry that he was dead when the wagon came to a halt, waking her fully. Her hands felt numb and her eyes were dry and painfully itchy. She blinked rapidly to moisten them. It was full day, and light filtered through the weave of the canvas as well as through the opening at one end.

Outside, she heard running footsteps again, then shouts. Then the shouts turned into screams. The incoherent thoughts became panicked. Lamprophyre heard the heavy, unmistakable sound of dragon wings, and she added her screams to those of her kidnappers, though joyful instead of terrified.

She wriggled her way toward the opening, thinking maybe in the commotion no one would be watching her. Above, beyond the canvas, the light grew orange and then gold. Lamprophyre realized what that meant in time to flatten herself into the wagon bed as Coquina's fire engulfed the wagon.

Lamprophyre had never felt the ferocity of fire before. Hot air parched her skin and filled her lungs, and the canvas caught fire. Breathless, Lamprophyre flung herself at the opening, desperate to get free before the flames consumed her. She rolled out just as the canvas disintegrated into a flaming mass that landed on the wagon's contents and started them burning as well. Lamprophyre drew in a cool breath untainted by dragon fire and lay with her face pressed to soft grass. No one shouted anything that might have been a warning that she was escaping; no hard hands grabbed hold of her to drag her away.

She rolled onto her side, realized there was nothing she could do in that position, and awkwardly got to her knees. Everything was in chaos. Dragons swooped overhead, taking turns making runs across the kidnappers' procession, which turned out to be several wagons drawn by horses that were either panicked or dead. The stink of acid filled the air, and little fires burned here and there on the ground. A couple of wagons, including hers, were on fire.

Someone grabbed Lamprophyre by the arm and hauled her to her feet. "You will get me out of here," Evart said. His face and clothes were singed, but he seemed unharmed. In his other hand, he held a slim wand that ended in long, thin claws at one end. Those claws clutched a fat rod of a green and black mottled stone Lamprophyre recognized as serpentine, half a handspan long and roughly faceted like a prism. Evart held the wand loosely, as if he'd forgotten it was there.

Lamprophyre tried to pull away, but his grip was implacable. "Turn me back, and I'll convince them not to kill you," she said.

Evart laughed. "You lie. You'd never let me go."

"Dragons don't lie. Release me."

Evart tugged on her arm and made her run with him, ducking and dodging the crippled wagons and the panicked horses. "If I die, you'll never return to your true form." He gestured with the wand. "You don't know how to use this."

"You're mad. This can't have been your whole plan—turn me human and extort money from me! Where did you even come up with such a ridiculous idea?"

Evart's grin was manic. "Night thoughts," he said, "ideas that come to you on the verge of sleep, like a little voice in your head whispering truth."

A chill struck Lamprophyre. "*Like* a little voice?" she said. "Or *actually* a little voice?"

A red wall dropped out of the sky before them. Lamprophyre screamed in terror and stumbled backward, dragging Evart with her. In the next breath, she recognized Porphyry. He was *enormous*. She'd been bigger than him her whole life and now he towered over her, wings spread, black acid dripping from the corner of his mouth. His wordless thoughts were filled with fury.

"Where is she?" he boomed, his normally pleasant voice deep and menacing. Lamprophyre, stunned, stared up at him, mute and terrified.

Evart looked at Lamprophyre, his expression confused. "But it should have worked. I was promised it would work," he said, mostly to himself. Then he took the wand in both hands. "Better a dead man than a live tool," he said, and snapped the wand across his knee.

White light flared, and something punched Lamprophyre in the chest, flinging her backward to slam into something hard and angular. Something snapped, sending pain coursing through her left arm. Barely conscious, she tried rolling away from the angular thing and managed to fall face-first to the softer ground. Grass filled her mouth and nostrils, and she coughed and raised her head. The pain in her arm was a dull ache so long as she didn't try to move it, and when she did, more pain shot through her, making her dizzy and sick. She lay still and concentrated on breathing.

Someone grabbed her arm—her left arm—and hauled her to her feet. She screamed at the pain and struggled to get away from her captor. To her surprise, the person let her go, thinking *didn't hurt her*. Beyond the pain, the thoughts sounded familiar. Lamprophyre took a couple of stumbling steps and crouched, head bowed, sucking in air and trying not to fall over.

"God's breath, you're a captive," Rokshan said.

She jerked upright and stared at him. Rokshan had drawn his belt knife and was approaching her slowly, his other hand spread wide to show he was no threat. His hair was a mess and soot covered his face and shirt, but he looked unharmed. He was taller than she now, something she observed with wonder—tiny Rokshan, taller than a dragon... a dragon in a human body, so that wasn't so strange... She realized her thoughts were running in mad circles and closed her eyes to make herself focus.

"It's all right," Rokshan was saying, "hold still and I'll free you." She felt the cold metal of the knife slip between her wrists, and then the ropes fell away. She opened her eyes and rubbed feeling back into her hands, then stopped doing that when another sharp pain shot up her arm. Rokshan was looking at her as if she were a stranger, and it felt as if he'd plunged that knife into her chest.

"Rokshan," she whispered, "it's me."

CHAPTER FOUR

Rokshan's eyes narrowed in puzzlement. "Do I know you?"

A tangle of emotions filled her, sorrow and fear and even embarrassment, as if their friendship was irrationally diminished by his inability to recognize her no matter her form. "I—he transformed me," she stammered. "It's me. Lamprophyre."

Rokshan blinked, uncomprehending. He took a few steps forward, his gaze fixed on her eyes. Then horror crossed his face. "*Lamprophyre*," he said, reaching for her shoulder but letting his hand fall before he touched her. "God's breath, what did they do to you?"

"He transformed—" She shook her head, clearing away the last of the confusion from being flung into whatever it was. "The wand," she breathed. "He broke the wand." She pushed past Rokshan and ran toward where she'd seen Evart last, her left arm folded across her chest.

Porphyry was gone. Part of Lamprophyre's awareness registered this, and wondered if he was all right, but the rest of her attention was on Evart. The man lay sprawled on the ground in the center of a bare circle of earth perhaps half a dragonlength in diameter. His eyes were open and staring at the sun in a way impossible for a human. Nothing was left of the wand.

Lamprophyre dropped to her knees and felt around with her right hand, hoping madly that her fingers might find the remnants of the wand where her eyes couldn't. Maybe the wand was broken, but the serpentine stone was still intact. The stone was what mattered, yes? An adept could put it back together if only she had the stone.

"Lamprophyre, what are you doing?" Rokshan said. He crouched beside her and put a hand on her shoulder. Lamprophyre wrenched away and continued searching. She fumbled through Evart's clothes, searching for the stone—maybe it had tangled in his shirt or embedded itself in his flesh. She found a quartz pendant streaky with chlorite inclusions attached to a chain around his neck and yanked it off, clutching it without being conscious of what she held. No serpentine.

Over her shoulder, she said, "He had an artifact. It gave me a human body. We need to find it, or what's left of it—"

"The wand he broke," Rokshan said. "I was about thirty feet away when it happened. He snapped it in half, and it released all its energy—Lamprophyre, it's gone. It's gone."

"It is *not* gone!" she shrieked. "We have to get it back—I can't live like this, don't you understand! I can't live in this horrible human body, with its hair and squishy parts and this *nose* that doesn't work right!" Her eyes ached and felt swollen, as if they were going to pop out of her skull, and she didn't understand why. She didn't understand a...a damn thing about this stupid human form.

Rokshan gently touched her shoulder again. "We'll find another artifact," he said. "If someone made it work once, someone else can do it again. It will be all right, Lamprophyre."

The pressure eased, and her eyes were suddenly hot and wet, with water trickling down her face. Tears. Humans cried when they were miserable. It was surprisingly soothing. At least one thing about this ridiculous body wasn't awful.

"We need to make sure Porphyry is all right," Rokshan said. "He was right next to the blast, too." He helped Lamprophyre to her feet and guided her away from Evart's body, toward where the dragons had gathered around a recumbent crimson form. Fear for her clutchmate made it impossible for her to fear for herself, and she ran with Rokshan toward the others.

"...just see double for a while," Porphyry was saying as they approached. He was lying on his side with his wings folded away beneath him. He didn't look injured, though the scales on his belly were a strangely mottled orange.

"She's not here," Orthoclase said. "We should have left some of them alive."

"She *is* here," Coquina said irritably. She wore an iridescent stone on a thin chain around her neck and an expression of extreme displeasure. "The stone is clear about it. I don't know why we trusted Manishi."

Flint glanced at Rokshan, then stared more closely at Lamprophyre. "I guess we did leave someone..." His voice trailed off, and he leaned close to Lamprophyre, peering at her face. *No*, he thought. "Stones," he swore. "It's you."

"What?" Coquina exclaimed.

"Her eyes...Lamprophyre, what happened?" Flint exclaimed.

"That man transformed my body into a human's," Lamprophyre said, feeling like crying again. She sniffled, wiped her eyes, and added, "I think he got the idea from someone else. Someone old and evil."

"But...how is that even possible?" Orthoclase said.

"The artifact had a serpentine stone," Lamprophyre said. "I was looking for it—"

"Everyone sniff around," Flint said. "Maybe it's not broken."

Dolomite grunted and bent to pick something up. He displayed a jagged shard of green and black stone. "Is this it?"

Lamprophyre sank to the ground and buried her face in her hands. "It's not enough."

"We don't know that," Flint said. "We'll ask an adept. Someone will be able to recreate it."

"That's what I said," Rokshan said.

"We can't," Coquina said.

Lamprophyre looked up at the enormous grass-green dragon. "Why not?"

Coquina looked grim. "We can't let anyone know dragons are vulnerable to this kind of attack. Anyone who wanted to hurt a dragon would be able to, with nothing more than that one artifact.

Stones, we can't even let people know it's happened to Lamprophyre!"

"But I can't stay in this form forever!" Lamprophyre exclaimed.

"I know. We'll have to figure something else out." Coquina crouched next to Lamprophyre. "We'll put it to Hyaloclast. She'll have a better idea of how to handle the politics."

"But she doesn't know anything about magic," Rokshan said. "We absolutely have to talk to an adept."

"But who?" Flint said. "Obviously not Manishi. Sabarna?"

"Sabarna is smart, but she's not a practicing adept, and I think creating one of these artifacts might be beyond her." Rokshan started to pace. "And we can't ask around, looking for someone who is capable, without giving the secret away. This is a thousand times worse than kyanite."

"We can start by finding out if people do other things with serpentine," Flint said. "I'd never seen it before."

"Neither had I," Lamprophyre said.

"I don't understand how you know what it is if you'd never seen it before," Rokshan said.

Lamprophyre drew in a breath. "Dragons know stones. It's something that's bred into us. Every stone, everywhere, regardless of whether it's a stone that's found where we live. There's no serpentine in our mountains, so we need to know if it's even a stone humans here know about." It should have cheered her to realize there was one more part of her that was still dragon, but recognizing stone seemed useless.

Bromargyrite, who'd been silent this whole time, stirred. "I can find that out," he said. "My adept contact still believes he's using me for information, and he doesn't know I can hear his thoughts."

"It's a start," Lamprophyre said, taking a few steps toward Bromargyrite. She moved her left arm the wrong way and hissed at the sharp pain.

"What's wrong?" Rokshan asked.

"My arm hurts. I don't know why."

Rokshan gently ran his fingers along her forearm, making her wince. "It's broken."

Lamprophyre blinked. "It's...dragon bones don't break." She grimaced. "And this isn't a dragon body. What do I do?"

Rokshan let out a deep breath. "We have to get you to a healing center quickly, before your natural processes start working on mending that bone. And after that...you can't stay at the embassy, and you can't survive a winter in the dragon caves. You'll have to live somewhere in Tanajital." His eyes widened. "In the palace."

"I can't live in the palace!" Lamprophyre exclaimed. "People will figure it out."

"No one will believe you're really a dragon, not the way you look," Rokshan said. "You'll be a guest here for the royal wedding. Maybe a distant relative. But we'll have to tell my father. Look, I know it's not ideal," he went on, fending off the dragons' protests, "but if the dragon ambassador just disappears, he's going to worry. He needs to know the truth. I promise he'll be discreet. He needs this alliance."

"I don't like it," Coquina said, "but you're right." She looked over her shoulder in the direction of distant Tanajital. "We need to clean this mess up. It can't look like dragons were here. And then somebody needs to tell Hyaloclast what happened. This isn't something we can communicate via the chalcedony artifact—we actually need to fly home."

"Not you," Lamprophyre said. "You'll need to be acting ambassador while I'm...let's see...gone home for the winter festivities."

"What winter festivities?" Dolomite said, looking puzzled.

"The ones we don't have," Lamprophyre said, "but humans will believe are a possibility. It's pretending, right? We're all going to pretend I went home for the winter, and that Coquina is in charge."

"I'll fly back," Orthoclase said. "But we have to clean this up fast, because the races are this afternoon and we need to act like everything is well."

"Stones, I forgot about the races," Lamprophyre said. "This is a nightmare."

"Flint, you and Dolomite take Rokshan and Lamprophyre back to the city," Coquina said, "then hurry back here. Lamprophyre, can you meet me at the embassy tonight? I really don't want your job. Too much diplomacy."

"It has to be a female to seem legitimate," Lamprophyre said. Her various aches were catching up with her, and she wanted nothing more than to fall asleep somewhere, preferably somewhere her arm could be fixed. "I'll be there at suppertime—oh, Stones, we can't tell my household the truth!"

"It's all right, Lamprophyre, I'll take care of them," Coquina said. "Now, get moving." She turned away and began tearing up the turf where acid had splattered long, jagged lines of black burn marks.

Lamprophyre looked up at Flint. He looked even bigger up close than Porphyry had. "I don't know," she said.

"Hurry, Lamprophyre, unless you want that arm to heal the slow way," Rokshan said. He had already climbed up into the notch behind Dolomite's shoulders.

Flint crouched low so Lamprophyre could climb up. One-handed, it was an ordeal to get herself settled, but finally she had a firm grip on Flint's scaly ridge and her knees clasped his shoulders tightly. "Hang on," Flint said, making Lamprophyre grab on more securely, and with a mighty thrust of his legs, he launched himself skyward.

Lamprophyre bit back a scream. Suppose it startled Flint, and he dropped her? She'd always loved flying under her own power, but this— this horrible, uncontrollable flight, all that empty air beneath her, terrified her more than being trapped in a human body had. She clutched her broken arm to her chest and focused on the back of Flint's head. No looking down. No wiggling. No letting go of the death grip she had on Flint's ruff. She forced her breathing to become calm and told herself it would be over soon. Rokshan was mad to think this was a wonderful way to travel.

She didn't realize they'd reached Tanajital until Flint banked slightly to pass a tower, tilting her sideways. She shrieked and grabbed for Flint with both hands, then yelped as the movement jarred her broken arm. "What's wrong?" Flint shouted. "Are you hurt?"

"No, just...get us there quickly," Lamprophyre said. Once again she made herself breathe slowly. Flint wasn't going to drop her, she wasn't going to fall screaming to her death, everything was fine.

They landed outside the palace, within the ring of the parkland circling it. Rokshan helped Lamprophyre down and kept a steadying hand on her right elbow when she reached the ground. "Tonight, at the embassy," he said.

"Take care," Flint said, and then he and Dolomite were gone.

Rokshan smiled reassuringly at Lamprophyre. "It will be all right," he said.

"Don't lie to me, Rokshan. This is bad."

The smile fell away. "It's bad," he agreed, "but we'll figure it out. And I won't abandon you."

"I know." Lamprophyre sighed. "Where do we go now?"

"The healing center." Rokshan tugged on her uninjured arm. "Everything else can wait."

CHAPTER FIVE

Past the parkland, humans thronged the streets, pushing and jostling and shouting at each other, their thoughts as much a din as their voices until she blocked them out. The sounds and movements made Lamprophyre feel sick and a little afraid. This must be what it felt like to be human and towered over by a dragon. She was nearly a head shorter than Rokshan, who she knew was of average height for a man, and it felt as if everyone she passed was taller and broader and heavier than she. She drew closer to Rokshan, using him as a shield, and tried not to let anger overcome her. She hated Evart for what he'd done to her, and for such a stupid, selfish reason.

But it hadn't been his idea, had it? She'd forgotten, in the chaos of deciding what steps to take, what Evart had said. "Little voices in the night," and something about how someone had promised him it would work. A little frisson of fear overrode her anger briefly. She'd heard that little voice in the night. It was the voice of their enemy—an ancient evil nobody knew more about than that it had corrupted one of Jiwanyil's own High Ecclesiasts and had a plan that would lead to utter destruction.

"Rokshan," she said, then spoke his name more loudly when he didn't hear her over the din.

He looked down at her. For a moment, he looked confused, as if he'd forgotten who she was. Then his expression became so neutral it made Lamprophyre feel sick again. It was the face of someone who'd seen his companion fatally wounded and didn't know how to tell her her fate. He took her hand to keep her from being buffeted away by the crowd. "Are you all right?"

"No. I mean, nothing new—never mind, we can talk about it later." This bustling, noisy, smelly crowd wasn't the place to discuss anything important.

The air was thick with dust and the stink of human bodies packed close together. For the first time since her transformation, it felt like her sense of smell worked properly. She wished it didn't. A lot of humans all in one place smelled sour and sweaty, the least pleasant odor Lamprophyre had ever smelled. She clung to Rokshan's hand, which was firm and a little rough—this body felt *everything*, as if she'd been skinned, except that would be painful and this was just unnerving —and looked around at the buildings. It was so different seeing them from this perspective, even the shortest ones much taller than she, looming over her as if they might fall and crush her.

She cringed away from a donkey that nosed her broken arm, hating herself for being so fearful. Dragons weren't afraid of anything. This was temporary. She wished again that Evart were alive, this time so she could boil the flesh from his bones. How *dare* he do this to her?

Rokshan tugged on her hand to guide her across the street, weaving between pedestrians who didn't pay any attention to them. She'd thought Rokshan was recognizable within the city, but everyone they passed looked intent on their own business. If they acknowledged him, it was with a grunt or a muttered word that might have been apology if they bumped into him. Rokshan ignored the other humans and led Lamprophyre to a low, squat building whose door was the color of green jade. There were no windows, nothing to indicate what the building was, but Rokshan opened the door with no hesitation.

Inside, the air was fresh and cool and smelled not of a musty, enclosed space, but of the outdoors. Lamprophyre couldn't understand it, because the place where they stood was a hallway with no other doors at this end but the one they'd entered by. A light breeze touched her cheeks, bringing with it the scent of cut grass like she'd only ever smelled in the parkland around the palace.

Rokshan drew her along after him down the hall to another door. This one had a big square hole cut in its top, large enough for Lamprophyre to climb through in her current form, and light came through the hole along with another breeze. Rokshan pushed this door open as well. "It's quiet today," he said. "They must not be very busy."

"Is that good?"

"In the sense that people aren't hurting, yes. They'd still care for you even if there were fifty patients waiting for treatment."

Lamprophyre followed him through the door, then stopped, amazed at what she saw. The room—if you could call it that, because it was as big as her embassy—was open above to the outdoors, with roofs circling a central garden through which flowed a tiny stream. Short, clipped grass covered the hilly ground, and stone benches dotted the low rises here and there. Most of them were occupied by pairs of men and women, apparently doing nothing but breathing in the warm, grass-scented air. Their thoughts were peaceful, even the ones that were tinged with pain. The soothing calmness relaxed her.

Wide patios surrounded the garden, and more people walked or sat beneath the sheltering roofs. Lamprophyre smelled the faint odor of blood, and watched as a man whose arm was a bloody mess took a seat in the shade next to a woman wearing a black sleeveless tunic. The woman held something in her right hand that she passed over the wound, and weak green light that would have been invisible in full daylight leaked between her fingers like iridescent water. Lamprophyre slowed to watch, but Rokshan pulled her along. "We don't have much time," he reminded her.

They circled half the garden before Rokshan approached a man dressed in the same black tunic. "My cousin broke her arm," he said. "Can you help us?"

"Have a seat," the man said. His skin was darker than Rokshan's, almost dark enough for him to be Sachetanese, but his accent was that of Gonjiri. Lamprophyre sat and extended her arm to him. He gently ran his fingers over the length of it, pressing down only slightly, but enough to send more pain shooting through it and make her gasp. "Sorry," the man said. "Wait here. I'll need an assistant."

Lamprophyre held her broken arm as still as she could manage. "Why does he need an assistant?"

"I don't know. I know very little about healing." Rokshan took a few restless steps around the bench, making Lamprophyre turn to watch him. He was looking at the sunny open grassy place, but his eyes were unfocused, as if he weren't actually seeing it.

"Rokshan," Lamprophyre said, then realized as he turned toward her that she didn't know what she'd intended to say. Talking about evil entities intent on cataclysmic destruction felt wrong in this beautiful, peaceful place. "Never mind," she said. "We should talk privately."

"Right," Rokshan said. He sounded distant and distracted, and the knot of fear in Lamprophyre's stomach tightened. She had never felt so small and alone.

The man returned, followed by an elderly man with thick white hair and a face so wrinkled his eyes and mouth were almost invisible. "My name is Rutin, and this is Harod. Harod will hold the bone in place, so sit still and this will be over in no time," the first man said.

"Give me your arm," Harod said in a creaky near-whisper Lamprophyre had to strain to hear. His touch was smoother than Rutin's, and when he took hold of her wrist and her arm just below the elbow, she felt barely a twinge of pain. Rutin held up something small that gleamed like jade—it was jade, and again Lamprophyre told herself to be happy that she'd recognized it deep within herself as she always did stone. She couldn't smell its clean, almost soapy scent, but she'd nearly resigned herself to the failings of her stupid nubbin of a nose.

Rutin extended the jade to Lamprophyre to examine. It was a flattened oval carved all over with letters that spelled out no words Lamprophyre was familiar with. "This produces healing magic that resonates with your body and alters it according to my intent," Rutin said. "It's not painful, but it may itch. Try not to wiggle."

He palmed the stone in his cupped hand and ran it over Lamprophyre's arm, not quite touching her skin. Pale green light leaked from between his fingers, like sunlight seen through trees. An itching tingle spread wherever the stone passed, ruffling the very fine hairs on her arm—Stones, humans were hairy!—but otherwise not having any obvious effect. After a few beats—seconds—Lamprophyre's arm felt as if tiny invisible bugs were crawling around on the delicate, sensitive skin. She clenched her teeth to keep herself still. Harod was the first human Lamprophyre had seen she felt she could physically resist, but she was afraid of what might happen if she pulled away from him.

Gradually, the itching subsided, as did the pain, the light faded, and Rutin took a step back, pocketing the jade. "There," he said. "See what you think."

Lamprophyre wasn't sure what he meant, but Harod let go of her arm, so she moved it back and forth and then felt along it with her right hand. No pain. She let out a deep breath. "Thank you."

"Anything to help," Rutin said. "Mareet will take payment. Have a nice day, your highnesses."

"But—" Lamprophyre began. Rokshan squeezed her shoulder gently in warning. "Um...thank you," she said.

Mareet was a round, rosy-cheeked woman with dark hair piled on her head and a sweet smile. "A sad accident, yes?" she said to Lamprophyre. "I'm glad we were close enough to help. And you'll be here for the wedding, I imagine. How nice."

"Yes, I...look forward to it," Lamprophyre managed.

"That injury would have put a damper on the festivities," Rokshan said, withdrawing a handful of coin from his belt pouch. "And we really should be getting back. Sorry to rush off."

"It's no trouble. I'm sure your family is very busy." Mareet smiled and put the coin into a metal box that wasn't locked or secured in any way. Lamprophyre wondered if that meant healing centers didn't worry about robberies.

"Busy is an understatement," Rokshan replied with a grin. "Let's go, La...Lelitha."

Lamprophyre, blinking at the sudden acquisition of a human name, let Rokshan tow her along behind him, out of the healing center and back into the busy street. "Lelitha?" she said when they were surrounded by the crowd.

"It was the first name that came to mind that started with L."

Rokshan looked embarrassed. "I knew a woman named Lelitha once. I think it's a pretty name."

"Oh. A woman you had sex with," Lamprophyre said, enlightenment dawning.

"I panicked, all right? Let's walk in the parkland for a bit. We need to make a plan."

Lamprophyre had never understood why the parkland, abutting so closely on one of Tanajital's main streets, was almost always empty of humans. She knew it was considered the royal family's property, but there were no walls to keep people out of it, and only a few soldiers patrolled its perimeter. At the moment, she was just grateful for that peculiarity. Being pressed closely on all sides by smelly humans made her uncomfortable. She refused to admit to fear.

Once they were free of the crowd, Rokshan let go of Lamprophyre's hand, and the two of them stood staring at each other. Rokshan still had that horrible neutral expression that made Lamprophyre feel like a stranger. "Stop it," she said.

"Stop what?"

"Looking at me like I'm...I don't know. Like I'm your enemy."

Rokshan closed his eyes briefly. "I keep looking for traces of you," he said. "Something in the shape of your face, or the way you move, but...it's a complete transformation, Lamprophyre. The only thing left of your physical form is your eyes. They're still copper."

"That's not good. Humans don't have copper eyes."

Rokshan bent to peer closely at her eyes. "I think most people will assume they're brown. I—God's breath, Lamprophyre, what are we going to do?"

Lamprophyre shuddered. "Don't panic. You can't panic, because I'm close to panicking myself."

"Sorry." Rokshan put a hesitant hand on her shoulder. "All right. No panicking."

Lamprophyre drew in a deep breath and let it out slowly. "Tell me what happened after I was taken."

"Walk with me. I don't want to draw attention from the soldiers. If we stand still, they'll want to know what we're up to." Rokshan strolled away through the trees, slowly enough that Lamprophyre with her shorter legs could keep up.

"Rassika came for me shortly after two o'clock this morning," Rokshan said. "It was enough of a disturbance we'll need an explanation—but I'll take care of that later."

"I thought you had family obligations this morning. What did you tell them?"

"That I'd been called away on diplomatic business. Another thing I'll have to make up a lie about." Rokshan sighed. "I hate lying to my family, but there's no alternative."

"All right. So you left the palace for the embassy after midnight. Then what?"

"Most of this, I only know from what Depik and Bhakriya saw. They were woken by your scream, and when they went to investigate, they were attacked by shadowy figures they couldn't describe properly. Depik thought they had some kind of magic on them."

"They seemed unusually dark to me, too. Go on."

"Depik and Bhakriya said they didn't fight long before they were put to sleep by some artifact. When they woke, you were gone, and there was blood on the floor. Depik went to the warehouses for the other dragons, and Rassika fetched me. When I arrived at the embassy, Orthoclase and Coquina were there—no room for everyone, you know—and Orthoclase said it was your blood. I guess he could smell your scent."

"We bleed so rarely, it's almost never an issue," Lamprophyre said, "but dragon blood is as unique to a dragon as the color of her scales."

"Well, Coquina started a search immediately, but even with me along to track, we couldn't find a single trace of you." Rokshan laughed bitterly. "Were you transformed already? Because we were looking for a dragon."

Lamprophyre scowled. "The transformation was how they were able to capture me at all. They said—no, go on."

"We searched for about an hour before realizing we needed a different approach. I had to beg Manishi for help."

Lamprophyre sucked in a sharp breath. "She hates us."

"I didn't tell her what we needed the tracking artifact for, and I had to promise her a favor. An unspecified favor, for her to redeem at any time." Rokshan shook his head. "I was desperate, and she knew it. No matter what I tell the family, she'll be suspicious."

"It's all right. We'll face that when it comes," Lamprophyre said. "So you borrowed the tracking artifact?"

"Yes, and it was as effective as ever," Rokshan said. "Coquina and I took the lead, and after a few false starts, we found the trail. It confused us because it passed through some very narrow spaces where we knew a dragon couldn't fit...God's breath, even that wasn't enough of a clue. Though how we could have expected you were changed, I don't know." He drew in a breath and released it all at once. "Eventually we followed the trail to that wagon train, and you know the rest."

"But Depik and Bhakriya are all right? And the children?"

Rokshan nodded. "It gave us hope despite the blood—that if your attackers weren't willing to kill your servants, they wouldn't kill you either."

"Unless they didn't want to kill fellow humans and were just fine with disposing of a dragon."

Rokshan stopped abruptly. "I'm glad that didn't occur to us. Now, what happened to you?"

Lamprophyre found her voice was unexpectedly shaky. She cleared her throat and started again. "I don't know where the blood came from, because I was uninjured until I broke my arm," she said, and went on to tell him everything that had happened up to the point where she met Evart. "He didn't seem mad," she said, "but he was totally convinced I had a hoard I refused to give him. And he said he had a reliable source for that fact. Rokshan, I think the entity spoke to him."

"The...what makes you say that?"

They had circled nearly halfway around the palace and were approaching the army barracks near the training ground. Lamprophyre hoped no soldiers would accost them. She felt tense enough that, human body or no, she might attack anyone who did so. "He said something about getting the idea from a little voice in the night. Later he mentioned a person who'd promised him this plan would work. That was just before he broke the wand."

"He could just have been delusional."

"Like I said, he seemed very sane aside from being completely misinformed. But..." Lamprophyre stopped, forcing Rokshan to stop as well. "I don't know. I could be completely wrong. But I have a feeling I'm right about this. The last thing he said before he died was 'better a dead man than a live tool.' Doesn't that sound like he realized he was being used by someone?"

Rokshan's brow furrowed. "Meaning that it was the entity who wanted you hurt?"

"Meaning," Lamprophyre said, "that it was the entity who wanted me *human*."

"And lied to this man about your nonexistent hoard to compel him to create an artifact that would do that." Rokshan nodded, slowly. "It's not impossible. But why would the entity want that?"

"I have no idea. I'm nothing special as far as dragons go. I mean, I'm not Hyaloclast—turning *her* human would devastate us."

"You're the first dragon to make contact with humans in modern times," Rokshan pointed out. "The first to make a human friend. If the entity doesn't want humans and dragons cooperating, well, you're arguably the one responsible for that. It could want to stop you making that happen."

"Or it could want me dead." Lamprophyre shivered. "I don't know how you humans bear the constant awareness of your own mortality. I feel as if danger lurks around every corner."

"Because we can't afford to be paralyzed by that knowledge, or we'd never do anything," Rokshan said. "And the world's not really that dangerous, not in a civilized era. It's not like you're going to be eaten by a crocodile or trampled by wild horses in the middle of Tanajital."

"That wasn't a worry until you mentioned it, thanks." With a sigh, Lamprophyre started walking again. She looked over her shoulder at Rokshan, who hadn't moved. "What?"

"You sounded like yourself just then," Rokshan said. "Your voice is higher, but the inflection of your words...I'm sorry, I'm having trouble with this, and I don't want to burden you with my confusion. Whatever I'm feeling has to be a million times worse for you."

Lamprophyre nudged one of her heavy breasts and regarded it as it shifted in that jiggling way. "This body is awful. I don't know how human women put up with it."

"It's actually a very pretty body," Rokshan offered, in the tone of someone trying to make the best of a bad situation. "But don't play with it in public. People notice that sort of thing."

"All right."

They continued walking through the trees, moving in a familiar, companionable silence that eased Lamprophyre's fears. At least one thing hadn't changed, which meant probably a lot of things hadn't changed. She and Rokshan were still friends. She was still part of her clutch, and part of the flight. She could still hear thoughts. She had her draconic sense of stone and, she was sure, her prodigious memory. And they would fix this.

"So we need a story to tell everyone," Rokshan said. "You'll be safest if you can live in the palace, but it's so busy with the wedding, you can't be a random stranger. I told the healers you were my cousin, and I think that's the best option."

"What's a cousin?"

"In human terms, it means one of two things. Specifically, it means the child of your parent's sibling. Like, if I had children, they would be Tekentriya's children's cousins. But it can also mean a more distant relationship. We call cousin anyone descended from a common ancestor. My mother's family is very large and spread throughout Gonjiri. We can say you're a distant cousin from...Adakavi, maybe. It's on the border near Sachetan, and we never see that branch of the family. I think they're fighting with the others."

"Won't that be dangerous if someone here is also from Adakavi?"

"It's a very small risk. Adakavi is a long way off. The alternative is me claiming I'm betrothed to you, and that will draw all manner of attention."

"Oh. Yes, let's not do that. All right, I'm Lelitha from Adakavi. I'm a distant cousin and I'm here to...mend the breach between our families by showing respect for Anchala's wedding."

"Good. And it's best not to go into too much detail about your nonexistent family. The best and most convincing lies are the ones you don't embroider. You're related to my mother through your father, whose name is Geret, and your mother is Balmina—can you...never mind, of course you can remember that."

"Geret and Balmina. At least my memory is intact."

"We'll keep you away from Manishi, because she's suspicious and might decide to ferret out your secrets if she has too much contact with you. It's unlikely she would ever jump to the conclusion that you're really a dragon, but no sense risking discovery." Rokshan ran his fingers through his hair distractedly. "And we should go to my father immediately. Before the races—God's breath, I almost forgot about the races. We only have a few hours before they start."

"Then we need to hurry." Lamprophyre sped up her pace, but stopped when Rokshan laid a hand on her arm.

"I don't know how well I'll be able to stay close to you," he said. "I'm worried about leaving you alone. Passing as human might be difficult."

"Rokshan, I've been observing humans for nearly eight months now," Lamprophyre said, resting her hand atop his. "I may not know everything, but I think I can pretend well enough to keep others from being suspicious. And I'll be able to come to you if I have problems, right?" She smiled for the first time since her transformation. Smiles were the same no matter your species. "Look, I even used months instead of twelvedays."

Rokshan nodded. His smile was more tentative, but it was still a smile. "And for all we know, the serpentine stone is common, and we'll turn you back in a matter of days."

"So optimistic. It's one of the things I love about you," Lamprophyre said.

CHAPTER SIX

Lamprophyre had been in the great entrance hall of the palace a handful of times. It was the only place she would fit. She was used to the snug feeling of its walls closing around her, of having to furl her wings so as not to clip the sides of the doorway and to duck to avoid hitting her head on the strange light fixture hanging from the ceiling, like a metal web that had swept up dozens of fireflies. It wasn't exactly homey, not the way the embassy was, but it was comfortably familiar.

Now she felt as if she'd never seen it before. The ceiling arched high above her head, dark at its farthest corners because the lights of the lanterns at ground level and the firefly glow of the ceiling light weren't strong enough to reach that far. The floor tiles, glossy squares of some substance that wasn't stone, were cool against her bare feet. The ticking sound her nonretractable toe claws usually made against them was gone, of course, and her feet were soundless against the tiles. She couldn't smell the familiar scent of dryness and dust and the smell of the tiles, which was almost like pumice, except as faint whiffs she had to strain to perceive.

Unusually for this hour of the day, the entrance hall was empty. "It's a private day," Rokshan explained as he led the way up the right-hand stairs. "No royal audience, so there are fewer people coming to have their grievances heard. And the servants never come here during the day."

"Why not?" That explained the smell of dust.

"It diminishes the grandeur if someone's mopping the floor. It gets cleaned late at night."

"That seems unpleasant for the servants, having to stay up late." Lamprophyre's breath was coming more heavily as she climbed. She'd never used human stairs before, had only rarely used natural stairs in the mountains, and her legs ached with exertion and her chest heaved with the effort of breathing. Once she was herself again, she would never take her wings for granted.

Rokshan shrugged. "They're paid very well, and it's not like they're forced to work for us. Some of them even see serving the royal family as a tremendous honor. And I think the late night cleaning duty is rotated—it's not always the same servants."

Lamprophyre didn't have the breath to reply, so she just nodded. She'd only ever been in the position of being waited on, so it wasn't as if she had objections to some humans acting as servants to others. It just seemed inconsiderate to expect servants to do things one wouldn't want to do in one's own position. Still, it was none of her business.

After an eternity, they reached the top of the stairs, and Lamprophyre perked up despite her wheezing. She'd always wondered what the interior of the palace looked like, whether the rooms were as small as the little houses behind the embassy where her household lived. There was an arched doorway opening off the stairway through which Rokshan went. Lamprophyre followed him eagerly.

But the space beyond was boring—a short, plain hall ending in three steps going up. "Is this what the palace looks like?" she asked, trying not to sound disappointed.

Rokshan glanced back at her. "The entrance hall was added on about a century ago," he said. "This connects it to the old palace." He stopped and gestured to her to precede him. "Go ahead and look."

Lamprophyre walked up the three steps and pushed open the door at the top. Riotous color filled the vast room beyond, and she gasped and walked forward slowly, turning to take it all in. The pillared hall was narrower than the entrance hall, but longer, and was painted in geometric designs of blue and green and red that managed not to clash with the black and ivory tiles in a different geometric pattern covering the floor. The pillars supporting the roof high above were a cobalt blue as deep as the steaming lakes above the flight's caves. In the distance, arched doorways ahead and to left and right let sunlight into the chamber, making the colors glow.

Lamprophyre took a few more steps, feeling dazed. "This is amazing," she said. "It's nothing like the exterior. Why keep all this color on the inside?"

"Because it would weather fast, exposed to the elements," Rokshan said. "Come along. We should go to my father before he leaves for the races."

Lamprophyre nodded, still staring at the walls and the pillars. "I think I should explore later," she said. "This isn't something dragons would normally be able to see. It's my duty to dragonkind to understand humans."

"You're just curious and you can't bear not knowing things."

"That's also true."

Rokshan led her through passages, not as colorful, and into a few larger rooms Lamprophyre itched to examine more closely: rooms filled with comfortable-looking sofas and chairs lit by ornate lanterns, rooms with fountains actually inside the palace that smelled of cool water, rooms whose walls were glass cut into many-colored shapes that made pictures. That was something dragons could learn to do, if Lamprophyre could just work out how they were made.

They passed people on their rapid journey, most of them apparently servants, or so Lamprophyre guessed from their plain clothing and the way they bowed to Rokshan. But others were dressed more finely, and those didn't acknowledge Rokshan, instead continuing their quiet conversations, by their thoughts not even aware of the two of them. Lamprophyre was relieved at not having to talk to any humans yet. Despite what she'd said to Rokshan about being able to pass as human after eight months of observing them, she knew there were things she wouldn't understand and things she wouldn't even know she wasn't doing right. Talk to the king first, and worry about the rest later.

Finally, they came to a door where a couple of armed soldiers stood. The door was narrower than the others they'd passed, and Lamprophyre eyed it and the passage they were in and concluded it would be very defensible if anyone attacked the palace.

The soldiers came to alert when Rokshan approached and saluted him. Rokshan returned the salute. "Is my father within?" he asked.

"His majesty hasn't yet left, sir," the soldier on the right said. He eyed Lamprophyre as if he thought she might be a threat, which pleased and amused her.

"This is my cousin Lelitha from Adakavi," Rokshan said. "She's just arrived and wishes to greet my parents."

The soldiers saluted again, and the one on the left opened the door. Lamprophyre nodded to them politely as she went through, then stopped. Rokshan, behind her, gave her a little nudge to keep walking, but once again she'd been struck motionless by the room beyond.

It wasn't large enough to fit a dragon, but that still made it enormous by her current standards. Unlike the others she'd seen, it was round, and a large section of wall was missing, letting light and the smell of cedar into the room. Lamprophyre walked forward and nearly toppled into a shallow pool, filled with lily pads and the darting golden shapes of hand-sized fish. Why anyone would want a pool indoors, let alone one filled with fish, she didn't know, but it was unexpectedly charming.

Heavy red and gold drapes blocked off some of the open section, which Lamprophyre now saw had stone balusters carved to look like trees she'd never seen before, with bulbous trunks and feathery branches sprouting from the tops of the trunks to support the railing. She circled the pool to stand by the railing and look out over the enclosed garden she had seen on flights over the palace. Tall, slender cedar trees with thick needles provided shade that would be especially welcome in the heat of summer, and more fountains sprayed water that caught the light like faceted diamonds. She'd never realized how beautiful the garden was.

She heard a knock, and turned to see Rokshan standing at a door half-shrouded by more of the red and gold drapes. Beside it stood a very tall wooden construction, a kind of furniture she didn't recognize.

Horizontal and vertical boards connected at right angles to make what looked like a very wide, very fat ladder. Stacks of books lay piled on it here and there, as well as a couple of small wooden boxes she did recognize as writing desks. Chairs and a little table with very thin legs stood near the books. It would be the perfect place for a human to sit and read.

The door opened. Rokshan drew himself up straight and addressed the unseen figure who'd opened the door. "Please ask my father if I can have a moment of his time," he said, more formally than Lamprophyre had expected. Rokshan's relationship with his father wasn't exactly friendly, but it wasn't antagonistic or distant either, and most of the time when Rokshan wasn't in a formal setting, he was almost casual with the king. His words now made it sound as if this were some official request, and maybe that was true.

Lamprophyre heard someone moving around in the other room, and she went to Rokshan's side just in time to see a servant return to the door. "His majesty asks that you attend on him," the man said in a quiet voice Lamprophyre had to strain to hear. It seemed her ears were as impaired as her stupid nose, which meant her eyes might be the same. This was turning out to be even more of a nightmare than she'd thought.

Rokshan put a hand low on Lamprophyre's back and gave her a gentle push to propel her through the door. The room beyond was more brightly lit than the antechamber and glowed with orange-gold draperies over the windows and the wide bed. Lamprophyre had never seen a bed like it. Pillars at the four corners nearly reached the ceiling, and the heavy golden draperies looked as if they would surround the bed completely if they were untied from the pillars. More chairs bearing cushions that matched the draperies lined the walls, as if waiting for supplicants to fill them. Though if this was the king's bedchamber, surely he wouldn't let just anyone in?

King Ekanath stood near the foot of the bed with his arms outstretched as a servant helped him don his familiar multi-colored robe. If he was going to watch the races wearing it, that meant he saw the races as more of a diplomatic function than Lamprophyre had thought. That was bad. A diplomatic function where the dragon ambassador wasn't in attendance suggested the dragons didn't respect the king. She was suddenly very glad they'd found the king before he left.

Queen Satiya sat on a low sofa beneath one of the windows. She, too, wore her formal robe over a plain white linen gown whose hem went only to the middle of her shins. One sandal-clad foot kicked idly at the leg of the sofa, but stilled when Rokshan and Lamprophyre entered. She wore her hair, as usual, in an elaborate construction of loops and curls that Lamprophyre had always been curious about. How long did it take to achieve that look? And was it a required hairstyle for the queen, or something Satiya personally preferred?

"Rokshan," the king said. "Who's this?"

"We need to speak with you privately, Father," Rokshan said.

Ekanath raised an eyebrow. "A serious matter?"

Rokshan said nothing, but he stood as straight as the soldiers at the royal suite had. Ekanath adjusted the robe across his shoulders and said, "Leave us." The servant bowed and left the room, closing the door quietly behind him.

"I hope this is private enough for you," Ekanath said, moving to sit beside Satiya. "Explain why you brought this stranger into my private rooms."

"You'll find it hard to believe," Rokshan said. "It seems someone created an artifact that can transform a dragon into a human. They used it on Lamprophyre, and…" He gestured at Lamprophyre, whose face warmed under the king and queen's close scrutiny. It made her feel as if there were something shameful about having been turned human. She drew in a calming breath, let it out slowly, and raised her chin the way she would if she still had a dragon body and was facing down a potential enemy.

The king's narrow-eyed gaze became an expression of stunned amazement. "Impossible," he said. "You can't expect me to believe this young woman is—this must be a joke."

"If it is, it's a joke that makes no sense," Satiya said. She stood and approached Lamprophyre, examining her even more closely. Even the queen, small as she was, overtopped Lamprophyre by a finger's breadth. "But her eyes…they're the same color as the ambassador's."

"I know it's hard to believe, but it's true," Lamprophyre said. "Your majesty, we came to you first because I thought you should know what happened. We can't reveal the truth to anyone else, which means I'll have to claim to have gone home for...for however long it takes to restore me."

"Did you destroy the artifact?" the king asked.

"Its maker destroyed it, which tells me it could have reversed the effect," Lamprophyre said, feeling angry and sick all over again. "We don't yet know how to make another."

"And you can't allow anyone to learn that it's possible to transform you. God's breath, are you fully human?" The king's expression grew briefly horrified.

"I think so," Lamprophyre said. "I have human senses and human frailties, and I've...anyway." She didn't like admitting to weakness, even to the king, who she didn't feel was a threat. "But yes, that means I'm vulnerable to anything that can hurt a human."

"Jiwanyil have mercy." Ekanath rose to stand by Satiya's side. "Shouldn't you return to the mountains? The dragons are far better able to protect you than we are. We'd do our best, of course, but if anyone finds out the truth..."

"It's winter in the mountains, and this body wouldn't survive the cold where the flight lives," Lamprophyre said.

"We've discussed it, and the best solution is to give her rooms in the palace," Rokshan said. "We can give out that she's a distant cousin of Mother's, come for the wedding. It's safer than finding her somewhere to stay in the city, or having her remain at the dragon embassy."

"We can, can we?" Ekanath said. "I'm not sure why you felt you needed to consult me, given that you seem to have made all the decisions already."

"I thought that was better than laying the whole mess on you and asking you to solve the problem. I—we—want your approval, but if you have a better idea..." Rokshan said, letting his voice trail off.

Ekanath eyed Lamprophyre again. "This will not be easy," he said. "In some ways, it would be better to find you a place in the city where you could be anonymous, but Rokshan is right that you will need protection in that body. Are you prepared to act like a human?"

"I'll do my best," Lamprophyre said. "And Rokshan says the city I'll claim to be from is far from here, so won't people assume anything I get wrong is because I'm provincial?"

Ekanath turned his gaze on Rokshan. "You really have thought of everything."

"Except her appearance," Satiya said. "Where did you get those clothes, ambassador?"

Lamprophyre somewhat self-consciously picked at the hem of her shirt. "The man who transformed me."

"Well, provincial or not, no one will believe you're attached to the royal family in that attire." Satiya clasped Ekanath's hand briefly. "I have some things she can wear. We'll follow behind."

Lamprophyre instinctively turned to Rokshan. "I thought I would stay with you."

"Mother's right, you need different clothes." Rokshan put a hand on her shoulder. "This is what we talked about. You can't stay with me all the time."

"I promise you'll be safe, ambassador," Satiya said with a warm smile.

Lamprophyre sighed. "Call me Lelitha," she said.

CHAPTER SEVEN

The royal litter moved so smoothly Lamprophyre could almost imagine she and Satiya were floating. The air inside, confined by the curtains that hung down on all sides, wasn't as stuffy as she'd expected, but it did smell of sandalwood, and Lamprophyre had to resist the urge to pinch shut her nose to avoid sneezing. Though at least now if she did, there was no chance of her setting the litter and its occupants on fire.

Satiya smiled at her again. "Are you comfortable, Lelitha?"

"Yes, your majesty," Lamprophyre said. She wasn't actually comfortable; aside from the smell, there were the sandals, which were almost intolerable in how they touched her feet just firmly enough for her never to forget she was wearing *things* on her feet for the first time in all her sixty years. But that wasn't what Satiya meant, so Lamprophyre felt confident in a tiny lie for the sake of politeness.

"I think you should call me Satiya, if we're meant to be related," Satiya said, her smile deepening. "You are the only child of my cousin... Geret, was it? And we want everyone to see how friendly the two branches of the family are."

"All right, your—Satiya." Now her discomfort extended into the emotional realm. "Thank you for helping me."

"I'm sure Ekanath would tell you it's a necessary diplomatic action," Satiya said, "but in truth I think he feels this redresses some of the inequity between Gonjiri and the dragons. Not that he would use your temporary weakness against you, but if he can garner goodwill from Hyaloclast by helping you, he'll take that opportunity."

"I understand. And I'm not offended."

The noise outside the litter had grown until the two of them were almost shouting to be heard over the crowd's roaring. Just as the bearers set the litter down, an enormous cheer rang out. Satiya sat up and swung her feet around over the side of the litter. "It sounds as if someone just won," she said.

Lamprophyre disentangled herself from the cushions filling the litter and managed to step out without falling on her face. The gown she wore was similar to Satiya's, though she didn't have a royal over-robe, and its narrow skirt bound her legs and made walking difficult. She followed Satiya, wishing she were wearing trousers instead.

The quartz and chlorite pendant she'd taken off Evart rubbed against her breastbone, concealed beneath the gown. She'd forgotten she had it until Satiya had started producing clothing for her to try. Wearing it had seemed the only option, not because she was afraid of having her thoughts overheard, but because she didn't want to lose it. Though it had occurred to her later that having a protection like that one might keep her from being found out. Nobody had yet claimed to have invented the artifact that would allow for hearing thoughts, but that didn't mean it hadn't happened. So Lamprophyre wore Evart's artifact and tried to think of it as a victory over him.

She tilted her head back and farther back to examine the wooden structures they now approached. When she had helped build the stands for humans to observe the races and put together the pillars and bars of the obstacle course, she'd wondered if they'd made everything tall enough. Now, looking up at the rows of seats in their wooden framework, she felt dizzied by their height, their wooden beams taller and slimmer than cypress trees and appearing to lean over her. She reminded herself that despite appearances, they were sturdy enough to support more than one dragon, as they'd proved by having Flint and Dolomite perch on opposite ends of the stands. Even so, they looked extremely unsafe.

Satiya, surrounded by her guards, had walked to the base of the narrowest of the stands and stepped onto the lift. "Lelitha," she said, and Lamprophyre hesitantly stood next to her and watched as the guards latched the short wooden half-door into place. This, the dragons hadn't tested, but Rokshan had and had pronounced it safe and comfortable. As the lift lurched into upward motion, Lamprophyre grabbed hold of the rail, trying not to show her fear. Satiya, calm as ever, looked around her with interest.

"It's remarkable, isn't it?" she said. "I think we should install one of these in the palace. So much more convenient than all those stairs. Though I'm not sure where they'd put it."

Lamprophyre made a strangled, wordless reply. She couldn't stop staring at the rapidly receding ground. So much empty space...if she fell from this height, would it kill her instantly, or would she lie in a heap of broken bones until death claimed her?

"It's perfectly safe, Rokshan assures me," Satiya said. Lamprophyre didn't dare look away from the ground, but the queen sounded as if she were soothing a wounded, frightened animal, and that made Lamprophyre ashamed of her fear. Of course it was safe. It was just her knowledge that she had no wings to save her from a fall that made this method of travel so difficult. She wrenched her gaze from the distant ground and made herself smile, hoping it didn't look forced.

"I've never been in one of these before," she said.

"This is the first one built outside the academy," Satiya said, as if Lamprophyre didn't already know this—but then Lelitha wouldn't have any idea about lifts, would she? "It's powered by an artifact, though I don't know any more than that. I am grateful not to have to walk up several flights of stairs. This stand is considerably taller than the one in the coliseum."

Lamprophyre suppressed the urge to tell Satiya about the race ground's construction—another thing Lelitha wouldn't know. "I expect taller is better when you're watching dragons race," she said instead.

The lift lurched again, coming to a halt. Guards at the top unlatched the inner door, and Satiya exited, not showing any nervousness at how the lift swayed with her motion. Lamprophyre followed as quickly as possible.

The top of the royal stand bore a canopy in bright green and yellow, the royal family's colors, sheltering the seats. Most of them were occupied, and Lamprophyre recognized Rokshan's sister Anchala on the front row and the dreaded Manishi near the back. That struck Lamprophyre as an odd seat for a princess, however unusual she was, but gratitude that Manishi wasn't anywhere near her made that oddity unimportant. A tangle of thoughts, most of them preoccupied with scanning the skies, left her feeling dizzy, and she blocked them, wishing once more that there was some way to selectively listen to one person's thoughts in the middle of a crowd. Hearing thoughts would be a serious advantage in her current state.

There was one empty seat next to the king that Satiya took immediately. A large, dark-skinned woman on her other side immediately engaged her in conversation, the woman's high-pitched voice reminding Lamprophyre of a twittering bird. Lamprophyre remained standing, looking out over the great fields filled with bars and pillars and one big hoop at the far end. Two other stands faced one another across the fields, crowded with humans. She saw no dragons anywhere.

"Lelitha," Rokshan said, startling her. He had just risen from a chair nearby. "Would you care to sit?"

Lamprophyre almost declined when she remembered she was human now, and humans had strange social customs with regard to men and women and politeness. "Thank you," she said, and sat. Rokshan remained standing nearby, which comforted her. "Where are the dragons?" she asked.

The stranger seated next to her said, "They're at the far end of the circuit. You can just see the specks if you look...there." His dark skin and the broad, elongated vowels of his accent proclaimed him to be Sachetanese. He pointed, and Lamprophyre looked in that direction and saw nothing. She squinted, trying to force her stupid human eyes into better acuity. Still nothing.

"They move fast," the Sachetanese man said, almost apologetically, as if it were his fault she couldn't see the dragons. "It's really extraordinary. The red dragon has quite a turn of speed for all he's smaller."

"P—" Lamprophyre closed her mouth on her clutchmate's name. There were so many things Lelitha wouldn't know. "I...haven't seen a dragon before," she said.

"Neither had I until today," the man said. "I'm Torannum. I don't think I've seen you before, either."

Torannum. Anchala's bridegroom. "I'm Lelitha," she said. "From Adakavi."

Torannum brightened. "Adakavi? I've been there often. How interesting to find...almost a fellow countrywoman, I suppose."

Lamprophyre's heart pounded against her ribs. "That is interesting," she managed. "I—"

"Lelitha has been studying at the academy in Kolmira for the past several years, so she hasn't seen Adakavi for a while," Rokshan interjected. "She's a distant cousin visiting for the wedding."

Anchala, sitting on Torannum's other side, leaned forward. "From Adakavi? That's distant indeed. Though I suppose if you've been studying in Kolmira it's not that odd to see you here. Who are your parents?"

"Look, they're coming back," Torannum said.

All eyes turned toward the distant specks of color that sped toward the stands. Lamprophyre's fists were clenched tight and her hands were inexplicably damp. She couldn't see who was in the front, though it was almost certainly Chrysoprase...yes, there was the dark green and maroon that was unique among the current flight as well as in the memories of the oldest dragons. Grass-green Coquina was just behind her, and Porphyry's bright crimson matched her neck and neck. Lamprophyre leaned forward, her heart beating rapidly again though she didn't have a stake in who won. How many humans had bet on the outcome of this race? Probably all of them. Humans liked wagering almost as much as they liked food.

The sounds of humans shouting drifted toward them from the other, distant stands, but the royal stand was quiet except for a low murmuring. Farther along her front row, the king sat leaning forward as she was, his gaze intent on the racers. Then someone behind her shouted, "Chrysoprase is ahead!" and the royal stand erupted into shouts and cheers that nearly deafened Lamprophyre. Torannum and Anchala stood and leaned against the railing in front of their seats, shouting with the rest. In another beat, the dragons were upon them, they'd flown past with a great wind that buffeted the canopy and blew Lamprophyre's hair around her face, and a great, deep voice shouted, "*Chrysoprase wins!*"

Lamprophyre turned to look for the speaker—Massicot, whom she hadn't seen at all—and caught Rokshan's eye. He was watching her with a strange, unreadable expression that turned into cheery good humor. He leaned down to whisper in her ear, "She's won the last two races. It's a good thing she doesn't live in Tanajital, because the races would become extremely boring."

"She's terrible at the obstacle course, though," Lamprophyre whispered back. It felt so odd, talking of ordinary things when nothing about this situation was ordinary.

"We'll have to see how that goes," Rokshan said. "There's a bit of a rest now," he said in a louder voice, "and then more races. We'll have dinner while we wait. Nothing fancy."

Lamprophyre saw the lift rattle into sight, bearing several men in royal livery carrying covered baskets. Human food. She hadn't eaten anything since that half a round of bread and now she was starving. She'd eat anything if it curbed the gnawing ache in her belly.

Torannum and Anchala resumed their seats. "That was invigorating," Torannum said. "Though I'm not sure it's fair to such magnificent creatures to make them race for our amusement. Dragons are as intelligent as humans, aren't they?"

"More intelligent," Lamprophyre said without thinking, and winced inwardly at Torannum's startled expression. "Or, not more intelligent, but they live longer and have better memories, so they must know more about some things than hu—than we do."

"And I understand racing was their idea," Rokshan said. "They intend to show humans that there's no reason to fear them."

Racing dragons had been Rokshan's idea, but Lamprophyre couldn't correct him on it—and it didn't really matter, did it? "They must enjoy racing, then," she said.

"Speaking of racing, where is Lamprophyre?" Anchala asked. "I wanted to introduce her to Torannum. She's the dragon ambassador to Gonjiri," she told Torannum.

"She's gone home for a few weeks," Rokshan said, as casually as if nothing about that was strange. "Some kind of winter celebration. Her mother, the dragon queen, insisted."

"That's too bad," Anchala said, "for us, anyway."

She leaned back in her seat and accepted an earthenware dish that was too deep to be a plate and too shallow to be a bowl, which were the only two kinds of dishes Lamprophyre knew. It was full of a thick yellow stew that smelled of lamb and spices that made Lamprophyre's stomach growl. Triangles of flat bread were arranged around the wide lip of the bowl-plate. Anchala picked up a piece of bread and scooped yellow stew onto it, conveying it dripping to her mouth. "Oh, lovely," she said with her mouth ungracefully full. "I do love simple food."

Lamprophyre was about to ask why this was considered simple when one of the servitors handed her her own bowl-plate of stew with bread triangles. Carefully, she dipped the bread into the yellow mess and took a bite. The flavor exploded on her tongue, so many spices she didn't know the names of, and she swallowed, then paused before taking another bite to savor the deliciousness of the morsel of lamb she scooped up. So much more subtle than cow or pig, even as well-cooked and -seasoned as Depik produced.

Silence fell as everyone ate. Lamprophyre felt paying homage to the delicious food was reasonable, and it would be impossible to talk around the stew, anyway. It occurred to her that she might have been disgusted by human food no dragon could digest, and for the first time that day felt grateful to her human body, for having normal reactions to food.

She ate until her belly was pleasantly full and handed off the empty dish to a servitor, who bowed to her exactly as if she were a lady. The stew was mostly lamb; suppose it was something dragons could eat, after all? Not the bread, naturally, but the stew juices might be edible. It was an idea she could put to Depik later. And now she was thinking optimistically. It was amazing how much better she felt about life now that she wasn't hungry.

"Lelitha, what are you studying at the academy?" Anchala said.

And there went her cheerful optimism. "I—several things," she said, her heart once more hammering. "History. Reading. Magic."

"You're an adept?" Torannum said.

Lamprophyre winced inwardly. "No, I was studying, not how to make artifacts, but their uses. I want to write about how magic works, and create a book listing what different stones can do. There isn't anything like that now."

"That sounds very scholarly indeed," said a new voice. Lamprophyre turned in her seat to observe the newcomer, also Sachetanese, and similar in features to Torannum, though his head was hairless where Torannum had thick black hair that curled around his face. His baldness would have reminded her of Evart if this man hadn't looked healthier and more fully-fleshed. "Tor, I insist you introduce me to the young lady."

"You would," Torannum said amiably. "Lady Lelitha, may I introduce my brother Sanyot. Sanyot, this is Anchala's cousin Lelitha. She's from Adakavi originally."

"Charmed," Sanyot said, bowing to Lamprophyre. "I can see the resemblance. Anchala, I had no idea you had such an attractive relation."

Lamprophyre's confusion over Torannum's interaction with Sanyot deepened. Resemblance to Anchala? Her body was shorter than tall Anchala's and rounder, with larger breasts and hips. And attractive? Well, Rokshan had said it was a pretty body, but Sanyot's voice had been heavy with meaning Lamprophyre didn't understand, as if there were something about being attractive that went beyond physical appearance. She tried listening to his thoughts, but was immediately overwhelmed by the noise of so many people together in one place, hearing only the words *lovely indeed*.

Sanyot took a few more steps until he was facing Lamprophyre, leaning casually against the rail. "I'm surprised there isn't such a book already," he said. "A compendium like that, I mean."

"So was I," Lamprophyre said. "You'd think it would be natural, if only for the use of non-adepts."

"It sounds like an ambitious undertaking." Sanyot smiled. "But I'm sure you're up to the challenge."

Lamprophyre wanted to ask him how he could be so sure, given that he didn't know anything about her, but Rokshan interrupted with, "It looks like the obstacle races are starting."

Sanyot straightened. "I hope to speak with you further this evening, Lady Lelitha," he said with another bow, and with a nod at his brother retreated to the back of the stand.

"He's a flirt, but harmless," Torannum said to Lamprophyre under his breath. "Don't mind his compliments."

"I...all right," Lamprophyre said. Compliments, huh? If that was flirting, it wasn't much like the way dragons did it. From context, she guessed to humans, a flirt meant someone who told people things that weren't entirely true for...actually, she couldn't think why anyone would do that. But Sanyot had been interested in her pretend course of study, and he seemed nice, and likely she would encounter him again, so she needed to be polite.

The clutch had returned to the field below the stands and appeared to be conversing. They were too far away for Lamprophyre to hear their words or their thoughts, even if she weren't blocking everything out. "The next races were my idea," Rokshan said. "I thought it might be fun to see how well dragons can maneuver through obstacles, the way chariots used to race twenty years ago."

"Is that what all the bars and pillars are for?" Anchala asked.

"Yes, they're to give the dragons something to avoid, or maneuver past. That hoop is my favorite." Rokshan pointed. "I've seen them practice, and it's remarkable. You never can tell who will win."

Lamprophyre's eyes felt hot and swollen again, and she pressed her palms against them. "Is something wrong, Lelitha?" Anchala asked.

"I just got something caught in my eye," Lamprophyre lied. That was something that happened to humans, right, because of having no nictitating membranes? Why she'd suddenly started crying, she had no idea, unless watching her clutchmates prepare to do something she'd enjoyed, something she couldn't do anymore, had saddened her. Yes, that made sense. She blinked away tears and made herself watch the races.

It was satisfying to hear the crowd roar their approval as each dragon sped through the obstacles. Someone at the far end of the course—it was Dharan, she thought—held an artifact that showed how fast each flyer had gone, and showed that speed on a giant slate specially prepared to be an artifact itself. The rankings were given in both human time units and dragon beats, so Lamprophyre could appreciate her clutchmates' speed. Dolomite and Orthoclase proved to be so fast they had to run the course a second time to determine who was fastest.

When Dolomite edged ahead of Orthoclase by only a couple of beats, Lamprophyre found herself on her feet, cheering with everyone else. Dolomite and Orthoclase flew slow loops over the fields, soon joined by the others. It was so beautiful Lamprophyre's heart ached along with her eyes. No one noticed her tears.

Then Ekanath and Satiya and the twittering woman walked past, on their way to the lift, and the races were over. Lamprophyre stood beside Rokshan and waited her turn on the lift, which could hold only four people at a time. She watched the other stands, where people descended steep stairs attached to the back sides, and wondered which would be more frightening, the stairs that surely shook with the passage of hundreds of feet, or the lift that wobbled as it descended. So much better to fly.

"I admit to being uncertain of that lift," Sanyot said from close beside her. She started, and he chuckled, not a cruel or mocking sound. "I apologize for startling you. The lift, though, seems an unnatural way to travel."

Lamprophyre looked at Rokshan for guidance, but his expression when he watched her was impassive, telling her that he couldn't intervene without looking suspicious. "I suppose everything involving artifacts is unnatural in some way," she said. "But I don't like heights—" *not in this body, anyway*— "and it shifts unpleasantly."

"You should ask one of the dragons to carry you to the ground." Sanyot's smile was pleasant, and his eyes gleamed with mirth. "Or would that be unpleasant as well?"

"I don't know," Lamprophyre lied. "I'm sure the dragons have better things to do."

"Better things than helping such a lovely young lady?"

"They're gone already, anyway," Rokshan said. "I'll have to introduce you, Lelitha."

"I didn't realize you were so close to them, Rokshan," Sanyot said.

"They're all good friends of mine." Rokshan extended a hand to Lamprophyre. "I believe it's our turn to descend."

"Thus robbing me of the opportunity to get to know you better, my lady," Sanyot said, making a sad face Lamprophyre thought was feigned. She didn't understand this man at all. "Perhaps later, after supper?"

"I suppose," Lamprophyre said, and Rokshan swept her away from the uncomfortable conversation. "What was that about?" she asked him in a low voice when they were safely—safely?—aboard the lift, accompanied by two people Lamprophyre didn't know.

"It's nothing. He's flirting with you. Some men are like that," Rokshan said in the same low voice. "He finds you attractive."

"Oh." The idea that she might be attractive to humans gave her a funny feeling in her stomach. Granted, she had a human body, and Sanyot didn't know she was really a dragon, but no one had ever found her attractive before, whether human or dragon. It wasn't exactly a comfortable feeling, but it wasn't disgusting or horrible, either.

She looked back up to see Sanyot was still watching her, and the funny feeling intensified. "What am I supposed to do? I don't want anyone paying that close attention to me," she told Rokshan.

"Be polite, but don't encourage him—yes, I realize you don't know what that would look like. Just be yourself, and he'll give up eventually."

Lamprophyre nodded. Be polite. Be herself. She could do that. She glanced up again. Sanyot had vanished. She gripped the rail of the lift more tightly as it came to a stop on the ground. Pretending to be human had already turned out to be more difficult than she'd imagined.

CHAPTER EIGHT

That evening, Lamprophyre and Rokshan walked to the embassy, once again dodging the tides of humanity swelling the streets as people left their places of employment for their suppers. Lamprophyre clung to Rokshan's firm hand and hoped she wouldn't be swept away. Again she felt small and weak, and the feeling angered her. She was a dragon, whatever body she currently occupied, and dragons weren't weak.

The crowds thinned somewhat as they turned onto the wide street that terminated at the embassy courtyard. There were no workshops or sellers of goods here; it was an entirely residential neighborhood, and Lamprophyre was acquainted with many of the residents. She passed her young friend Anamika's house and slowed to say hello to Anamika's mother, standing on the doorstep to call her children in for the evening meal. Rokshan tugged on her hand to move her along. "But I want——" she began.

"She doesn't know you, remember?" Rokshan said in a low voice. "None of these people do."

A sick, uncomfortable feeling passed over her. "I forgot," she said. She saw Anamika and her brother Varnak approaching from the direction of the embassy, racing as they always did, and the sick feeling intensified when they ran past her without a second glance, just a wave at Rokshan.

"It will be over soon," Rokshan said.

She eased her grip on his hand and nodded. Just then she felt the ordeal would go on forever.

The courtyard was full of beggars as usual, there for a free meal. Lamprophyre released Rokshan and stood watching the crowd. It was so different being on their eye level, or just below it—most everyone except the children was taller than she. For the first time, she wondered why she was in the body she currently occupied. Not why she was human, but why she was shorter than average and plumper than average, why she had long hair instead of short. Why she was female, for that matter. Something had made that determination, but did it mean this was her essence, expressed in human form, or had Evart chosen it because it made her even weaker in human terms? As a dragon, she was slightly bigger than average for a female, and she hadn't yet achieved her full growth. Nothing about this made sense.

She turned away from Bhakriya, who was serving soup. It was too hard to look at her and know if Lamprophyre approached, Bhakriya would treat her like a stranger. Instead, she went into the embassy. No beggars ever did that, and Lamprophyre hoped she wouldn't be noticed. She didn't feel like making up any more lies.

Coquina wasn't there. A large, dark splotch that smelled faintly of blood marked where Lamprophyre had been transformed. She avoided looking at it. Rokshan, who'd followed Lamprophyre into the embassy, said, "We could eat while we wait."

"I don't think I could bear it." Lamprophyre picked over the piles of books, some of them Dharan's on loan, some of them her own. She chose one that had formerly been too small for her to read, even with the help of her giant magnifying lens, and leaned against the wall. "I'll wait here. You can eat if you want."

"Lamprophyre," Rokshan said. His tone of voice, a mix of resignation and exasperation, made her raise her head. "Quit sulking."

"I'm not sulking."

"You're feeling despondent and you've given up. That's sulking."

69

Lamprophyre closed the book. "Fine. I'm sulking. You don't think I have reason?"

"I think you need to stop feeling sorry for yourself. That's not going to help."

"Everything is wrong!" Lamprophyre exclaimed. "I don't know what to do about that. And I didn't know how bad it would feel to have none of my friends recognize me."

"The clutch recognizes you."

"You know what I mean."

"I do." Rokshan sighed and put his hand on her shoulder. Her tiny, soft, human shoulder. "But you can't wallow in despair. Think of what Hyaloclast would say."

Hyaloclast. Lamprophyre shuddered. "She'd give me that *look* of disappointment, like I'm letting down all my ancestors by not taking this challenge by the throat."

"And she might be on her way here now. Time to stiffen your spine, Lamprophyre, and stop despairing."

Lamprophyre drew in a deep breath. "All right. Let's eat."

Bhakriya greeted Rokshan with a gasp, dropping her ladle into the soup cauldron so it splashed a few drops onto her shirt. "Your highness, is there more news? What happened to my lady?"

"Didn't anyone tell you?" Rokshan sounded dismayed, and Lamprophyre heard a scrap of powerful thought despite her deliberately not listening in: *should have told them something.* "Lamprophyre was called home for the winter festivities. Her mother insisted."

"But there was so much blood! What happened, your highness?"

"Orthoclase told me it was some kind of natural process. Like...like a woman's time of the month." Rokshan was crimson to his hairline. It amused Lamprophyre that Rokshan still got embarrassed when talking about reproductive matters, even ones he made up. "But it was something Lamprophyre needed to be treated for at home. Especially since she, um, since her delirium made her wander. Because of losing blood."

None of that made sense to Lamprophyre, and she could tell Bhakriya was confused as well. But Bhakriya just said, "So she was delirious, and that's why you and the dragons had to search for her?"

"Yes. That's it. Exactly. She wandered off, but she was fine when we found her. She just had to go home for treatment. And rest. She's been so busy as ambassador."

That seemed to make more sense to Bhakriya, because she nodded and smiled. "She really does do so much for all of us. I hope she recovers quickly. Now, did you—" Her eye fell on Lamprophyre. "Is this a friend?"

"This is my cousin Lelitha from Adakavi." Rokshan drew Lamprophyre forward. "She's studying in Kolmira and she came for the wedding."

"How nice!" Bhakriya's smile softened the way it always did when she talked about the royal wedding. "Please, have some soup, and feel free to use the pavilion."

"We'll wait in the embassy," Rokshan said. "I need to speak to Coquina. She's acting ambassador while Lamprophyre is gone, and there are things we have to discuss."

Bhakriya nodded. "Have a good evening, your highness, Lady Lelitha."

Lamprophyre hurried back to the embassy, where she knelt on the floor and set her bowl to one side. "Natural process? Time of the month? You know dragons don't have reproductive cycles like women do."

"I panicked, all right? I think I made it all sound reasonable." Rokshan folded himself into the cross-legged position he commonly used and spooned soup into his mouth as fast as he could.

Lamprophyre eyed his legs. "How do you do that?"

"What? Sit like this? It's just the way legs bend. Human legs. Look." Rokshan stood and then lowered himself to the ground, bending first one leg and then the other slowly to demonstrate. Lamprophyre made an attempt, but found the narrow-skirted gown kept her from bending properly. She went back to kneeling and picked up her bowl.

"I'll try it again sometime when I'm wearing trousers," she said. Trousers. She groaned and lowered the bowl again. "I need clothing. I can't borrow from your mother forever, not to mention that all her clothing seems formal."

"We can go shopping tomorrow. You'll be all right for tonight."

A shadow passed over the doorway, something very large, and then

Coquina put her head inside. "I'm glad you're here," she said, somewhat breathlessly. "What do we tell the humans? Bhakriya and Depik?"

"Rokshan made up a story that almost makes sense," Lamprophyre said, ignoring Rokshan's scowl. She told Coquina the details of Rokshan's story, then added, "We just have to pretend the blood means nothing, which should be easy because we don't know where it came from."

"And press forward with 'oh, Lamprophyre just needs to recuperate, it's not important,'" Coquina agreed. She came fully into the embassy and sat in front of the door, blocking it so only a little light came through. Rokshan rose and lit several lanterns, filling the embassy with warm, flickering light. With the doorway invisible, Lamprophyre could almost imagine she was in one of the flight's caves, cozy and warm for winter.

"So what do I do?" Coquina said, almost plaintively. "I'm not good at talking to angry people. I get angry myself and then I shout. But you never do that."

"Patience is important," Lamprophyre said. "Patience, and listening to what others have to say."

"I can listen!"

"I didn't say you couldn't." Lamprophyre tipped up her bowl to drink down the last of her soup. "It's just that people will come to you with troubles, and you listen to their stories and decide whether there's anything you can do for them. Whether it's anything you *should* do. Rokshan will help when it's a matter of human law or custom."

"I can't be in two places at once, Lamprophyre," Rokshan pointed out. "What if you need me?"

"It's more important that the dragon presence in Tanajital remain unobjectionable." That wasn't the right word, but Lamprophyre couldn't think of a better one. She regarded Rokshan, then Coquina, with a stern gaze. "I've worked too hard to get humans not to be afraid of dragons to let that fall apart just because I'm gone. You can do this, Coquina. You're clever and you see things differently than I do, and you'll probably be better at spotting liars than I am. It will be all right."

"I wish you hadn't put it in those terms," Coquina said with a sigh.

"I hadn't even thought about this being a matter of international relationships. But it is. And I'll do my best."

"I'll help when I can," Rokshan said. "But, Lamprophyre, you *will* need help. And that's just as important as diplomacy. If anyone finds out the truth about you, that will be as bad in a different way as if some diplomatic incident occurs."

Lamprophyre grimaced and rose to pace between Rokshan and Coquina. "I know you're right. I was just hoping, if I pretended hard enough, this would all be easy." She stopped pacing and looked up at Coquina. How strange, that Coquina was now the largest dragon in Tanajital. "Did Orthoclase come back?"

"I haven't seen him." Coquina breathed out a ring of smoke. Lamprophyre had never been able to make smoke rings and she'd always sort of envied Coquina the ability. "I thought he'd be back a thousand beats ago or more. How much could Hyaloclast possibly have to say?"

"There's nothing she can do," Lamprophyre said. Deep down, she hoped she was wrong, that Hyaloclast would swoop in and solve this problem as she had so many others. It was what made her a great dragon queen. But this was a matter of human magic, and dragons, even dragon queens, were at a loss confronted with that.

Coquina jerked, then looked back over her shoulder. "Orthoclase," she said. "What news?" She shifted forward, forcing Rokshan and Lamprophyre to move out of her way.

Orthoclase poked his head inside. "Good, you're here," he said to Lamprophyre. "Hyaloclast wants to see you."

The thought of the thousands of beats-long flight to the mountains made Lamprophyre feel sick and terrified again. "Right now?"

"She came with me. She's waiting outside the city. Hurry, Lamprophyre, we don't want any humans wondering what's going on with the big black dragon sitting in the fields."

Coquina moved so Lamprophyre could exit. Orthoclase gleamed in the light of the setting sun, his scales looking like silver brushed over sable. Forcing her fears aside, Lamprophyre clambered up to the notch behind his shoulders. It was so much easier with two hands. Orthoclase didn't wait for her to tell him she was ready; he leaped into the sky with a tremendous jerk that nearly made Lamprophyre lose her seat. Terror struck her despite her best efforts, and she clung to Orthoclase and squeezed her eyes shut.

Almost immediately, she discovered being blind was even worse than seeing the vast gulf beneath her. She opened her eyes and fixed her gaze on the back of Orthoclase's head. He had a round patch of scales just above the base of his neck, the scales finer and smaller than the ones surrounding it. It was exactly in the place Lamprophyre had a sensitive spot, one that had been exploited by a Fanishkorite spy intent on killing her to start a war between his country and Gonjiri. How strange that it was visible. Surely someone else must have noticed it, but then dragons didn't spend a lot of time staring at the backs of each other's heads. Maybe it was something everyone knew about except her.

Her reverie kept her from noticing her potential grisly death by falling, and only Orthoclase's rapid descent outside the city wall, forcing her to cling more tightly, brought her back to herself. As soon as his feet touched earth, she tumbled off, landing gracelessly on her hands and knees and breathing heavily. The dry, prickly ground tore at her hands, but she didn't care, she was so grateful for the nice, unmoving surface.

"Stones," a deep voice said. "There's nothing left of you."

Lamprophyre, still crouching, lifted her head to look at Hyaloclast. She had a flash of a memory of Rokshan facing the dragon queen down, how small he'd looked. Now she was even smaller and in the same position, and she thought it was a miracle that Rokshan hadn't quailed before Hyaloclast. She made herself get to her feet and meet the dragon queen's gaze. "I'm still myself," she said. Her voice was thin and tiny compared to Hyaloclast's deep boom.

"In spirit, perhaps," Hyaloclast said. "Your body...how is it even possible?"

Lamprophyre's eyes swelled with hot tears. She had hoped Hyaloclast would reassure her, tell her she had a solution, but Hyaloclast's genuine dismay hurt Lamprophyre to her core. She wiped her eyes furiously and said, "I don't know. But I still hear thoughts, and I know stone, and I remember everything that makes me myself—I refuse to call myself human when everything inside me is still dragon!"

Hyaloclast lowered herself so her head was on a level with Lamprophyre's. "It is dangerous for us to claim anything else. Orthoclase told me the artifact that did this is broken, but where one human has created magic, another may repeat that creation. If humans believe dragons can be reduced to their condition, then... You were wise to conceal your transformation. I assume you were successful."

"So far." Lamprophyre breathed out slowly, waiting for the hot wet feeling in her eyes to subside. "Hyaloclast, what do we do?"

Hyaloclast shook her head slowly. "I wish I had an answer for you. Finding a human who can create the right artifact is difficult if we want to keep this a secret."

"That's what we thought. Doesn't that mean we have to trust someone?"

"Trust whom? We know so little of magic, and the one adept you do know is an enemy, or so I understand."

"Manishi is definitely an enemy. And Rokshan is already in her debt for the artifact that let them find me. More than that, she would find a way to use this against us somehow."

"Yes." Hyaloclast's gaze went distant, as if she were looking far beyond Lamprophyre at something only she could see. "What stone was this artifact?"

"Serpentine."

"I've never seen it. But..." She fell silent. Lamprophyre knew better than to interrupt her when she was thinking. She waited patiently until Hyaloclast said, "There is something I barely remember. Something to do with serpentine. An old, old story about transformation. Not dragons, but other creatures. I thought it was a myth, but now I wonder."

"Wonder what?"

Hyaloclast smiled. "Still impatient?"

"Sorry."

"Don't be. Impatience in your situation is natural. If it were me, I'd be clawing stone in my desire to be restored." Hyaloclast pursed her lips in thought. "I will ask Scoria. She'll remember the details. But it was a story in which a carving blessed by Mother Stone had the power to change creatures from predator to prey, and I'm almost certain the stone was serpentine. Though it might have been travertine."

"But will that help? An old story?"

"Most of our stories have truth at their heart. Humans have been creating artifacts for centuries, easily since the time of the Great Cataclysm, and it's possible the carving in the story was an artifact rather than a blessed stone. After all, there's never been any evidence that Mother Stone acts on the natural world that way."

Lamprophyre sucked in a breath. "That's almost blasphemy. Suggesting that Mother Stone isn't as powerful as a human-made artifact."

"I didn't say she was less powerful. I said it wasn't the sort of thing she does. If the story is even a little true, it's far more reasonable to think a dragon somehow got hold of a human artifact. And stone is forever. That artifact, if it exists, is still around."

Hope sprang up in Lamprophyre's heart and she quashed it. "There's so many 'ifs' in this plan."

"It's one possibility. The other is finding a trustworthy adept to make a new artifact. And *you* will pursue that possibility." Hyaloclast's gaze was now terribly acute and fixed on Lamprophyre. The dragon queen's blood-red eyes were the size of Lamprophyre's human hand and unblinking. "Carefully, of course. Investigate the human who did this to you. If he had colleagues, one of them might be...persuaded...to repeat his work. And speak with other adepts in the city."

"But we can't trust them!"

Hyaloclast smiled again. "Lamprophyre, if you were an adept and someone came to you wanting a reversal of this transformation, would you use that knowledge against her?"

Lamprophyre, startled by this change of subject, said, "Of course not."

"And you are not the only one. Somewhere in this city is an adept who feels as you do, who has an honest heart and a desire to do good. Find that person, and you find your solution." Hyaloclast reached out with one giant hand and gently touched Lamprophyre's head, so lightly Lamprophyre almost couldn't feel it. She'd never have guessed the dragon queen had so much gentleness in her.

"I'll do my best," she said.

"And so will I," Hyaloclast said. "Whatever it takes."

Lamprophyre blinked. "But what does that mean?" Hyaloclast had sounded grim, as if she were pronouncing Lamprophyre's doom.

"You are my daughter as well as a dragon in my care. You think I wouldn't do everything in my power to see you restored?" Hyaloclast stood to her full height. "Good luck, Lamprophyre. Send word when you've succeeded—or better yet, come to the mountains yourself. And take care. If you're harmed in human form, I will have trouble justifying the destruction of whoever hurt you." She spread her wings, which filled the evening sky like a second crimson sunset, and took off, knocking Lamprophyre down with the force of the wind she made.

Lamprophyre lay sprawled on the ground, watching Hyaloclast fly away, until Orthoclase said, "Lamprophyre, are you all right?"

She'd forgotten he was there, and hoped he hadn't heard that. Hyaloclast never admitted to sentimentality, and she never treated Lamprophyre differently from the other dragons just because she was her daughter, but that had been embarrassingly personal. Climbing to her feet, Lamprophyre said, "I'm fine. Hyaloclast will look for a solution, and we're to see about finding an adept who can restore me."

"It will work out," Orthoclase said, bending to give Lamprophyre a leg up.

She didn't need to hear his thoughts to know he was being falsely optimistic. "Let's just stick with finding a solution, all right?" she said, feeling weary down to her human bones. "It's all right if we feel discouraged so long as we don't give up."

"Then can I say better you than me?" Orthoclase took to the skies, making Lamprophyre clutch at his ruff. "I'd have gone mad two thousand beats ago if it had happened to me. You're tougher than I am."

"Well, I *am* female," Lamprophyre teased, making her clutchmate laugh. "You males are all puny by comparison."

"Be nice, or I'll squish you," Orthoclase retorted. "Stones, but you're small. I can barely tell you're there."

"No fancy flying, or I might not be." Lamprophyre held on tighter. "I hate this. Flying like this."

"We will fix this, Lamprophyre," Orthoclase said, sobering. "No false optimism."

"I know," Lamprophyre said. "But I'm not looking forward to what comes next."

"What's that?"

Lamprophyre sighed. "More pretending to be human. Talking to strangers. And if I'm really unlucky, I'll have to endure the human kind of flirting."

CHAPTER NINE

Orthoclase returned Lamprophyre to the embassy, and she and Rokshan walked back to the palace. The flood of humanity had ebbed, and Lamprophyre didn't need to hold Rokshan's hand to keep from being lost. She held it anyway, feeling the need for comfort that hand-holding surprisingly gave. It was this skin, she decided, this thin, sensitive human skin that felt absolutely everything from the brush of fabric to the poke of an incautious elbow to the hard, callused surface of Rokshan's hand.

His palm was rougher than hers, with stripes of even rougher skin in places, and very warm, and his hand closed on hers firmly but not painfully, enveloping hers entirely. Either his hand was large, or, more likely, hers was unusually small. She was becoming used to her size, how much shorter she was than everyone else—and yet she couldn't be that small, because no one looked at her as if she were unusual in any way. She looked just like every other human woman in the essentials. It was an unsettling thought.

Rokshan slowed his pace when they entered the parkland, which was dark and shadowy now that the sun had fully set. Lamprophyre was used to seeing more clearly in the dark, and the discovery that this wasn't a draconic trait she'd retained made her angry. After stumbling a few times, she halted, bringing Rokshan to a stop as well. "I hate this," she said. "I'm sorry, I know I said I wouldn't be discouraged, but I can't see a thing."

"We'll go more slowly," Rokshan said. "I can't see well either, if that's any comfort."

"Only a little."

She let him lead her on through the trees until they came out into the great grassy open space between the strip of trees and the palace. Lights gleamed at all its windows, illuminating the ground, and lanterns burned on poles lining the main path that led to the front doors. Lamprophyre, who'd begun to feel permanently blinded, walked faster.

The guards at the front doors, which were closed now that it was full dark, appeared to ignore them when Rokshan didn't approach, but Lamprophyre could hear their thoughts, and they were full of speculation about where the prince was going and who his attractive companion was. Once again Lamprophyre felt uncomfortable. She didn't understand what about her new body made her attractive to humans, and she didn't understand what she was supposed to do about it. Did women flirt, or was that a thing only men did? She had so many questions she was bursting with them. "Rokshan," she began.

Rokshan had led her around the side of the palace to a door she'd seen a few times before. This one was also flanked by guards who saluted Rokshan when he approached. Their thoughts were identical to the other guards', and the taller of the men regarded Lamprophyre closely. His thoughts were centered on her breasts, and she almost put her arm across her chest to cover them before remembering that would give her secret away. She knew from Darsha's stories that men found female breasts enticing, but she'd thought that meant when they were visible. The guard seemed more interested because he *couldn't* see them. More questions for Rokshan.

The door was smaller than the grand front entrance and opened on a narrow little hallway like the one that connected the great hall to the "old" palace. "Rokshan," Lamprophyre said as soon as the door closed behind them, "why do men like breasts?"

Rokshan made a choked sound and stopped walking. "God's breath, La—Lelitha, where did that come from?"

"That guard was looking at my breasts."

Rokshan was once more crimson with embarrassment. "I don't—I suppose it's because women in our culture keep them covered, and... Lelitha, this is not the sort of question I'm comfortable with."

"Well, who would be? Because it seems to me, if men find this body attractive, I'm going to have a lot more questions like that one!"

The red was fading from Rokshan's face. "I'm sorry. Those are natural questions, it's just that I'm not used to talking about such things with a woman I'm not intimate with. You're right, I'm going to have to get over that embarrassment if I'm to help you."

"I wish I could ask Darsha, but she can't know who I am either."

"Darsha?"

"The Sister of the Red who comes for soup sometimes."

"I didn't know you were on a first-name basis." Rokshan resumed walking.

"She's told me all sorts of things about human sex. I wish I knew anything about dragon sex so I could compare."

That stopped Rokshan again. "How do you not know about dragon sex?"

"It's something our parents explain to us when we're old enough to choose a mate. We don't really talk about sex otherwise."

"Huh. I suppose that makes sense, since dragons don't experiment before they're married the way humans can." He sighed. "I wish I could justify sending you—oh, damn, we didn't get you a room yet."

"You mean, a place to sleep? I can't sleep with you?"

He grinned. "No, Lelitha, you can't sleep with me. And you'll want a place to retreat to when the demands of human life get to be too much."

"I like the sound of that. And you were about to say we can't justify me going to that room I don't have yet and avoiding talking to people tonight."

"You'll have to start interacting sometime, and a private family gathering is as good an opportunity as any. Far better than navigating a public entertainment or paraveti tangal performance. We—my family and Torannum's—occasionally come together after supper for conversation and drinks and sometimes games of chance. You shouldn't drink. We don't know how liquor will affect you, and if it makes you talkative, that could be a problem."

"I don't want to drink. It smells nasty."

"Fair enough." Rokshan sighed. "If I show you where to go, can you handle conversation on your own while I arrange for a room for you?"

The thought sent a nervous chill up Lamprophyre's spine, but she nodded. "I think so. Torannum is nice, and I like Anchala. Will Manishi or Khadar be there?"

"Khadar lives in the Archprelate's palace and almost never dines here. It's possible Manishi will be there, but she doesn't like small talk and is terrible at games, so the odds are in your favor."

The narrow corridor opened into one of the large rooms with colored glass walls, this one holding a few upholstered couches and a low table. Rokshan led her through this room, past an even larger, brightly lit room with a long table and dozens of thin-legged chairs lined up along it, filled with servants collecting dishes, and through a door that swung freely on its hinges.

Lamprophyre came to an abrupt halt just inside the swinging door and felt it smack her lightly on her tailless backside before settling into place. The room glowed in the light of a dozen golden lanterns, their light picked up by the walls tiled with more gold and reflected a dozen times. A shallow, oblong pool, this one empty of fish or plants, occupied the center of the room, with little trees in pots flanking it on all four sides. The smell of the water made Lamprophyre thirsty, and she ran her tongue around the inside of her mouth to moisten it.

Past the pool, the floor rose abruptly a handspan so the rest of the room was elevated. Four steps led up to this upper level, which circled half the room. Tables and chairs and couches stood in little groups here and there, as if inviting people to gather in threes or fours. It reminded Lamprophyre of the flight's caverns, some of them small enough for only a few dragons to fit at a time, and how cozy it was to snuggle in with a couple of clutchmates and tell stories and recite poetry into the dreaming hour.

But it didn't look like the people in this room had taken the hint.

There were at least two dozen men and women, and none of them were sitting. Instead, they had gathered in larger groups in whatever open spaces there were and stood talking quietly. Most of them held glasses, which still fascinated Lamprophyre; dragons could create glass, but no dragon had ever done anything so creative with that glass as humans seemed to do without a second thought. Glass cups to hold water, or liquor. So intriguing.

"Anchala," Rokshan said, raising his hand in greeting. Anchala, dressed more formally than she had been that afternoon, turned to acknowledge him. "Lelitha would like to get to know more of the family," he continued, steering Lamprophyre in Anchala's direction, "and I need to arrange for a bedroom for her. Introduce her, please?"

"Of course," Anchala said. She extended a hand to Lamprophyre and beckoned to her. "Join us, won't you?"

Lamprophyre managed not to look back over her shoulder at the departing Rokshan. That would make her look weak, as if she depended on him for security. She had to look strong, confident, completely at ease with her humanity just the way all these people were.

She went to Anchala's side, noticing again with an inward sigh that the princess was, like everyone else, taller than she was. Torannum, also in the little group, was even taller. Lamprophyre looked him over curiously, wondering what had brought him together with Anchala when they were of different countries. She decided she liked his black hair, which curled around his face and highlighted its angular bones. If that was what human male attractiveness meant, she could understand Anchala liking the way he looked, but surely even for humans there was more to love than that?

"Lelitha," Torannum said. "Nice to see you again. How did you like the dragon races?"

A pang shot through her, and it took some effort to reply casually, "They were so exciting, and the dragons are all so beautifully colored. I think the dark blue one is the handsomest."

Anchala smiled. "I wouldn't have thought to call a dragon handsome, the way I would a man, but they're all very shapely. I wonder what they consider attractive among themselves?"

"I wish we could ask them, but I feel uncomfortable approaching them, they're all so majestic," another woman said. "Anchala, introduce us."

"Oh, how stupid of me," Anchala said with a laugh. "Everyone, this is my cousin Lelitha from Adakavi. Lelitha, this is my dear friend and attendant Kalivati and her husband Harek, and this is my cousin Shekhar. Shekhar, how are you and I really related?"

Shekhar, a thin man whose hands moved restlessly, startled as if he hadn't been paying attention. "Second cousin once removed, on his majesty's side," he said. His voice was bland and as distant as his manner.

"I never can remember what that means, except that it's fairly distant, isn't it?"

"Your great-grandfather was my great-great-grandfather," Shekhar said in the same dull voice. "That generation was a big one. Fifteen children." Lamprophyre thought he sounded bored with the conversation. She listened to his thoughts and heard *fifteen children, twenty-seven years between oldest and youngest, enough to spread out the generations*. She wondered why Anchala didn't look offended at his tone. If a dragon had spoken to Lamprophyre that way, she would have excused herself to find someone who actually wanted to talk to her.

But Anchala just said, "That's so interesting. You'd think, with everything I've studied about our ancient history, that I'd know at least a little about my own family. I suppose it's too recent to interest me."

"I suppose," Shekhar said with a shrug. Anchala's thoughts still didn't sound irritated. Lamprophyre didn't understand that interaction at all.

Kalivati, taller even than Anchala and slender enough to resemble a willow branch, said, "So how are you related, Lelitha?"

Lamprophyre had been listening to Kalivati's thoughts, *nice girl, so quiet*, and she was caught off-guard. Her mind became a white blank. "Oh, you know, I don't remember the details?" she said, grateful that her voice didn't shake. "It's more distant than second cousins, I know, and my father is related to the queen in some way. We don't see this part of the family often." Why hadn't Rokshan primed her with the answer to this question? There were going to be a dozen other things she didn't know, and she would give herself away...except she wouldn't, because her greatest protection was that no one even suspected a transformation like hers was possible.

She decided to stop listening to their thoughts. She needed to pay close attention to what they said verbally if she didn't want to be caught like that again.

"I only know we have a hundred cousins all over Gonjiri," Anchala said, "and it would take a Shekhar to keep track of them all."

Shekhar shrugged again, but said nothing. Lamprophyre was starting to wonder why he was at this gathering, if he wasn't going to participate in the conversation. Or maybe that meant it was acceptable to stay silent, and she could get away with saying nothing that might expose her.

Harek put his arm around Kalivati's waist. "I know marrying Kalivati, with her seven siblings, was a shock. I'm an only child and I had no idea families could be so loud."

"You love it," Kalivati said with a smile.

"What about you, Lelitha? Do you have brothers or sisters?" Torannum asked.

Again Lamprophyre's mind went blank. What had Rokshan said about her imaginary family? The only thing she remembered was the thing about lies being most believable when you kept them simple. And she could think of only one way to keep a fictional family straight in her head, short of pretending the clutch was her siblings, and that could lead to revealing things no one would assume were human. "I'm an only child, too," she said. This was entirely true. "And we live so far south, I haven't ever met my cousins, even the nearest ones."

"We're glad you came," Anchala said. "I'm sorry we didn't know you currently live so close, or we would have invited you to family gatherings." She made a face that came and went so swiftly Lamprophyre would have missed it if she hadn't been looking right at her. "Though our family gatherings are often...strained...so you might consider our oversight a blessing."

"Anchala, remember what you swore," Kalivati said with an impish grin.

Anchala rolled her eyes. "I swear not to say bad things about my siblings until the wedding is over," she chanted. "Even if I really want to," she added in a more normal voice. "Manishi is driving me mad. She refuses to do even the smallest thing in any of the activities and ceremonies. Did you notice how she sat in the back at the dragon races today? She——"

Kalivati cleared her throat. Anchala pressed her lips together as if that would keep more words from escaping. "I'm done now," she said.

"Good," Kalivati said. She sipped from her glass, which contained a rosy liquid, and added, "Speaking of siblings, Tor, here comes your brother."

Torannum shifted to make room for Sanyot. He held not one, but two skinny glasses filled with something pale. Lamprophyre hadn't seen anyone else with two glasses and wondered how fond of liquor you had to be to need both hands occupied with drink.

"I didn't realize yours was the most interesting conversation," he said, addressing Torannum but smiling at Lamprophyre. "For shame, Tor, not offering our newest arrival refreshment." To Lamprophyre's surprise and consternation, Sanyot extended one of his glasses to her. She took it without thinking. The smell of alcohol coming off it was faint, but that might just be the limitations of her human nose. She hadn't considered that someone might force liquor on her, and she had no idea what the protocol was.

Sanyot took a sip of his liquor—wine, Lamprophyre guessed, though she only knew the names of two kinds of liquor and there were likely hundreds, given how fond humans were of being inebriated—and said, his eyes still fixed on Lamprophyre, "And what have we been discussing? Something interesting, I hope?"

"Family relations," Anchala said. "You'd probably find it boring."

"Not at all," Sanyot said. "I'm about to acquire a royal family, however indirectly. How closely related does this make us, Lelitha?"

"I don't know. Not very closely, I think. I'm sorry," Lamprophyre said, wishing herself far from this conversation and the undertones in Sanyot's voice she didn't understand. She chanced listening to his thoughts and heard only a snatch of emotion she didn't recognize.

"You're not related to her at all, not by blood," Harek said.

"True." Sanyot sipped again. "Lelitha, tell us more about your course of study at the academy. *That* sounded interesting. I didn't know anyone studied magic who wasn't an adept."

Lamprophyre felt a surprising rush of gratitude toward Sanyot. This was something she could talk about that wasn't a lie, except for how she wasn't a student at the academy. "I just think magic is so much a part of our lives, it makes sense for people to want to understand how it works. And when I began my studies, I discovered there was no simple book or even a list that showed what stones had what magical effect. And none of the adepts I spoke to were interested in compiling one. So it's my project, I suppose you could call it." It was something she and Porphyry had been working on in the past months and had been oddly difficult to assemble, as if the adepts weren't just uninterested, they were actively opposed.

"You're right, that is interesting," Kalivati said. "I never thought about it, but why shouldn't we know what the stones we buy and sell are used for?"

"I only know jade and moonstone are used in healing," Torannum said. "And Sanyot has a sapphire chip he used to cheat at lessons."

"I did not, and you're going to give everyone a bad impression of my character," Sanyot said, his gaze once more fixed on Lamprophyre so there was no question which part of "everyone" he cared about. "It was an artifact to stimulate my memory when I studied. Nothing illicit about that."

"Except when you used it during examinations."

"Which I did exactly once. And it's not as if you were innocent of cheating yourself, Tor."

"You see what we missed out on, not having siblings?" Harek said to Lamprophyre.

Torannum and Sanyot both laughed. Lamprophyre, who'd grown tense with their sharp exchange, relaxed. They'd just been teasing each other the way the clutch usually did—and with that thought, Lamprophyre was struck so hard by homesickness she felt her eyes burn the way that signaled tears were coming. She blinked hard and fast to hold them back.

"Anyway, Lelitha, do you plan on publishing your research? It seems there's interest," Sanyot said.

"I do," Lamprophyre said. "But that's still a ways off."

"Attractive and intelligent," Sanyot said with another of those smiles Lamprophyre couldn't interpret. "What a combination."

Shekhar, who'd been silent throughout this conversation, abruptly turned. "I'm going to talk to Mother," he said, and walked away without waiting for acknowledgement.

Anchala watched him go. "Don't worry," she told Lamprophyre. "Shekhar's just like that. Very focused, only talks when he has something to say, and he never met a social grace he didn't ignore. But if you can get him going on some subject he cares about, he sounds perfectly normal."

"I wondered," Lamprophyre admitted. "He was so quiet, I thought maybe he was uncomfortable." More uncomfortable even than she was.

"He's brave, if he's willing to risk the aunties," Torannum said, lowering his voice as if confiding a secret. "They've already cornered Tekentriya and are probably lecturing her about her familial duties. I hope they don't decide to descend upon us."

Silence fell, but it was a comfortable silence, as if everyone was considering what to talk about next. Lamprophyre took the opportunity to look around the room. Shekhar had joined a group of what looked like older women, not truly aged with white hair, but not as young as Anchala or Kalivati. Tekentriya, the crown princess, was at the center of that group. She looked more sour than usual, though that might have been because the older women all appeared to be talking to her at once. If they were the aunties Torannum had mentioned, they seemed formidable. She tucked the unfamiliar word away to ask Rokshan about later.

Beyond Shekhar, Satiya was conversing with the large woman Lamprophyre had heard twittering to the queen at the races. The king wasn't in attendance, but Lamprophyre's impression of him over the past several months was that he didn't care for social gatherings that didn't have a political purpose.

"That's our mother," Torannum said, following Lamprophyre's gaze. "She and Queen Satiya don't usually get along, so I wonder what they've found to talk about so amicably."

"Why don't they get along? Or—I'm sorry, that must be personal," Lamprophyre said.

"It's not," Sanyot said, for once not sounding flirtatious. "Mother is very conscious of our family's social standing. We're of very high rank in Sachetan."

"And *my* mother, for all she's queen, cares very little for rank," Anchala said. "So it's not that they don't get along so much as they have very different views of the way the world works."

Lamprophyre felt uncomfortable at how readily the three discussed their mothers. She would never have dared to criticize Hyaloclast's behavior in any way, not to others and certainly not to her mother's face. And yet they didn't seem disdainful of their parents' failings, just matter-of-fact.

"Well, that's one thing going my way, if they can keep up the civility," Anchala said. "I wish my wedding didn't have to be so political."

"It could be worse. You could be heir. Or queen," Torannum said, taking her hand and raising it to his lips in a gesture Lamprophyre found even more uncomfortable than the conversation. Humans and their casual displays of affection. She tried to imagine one of her clutchmates kissing her hand and came up blank.

She looked past Torannum so she could pretend she hadn't seen it and, to her immense relief, saw Rokshan approaching. "It's all taken care of, Lelitha," he said. "Shall I show you to your room? I know you had a long journey to arrive this morning and you must be tired."

"You came from Kolmira this morning?" Sanyot said. "I'm amazed you have the energy to socialize." He smiled and bowed. "Rest well, my lady, and perhaps we can speak again in the morning."

"Yes, um, that would be nice," Lamprophyre managed. She bowed politely to the others and followed Rokshan at the fastest pace that was still polite. She didn't want to look like she was running.

"I thought you weren't going to drink," Rokshan said when they were back in the hall. He took the glass from her and set it on a table in passing.

"I wasn't. I didn't. Sanyot gave it to me."

"He did, did he?" Rokshan scowled. "He might become a problem."

"I don't know. At least he's nice, even if he is flirting. I just don't know how to respond."

"Are you attracted to him?"

Lamprophyre shot him an astonished look. "He's human, Rokshan. How could I be attracted to him?"

"I don't know. I thought, if you're in a human body…but I suppose that doesn't make sense." Rokshan sighed. "Just do what I said before. Be yourself. He'll eventually realize you're not interested and stop pursuing you. At least, I think he will. I don't know him very well."

Lamprophyre nodded. Flirting. Conversation. Families. She hoped more than ever they would find a solution soon.

CHAPTER TEN

Lamprophyre woke slowly, disoriented by her surroundings. The floor shifted beneath her as if she were sleeping in mud, except mud would be clingy and this was dry and smooth like polished marble, if marble were soft. She opened her eyes and saw, not the cool white walls of the embassy curving until they met high above, but colored tiles covering a flat ceiling, rimmed with gold. The gold gave off no smell, but she felt certain it was real gold and not imitation the way some of the roofs in the city were.

She realized she was lying on her back with no discomfort from her wings being trapped under her. In that moment of realization, she remembered where and what she was. The palace. She had a human body. She sat up and buried her face in her hands, but no tears came even though she was certain this body had an unlimited supply of them. No tears. It was time to act.

She got out of the bed and regarded it with interest. Dragons didn't sleep on anything but bare earth or stone, which was extremely comfortable as well as smelling nice. Humans, though, needed beds to cushion their frail bodies. She had to admit the bed felt nice, but would she have felt the same if she were still a dragon sleeping on a human bed? Assuming she could find one big enough to fit her.

The bedroom Rokshan had found for her wouldn't fit her in her actual form, but to "Lelitha" it was proportionally the same as the embassy was to Lamprophyre. It had furnishings Rokshan had had to explain to her: a clothespress to store her clothes when she finally had some, a dressing table with a mirror for her to examine herself after she dressed, which made no sense, and a padded chair with a footstool for relaxing. There was also another mirror, this one long enough to show her whole body, mounted on the wall beneath the row of round windows that let in plenty of morning sunlight.

Now she stood in front of the long mirror and examined her human body for the first time. It was curvy, with smooth brown skin that dimpled when she pressed a finger to it, far more rounded than Rokshan's angular chest and legs. That was the only other human body she'd seen enough of to compare, though she remembered what Darsha and Bhakriya and Anchala looked like and even through their clothes she thought she was rounder than they were.

She poked a finger into the deep hole in the middle of her belly. It didn't go through her skin to her internal organs, and she couldn't imagine what it was for. Rokshan had one, as she recalled from seeing him swimming, and he never did anything to conceal it, so it must not be private. Touching it made her feel strange, with a sort of itchy feeling that tingled and made tiny bumps rise up on her skin. It was a sensation she had no name for.

Lamprophyre twisted to look at her backside. More curves, from which extended her legs, which also curved. This body was surprisingly appealing to her, like river rocks smoothed by centuries of flowing water. It was symmetrical, something dragons found attractive, and the skin was beautiful, almost glowing. If it weren't for the fact that she was trapped in it, she might have actually liked it.

She pushed up on her heavy breasts and looked at how that changed their appearance. They were tipped with darker, rougher skin that was nevertheless very sensitive. The breasts were as curvy as the rest of her, a part of her overall appearance, and yet it felt like they were their own entity. She let go of them and hopped up and down, making them jiggle uncomfortably. Really, breasts were annoying. She couldn't understand why men liked them, unless it was out of relief that they didn't have to endure how they moved.

With a sigh, she wiggled back into the gown Satiya had given her. She was sure it was wrong for daytime wear—humans had such interesting customs with regard to clothing—but she didn't have anything else, and she certainly couldn't go naked.

Then she crossed the room to the door, and hesitated with her hand on the latch. Her body had begun signaling its hunger, as well as other needs. However nice it was to know there were some physical reactions humans and dragons had in common, she still didn't know how to get food and she certainly didn't know how to relieve herself. Rokshan had said he would come for her in the morning, but she had no idea when he intended to arrive. Wandering the palace, which was enormous and confusing, struck her as a bad idea.

Her stomach growled again, and Lamprophyre made a decision. After a little pushing and pulling, trying to figure out how to work the latch, she managed to get the door open and stepped out into the hall. It was long and covered in sheets of embossed gold, and the floor was wood and cool against her bare—

Lamprophyre grumbled. She'd forgotten the sandals. She thought she might have forgotten them on purpose, her mind deliberately overlooking putting them on. She returned to sit on the chair beside the dressing table and fumbled into the many thin straps. It took almost as long to figure out the buckles as it had the door latch, but eventually she felt she'd done it properly.

The door opened. "Good morning," Rokshan said. "Did you sleep well?" He had a silver tray in one hand and held the door open with the other.

"I think so. I didn't dream," Lamprophyre said. She stood, wobbled a little at not having direct contact with the floor, and added, "I don't know how this body relieves itself, but I feel pressure—Stones, Rokshan, don't get that look! I need you not to be embarrassed about this!"

"Sorry," Rokshan said. "I doubt it's much different from how dragons do it, but we use artifacts to dispose of the waste." He took hold of a knob embedded in the wall and pulled to reveal a cleverly concealed door and cubby. Within the cubby, which would fit someone twice Rokshan's size and was therefore perfect for her, was a wooden box with a hole cut out of the top. Rokshan reached inside and grasped a second knob, this one attached to the side of the box.

"You sit on top and relieve yourself into the box," he said, "then you turn the knob like this—" He demonstrated. A brief flash of pale light, not bright enough to hurt her eyes, flickered out of the hole. "The artifact destroys the waste."

Lamprophyre peered past him at the box. "Will it hurt if I'm on the box when I turn the knob?"

"No. It is kind of a strange feeling, though." Rokshan stepped back and went to sit on the edge of the bed. "Go ahead and try it."

Lamprophyre shut herself into the cubby. It was warm and dimly lit by a couple of small window holes near the ceiling, and felt comforting, like snuggling up with friends in a cozy cave. She couldn't smell any waste products, so either no one had used this cubby for a while, or the artifact was extremely efficient.

Fortunately, there were only so many ways a body could be arranged and still function, and Lamprophyre's guess about where her bodily wastes were excreted was right. She held her dress high above her waist, did her business, and twisted the knob. The faintest tugging sensation on her rear end was the only sign the artifact had done anything. She hopped down and peered into the box, and saw nothing. Fascinating. She should see about getting one of these boxes for the embassy. A big one. Having to fly outside the city to relieve herself was tedious.

She emerged from the cubby and shut the door behind her. "I promise this is the last time I'll say this, but I wish this was over."

Rokshan smiled. "After you eat, we'll go to the warehouses and see what progress the others have made. Maybe they've found someone who can create the artifact already."

Lamprophyre shook her head. "That's more optimistic even than I'm willing to be." She nodded at the tray. "Is that food? It smells like food."

Rokshan had set the tray on the end of the bed, and now he

removed the cover. "I wasn't sure what you'd like, so I had them give me some of everything."

"Is it appropriate for a prince to bring food? I thought you had servants for that." There was meat in varying cuts she didn't recognize, and a pile of something yellow that smelled a little sulfurous, and some silvery finger-long things that smelled like nothing she'd ever smelled before. She prodded the pile with a finger and sucked on it. It didn't taste terrible, so she picked up one of the things and bit it in half.

"We do, but—Lelitha, don't eat with your fingers. Use a fork and knife."

Lamprophyre regarded the silver sticks with dismay. "How?"

Rokshan showed her how to hold the fork, which was the stick that divided into two prongs at one end, and then how to stab it into the food. She managed to convey one of the silvery things to her mouth without it falling off the fork more than twice. "This is delicious. What is it?"

"You've never had fish before?"

"Fish are too small to be more than a nibble, and dragons don't cook them. They just catch fire and burn to ash." Now that she was chewing, she could identify the similarities between the tiny fish on her tray and the larger ones she'd occasionally consumed, though she'd never chewed those, just swallowed them whole.

Using the knife and fork together was much harder, but eventually she sawed off a piece of a cylinder of meat, also the size of her finger, and took a bite. "Oh," she moaned, "this is *amazing*. Why haven't I had this before?"

"It's sausage," Rokshan said, "and I'm sure Depik hasn't served it to you because it would take a thousand sausages to satisfy you. Easier to feed you a pig."

"I think I should have sausages occasionally. Even if it takes a thousand of them to feed me. It would be a lovely treat."

She didn't care for the yellow stuff, which Rokshan said was eggs; it was blander than the sausage and the fish, and Lamprophyre decided she liked strong flavors in this body. She also didn't care for the black liquid called coffee, which tasted like turquoise, bitter and strong, but drank the hot tea happily. She ate until she was full, then said, "Do we take the rest back to the kitchen?"

"No, the servants will fetch it later," Rokshan said. "It's common practice for us—the nobility who live in the palace—to have breakfast brought to our rooms. I told them I would take yours. And yes, they did give me funny looks, but Akarshan won't let anyone argue with the royal family no matter how crazy their requests."

Lamprophyre remembered Akarshan, the chief cook, from her early days in Tanajital, how kind and obliging he'd been. "Do the servants come into my room, then?"

"They'll make your bed and tidy up. More or less what Bhakriya does for you." Rokshan rose from the chair where he'd been sitting with his feet up on the footstool. "Let's go. We also have to buy clothing for you so you'll be properly dressed tonight."

Lamprophyre made a face. "And tonight is what?"

"A paraveti tangal performance."

That cheered Lamprophyre. "I do like paraveti tangal. I didn't know you need special clothes for it."

Rokshan opened the door for her. "You need clothes for everything. Everyday wear, afternoon wear, evening wear to dine, evening wear for a performance, formal robes for religious ceremonies—"

"You're making this up."

"By Jiwanyil, I'm not."

Lamprophyre's cheerful feeling faded. "But I don't want to be in this form that long!"

"I know, and we're hoping you won't be. But we have to be prepared."

Lamprophyre felt like grumbling again, but she kept it to herself. Someday soon, very soon if she was lucky, she wouldn't have to worry about strange human customs anymore. That day couldn't come quickly enough.

The streets surrounding the dragons' warehouses were free of humans. Lamprophyre had known this was so, because she'd seen how men and women gave the dragons plenty of room when the clutch had first come to Tanajital, but she hadn't expected how odd it would feel to walk those streets without being thronged by people. If not for the steady murmur of movement nearby, people heard but not seen, she might have thought the city abandoned. The feeling was unexpectedly melancholy.

Only Orthoclase and Porphyry were visible when she and Rokshan arrived. "Stones, I forgot how small you are now," Porphyry said. "We have got to get you changed back."

"Bromargyrite went to talk to his adept contact," Orthoclase said. "If humans know about serpentine, we'll find out soon."

Dolomite poked his head out of his warehouse. "I had a dream that Lamprophyre regained her dragon body," he said. "It was so real—but I suppose not. I'm sorry, Lamprophyre."

"For what?" Lamprophyre asked.

"Oh, that my dream couldn't be true. You must be miserable."

Trust the guileless Dolomite to cut straight to the heart of things. "It's not so bad," she reassured him. "I mean, of course it's bad, but at least I'm not a mindless animal."

Dolomite brightened. "That's true. I wonder if such a transformation is possible."

"I think if it was, our enemy would have arranged for it," Lamprophyre said.

Dolomite's brow furrowed. "Enemy? We have an enemy?"

Lamprophyre realized she hadn't told anyone but Rokshan about her suspicions that the ancient entity was behind her predicament. "Evart said he was influenced by a voice in his head," she said. "Something that told him dragons have hoards of gold and gems. He transformed me so he could capture and compel me, but I think the entity wanted me human and was just using him to accomplish that."

"What would be the point?" Orthoclase said. "So you're in a human body. You're still a dragon in the essentials."

"Because she's vulnerable now," Porphyry said. "If the entity wants her dead, that's suddenly become a thousand times easier."

"That's what we thought," Rokshan said. "But we don't know what the entity is capable of. So far, it hasn't spoken to more than one mind at a time, but is that because it can't or because it just hasn't needed to? And can it only speak to certain people, or is anyone potentially a tool?"

"Even if it can speak to anyone, I don't think everyone is vulnerable," Lamprophyre said. "When it spoke to me, it tried to convince me that I was special and that it could give me my heart's desire. Maybe I'm wrong, and humans are different, but not every dragon would listen to that kind of persuasion, even if we didn't know who the entity was."

"No, you're right, not all humans are greedy and prideful," Rokshan said. "So we only have to worry about humans who can be motivated by the promise of power or wealth."

"Or revenge," Orthoclase said. "Or love. Don't humans act irrationally when it's a matter of love?"

"Are you saying dragons don't?" Rokshan said, his voice sharp.

"Not the way humans do in the stories I've read," Porphyry said. "A dragon might pine after another dragon, or pursue him or her relentlessly, but if the one they're interested in makes it explicit they won't love them in return, that's the end of it. You can't force someone to love you, and dragons always know when their feelings are unrequited."

"But that doesn't stop you from feeling them," Rokshan said.

"No. But we do what we can to turn our interest elsewhere. Dragons don't kill in a fit of romantic passion, for example."

"You've been reading too many romantic poems," Rokshan said. "Most humans don't do that either."

"Stop," Lamprophyre said. "You're arguing over irrelevancies. Porphyry is right that there are some humans who might be motivated to listen to the entity if it promised to give them someone they love. That doesn't make humans weak or inferior to dragons. It doesn't matter whether dragons behave like humans. Can we focus on figuring out what the entity might try next?"

Porphyry's crimson scales darkened with embarrassment. "Sorry," he said. "That was rude."

"No, I was too quick to take offense," Rokshan said. "I didn't realize how on edge I was."

"Good," Lamprophyre said. "So it seems our guess is that humans who desperately want something the entity can promise to give them are the ones we need to worry about. Which means Manishi just got about a hundred times more dangerous."

"Maybe," Rokshan said. "I can't see Manishi believing the promises of anyone she can't see, no matter what they promise."

"We should still be careful of her," Orthoclase said. "But we already knew that. Also, someone needs to return the tracking artifact, and I don't want it to be me."

"I'll do it," Rokshan said. "I'm the one who negotiated for it. Where is it?"

"Coquina still has it."

"We have to go to the embassy anyway, to see if Coquina needs anything," Lamprophyre said.

She looked up as a huge shadow passed overhead and managed not to duck as Bromargyrite descended. The big male landed some distance from Lamprophyre and turned around carefully as if afraid he might squash her. Given his general awkward clumsiness, Lamprophyre was grateful for his caution.

"Bad news," he said as he approached the others. "Or at least I think it's bad. My adept friend had never heard of serpentine."

Lamprophyre's heart felt dipped in lead. "Not even heard of it?"

"It could still exist," Bromargyrite said. "He's just one adept. He can't know everything."

"Yes, and if serpentine is rare, maybe only a few people know about it," Porphyry said.

"But we can't go around asking to find those few," Orthoclase said.

Lamprophyre drew in a deep breath. "So we'll take a different approach. We'll go to the academy's library and search for it there."

"That will draw all sorts of attention, if a bunch of dragons, or even one dragon, shows up on their doorstep asking to look at their records," Porphyry objected.

"It won't be a dragon. It will be a human visiting from another academy," Lamprophyre said. The prospect of taking action cheered her tremendously. So did the idea of going inside the academy, something she'd never done because none of the buildings were sized for dragons.

"It's dangerous," Bromargyrite said, but let his voice trail off. "Or, actually I suppose it isn't. At worst, they'll refuse you entrance."

"And if I have Dharan along, they won't do that," Lamprophyre said. "We need to bring Dharan in on the secret."

"He won't betray you, that's certain," Rokshan said. "All right. I'll talk to him this afternoon and we'll see how soon you can get into the library."

"I'm so jealous," Porphyry said. "You should take advantage of the opportunity to get more information for our book."

Lamprophyre had forgotten, in the excitement of pursuing a cure, that there were other things she might learn from a human library. "I'll see what I can learn," she said. "For now...wait, where's Flint?"

Porphyry and Orthoclase exchanged meaningful glances. "He went to the embassy to 'help' Coquina," Orthoclase said with a grin.

Lamprophyre heard the emphasis on "help." "What kind of help?"

"The kind you give someone you're interested in," Porphyry said. "I think Flint has started to appreciate Coquina's virtues. Now that she's stopped flirting so relentlessly."

Lamprophyre gasped. "Are you sure? That would be wonderful for them, obviously, but how strange."

"It's a theory," Orthoclase said, "but he has been rather attentive lately. And Coquina has singled him out often in the last several twelvedays."

A squirmy, uncomfortable feeling began in the pit of Lamprophyre's stomach. If Coquina and Flint became pair-bonded, she would be happy for them, but it brought up once again the issue of who *Lamprophyre* would choose. She still didn't feel an attraction to any of her clutchmates, and it made her feel guilty because all of them were interesting in their own way, even Dolomite, who acted younger than his years and was definitely not a possibility. She didn't think any of them were pining after her, or even watching expectantly to see if she'd choose him, but surely they couldn't *not* wonder?

"So we'll stop at the embassy," Rokshan was saying, "and then Lelitha and I need to buy clothes for her. And set up fittings for formal wear."

"What does that mean, fittings?" Lamprophyre asked.

"Formal clothing is made to fit your body exactly," Rokshan said, "not like shirts and trousers which are ready-made. I asked Anchala for the name of a tailor—told her you'd never needed formal wear before, and I don't think she was suspicious. He'll measure you, and he and his assistants will sew clothes to those measurements."

"That sounds tedious."

"It is." Rokshan shrugged. "Fortunately, the embassy is rather overflowing with riches at the moment, because formal clothing is also expensive."

Lamprophyre made a face. "Then let's get it over with." Her resentment over needing clothing for her human body deepened when she considered how much that clothing would cost—money that could have gone to buying sausages, for example. She made herself think about seeing the paraveti tangal performance instead. Clearly there were some compensations for being human.

CHAPTER ELEVEN

They heard shouting before they came in sight of the embassy, not the sound of a mob, but of many voices all trying to be heard over one another. Rokshan and Lamprophyre looked at each other in alarm. Then they ran.

Rokshan quickly outpaced Lamprophyre, with her shorter legs and jiggling parts. Panting, Lamprophyre pushed herself faster. She'd only been running for a handful of beats and already she was short of breath. This body had more shortcomings than she'd originally thought. If Evart, or the entity, had had a hand in designing it, they'd been unusually clever in creating one that would hamper her.

She reached the embassy courtyard and stood with a hand pressed to the ache in her side, sucking in air and cursing mentally. She didn't have enough breath to curse aloud. Ahead, Coquina sat on her haunches in front of the embassy, facing a crowd of perhaps a dozen men and women. The noise of their shouting was great enough that their words were as unintelligible as their thoughts.

It didn't take hearing thoughts to see how dismayed Coquina was. Her head moved restlessly as she tried to focus on one speaker only to be distracted by another. Flint sat in the entrance to the dining pavilion, his expression the kind of neutral that said he was concealing worry. He shifted, too, looking as if he wanted to fly for help, but didn't want to abandon Coquina.

Rokshan was pushing through the crowd, shouting as well. Lamprophyre couldn't hear him either, though she could guess he was calling for quiet. Coquina hadn't noticed him yet, as far as Lamprophyre could tell. Lamprophyre surveyed the crowd. Some of the people, she knew, and others were strangers, but all of them were like every other petitioner: they wanted something from the dragons.

Drawing in a deep breath, she trotted—she didn't feel like running again—around the crowd and to the back door of the embassy. It was heavier than she'd imagined, but once she got it moving, it opened smoothly on its oiled hinges. She slipped through the opening and came up behind Coquina. Her clutchmate had started moving restlessly, a sign that Coquina was about to lose her temper. Lamprophyre shouted her name, then shouted it again, putting her whole body into it.

Coquina jumped, startled, and swung around fast enough that Lamprophyre had to move to avoid being hit by Coquina's tail. "Lamprophyre," she breathed. "I am so glad to see you. There's a mob, and I don't know what they all want!"

"It's not a mob," Lamprophyre said. "Get them to shut up, tell them they have to wait a few minutes, and I'll tell you what to do."

Coquina nodded and turned back to face the crowd. "*Quiet!*" she bellowed, her deep voice cutting across even the loudest shouts. The noise dwindled to almost nothing. "I can't help you all at once," she said, still in that loud voice. "Wait a few...minutes...and I will meet with each of you."

A few people began shouting again. Typical of some humans, Lamprophyre thought, to imagine instructions didn't apply to them.

"Shut up, or I'll kick you out," Coquina snarled, lowering her head to stare down the offenders. They shut up.

Coquina backed into the embassy, followed by Rokshan. "I can't do this," Coquina said. "They all want to talk at once, and their thoughts make me dizzy so I can't even depend on that to help me. What the Stones am I supposed to do, Lamprophyre?"

"Rokshan, will you go out there and see if you can't get them to queue up or something?" Lamprophyre looked past Coquina's bulk to assess the crowd. She'd grown used to seeing crowds as their own entities rather than as a group of individuals, getting a sense for their moods and how to treat them. This one didn't move like an angry thing, but it was definitely impatient, which meant it needed to see progress of some kind.

With her eyes still on Rokshan as he moved through the crowd, she said, "Some of those people come here often, always with minor or manufactured complaints. I think it's past time we stopped coddling them. Tell Kaumat, Viveki, and Saretha that they're to stop wasting our time and the embassy won't hear any more of their demands."

"That doesn't sound diplomatic," Coquina said.

"It's a different kind of diplomacy. And we can get away with it because you're unfamiliar and scary and might do anything."

"I'm not scary!" Coquina looked at her wings as if expecting them to sprout barbs or fling spikes.

"Humans fear anything new. Those three got used to me being polite and know I won't hurt them. They have no idea what you might do to them." Lamprophyre scanned the crowd. "As for the others, Syotin had an appointment to return today because I had to investigate his claim. Tell him we've determined he's due ten rupyas in reparations and that Bromargyrite apologizes for the damage. I think he'll be satisfied with that. And you'll have to tell Marani I've gone back to the mountains and can't visit her school to talk about dragons, but see if she'll accept someone else in the clutch. That's got to be up to you to figure out."

Coquina's lips moved as she memorized the names. "And the others?"

"The others are strangers, but I'll stay here and help determine judgments. That should give you a feel for how it's done."

"I'm still not sure this is a great idea, but we don't have a choice, do we?"

"You'll be fine." Impishly, Lamprophyre added, "Just think how impressed Flint will be."

Coquina's scales turned faintly brown as she blushed. "He won't care. I'm just doing what's needed."

"Males always admire a confident, take-charge female. You didn't say things were serious between you."

Coquina blushed harder. "I didn't know they were. I flirted with him because he's handsome, but I didn't think it would amount to anything, and now, well, I've never felt so foolish in my life."

Lamprophyre patted Coquina's leg. Her scales were smooth, barely bumpy, and warmer than Lamprophyre's human skin. "We'll all be so happy for you, you know. Now, get out there and impress everyone."

Rokshan had managed to coerce everyone into a rough line, and as Coquina stepped forward to address the first, Lamprophyre stood in the shadows where she couldn't be seen and observed her clutchmate's interactions. Coquina sounded as confident as if she had no reservations whatsoever, something Lamprophyre remembered had always been one of Coquina's traits, never looking uncertain no matter the situation.

She looked past the crowd of humans to Flint, who was watching Coquina closely. Lamprophyre couldn't tell from this distance how he felt, but she hoped he was impressed. It was hard to remember now how she'd spent so many years envying Coquina and wanting to best her at the things Coquina excelled at, when she had her own talents Coquina couldn't match.

She brought her attention back to the present when Coquina nudged her, a prod that sent her stumbling a few steps. "Oh," she said, seeing Coquina looking down at her. "Tell her dragons aren't messengers and they don't give rides to strangers, so we can't convey her goods to Kolmira. But be sympathetic. It's good that she isn't afraid of us, and we want to encourage that."

It took a few thousand beats to deal with all the petitioners, at the end of which time Lamprophyre felt a little easier about leaving Coquina in charge. When the last of them was gone, Lamprophyre leaned against the wall, feeling as if she'd run to the palace and back, and said, "See? It's not so bad."

"Not so bad? I feel as if I've flown to the mountains and back a dozen times without stopping. I never really appreciated what you do before." Coquina settled on the floor of the embassy with her wings spread wide to cover her.

"It was good," Flint said from the doorway. "They all went away... not satisfied, all of them, but they were convinced you had the right to pass judgment. That's important in a diplomat, I think."

"It is," Lamprophyre agreed. "Even so, it's good we only have three judgment days in a twelveday."

Coquina perked up. "So I have three days before I have to do that again? You might be cured by then!"

"I don't know," Lamprophyre said, and repeated what Bromargyrite had learned from the adept and what she and the others had discussed. Flint and Coquina stilled as she spoke. Finally, she said, "I'm hopeful I can find something in the embassy library, so it's not all bad. It just might take a while."

"What's a library?" Flint asked.

"It's a collection of books and scrolls, organized so people can find information they need," Rokshan said. "The Tanajital academy library is the largest public library in Gonjiri—though it's only public in the sense that it isn't owned by an individual, the way the palace library is. They don't let just anyone in, which is why we need Dharan's help."

"I choose to remain optimistic," Coquina said, "though it's completely self-serving."

"I think you were wonderful," Flint said. Coquina ducked her head and blushed again. Lamprophyre caught Rokshan's eye and grinned. Really, she liked romance so long as it was other people's.

"We're going to buy clothing for this body now," she told her clutchmates, "and Rokshan says that will take time. And there's a paraveti tangal performance tonight."

"That sounds nice," Flint said. "You'll have to tell us about the inside of the recital hall. I've always been curious."

"I'm trying to stay optimistic myself by remembering how many places I fit now," Lamprophyre said.

When they were back on the street, Rokshan said, "So. Flint and Coquina. It looks like Porphyry and Orthoclase were right. How do you feel about that?"

"Happy for them. And surprised. I thought Coquina's flirtation would guarantee Flint never looked at her that way, but I suppose she hasn't flirted with him in...months. Months, right?"

"That sounds right. At the very least it's been since midsummer, so that makes it months." Rokshan took her hand to keep her close to him. "The shop I have in mind is around the next corner."

The shop in question smelled dry like cloth, which made sense because its walls were lined with wide wooden ladders whose rungs were piled with folded cloth in various shades of white and cream and beige. More colorful fabrics hung from the walls or were folded on other ladders. Lamprophyre reminded herself to ask why the ladders were so wide and appeared to be fixed in place. Humans had the strangest furnishings.

The shopkeeper didn't seem at all overawed by waiting on a prince and didn't ask any questions about the prince's cousin. She just removed cloth piles from the ladder rungs and pressed them on Lamprophyre, directing her to a little room that held a short stool and nothing else.

"Try them on, dear, I have an eye for sizes," the woman said. Left alone, Lamprophyre stripped out of Satiya's gown and pulled on shirt and trousers. The trousers were too tight around the hips, but the shirt fit perfectly. When Lamprophyre emerged, the shopkeeper looked at Lamprophyre's hips and handed her a different pair of trousers. These fit too loosely, but the shopkeeper just said, "You'll want to have them fitted," and gave Rokshan several piles of folded cloth, mostly white, but also red and gold. He gave her a handful of rupyas in exchange and said, "Bring that gown, Lamprophyre, and let's hurry. Kulat gets testy if his clients are late."

Hitching up her trouser waistband, Lamprophyre trotted after Rokshan. She felt better in trousers, more in control, even if they didn't fit quite right. "How can that woman afford to make all those clothes when she doesn't know if anyone will wear them?" she asked.

Rokshan glanced back at her. "It's an innovation," he said. "Mostly people make their own clothes or pay someone to make clothes for them. Either way, clothing is made with a specific person in mind. Madhya's idea is to make clothing for an imaginary average person— actually, several imaginary people of different sizes—more cheaply than people can make them for themselves, and save people the time and effort of sewing. They're not perfect fits, as you saw, but the time it takes to alter clothing is far, far shorter than making it from scratch."

Lamprophyre hitched up her trousers again. "It's certainly convenient for us. I don't know how to make clothing."

"Neither do I, but I know it takes time. As you'll see here." Rokshan pushed open a door which bore a brass rectangle with the word KULAT engraved on it so ornately Lamprophyre could barely make it out. "Just be patient," he said in a voice so low it was almost a whisper. "I'm told Kulat can be...difficult."

Lamprophyre was about to ask what he meant when a curtain in the far wall moved and a man emerged. The store they'd entered was vividly colored, with cloth in every color imaginable draping the walls, but the man facing her was so brightly garbed he made the walls fade by comparison. His shirt with wide sleeves that fell below his elbows was a bright magenta, his trousers were as orange as Bromargyrite, and the filmy scarf around his waist was the exact color Lamprophyre had been before Evart's magic artifact had transformed her. Gold filigree decorated the legs of his trousers, and more gold embroidered across the ends of the scarf echoed the design. A round hat with a stiff, flat top matched the scarf in color and embroidery. He was as garishly beautiful as a dragon.

"You're late," he said in a rough voice that didn't match his clothing at all. Lamprophyre felt disappointed. She'd expected him to sound beautiful, melodic like a songbird, but this was more like the crunch of a foot on gravel.

"We apologize, sirrah," Rokshan said with a slight bow. "I hope you'll still agree to clothe my cousin. We would hate to have to go to some other tailor."

The man sniffed. "I suppose I can make an exception." He advanced on Lamprophyre, one hand dipping into his sleeve and bringing out a knotted cord. "My name is Kulat, young lady. Now, do as I tell you and let me work."

Lamprophyre raised and lowered her arms at his command as his knotted cord whipped around her, measuring her waist and hips and around her breasts. "Very nice proportions," Kulat murmured to himself, "very nice indeed. In fact..." Lamprophyre longed to ask him to complete that sentence, but for the first time in her life she felt intimidated by a human. She snatched the waistband of her trousers, which had begun to slip when she let go to raise her arms, and turned slowly in a circle while he stared at her, rubbing his chin in thought.

Finally, Kulat stepped back. A tiny blank book the size of his palm appeared from nowhere, and he scribbled on it with a slim stick of charcoal. "It will be a pleasure designing for madama," he said. The blank book disappeared into his sleeve along with the knotted cord. Lamprophyre listened to his thoughts and was surprised to find him thinking of how she would make him famous at court. She had no idea how wearing clothing could make anyone famous, but if it motivated him to do a good job, he could believe whatever he wanted.

Kulat turned to the walls and walked slowly around the room, fingering some fabrics, casting others aside. A few he unhooked from the wall and examined more closely, muttering words that his thoughts didn't much clarify. She knew the words he was thinking, tone and depth and richness and texture, but aside from the last, she didn't understand what they meant when he thought them.

"Hold this," Kulat told her, tossing a length of cloth that shone like sun on water over her shoulder. Lamprophyre admired the blue fabric with its darker blue embroidery until he threw a different length of cloth over it, obscuring it. The second was even prettier, woven in a pattern of purple flowers and green twining vines on a white background. More cloths joined those two until Lamprophyre was staggering under the weight of a dozen fabrics.

"Should Lelitha choose from those?" Rokshan asked.

Kulat shot him an irritated look. "People can't be trusted to choose what will suit them," he said. "I have an eye for color and pattern that is far superior to the average man or woman's. I will decide which of madama's clothes to make up in these fabrics, and I guarantee the results will be stunning."

"How soon? Lelitha is attending the paraveti tangal this evening—"

"Don't rush me, your highness," Kulat said, sounding even more irritated. Then his eyes narrowed, and he examined Lamprophyre so closely she felt he was seeing through the pile of fabrics and her own clothing all the way to her skin. "However..."

He snatched the pile of cloth from Lamprophyre and disappeared through the curtain. Lamprophyre sagged as if the cloth had been a pile of metal links instead. "He's very proud, isn't he?"

"Deservedly so. He has quite the reputation."

Lamprophyre almost asked why he'd thought she would make him famous, given that it sounded as if he was already famous at court, but at that moment Kulat came back through the curtain, carrying something in emerald green fabric that shimmered in the soft lights of the shop. Lamprophyre, mesmerized, stepped forward to meet him, reaching out to touch the cloth. It looked as if it might flow like water if Kulat dropped it.

"The woman this was made for refused to pay for it," Kulat said. He sounded affronted, as if the woman in question had spat in his face. "It is too long for madama, but the bustline and hips will fit perfectly. I would be willing to alter it for the right sum."

"Lelitha, what do you think?" Rokshan said.

The idea of wearing this soft, shimmering fabric almost reconciled Lamprophyre to the stupid human body. It would feel like wearing a rippling stream. "I love it," she said.

"Return in two hours and it will be ready," Kulat said. "The first of the other gowns will be finished in two days."

Rokshan dug out a substantial handful of coins and handed them to Kulat, whose thoughts about being asked to sully himself by handling money were disgusted, but who showed no sign of those thoughts on his face. He disappeared beyond the curtain again without saying goodbye, leaving them alone in the shop. "Is he—" Lamprophyre began, but Rokshan made a shushing gesture and ushered her out of the store.

"I warned you he could be difficult," he said when they were safely back on the street.

"I didn't realize you also meant eccentric and proud," Lamprophyre said. "But that gown..."

"I've never seen silk that color," Rokshan said. "It suits you. Your coloring, I mean."

"I'm glad, because it's beautiful." Hitching up her trousers again, Lamprophyre said, "I forgot humans eat at noon. I'm starving."

"Let's return to the palace and put these things away, and ask the chatelaine for a servant who can alter them." Rokshan offered her his hand.

"We can't have Kulat do it?"

"We could ask, but I'm certain he'd look at us like we'd offered him a giant bug to eat. Basic alterations are beneath him. No, the chatelaine will send someone who can do that kind of sewing. We'll have a meal, then find Dharan."

"And then return for the gown."

Rokshan laughed. "You sound so eager. I'm afraid you're going native."

Lamprophyre shuddered. "Never that." But she remembered the beautiful green silk gown, and pictured herself wearing it, and for the first time felt a human body wasn't all bad.

CHAPTER TWELVE

The emerald green gown was even more beautiful on her body than it had been in the shop. Lamprophyre turned before her mirror, twisting to see how the silk fell over her hips and backside. It shimmered when she moved, the loose fabric of the sleeves fluttering like butterfly wings if she lifted her arms. The hem fell to her ankles so she wouldn't have to lift the skirts to keep from tripping.

She turned back so she was facing the mirror and smoothed the silk over her stomach. The thin white underdress kept the hole in her stomach and the pointy parts of her breasts from being obvious. She looked...well, she didn't know how humans would see her, but to herself, she looked beautiful.

She did her best to fold her shirt and trousers, guessing that wadding them up and throwing them into the clothespress wasn't appropriate, and left the room to go in search of Rokshan. He'd said he would be in the east waiting room, which was the room with the glass walls, and while she was sure he wouldn't leave without her, she didn't like to keep him waiting.

The embossed golden walls reflected her as no more than a green blur topped with a darker blur that was her hair. She hadn't known how to arrange it in the elaborate manner many of the court women used, so she had fastened it at the nape of her neck with a thing she'd found in the dressing table she hoped was used for that purpose. After a day spent shoving hair out of her face, she wondered why she hadn't done that in the first place. Hair was annoying.

Rokshan was seated on one of the sofas in the east waiting room, talking to a woman Lamprophyre didn't know. He glanced her way when she entered, started to look away, then jerked his head back to gaze at her, so swiftly Lamprophyre wondered if he'd hurt his neck. A strange expression crossed his face, faster than a lightning strike, and she heard an unfamiliar emotion echoing through his thoughts, loudly enough that she heard them despite her resolve not to listen in: *looks beautiful*. Then he smiled, and he was himself again. "Lelitha, you look lovely," he said. "I can't imagine how you'll look in a gown actually made for you, if this is how you look now."

"Rokshan, you should never suggest a noblewoman's gown isn't specially made just for her," the woman chided him, but she was smiling. "That implies she has to wear hand-me-downs." She rose and walked toward Lamprophyre, extending her hand. "I'm Zefira," she said. "You're Rokshan's cousin?"

"Yes. It's nice to meet you," Lamprophyre said. Zefira was, of course, taller than Lamprophyre, but she nearly matched Rokshan in height, so Lamprophyre concluded she was unusually tall for a woman. She was slender, too, with small breasts and narrow hips, and reminded Lamprophyre even more of a willow tree than Kalivati had. Her symmetrical features appealed to Lamprophyre, and she made a mental note to ask Rokshan later if Zefira was considered pretty.

"Zefira is an old friend of mine from my academy days," Rokshan said, rising to join them. "Her parents are the rulers of Manjaret, which is a city east of here. They've come to attend the wedding."

"Like everyone else," Zefira said with a laugh. Lamprophyre heard her think *so nice to see Rokshan again*, and with that thought came a whisper of emotion that startled Lamprophyre. So Zefira had romantic feelings for Rokshan. That was interesting. Lamprophyre didn't want to break her rule about not listening to Rokshan's thoughts, especially since learning how Zefira felt had just happened by accident, but it was tempting to see if he felt the same way about Zefira. He didn't look at

Zefira the way a man who was attracted to a woman might, but Lamprophyre was still new to interpreting human body language and she could be wrong.

"Our seats at the paraveti tangal are reserved, but we're leaving early to avoid the crowds in the streets," Rokshan said. "Shall we?"

Lamprophyre had wondered, as she was dressing, whether they would walk to the performance. She'd never seen anyone dressed as finely as she was walking through the streets unless it was a Sister of the Red. But it turned out there were three litters waiting at the front door of the palace. Lamprophyre needed Rokshan's help to get into the litter, what with the gown tangling itself around her legs and the sandals she still wasn't used to binding her feet.

"I should have brought a stick to beat the men off with," Rokshan murmured as he helped her settle herself on the cushions.

"Men? What men?" Lamprophyre said, alarmed. She leaned past him to look for assailants.

Rokshan laughed. "I meant that you're beautiful," he said. "Between that and your status as mysterious stranger to the court, I predict you'll be thronged with suitors."

The alarm threatened to become panic. "But I don't want suitors!"

Rokshan's laughter died. "That was mostly a joke," he said. "I'm sorry. Stay close to me, and everything will be fine." He let the curtain fall, and she heard him say something to the bearers. They lifted the litter, and Lamprophyre felt the bobbing, swaying motion that said they were on their way.

She leaned back against the cushions. Being beautiful was nice, but if beautiful meant men would pursue her romantically, she wanted no part of it. It wasn't fair to them, really, because she was a dragon and could never return their interest. So in a way, her beauty was a tease, and that made her feel uncomfortable. She didn't think she had a duty to make herself unattractive just to protect those men, but suppose she was wrong?

The sounds of Tanajital's streets rose up around her. It was the quiet hour during which most people were indoors at supper, the hour before the evening city came to life with people shouting and singing and enjoying themselves, but the hum of the city went on nonetheless.

Lamprophyre closed her eyes and let her mind wander. Rokshan had been joking. Yes, this body was beautiful, but humans weren't animals and they didn't attack women just because they were attractive. The men at the performance would be more interested in the paraveti tangal than in pursuing her.

After a few hundred beats, during which time the noise of the city grew louder, the bearers set the litter down, and one of them gave her a hand so she didn't trip emerging from the litter. Nearby, she saw Rokshan assisting Zefira, and beyond them a white wall rose more than three stories, blank-faced and unadorned except for a door that stood open at its center.

Two men dressed in an unfamiliar uniform, but bearing very familiar and deadly-looking weapons, flanked the door, their hard, cold gazes examining anyone who passed too close. A man and a woman dressed in colorful finery approached the door and were examined closely by the guards before being allowed inside. Whatever the guards were looking for, Lamprophyre hoped she and her companions had it.

Rokshan came toward her with his hand outstretched. "This way, Lelitha," he said, beckoning. Lamprophyre went to his side, and he guided her through the door with a hand on the small of her back. The silk gave his light touch that itchy, tingling feeling she'd had poking the hole in her belly, and she had to resist the urge to step away from it. The guards made no move to stop them; they didn't so much as acknowledge their presence. Maybe royalty got in without question.

Zefira followed them, her thoughts focused on Rokshan. She was wondering what his relationship to his "cousin" was, and Lamprophyre almost laughed. Zefira wasn't exactly jealous, but she certainly wished Rokshan wasn't so attentive to Lamprophyre.

The passage beyond the door was narrow, barely wide enough for two people to walk side by side. "This is the back entrance," Rokshan told Lamprophyre. "My family always uses this way so we aren't pressed by the crowds."

"How do the guards know who to let through? I assume they know the royal family by sight, but what about other people?"

"Some people pay for the privilege. They're given an artifact that resonates with ones the guards carry, and the guards know to let them through. Anyone else..." Rokshan made a dismissive gesture with one hand.

"Which is why I'm grateful to have Rokshan's escort tonight," Zefira said. "I hate crowds."

The passage gradually sloped upward, finally ending at the foot of a steep staircase. Lamprophyre began to hear the noise of many conversations going on at once, but she and Rokshan and Zefira were the only ones on the stairs. "Where is everyone?" she asked.

"Beyond the wall. It must be busy tonight for us to hear them through it," Rokshan said. "These stairs are the back wall of the central gallery, the one the main doors lead to. The stairs lead to the first level. You'll understand better when you see it."

Lamprophyre nodded. She was already breathing heavily from the climb. Evart had a lot to answer for.

The stairs ended at a curved hallway, with walls painted with colorful pictures and a ceiling of hammered copper. It reflected the three of them as imperfectly as the palace hallway had, making them look like three black blobs haloed in the faint colors of what each of them were wearing. The smell of paint stung Lamprophyre's nose, and much fainter, the smell of varnish. "Is this place new?"

"It's old, but the murals were newly painted, just a few days ago," Zefira said. "And I think they refinished the floors."

Lamprophyre looked down. The floorboards did seem bright and new, their surfaces free of scuff marks and reflecting her even more dimly than the ceiling. It felt like being caught between two dirty mirrors. The floorboards curved to match the curve of the hallway, something Lamprophyre observed with astonishment. She knew humans were clever with their building, but all the buildings she'd ever seen were angular, with everything as regular as straight-sided crystals. That they could make straight boards curve—or were there trees that produced curved boards? It was fascinating.

Doors along the inner curve drew Lamprophyre's eye, and she saw a group of men dressed like Rokshan in wide-legged trousers and wide-sleeved shirts in a variety of colors enter one of the doors some distance away along the curve. She stopped to watch them, wondering if they were nobles or just very wealthy, and was called back to the present by Rokshan, who was holding a door open. She hurried to join him.

"Anchala and Torannum will be here shortly," Rokshan said, "but you can sit anywhere you like. These boxes are made to have good views of the proscenium from any seat."

Awed, Lamprophyre walked forward to the front edge of the—it was a box? This didn't look like any kind of box she was familiar with. It was more like a square hole cut out of the wall, with a railing across the front so no one could walk out of it accidentally. She looked out over the ground beneath. The floor was more than a full story beneath them, and it was covered with chairs that all matched each other with bright turquoise and orange-patterned cushions.

About half the chairs were occupied, but many people stood in the open spaces between sections of chairs, talking and laughing as if that was why they'd come and not a desire to see the paraveti tangal. The hum of conversation was much louder than it had been in the passage, and Lamprophyre blocked their thoughts, regretting as she did that she wouldn't be able to listen to Zefira's thoughts about Rokshan.

Conscious of how short she was sitting as well as standing, Lamprophyre took a seat near the front of the box. She leaned on the railing, decided that might seem too casual for such a formal event, and sat back.

Beyond the chairs on the floor below was a semi-circular platform with a curtain concealing its back. It might have been fully circular and divided in half by the curtain, though Lamprophyre didn't know what the point of building a platform and then using only half of it would be. The curtain was turquoise with orange patterns, just like the cushions—at least, the colors were the same, but the patterns were different from the cushions.

People dressed all in tight fitting black clothing passed across the platform, carrying boxes or stools, some of which they set at random on the platform. Some of them ducked through the curtain and returned empty-handed. Or maybe they were different people. It was hard to tell when they wore the same clothes and were mostly shaped the same.

The door opened again, and Lamprophyre turned to see Torannum holding it open for Anchala. Behind her came Kalivati and Sanyot. "Oh, good," Anchala said. "I told Lady Risha and Auntie Piya there wouldn't be room in this box and they'd enjoy the royal box better. I do *not* want to see the paraveti tangal with Auntie Piya offering very loud-voiced commentary throughout."

"Mother is much the same," Torannum said. "We don't have paraveti tangal in Sachetan, and I'm afraid Mother sees nothing wrong with asking 'What did he say?' or 'What does that mean?' in the middle of a performance."

Sanyot took the seat beside Lamprophyre. "Good evening, Lady Lelitha," he said with a smile. "Are you fond of paraveti tangal?"

"I am, though I haven't seen much of it." Lamprophyre eyed him warily, in case he was about to break out into protestations of love over her extraordinary beauty or something similarly dire, but he just nodded. His clothing was a subdued maroon that coordinated unexpectedly well with her green gown, and like the other men, he wore a scarf draped around his neck, gray with silver embroidery on the ends. Lamprophyre liked it. "So have you not seen it before, if you don't have paraveti tangal in Sachetan?"

"Only one or two performances. You will have to explain it to me. During intermission, naturally. I would never dream of talking through a theatrical performance." Sanyot's smile widened.

Rokshan sat on Lamprophyre's other side, with Zefira just beyond him. "Tonight's tangal is dedicated to the happy royal couple," he said. "Paired performances of famous lovers throughout history and myth."

"I hope that includes Hirut and Gethira," Anchala said. "That's one of my favorites."

"So am I right that the tangal performers recite poetry about the people they portray?" Sanyot asked, his attention still on Lamprophyre. The intensity of his gaze made her feel a little uncomfortable, as did the question—she knew the answer, but Rokshan was the paraveti tangal expert.

"That's mostly true," she said when Rokshan didn't intervene. "The performers take on a role and recite or even compose poetry as they speak. Their intent is to reveal the nature of the person they're portraying, or show how that person experienced some famous event. I don't think I've ever seen a performance like Rokshan says this one will be, though." She didn't tell Sanyot that she only barely understood paraveti tangal because as a dragon she lacked the knowledge to appreciate it fully.

"It does sound fascinating," Sanyot said. "We will have to discuss, afterward, whether I understood it properly."

As he spoke, the lights dimmed as smoothly as if someone had slid a black cloth over the lantern. Lamprophyre knew from what Rokshan had told her a long time ago that the lights in the recital hall were actually artifacts rather than lanterns, made to dim or brighten with a touch. "Expensive artifacts, too, made of diamond chips," he'd also said, and Lamprophyre looked around avidly for a sight of them, but wherever they were, they were well concealed.

Two spots of light appeared on the wooden platform. Each was centered on a box or a stool, upon which stood or sat a black-clad figure. Those figures wore black scarves wrapped around their heads, completely concealing their hair, and their feet were bare. The hall went perfectly still.

Lamprophyre had seen many paraveti tangal performances, but they had all come to her, so to speak—arranged by Rokshan to be held in the public coliseum, which was one of the few places in Tanajital dragons would fit. She had never seen one in this way before, surrounded by humans, all of them waiting to hear what words the first performer would utter. She felt poised on the edge of a precipice, pleasurably tense, and realized she was leaning on the railing again and sat back in her seat.

The woman seated on a pile of boxes left of center raised her head and spoke. Her accent was unfamiliar, and Lamprophyre had to strain to understand it at first. Something about love lost, and love found. The words became more intelligible as Lamprophyre listened, and soon she was swept away in the woman's story of leaving her true love behind.

A second voice spoke up, this one male, and although the woman didn't stop speaking, the man's words harmonized with hers to be surprisingly easy to understand. He spoke of being left by his true love, and even Lamprophyre understood the two were talking about each other. Mesmerized, Lamprophyre's gaze went from one to the other as their poems intertwined and rose to a satisfying conclusion that brought the two together, physically as well as verbally.

As they joined hands and spoke their final words in unison, the lights went out, and a roar of applause filled the recital hall. Lamprophyre clapped with the rest—she'd learned about clapping from Rokshan, but she hadn't realized the stinging sharpness of human skin striking skin could be so satisfying.

"How did they do that?" she exclaimed. "If they're both making up the poems as they go, how could they know to end with the same words?"

Rokshan, to whom she'd addressed this, looked briefly dismayed before saying, "Well, I suppose it's because those are famous quotes attributed to the people they portrayed, and it was a natural conclusion. Doesn't that make sense, Lelitha?"

Lamprophyre didn't need to hear his thoughts to know she'd blundered. Famous quotes that any Gonjirian would recognize? That *she* should have recognized? "Oh, of course," she said, "I meant that it was remarkable that they both had the same idea."

"That was lovely," Sanyot said. "Didn't you think it was interesting, Lelitha, how the story began with such a distance between the lovers and progressed through their reconciliation? Quite the transformation."

Lamprophyre relaxed. She'd expected him to say something flirtatious. "And how the language of the poetry became more intense the closer the performers grew physically," she said. "You seem to understand it very well."

"Well, I like to think I understand love," Sanyot said with a smile, and once again Lamprophyre felt dismay, because it was one of his smiles that concealed a deeper meaning. If Sanyot was attracted to Lamprophyre—more specifically, to this body—she had no idea what to do about that. She smiled back cheerfully, willing him to see innocent pleasure in her expression and not anything that might encourage him.

"Shh," Rokshan said. More spots of light illuminated the platform, this time three of them, and Lamprophyre settled in to enjoy the performance.

She didn't understand this one as well as the first, though the performers' accents were perfect Gonjirian; one person loved another, who loved a third, and the third loved neither, and there was a lot of talking and weeping Lamprophyre felt could have been avoided if they'd all sat down together to discuss the situation. Still, the poetry was nice, and Lamprophyre was deep in enjoyment of it when she felt something touch the back of her left hand.

In the next moment, she realized it was Sanyot's finger, stroking her skin. Before she could do anything, Sanyot's hand closed gently around hers, twining their fingers together.

CHAPTER THIRTEEN

A jolt of mingled embarrassment and nervousness shot through Lamprophyre. She glanced at Sanyot, but his attention was apparently on the performance. Now what? She twitched her hand slightly, but Sanyot only tightened his grip, still not painfully, but enough that removing her hand from his would be noticeable by everyone in the box. What did this mean? When Rokshan held her hand, it was to keep them from becoming separated in a crowd. Obviously there was no danger of that now, so Sanyot must have something else in mind.

Lamprophyre realized she was breathing heavily and calmed herself. All right. This had to be more flirting, or whatever humans called it when they were heading toward intimacy. Sanyot was nice, for all he liked to flirt, but she had no interest in a human despite her being in a human body. But she didn't know how to tell Sanyot that. Even if she weren't keeping her identity a secret, she knew humans weren't as straightforward about such things as dragons. If she and Sanyot were both dragons, she could have simply told him she wasn't interested, and he wouldn't take offense.

But humans weren't like that. They required subtlety, Lamprophyre knew from reading romantic stories Dharan didn't approve of.

She thought it was because human males in particular were very sensitive about their sexual prowess, and they didn't like being told they weren't attractive in that way. She didn't want Sanyot to feel bad about himself just because she wasn't interested. Stones, this was difficult! She needed to get Rokshan alone and ask him what to do. In the meantime, letting Sanyot hold her hand might put off the inevitable long enough for her to learn how to turn him down properly.

The lights changed again, the spots disappearing and the hall lights rising. Sanyot let go of her hand so he could applaud, and Lamprophyre clapped too, grateful to be free. "This is intermission, right?" she said, maybe a little too eagerly.

"Yes, and I'm going to refresh myself. Ladies, would you care to join me?" Anchala said. Lamprophyre rose swiftly and followed Anchala out. The last thing she heard before the door closed was Sanyot saying, "What is it about—"

"The refreshing rooms are this way, Lelitha," Anchala said. She and Kalivati hooked their arms together at the elbow and strolled away, Kalivati starting in on a story about a woman both of them knew and Lamprophyre didn't. She and Zefira followed at a slower pace, though not so slow as to lose sight of the princess. The hall was growing busier now, full of women in bright gowns and men in subdued shirts and trousers. Most of them were moving in the same direction Anchala was, but others stood in small groups, talking in low voices.

Lamprophyre drew nearer to Zefira as a couple of men brushed past, not making way for her. Zefira put a hand on Lamprophyre's arm and guided her around them. "I hate it when men act like they have the right of way," she said, loudly enough that the men looked her way. Lamprophyre felt uncomfortable being regarded so closely by strangers, but the men did step wide of the next women they passed.

"Though some of them are simply oblivious," Zefira went on, "and when they become aware and change their behavior, I don't hold that against them."

"I'm used to Rokshan clearing a path," Lamprophyre said. The halls were too crowded for her to listen in on Zefira's thoughts, but she saw the briefest look of annoyance cross the woman's face. Well, Lamprophyre wasn't going to avoid her best friend just so Zefira could pursue a romantic relationship.

"I didn't realize you and Rokshan were so close. You don't spend much time in Tanajital, do you?"

Even Lamprophyre could tell that was a leading question. "We, um, correspond frequently," she said, "and we have much in common. We've been friends for a while. You knew him at the academy?"

"Yes, when we were young. Then I returned to Manjaret to take up my duties there. I'm my mother's heir to the principality. It's a big responsibility." Zefira sounded as if she were talking about something other than ruling a city, but Lamprophyre couldn't tell what.

The refreshing rooms were a line of small doors in the outer curve of the hall, painted to continue the murals decorating the wall. Women clustered in little groups around them, making Lamprophyre wonder if it was enough refreshment just standing near the rooms. Occasionally a woman entered or left. Anchala and Kalivati were just disappearing into two of the little doors when Lamprophyre and Zefira approached.

"And you and Sanyot are...?" Zefira let the end of her question hang in the air like dandelion fluff.

"Are what?" Lamprophyre said, confused.

"I saw him take your hand. Are you courting?"

"No!" That had sounded too horrified for politeness. "That is, no, we're not courting. He just...it was just friendliness." And *that* had sounded so stupid it was a wonder everyone in the hall didn't stare at her for saying it.

Zefira arched an eyebrow. "I don't know him well, but men like Sanyot don't hold hands out of friendliness. You shouldn't encourage him."

"I didn't encourage him! I've barely said three words to him since we met, and none of those were flirting. I don't know what he wants from me."

Zefira gave her a long, calculating look. "It's up to you how you behave," she said, "and maybe it's different in Kolmira, but in Tanajital, women who play games with men aren't respected." One of the little doors opened, and she turned and entered the refreshing room, closing the door before Lamprophyre could respond.

Lamprophyre gaped at the closed door. That part of the mural was of a pack of gamboling dogs chasing a stag. She felt like the stag, stumbling along pursued by some implacable force she didn't understand. Another door opened, and she pushed past a woman to enter it, ignoring the woman's angry protest. There was a latch to hold the door shut, and after some fumbling she fastened it in place. Then she leaned against the wall and buried her face in her hands. Would *everyone* assume she was playing some game with Sanyot when she didn't return his interest?

The faint smell of waste brought her back to herself. So that was what refreshing oneself meant. She assessed the state of her bladder and decided she might as well use the refreshing room for its actual purpose. This one was a larger version of the cubby in her bedroom, and not at all confusing. It took some doing to keep her beautiful gown clean, but when she was done, she felt better. It was funny how similar human bodily waste elimination was to the draconic way.

She straightened her gown and left the room. Her companions were nowhere in sight. She walked back the way they'd come, counting doors on the inner curve until she came to Rokshan's box. To her immense relief, Rokshan was alone. She shut the door and discovered it, too, had a latch on the inside. She fastened it and said, "Sanyot held my hand during the last performance. What do I do?"

Rokshan looked startled, then angry. "He did *what?*"

Lamprophyre covered her face with both hands. "I knew it was terrible. Why did he do that?"

"Obviously he's more attracted to you than I thought. Why didn't you make him stop?"

"I couldn't do that! It was the middle of the performance and it would have caused a scene. And why is this my fault?"

"I didn't say it was your fault."

"If you think I'm the one responsible for making *him* change his behavior, that's like saying it's my fault."

Rokshan sighed. "I'm sorry. I misspoke. You're right, his behavior isn't your responsibility. I just don't like the idea of him forcing himself on you." He took a few steps toward her, but stopped when he was still several paces away. Lamprophyre observed how tense he was and wondered just how much danger she was in from Sanyot. He hadn't seemed dangerous.

She said, "It seemed awfully subtle to be considered forcing himself on me."

"Well, yes, but...all right, forcing is a bit of an exaggeration. But you shouldn't have to put up with any amount of intimacy you don't want. You *don't* want intimacy with Sanyot, right?"

"Of course not! But I don't know what to do about it. Should I have yanked my hand away, after all?"

"No, making a scene would have looked bad." Rokshan closed the distance between them and put a tentative hand on her shoulder. "Look. Torannum tells me Sanyot is sort of a ladies' man. That means he likes to flirt and he's always moving from one woman to the next. If you tell him you're not interested, he'll stop bothering you."

"But *you* told me men don't like being turned down."

The door rattled as someone tried to open it. "Hey," Torannum's muffled voice said. "Who's in there?"

"Yes, but that doesn't mean you shouldn't do it. Especially if the man is a pushy ass." Rokshan rose and went to the door. "Just be firm and it will all work out."

He slid the latch back just as the door rattled again, this time with the thump of a fist on wood. "Finally," Torannum said. "What were you two doing in here that you needed to lock the door?" He grinned. "Not another romance brewing?"

Rokshan shrugged, ignoring how Sanyot gave him a close, considering look. "The latch sometimes falls shut when the door is closed too fast. Lelitha didn't realize that."

"That's good to hear. I'm a jealous man and I don't want you monopolizing the loveliest woman in Tanajital," Sanyot said. He resumed his seat, looking at Lamprophyre in invitation to join him.

Rokshan's eyes met Lamprophyre's. He opened his mouth to speak, then frowned and turned away. Lamprophyre, who'd hoped briefly that he would say something to dissuade Sanyot, felt a moment's irritation that quickly disappeared. Even her limited understanding of human romantic customs knew if Rokshan told Sanyot to leave Lamprophyre alone, everyone would assume Rokshan was interested in courting her, and they would have a different problem. Besides, just because she was temporarily in a human body didn't mean she was helpless. She would deal with Sanyot herself.

Even so, when Rokshan sat between her and Sanyot, she was relieved. She'd planned to clasp her hands in her lap to keep Sanyot from holding her hand again, but instinctively she felt that was more of a rebuff than he deserved. She was able to listen to the rest of the performances with enjoyment, though two of them made no sense to her. Anchala applauded loudly for the last one, suggesting that it was a favorite, and Lamprophyre hoped she wouldn't try to discuss it, because Lamprophyre's ignorance would show.

When the lights grew brighter, Rokshan stood, and Lamprophyre hurried to follow him. She covertly watched Sanyot, but his attention was on his brother and not on her, which relieved her mind. She took a few steps toward the door, smiling politely at Anchala. "That was lovely," she said.

"It was," Sanyot said from close beside her. Startled, she turned to find him offering her his hand. "May I escort you, my lady? I would like to hear your perspective. And I hope you'll feel free to correct my interpretation."

Lamprophyre gazed at him in dismay. She couldn't look away to discover if Rokshan was watching this or if he meant to intervene. Sanyot's smile was friendly, though, without that funny crook it got when he was saying something flirtatious. She suddenly felt impatient with herself. She was acting like a dragonet afraid of her own shadow. This was just a man who found her body attractive, and there was nothing wrong with that. She would behave normally, and if he said anything to overtly court her, she would turn him down politely.

She smiled at him in return and accepted his hand. He tucked hers into the crook of his elbow. "Now, the last one struck me as particularly memorable," he said. "I suppose they chose it to leave the audience with a good feeling."

"That was what I thought," Lamprophyre said, hoping that would be enough to end that line of conversation.

She and Sanyot walked behind Rokshan and Zefira into the hallway, with Anchala and Torannum close behind and Kalivati bringing up the rear. The murals seemed dimmer, or maybe it was the lights that were lower, but it felt cozy. Sanyot drew her closer. He smelled faintly of sandalwood, and the low lights gleamed off his shaved head. Lamprophyre wondered about his baldness. She knew some men shaved their heads when their hair started falling out, though humans in general seemed so proud of their hair she didn't know why they wouldn't want to keep what little they had left. She couldn't tell from looking if Sanyot was one of those balding men, or if he just disliked hair. She could sympathize if it was the latter.

"I confess to enjoying romantic stories where the man has to work to earn the woman's love," Sanyot went on. "It's the fun of the pursuit that does it, I think."

"Pursuit? You mean, chasing her down?" That made no sense. Ahead, Rokshan's shoulders tensed, and she was sure he was listening to this conversation. Sanyot didn't seem to be flirting, but what if there were subtleties to his speech Lamprophyre wasn't aware of?

Sanyot laughed. "I suppose that's one way of looking at it. But no, I mean the kind of romance where the man must convince the lady that he is worth her attention. As with the story of Hirut and Gethira, there at the end."

They'd reached the stairs and were descending. Lamprophyre hitched up her gown to keep from treading on it and tumbling to the bottom. "That was the part I *didn't* like," she said without thinking. "Hirut kept courting Gethira even though she said she didn't care for him. Shouldn't he have stopped when she made it clear she wanted him to?"

"That was her words, Lelitha," Anchala said. "Her actions said otherwise. She chose to be in the places he went, she went out of her way to speak to him. She told him she wasn't interested in him, but she didn't mean it."

"But that seems very hard on Hirut," Lamprophyre persisted. "What if he hadn't known what her actions meant? Then he *would* have stopped courting her, and they both would have been miserable. I think Gethira should have been more straightforward."

Rokshan chuckled and glanced over his shoulder at her. "You have touched on the key point of disagreement between interpreters of that story," he said, "and Anchala will no doubt argue it with you for as long as you let her."

"I don't want to argue," Lamprophyre said quickly. "It was a romantic story. I loved how they saved each other, in the end. It's just that it wouldn't work nearly so well if it was real life."

"That's certainly true," Kalivati said. "But then, most romances aren't nearly so complicated. Anchala, your love story would make a terrible poem."

Lamprophyre glanced back to see Anchala rest her head on Torannum's shoulder briefly. "We met, we courted, we fell in love. I'm perfectly satisfied with how it turned out."

"I'm glad I didn't have to rescue you from bandits," Torannum said. "I'm terrible with a sword."

Sanyot's hand rested briefly on Lamprophyre's. "What about you, my lady? If you wouldn't want to be pursued, how would you like your heart to be won?"

Lamprophyre's mind went blank. "Um," she said, "I suppose I've never thought about it."

"That's impossible," Sanyot said. "I can't believe a lovely lady like you has never thought about love."

His tone was light and teasing, but it struck a nerve she'd thought long buried. Her feelings of guilt and embarrassment at not finding any of her clutchmates—any of the flight—attractive, her fears of never being mated, all rose up within her at once. "I never have," she said, managing not to sound angry and fearing she only sounded haughty, "but I imagine I'll find love when I least expect it."

"Excellent answer," Sanyot said with a laugh. He didn't sound offended by her sharp response. "That would be romantic indeed."

Confused by his reaction, Lamprophyre said nothing. So, her anger amused him? Or did he think—Stones, he didn't think she was flirting with him, did he? What if, like Gethira, her actions toward Sanyot indicated an interest even though her words didn't? She'd accepted his escort, and that might have been a mistake.

Sanyot released her to allow her to pass through the outer door, but followed her to her waiting litter and helped her into it. Once she was settled, though, he didn't let go of her hand. "I understand you better now," he said. "You don't appreciate pretty compliments or hinting at intimacy. I hope to speak with you again soon."

Lamprophyre stared at him. Gone was the sly, flirtatious smile; Sanyot's gaze was open and friendly. It made her wonder if she'd misjudged him, hand-holding aside. "I...all right," she heard herself say.

Sanyot's smile broadened. "I look forward to it." He raised her hand as he bowed to her, pressing her hand lightly to his forehead and then releasing her. The curtain fell, the bearers lifted the litter, and Lamprophyre leaned back against the cushions, feeling as if a weight were bearing down on her. He wasn't a bad man, she'd heard nothing evil in his thoughts, and when he wasn't flirting, he was pleasant enough. She'd done the right thing in not rebuffing him. She hoped. So why did she feel as if Sanyot had won a game she hadn't known they were playing?

She closed her eyes and swore, softly. If she'd made a mistake, and this was Sanyot's way of courting her without flirtation, she would just tell him she wasn't interested. He wouldn't persist in courting her even if he did love that kind of romantic story. Though after hearing the story of Hirut and Gethira, she felt even more nervous about inadvertently encouraging Sanyot. Rokshan had never said she'd need to worry about her behavior as well as her words. Human romance was so complicated.

The litter lurched. Someone very nearby screamed, and then there were shouts, and the litter hit the ground with a crash, tilting further and throwing Lamprophyre forward against the curtains. She listened for thoughts and heard nothing but chaotic fear and, more distantly, a cruel eagerness for blood. A jolt of fear shot through her, driving her to fumble her way through the curtains and out into the fresh, chilly air.

Shouts and screams echoed in the night. The street was unexpectedly dark, with no lanterns illuminating it and very few lights behind the windows of the buildings lining it. Lamprophyre registered this strangeness with part of her mind, but most of her was preoccupied with her bearers, who were crouched over a fallen form nearby.

Lamprophyre cast about for the other litters, and saw only two— but there had been several of them, including the large one Anchala and Kalivati had gotten into. That one and one other were down, and the bearers crouched beside them as if taking shelter against a storm.

Something whistled past, making Lamprophyre duck. She ran, crouching, to the bearers and knelt beside the man lying in the street. He was the fourth of her bearers, and he was dead, a short stick emerging from his chest, his eyes open and staring. Lamprophyre touched the bloody mark in a daze. His death was impossible. None of this made sense.

She straightened and stared down at the dead man. Rokshan would know what to do. She needed to find Rokshan.

Backing away, she looked again for the litters, but in the darkness she couldn't tell if the other litter belonged to Rokshan. The street was deserted, all except half a dozen dark-clad figures who darted here and there. Lamprophyre peered into the dimness. What—

A figure appeared not half a dragonlength away. In perfect silence, the man raised a crossbow and fired directly at her.

CHAPTER FOURTEEN

Lamprophyre screamed. Something hit her from the side, a heavy weight that bore her to the ground, and the crossbow bolt whistled past overhead. "Stay down!" Rokshan commanded. He rose to his feet and charged at the shadowy figure, which turned and ran. Lamprophyre pushed herself up just enough to be able to watch the two as they disappeared into a side street. Her heart was pounding with fear —for her narrow escape, and for Rokshan, unarmed and unarmored.

"My lady?" One of the bearers crouched by her side. "You are unhurt?"

Her arm and hip were sore where she'd hit the ground, but she wasn't bleeding and the bolt hadn't struck her. "I'm fine," she said, not very truthfully. "What happened?"

"We were attacked by ruffians. We aren't soldiers, my lady, we had no way to fight back," the bearer said. He sounded fearful, as if he expected Lamprophyre to shout at him for letting this happen.

"I understand. And one of you was killed," she said. "What do we do?" She couldn't see any more dark figures, but people were emerging from the buildings lining the street, moving uncertainly and calling out to one another. Then she heard more shouting coming their way, and her pulse raced once more. She got to her feet, not wanting to lie helpless and wait to be shot.

"That is the city guard, my lady," the bearer said. "They will help drive off the attackers."

"But Rokshan—aren't they already gone? Where is Rokshan?" Fear shot through her like a knife to the chest.

The bearer wiped sweat from his forehead. "He went after them, my lady."

Men appeared from the shadows, running toward them, and Lamprophyre bit back a shriek. This stupid body had her behaving like a helpless woman. But these figures bore fat, arm-length sticks instead of crossbows, and they slowed as they approached rather than stopping at a good shooting distance. They spread out, approaching the downed litters. Lamprophyre watched the one coming toward her. He was almost certainly a guard, but she assessed him, working out how she would defend herself if she was wrong.

"Are you all right, my lady?" he said when he was close enough. He was breathing heavily from running and held his stick loosely, not in readiness to use it. In the dimness, Lamprophyre could barely make out the sky-blue color of his tunic. Definitely a guardsman.

"I'm well," she said. "You should go after our attackers. Prince Rokshan was pursuing them and he might be in danger."

"Tell me about these attackers," the guard said, not seeming interested in the fate of Rokshan. "They came after your litter?"

"After all of us. They had crossbows—please, you need to pursue them!"

"Crossbows?" The guard said the word dubiously, as if he didn't know what a crossbow was—except surely that was impossible. "Thugs with crossbows? You must be confused, my lady."

It infuriated Lamprophyre that this stupid man wasn't listening to half of what she said and apparently didn't believe the other half. "My bearer is dead with a crossbow bolt in his chest," she said hotly. "I am *not* confused. And if you don't go after those attackers this instant, I'm going to have words with your captain about your disrespect for a lady of the court."

The guard jerked as if she'd shot him with a crossbow. "I—wait here where it's safe, my lady," he said, and ran off to where the rest of his companions milled around the other litters, which were closer to each other than to hers. Lamprophyre scanned the street. It was empty of assailants. Gingerly, she took a few steps away from her downed litter, wincing at the pain in her hip and shoulder. It was better than being dead with a crossbow bolt through her body, but it still hurt. She wasn't used to injury and wondered how long the pain would last, though it was already fading.

The people from the buildings approached cautiously and were waved back by the guards. Most of them ignored the warnings and surrounded the litters, stopping at a dragonlength's distance. Most of them were thinking excited thoughts about the drama playing out in their street, which angered her. A man was dead—possibly more than one—and they could only think about what they would tell their friends in the morning!

Across the street, within an alley that cut between two dark buildings, a figure emerged. Lamprophyre opened her mouth to shout a warning, then recognized the shape of the man's head and shoulders and ran to meet Rokshan. He walked slowly, but he didn't look injured. Even so, Lamprophyre hugged him tightly, relieved beyond words that he was well.

She'd hugged him before when she was in her own body, but this felt so different, and not only because he was now bigger than she; her sensitive human body felt the hard outlines of his muscles and the softer flesh of his belly, and she was close enough that even her inadequate nose could smell his familiar scent, musky and warm like living wood.

Rokshan put his arms around her and held her close, one hand touching the small of her back again, the other cradling the base of her head, just as if she were a dragonet needing comfort during a thunderstorm. "I hope I didn't hurt you when I knocked you down," he said. "You just stood there like you were stunned instead of getting out of the way. You aren't invulnerable, Lelitha."

"I know. I was so surprised. What happened? Who were those men?"

"I don't know," Rokshan said grimly. "Let's see if everyone's all right. If anyone was killed..." His words trailed off. Lamprophyre didn't know how he might have concluded that sentence. She released him, and after a moment, his hands fell to his side. She thought about taking his hand to reassure herself that he was well, but the idea made her obscurely uncomfortable, given that he was clearly well and she was not a foolish woman always in need of protection. Of course, he'd protected her just now, but she chose not to dwell on that.

Zefira stood beside her litter, which didn't appear damaged. "Rokshan, are you mad?" she exclaimed. "Running after those men, unarmed —you might have been killed!"

"So might any of us," Rokshan said. He continued past her to the large litter. Anchala sat on the ground, with Kalivati kneeling beside her and pressing a wad of cloth Lamprophyre recognized as part of Kalivati's gown to the crease of her shoulder. The lavender silk, gray in the dim light, was streaked with darker splotches. Blood.

"No, it's not bad, Rokshan, it just grazed me," Anchala was saying to him as Lamprophyre approached. "Where's Torannum? Why isn't he here?"

"He and Sanyot left before we did," Rokshan said. "They're probably at the palace now, wondering where *we* are."

"I don't understand. Why attack us and run away? They should have tried to steal from us. Such a waste of time," Anchala said with a weak laugh.

"Your highness," one of the guards said to Rokshan. "Can I have a word with you?" The guard wore insignia pinned to the right breast of his tunic and seemed to Lamprophyre to be calmer than the other guards, who milled about staring into the darkness.

Lamprophyre turned away from Anchala and Kalivati, surveying her surroundings. Now that she wasn't terrified, more oddities occurred to her, such as why this street had been deserted. Even at night, Tanajital was thronged with men and women seeking entertainment or going about their night jobs. And the lanterns should have been lit. That was a law, that householders or business owners had to provide a lamp to light the street. It was why Lamprophyre lit her embassy's courtyard every night.

She peered at the nearest lantern pole. The lantern was there; it just wasn't lit. She walked closer to it and sniffed, but couldn't tell how recently it had burned. It was too much of a coincidence that several householders along this street had forgotten to light their lamps tonight. Someone, probably their attackers, had extinguished them to give themselves cover of darkness.

"Lelitha," Rokshan said. She turned and saw him beckoning to her. "You'll take my litter and go back to the palace with the others. You ladies need to get to safety in case they come back."

"But you don't think they'll come back."

Rokshan looked grim. "I think they accomplished what they came for." He lowered his voice. "I'll come to you when I'm done here, so don't go to bed. We need to talk."

Lamprophyre nodded. She climbed into Rokshan's litter and felt it lifted and carried off. She curled up around her aches and tried not to see the body of the dead bearer. Anchala was right, she thought to distract herself, it was a waste of time for those attackers to shoot at them, injure or kill some of them, and then not steal their things.

Unless...Rokshan had said they'd done what they wanted, but why was killing and injuring the royal party something anyone would want? She remembered the guard's surprised expression when she'd mentioned crossbows. She didn't know much about the criminal element in Tanajital, but she didn't think crossbows were a typical weapon. Coquina's human friend Melika had been attacked a few months back, and her assailants had used sticks and their own fists, not martial weapons. The crossbows, combined with the deliberate extinguishing of the lanterns, suggested something else was going on.

When they reached the palace, Anchala could barely walk. Kalivati and Zefira supported her on either side while Lamprophyre ran ahead to open doors. She grabbed a servant tidying the east waiting room and said, "Princess Anchala has been injured. Go fetch a physician or a healer."

The servant, her eyes wide, ran off. Lamprophyre waited for the three women to appear, then said, "Who should I call? I sent someone for help."

"I need to sit," Anchala said. Zefira and Kalivati brought her to a sofa and helped her sit and then lie down. The cloth pressed against her shoulder was almost entirely red with blood now. It didn't look as insignificant a wound as Anchala had said. Lamprophyre hovered, uncertain of what else she could do but unwilling to simply say good night and walk away.

Anchala lay with her eyes closed, her skin ashen in the bright light of the waiting room. Lamprophyre thought she'd fallen asleep, but then she said, "Someone needs to find Tor. I need him."

"I'll—" Lamprophyre began, but Kalivati said, "Wait here, I know where he'll be," and hurried away.

Zefira knelt beside Anchala to hold the cloth pressed over her wound. "Don't just stand there, Lelitha, find out where the healer is," she said irritably, thinking *pretty and useless*. Lamprophyre, stung by the harsh tone of her words and her thoughts, ran off in the direction the servant had gone.

Almost immediately, she was lost. Her draconic memory had learned the path from her room in the guest quarters to the side door and everything in between, but that left most of the palace unexplored. She wandered helplessly for a few hundred beats, cursing herself for a fool and feeling embarrassed about Zefira's harsh words and thoughts. They had made her feel awkward and stupid, and she wasn't used to feeling awkward and stupid. Zefira clearly didn't like her, and Lamprophyre was prepared to wager like a human that it was because of Lamprophyre's closeness to Rokshan.

She took another turn that led to yet another wide hallway, this one walled with a blue and green mosaic of tiny glossy tiles that made her feel like she was underwater, and ground her teeth in frustration. She didn't really care if Zefira liked her, and she wasn't going to stop being close to her best friend just to satisfy the stupid woman, so she didn't know why had it hurt when Zefira had been so dismissive of her. It made no sense. Humans made no sense. She hated even looking like she was one of them.

To her surprise, her eyes grew hot and swollen with unshed tears. Apparently humans cried when they felt angry and humiliated, or maybe it was just this body's way of coping with unfamiliar emotions. Irritated and ashamed of herself, she swiped a hand across her eyes, dashing away tears. Crying over how Zefira had made her feel was ridiculous, and she refused to be ridiculous. She wiped away more tears. She was a dragon, not some weeping woman. Even so, she was grateful no one was around to witness her moment of weakness. Being lost was good for something, it seemed.

CHAPTER FIFTEEN

Finally, after what felt like a thousand beats but was probably less than half that, Lamprophyre reached a corridor she knew, and from there she found her way easily back to the east waiting room. Now the room teemed with people, servants and Torannum and Sanyot and the king and queen as well as the injured princess and her companions. A man in the black sleeveless tunic of a healer sat on the edge of the sofa next to Anchala. He wasn't doing anything, but Anchala was sitting up, so Lamprophyre concluded she'd missed the healing.

She hovered in the doorway, uncertain of what to do. The healer rose, making way for Torannum, who put his arms around Anchala to support her and lightly pressed his lips to the top of her head. It was such a tender gesture it made Lamprophyre's heart give an extra little thump, as if he'd kissed her instead. Kissing was one of the things humans and dragons did not have in common, and everything Lamprophyre knew about it, she'd learned from romantic stories Dharan didn't know she read. This was the first time she'd seen a kiss, and she felt the beginnings of understanding of why it was so powerful.

Sanyot turned away from the two and saw Lamprophyre standing in the doorway. A look of dismay crossed his face, and then he came to her side and took her hand. "You disappeared," he said. "Are you all right? Where did you go?"

"I got lost," Lamprophyre confessed. "The palace is still confusing to me."

Sanyot smiled. "Try not to become permanently lost. I would be devastated if you were gone." He winked at her to show he wasn't serious. "Anchala is healed, and everything is well."

"Everything is *not* well," King Ekanath said in a voice like thunder. "Why did none of you think to take soldiers? Outriders, at the very least? You were all dangerously irresponsible, and Anchala nearly died!"

"It wasn't that serious an injury, Father," Anchala said. "And we never take soldiers when we go into the city. What would be the point? No one's ever attacked us when we travel in a group like that."

"Apparently we've just been lucky," Ekanath said. "You're not to leave the palace unescorted again, do you hear me? We're preparing for a wedding. I don't want to prepare for a funeral instead."

"I don't think that will be an issue," Rokshan said as he entered the room. Lamprophyre looked him over, just in case, but he showed no signs of injury. "Though an escort wouldn't be a bad idea."

"What did you learn?" Ekanath demanded.

Rokshan sighed. "Not much. It was a planned attack, with our assailants concealed around the place they'd chosen for their ambush."

"So someone knew we were coming," Torannum said. "Who could have that information?"

"Practically anyone," Rokshan said. "That's the route we always take to and from the paraveti tangal. It's a nice, quiet side street, mostly residential, and allows us to pass freely without being delayed by crowds. And I blame myself for not realizing that route could encourage exactly this kind of attack. In future, we'll go by different streets chosen at random."

"So these assassins wanted Anchala dead?" Ekanath said.

Anchala sucked in a breath. Torannum held her more closely. "You think it was assassins?" he said.

Rokshan's gaze flicked swiftly to Lamprophyre and just as swiftly rested on his father. "I don't know," he said. "They ran rather than press the attack, which is strange given that I was the only trained soldier in our group and I was unarmed. I think they were interested in scaring us, and injury or death were secondary intents."

"And yet Anchala was the one injured," Ekanath said. "Were they Gonjirian assassins, or Sachetanese?"

Rokshan shrugged. "I didn't get close enough to see. But I really don't think this was the work of Sachetanese dissidents, if that's what you're getting at."

"There are plenty of those in the opposition who would like to disrupt my marriage out of spite," Torannum said. Lamprophyre had never heard him sound so dangerous. It was completely at odds with the kind-spoken, easygoing man she'd thought he was. "And others who don't want a prominent representative in our government tainted by marrying a non-Sachetanese."

"That's true," Rokshan said, "but—"

"I'm not risking my daughter's life on the possibility that she wasn't the intended target," Ekanath said. "From now on, all members of the household take a soldier with them when they go out. No exceptions."

Rokshan sighed. "I can't argue with that." His gaze fell on Lamprophyre again, and this time his expression was unreadable.

Satiya, who'd been silent throughout, laid a gentle hand on her daughter's arm. "Anchala needs rest," she said, "and I'm sure the rest of you are tired. Let's all sleep, and we can worry about this tomorrow."

Lamprophyre moved to follow the king and queen out of the room, but Sanyot grasped her elbow and brought her to a halt. "You're sure you're all right?" he said.

His intent gaze made her feel uncomfortable. "Just sore," she said. "And I can still see the dead bearer when I close my eyes. I feel so bad for his family. I'm sure none of them thought litter bearer was a dangerous occupation."

"I hate the idea of you being exposed to such horrors," Sanyot said. Once again, there was no slyness in his tone of voice, just concern, and it increased her discomfort.

"Let Lady Lelitha return to her room, Sanyot," Rokshan said. There was a sharpness in his tone that confused Lamprophyre, given that she thought Rokshan had told her that she was to deal with Sanyot herself. She both liked and disliked the idea of Rokshan doing it for her: liked, because it spared her the confusion and potential guilt of hurting an innocent man's feelings; disliked, because she was strong and capable of handling her own suitors.

"I'll be fine," she said to Sanyot, and gently disengaged from his grip.

Sanyot ignored Rokshan and repeated the strange gesture he'd made back at the paraveti tangal building, clasping her hand and raising it to his forehead briefly. When he let go of her, Lamprophyre hurried off to her room as quickly as she could.

She closed the door behind her and leaned against it as if warding Sanyot off. She really didn't understand him, and that troubled her. She'd been overwhelmed enough that she'd forgotten to listen to his thoughts, but she wasn't sure that would have helped. If he would just do something unequivocally romantic, she could tell him she wasn't interested and that would be the end of it. But all this friendliness—that, she couldn't deal with short of being rude, and she didn't want to do that.

Someone knocked lightly on her door, three times, and she opened it to let Rokshan in. "Sanyot is becoming a problem," he said.

"But he's stopped flirting. I can't tell him to leave me alone if he's not doing anything but being friendly."

"He's just good at concealing his interest." Rokshan leaned against the door and crossed his arms over his chest. "You need to tell him to back off. Or I can do it."

Lamprophyre eyed him curiously. "Rokshan, is something wrong? You're acting as if Sanyot is my enemy."

Rokshan let out a sharp breath. "He's not, but he...never mind. We'll keep an eye on him, and I promise I won't let him impose on you." He shook his head. "Maybe I'm wrong."

"It's all right. I can take care of myself. Mostly right now I'm glad Anchala wasn't killed. And I feel so terrible about the bearer who was."

Rokshan nodded. "I can't tell you how glad I am you weren't injured," he said. "Not just because I couldn't bear it, but because that would put you under scrutiny I don't think you'd withstand."

"You can't believe they'd find out the truth just because I was shot?"

"I don't know what they'd find, but if they believed you were the target of assassins, they'd want to know why, and then it would come out that you're not a student at the Kolmira academy, and you're not from Adakavi, and at the very least they'd kick you out for being an imposter. I'm not sure how far my father is willing to go to protect you, alliance or no."

Lamprophyre sighed and sat on the bed. It was tall, and her short legs dangled half a handspan above the floor. "So what really happened?"

"Just what I said. I didn't catch any of the attackers, but that was probably just as well. We couldn't withstand what they'd reveal."

"Rokshan, you're being cryptic. You know I hate that."

"Sorry." Rokshan dropped heavily onto the seat in front of her dressing table. "I think you were the target. And I think our enemy is the one who sent them."

The room seemed suddenly airless. Lamprophyre's pulse thudded in her ears. "That's impossible," she heard herself say in a weak voice.

"The bolt that hit Anchala flew wide. It wasn't aimed at her. You," Rokshan said flatly, "were the only one other than your bearer who was shot at directly. And the bearer was clearly targeted to make you vulnerable."

Lamprophyre's hands closed tightly on the bedclothes. "I know we said the enemy made me human to make me killable," she said, "but somehow it's different when they nearly succeed."

"I can't believe how stupid I was," Rokshan said. "I should never have let you go out unprotected. I thought, if you were in company, there was less danger. At the very least, I should have gone armed."

"Neither of us were thinking defensively," Lamprophyre said. "We just have to be more careful."

"What worries me is how those men knew where to attack." Rokshan stood and paced, running his fingers distractedly through his hair. "It's true what I said about that place being chosen for an ambush, but how did they know you would be at the paraveti tangal tonight? We didn't announce Anchala's movements, and even if we had, no one could know you'd accompany her."

"You mean there's someone in the palace who's the enemy's spy."

"I mean the enemy has made contact with someone who knows what goes on here. And it could be anyone."

An icy chill straight from the heart of her mountain home ran through Lamprophyre's veins. "The servants go everywhere. What if it's one of them? Someone who might enter my room at night?"

Rokshan swore. "I hadn't even considered that. You'll need to lock your door—do you know how to do that?"

"Rokshan, I can barely figure out how to open the door, let alone lock it."

Rokshan demonstrated the lock, which came in two parts. One was a hole into which a key fit. "For locking while you're away," Rokshan said. The second was a metal bar half a handspan long that slid across the door frame to block the door from being opened from the outside, sturdier than the latches at the paraveti tangal. Lamprophyre tried it and found it very effective.

"A dragon could open it, though," she said.

"A dragon couldn't fit into the hallway," Rokshan said. "Bar the door after me and don't open it to anyone except me, all right?"

"All right." Impulsively, Lamprophyre put her arms around Rokshan's waist and hugged him. "I was so afraid for you, running into the darkness after those men without even a sword," she said. "That was foolish."

"I wasn't thinking clearly," Rokshan admitted. "I saw that man aim his crossbow at you, and you just stood there like a ninny, and everything after that is sort of a red haze in memory." He hugged her tightly, his hands once more touching her lightly enough to send a shiver of that unnamed sensation through her. "Now, go to sleep, and in the morning you and Dharan are going to the academy library."

"Not you?"

"I'm going to pursue our mystery attackers, see if anyone knows who they were. It's a long shot, but worth the effort. And I'll tell my father my suspicions. He needs to know where the true threat is."

"Good luck."

When he was gone, Lamprophyre slid the bar across. She liked the metal *snick* sound it made when it shot home, and she worked it back and forth a few times before securing it. Then she took off her beautiful gown and folded it into the clothespress. It had a smear of dirt along the hip where she'd landed, and that made her angrier still. She hoped Rokshan would find those attackers and make them pay for everything they'd done, starting with the death of the bearer and finishing with damaging her gown.

She turned out the lantern and settled in to sleep, but once more the image of the dead man, his eyes staring, intruded on her peace. She tried to think of other things—how grateful she was to be alive, how glad she hadn't been listening to his thoughts when he was killed—but ultimately she rose from her bed and stretched, bending and twisting until she was exhausted. It was something her father Aegirine had taught her to do when she had a restless night.

Tired, she returned to bed and stretched again, this time to feel the smooth sheets against her skin. She didn't know what they were made of, except that it didn't feel like silk, but they were cool and soft and her skin loved the way they felt. She curled up on her undamaged side and finally slept.

CHAPTER SIXTEEN

Lamprophyre cringed away from a passing woman who brushed against her arm and immediately felt foolish. Maybe the enemy wanted her dead, but it couldn't control *everyone* in Tanajital, and with Dharan and her soldier guard flanking her, it would have trouble reaching her anyway. Even so, she edged closer to Dharan, whose tall form broke the crowds ahead of their little procession.

Dharan slowed, and Lamprophyre bumped into him. "Sorry," she said.

"Try not to walk so closely," Dharan said. "I don't want to tread on your toes."

Lamprophyre eyed his sturdy sandals and big feet. "That would be bad."

Dharan laughed. "We're almost there, Lelitha. See, there's the commons."

Lamprophyre looked past him. The street they were on came to an abrupt end about five dragonlengths ahead, much the way the street leading to the embassy did. This one, however, ended in a patch of greenery filled with tall, spreading trees Lamprophyre didn't know the name of. Even her nubbin of a nose could smell the scent of a lot of plants growing in one place, overriding the stench of the city streets and the humans thronging them.

"Why is it called the commons?" she asked.

"Because it belongs to all the students, and all of them are allowed to use it," Dharan said. "I suppose technically it belongs to the academy, but the students pay to attend, so in a different sense, it's theirs."

Lamprophyre felt slightly confused by this explanation, but she could understand property that belonged to everyone. She almost told Dharan it reminded her of the hatching cavern back home, but remembered in time the soldier sweating along behind her in full hardened leather armor and refrained.

"So why do they have a parkland as commons?" she asked. "Wouldn't it make more sense to have some building where they could all meet together?"

"They have those too. But in a city as big as Tanajital, with all these hot, stinking streets, it's good to have a place to go that's fresh and green."

"Is that why the healing center has a grassy courtyard?"

"I suppose. I've never been to one, so I didn't know they did."

Lamprophyre thought of the parkland reserved for the use of the royal family and felt a moment's discomfort. Surely the common people needed refreshment as much as the king did? On the other hand, if everyone in Tanajital were allowed to roam that strip of land, it would be destroyed in a twelveday. "It's too bad there aren't more parklands," she said.

"Most people go to the riverside when they have time," Dharan said. "Swimming is popular in Tanajital. More so even than parklands."

Lamprophyre slowed as they entered the commons. It was twice the size of the embassy courtyard and was surrounded by white-walled buildings that rose high above Lamprophyre's head, blank faced and impassive like stony cliff walls. She wasn't sure how humans kept track of which buildings housed which parts of the academy, since all the buildings looked the same. For her, with her excellent memory, it would be no trouble.

There weren't many humans there, though all of them appeared to be students; they wore mostly light-colored shirts and short-legged trousers with colored ankle-length robes, grass-green like Coquina or red like Porphyry or blue like herself, but faded, not vibrant. By the way all the robes were the same washed-out hue, Lamprophyre concluded it was on purpose.

Dharan strode toward one of the buildings, which had a brass-bound wooden door with an ornate thumb latch shaped like a cluster of leaves. He held the door open for her, a gesture Lamprophyre still wasn't used to—did men think women were too weak to open doors, or was it simple politeness?—and motioned her to enter.

Something Lamprophyre *was* getting used to was the difference between the outsides and the insides of human buildings. Rokshan had told her once that houses in Tanajital were taxed according to how ornate they were externally, so most buildings were plain, painted white or cream and roofed in dull tiles.

But the interiors were a different matter. Gonjirians expressed their love of color and pattern freely inside their homes. Lamprophyre had seen this already in the palace, with its extraordinary painted walls and the colored glass and woven rugs that were a riot of color. The academy wasn't as dramatic, but it was still beautiful, with mosaics of tiny blue and purple tiles covering the walls and thick rugs muffling her steps. The room was round, and a staircase with a wrought iron handrail curved along its wall up to an arched opening more than a story above.

"Through here," Dharan said. Another arched doorway beneath the curve of the stair led deeper into the building, and warm lamplight spilled through it, as if windows weren't enough.

But when she entered the room, she discovered there were no windows, just dozens of lamps in peculiar glass cages. The light didn't flicker the way lanterns usually did, just burned steady and bright. Lamprophyre took a look at the nearest lantern, attached to the wall just above head height, and saw to her surprise that water moved within the glass without extinguishing the flame. "What the St—I mean, why is there water in those lanterns?" she exclaimed.

Dharan, who'd kept moving, stopped and returned to her side. "Safety lanterns," he said. "If they break, the water puts out the fire before it can burn anything. Like, for example, the books."

Lamprophyre turned her attention to the rest of the room. "But there aren't any books here."

Dharan took her by the elbow and steered her away from the safety lantern. "Nobody gets into the stacks—the place the books are stored —but the librarians," he said. "Not even me. We request a book, and the librarian brings it to us, if we have authorization."

"That seems so...regimented, maybe? Do we have authorization?"

Dharan chuckled. "Sometimes being a known genius has advantages. I have the highest authorization, and with me to vouch for you, so do you."

Lamprophyre was only half-listening. Her attention was on the room, which was crowded despite not having any books except the few on the tables. There were a lot of little rectangular tables, arranged in neat rows, each with two chairs that faced each other. Only a few of the chairs were occupied, and those people only glanced at Dharan and Lamprophyre before returning their attention to their books.

Lanterns hung from the ceiling above each table, low enough to thoroughly illuminate anything on the tables. Lamprophyre liked the iron frames of the lanterns, like metal lacework. So much prettier than the ones in the embassy. Maybe she could have hers replaced.

At the far end of the room from the door, an enormous window had been cut out of the wall, looking not out on the commons or whatever was outside at that point, but on another room. That one was full of those odd wide-rung ladders, impossibly free-standing, extending out of sight away from the window. A waist-high shelf—waist-high to Dharan, which put it considerably higher to her—ran the length of the window, and two humans stood on either side of the half-wall, talking intently. Dharan approached, not too closely, and stood with his hands clasped loosely behind his back. Lamprophyre stood beside him, wondering what came next.

She didn't intend to eavesdrop, but the two men's conversation was loud enough she couldn't avoid hearing it, even with her limited human hearing. "I told you," the man on their side of the wall said in a rather heated tone, "I need that book for my thesis."

"And *I* told *you*," the other man said, as placidly as if this conversation didn't matter to him, "Lector Bharin has the book until a week from yesterday. I'll put your name on the reserve list."

"My thesis is due in five days! A week from yesterday will be too late!"

"Then I respectfully suggest you shouldn't have procrastinated your research." Now the second man's tone was smug enough that even Lamprophyre itched to slap him, even though she had to admit he had a point.

"I didn't procrastinate," the first man said through gritted teeth. "Lector Bharin has had that book for two months. That's a month longer than the allotted time. I've been asking for it—"

"Lectors are free to extend the loan period if they need a book longer than a month." The second man smiled. Lamprophyre heard him think *Jiwanyil save me from students, probably spill food on it.*

"Excuse me," Dharan said, stepping forward. The first man startled at Dharan's sudden appearance beside him. The second man's smile grew wider, and his thoughts became more pleasant and focused on Dharan's good qualities, which to him meant punctuality and respect for the books.

"Lector Dharan," the second man said. "Can I help you with anything?"

"Actually, I thought I might help you," Dharan said. "Scholar, I apologize for eavesdropping, but do I understand you need a book that Lector Bharin has?"

"That...yes, Lector," the first man said. His thoughts were stunned and surprised at being addressed by someone as famous as Dharan. Lamprophyre's assessment of Dharan's reputation moved up a few notches. She was used to treating him with the same casual respect she gave all her friends, and she'd never realized how honored he was in the academy.

"I'm sure Bharin wouldn't mind letting you look at the book for a short time—if your thesis is due in a few days, it must be nearly finished, yes? So you won't need the book for long." Dharan extracted the blank book he always carried with him and a pencil from inside his shirt. "I can write you a note of introduction so he'll take you seriously. I'm afraid Bharin sees students as a necessary evil." He scribbled a few lines on the blank book, then tore the page off and handed it to the student.

The student clasped the paper to his chest like a shield, his eyes wide. "Thank you, Lector Dharan," he said.

"Bharin should be in his office in half an hour. Don't dawdle," Dharan said.

The student bobbed his head in a nervous nod and almost ran for the door.

"That was generous of you, Lector," the other man said.

"Yes, and you could have easily done the same for him," Dharan said. His voice was pleasant, but his eyes were cold. "I wonder why you didn't."

The man swallowed. "I...it didn't occur to me. You know what Lector Bharin is like. Probably a note from me would have gotten that young man nowhere. And it's not my job to look out for students who put off their work."

"I see," Dharan said.

Lamprophyre listened to the man's thoughts again. This time, he was thinking *not my job* and *students are pests* and *hope Lector Dharan doesn't take against me*. He clearly couldn't see Dharan's displeasure, which was as clear as day to Lamprophyre even without hearing her friend's thoughts.

"This is my friend and colleague Lady Lelitha," Dharan said, apparently losing interest in the other conversation. "She's here to do some research and she's to be accorded the same respect you would give my requests. Is that clear?"

The man flinched, not much, but enough that Lamprophyre noticed it. "Of course, Lector," the man said. "Scholar, are you familiar with our cataloguing system?"

"I'll explain it to her," Dharan said. "But you can answer any questions she might have later. I have a lecture in half an hour." He steered Lamprophyre away from the window without acknowledging the man's polite nod.

"I hope that's enough," he whispered in Lamprophyre's ear. "You saw how he treated that unfortunate man. With luck, some of my reputation will rub off on you, enough that he'll behave better."

"He's afraid of you taking a dislike to him. Could you hurt him? I mean, his reputation or his standing in the academy?"

"If I really wanted to, yes, but I don't go out of my way to ruin people. He's just smug and secure in his position and he likes exercising power over others." Dharan sighed. "Sometimes I worry for the fate of humanity, if there are so many people like him. Maybe we should be learning from dragons."

"Dragons have their own flaws," Lamprophyre said, though truthfully she'd been thinking how nice it was that dragons didn't behave in mean and petty ways. "But if you have a lecture soon, we should get to work."

"Yes. Come with me." Dharan waved a hand at the walls. "Let me introduce you to the magical world of research."

Lamprophyre's eyebrows went up. "Magical? There aren't any artifacts here."

"Oh, Lelitha," Dharan said. "There are so many kinds of magic."

Cabinets like the many-drawered ones in Rokshan's sister Manishi's workshop lined the walls. Manishi's cabinets were made of heavy oak and the drawers were of many sizes. These were of a fine-grained wood so dark it was nearly black, and all the drawers were the same size, just a little larger than Lamprophyre's human palm. Each drawer had a silver knob in its center and a scrap of paper framed in silver above the knob. Lamprophyre peered at one of the papers. "ALG—ARS," she read. "I don't recognize that word."

"It's letters. All these records are arranged in alphabetical order." Dharan opened the drawer to reveal its contents: many, many pieces of thick, square paper cut to fit the interior of the drawer exactly. "Each card lists a book title, or an author, or a subject. If you wanted to find a book by Alharet, you'd look in this drawer, and see, the library has four of Alharet's books. Then you write the title of the book you want on one of these papers—" He indicated a messy stack of much thinner papers atop the cabinet— "and take it to the librarian to fetch it for you. If someone else has it, he will let you know when it will be available."

"But I don't know who wrote the books I need. I don't even know what those books are."

"That's why you'll search by subject." Dharan walked down the row of cabinets until he came to a drawer marked SEF—SET. "Let's try the most obvious one first. Go ahead."

Lamprophyre slid the drawer open and flicked through the cards. Each had a pair of holes cut into their bottom edge, and two metal rods went through those holes, keeping the cards in place. "I suppose taking them out of the drawer would be bad," she said.

"Terrible. That's how disorganization happens," Dharan said with a grimace, as if disorganization was a sin.

Lamprophyre mentally ran through the alphabet Dharan had taught her and how to use it to find things in alphabetical order. She'd thought it unnecessary at the time, one of Dharan's intellectual quirks, but now she was grateful for the skill. "*Serious Studies in Agriculture*... Serlik...serpent...no serpentine. Wouldn't it be better if all the subject cards were in one place? You wouldn't have to look through so many cards."

Dharan grimaced again. "That didn't occur to me until they'd already implemented the system. I originally thought it would be better to have the whole thing as one unit, but it turns out that's not how people use it."

"*You* thought? Dharan, was this your idea?"

Dharan tapped the side of his head and grinned. "My gift to the academy, revolutionizing how we do research. I was twelve—no, thirteen. Though it's due to Rokshan that they even listened to me. He was extremely convincing."

Lamprophyre regarded the long row of cabinets with amazement. "You thought of this when you were thirteen? Is it normal for hu—for boys to focus on academics to that extent?"

"I was far from being a normal child. And at the time, it just seemed obvious. I was trying to establish a history of some mathematical theory and it was impossible to find anything to support my research. I griped about it enough to Rokshan that he finally challenged me to take action. And Lector Karuna, the head librarian at the time, was willing to be talked into testing my ideas." Dharan slid a drawer open and shut a few times, idly. "Then it took five years to catalog the entire library. That was an exciting time, if by 'exciting' you mean 'tedious and exhausting.' But it was worth it."

"I'm very impressed. Except that there isn't anything about serpentine. I realize I shouldn't have gotten my hopes up, but you said such wonderful things about this place."

"You already knew the odds were poor. But the thing about the subject listings is that they are limited to what people knew about the books they catalogued, which means the information might still be here, just hidden." Dharan took out his blank book and tore off the top page. "I suggest you write down all the possible subjects that might relate to the serpentine artifact, then look those up. When you find a book that's valuable, look up that author and see if he or she has written any other similar books. And don't forget about synonyms. We found 'serpent,' but there might be other books under 'snake.' If that's what we were looking for."

"That makes sense. Are you leaving now?"

"I have a few minutes. I'm going to look for that story you said Hyaloclast referred to." Dharan walked away, scanning the drawers. Lamprophyre, after a moment's hesitation, sat at one of the tables. She didn't think they were assigned to specific people, but she was conscious of being an outsider and secretly a fraud, and sitting seemed like a declaration that she wasn't actually either of those—a declaration someone more worthy might challenge. She reminded herself that she was there under Dharan's protection, so to speak, and no one in the academy was likely to challenge that.

She filled the page with as many words as she could think of. Artifact. Wand. Transformation. The list went on. Finally, her mind buzzing with possibilities, she took her list to the cabinets and started her search.

She'd been taking notes for a few hundred beats—a few *minutes*—when Dharan appeared beside her with a couple of books under his arm. "These are very old, and they won't let us borrow them, just read them here in the scriptorium," he said. "I didn't have time to examine their contents, but if Hyaloclast's story is as old as she said, these books would be the ones containing it. I have to leave now—are you all right alone for an hour and a half? I'll be back when I finish."

Lamprophyre glanced at the guard, who'd stayed stolid and unmoving by the door the whole time, carefully examining anyone who entered. "I'll be fine. This is actually fun."

"Welcome to my world," Dharan said with a grin. He handed her the books, squeezed her shoulder, and left the room.

CHAPTER SEVENTEEN

L amprophyre set the two books on what she'd come to think of as "her" desk. The books were bound in worn leather frayed at the corners, with the page edges rough and the spines tilted. One of them smelled faintly of smoke, though it showed no sign of burn damage. She opened the other and found its front pages speckled with water spots. How old it was, she couldn't tell, but she could believe it had survived at least a century. That was young for a dragon, but old for a book. She hoped it was old enough.

She carried her notes, scrawled on the pieces of paper left untidily on top of the cabinets, to the window. "I'd like to look at these," she said, handing over the little pile to the librarian.

The man smiled pleasantly at her, but his thoughts were less nice. Lamprophyre managed to keep a pleasant smile of her own firmly in place, but she felt like slapping him for wondering if she was sleeping with Dharan and that was why Dharan insisted on her receiving good treatment. She'd never realized humans were so obsessed with sex despite her many conversations with the prostitute Darsha.

"I'm afraid you can only have five books at a time," the librarian said. Lamprophyre listened to hear if he'd made up that policy to exercise power over her, but apparently he was telling the truth. "So, if you'll choose five?"

At least he wasn't going to count Dharan's ancient books against that total. Lamprophyre shuffled through the papers and handed over five. "It will take a few minutes," the librarian said, and walked away among the bookcases.

Lamprophyre waited for a few minutes, then, growing bored, returned to her table and neatly squared up her remaining papers. She flipped open the water-spotted book again and turned to the first page. Modern books often had lists in the front, showing what was inside, especially if what they contained were collections of stories or poems or essays. This was old enough not to have that innovation. She would have to read the whole thing, or at least skim through it. Well, maybe the stories were interesting.

She'd gone through a handful of its pages when the librarian called her name. She looked up to see him set a stack of books on the shelf. "I'm afraid the Kalivas is not available. It seems to be missing," he said when she approached. "Here are the other four."

"Missing? Do you mean stolen?"

The librarian shook his head. "I couldn't say. Sometimes books are put away in the wrong place, and no one knows about it until someone requests those books. Occasionally a borrowed book is lost by a student." A look of distaste flitted across the librarian's face. "And yes, sometimes a book is stolen. But that is very rare. In this case, it's more likely the Kalivas was simply misplaced. We will have an apprentice search the shelves for it."

His tone was decisive enough that even without listening to his thoughts, Lamprophyre could recognize a brush-off. She collected the books, nodded at the librarian politely, and returned to her table.

She'd chosen books relating to artifacts in general, books about how artifacts were created and books focusing on different types of artifacts. It had occurred to her while searching that she didn't know whether the shape of an artifact mattered. Was it important, for example, that Evart had built the serpentine stone into a wand rather than a pendant or a coronet? If the transformation could only happen through a wand, that might be information they could use.

She skimmed through the volumes, returned some, accepted others. None of her other requests were denied, but few of the books contained anything useful. Superstitiously, she thought about the missing book by the adept Kalivas and whether it might not be the key to her search. She reminded herself that it was just as likely to be useless and turned her attention to the one book that seemed to have the most information about artifacts. After only a few minutes, she closed it and let her eyes go unfocused in the direction of its cover, which was leather dyed a bright green. This one, she'd need to read carefully, but that felt like a waste of her library time. Maybe they would let her borrow it.

She left that one at her table with Dharan's ancient books and took the remaining two back to the librarian. "I'll have more requests in a little while," she said.

"I hope they are more serious than your previous ones," the librarian said coldly. "I dislike having my time wasted. If you're not going to read the books, don't bother requesting them."

Too late Lamprophyre realized what her search must look like to the librarian. Dharan had told her she was an unusually fast reader and guessed it was related to the way she'd learned to read and her memory, extraordinary even for a dragon. It must seem as if she was just flipping pages and discarding books. She listened to the librarian's thoughts and heard him think *pet pupil, obviously more than just a student* and *Dharan playing a game with me.* Stones take humans and their prickly pride.

"Would you humor me for a moment?" she said. Without waiting for his assent, she retrieved the topmost book and opened it at random. She silently read the first dozen sentences from the top of the page and spun the book around so it was right side up to the librarian. "Cover that so I can't see it," she said, and immediately started reciting back what she'd read.

It took the librarian a moment to catch on. His eyes widened as he realized what she was doing. Lamprophyre reached the end of the passage and fixed her gaze on the librarian. "Does that clarify anything for you?" she said, enjoying his look of amazement.

The librarian swallowed. "I've never—that is, I understand now why you are Lector Dharan's student. My apologies. You must know why I misunderstood."

"I think you are a good librarian," Lamprophyre said, not sure if it was true or not, but willing to throw him a bone. "But you could stand to make fewer assumptions."

That angered as well as embarrassed him, but he concealed it well. "We have students who aren't very respectful of my time. They play all sorts of games. How was I to know you weren't one of them?"

"Because Dharan vouched for me?" Lamprophyre said sweetly. "It's all right, sirrah, we understand one another now and I'm sure there will be no more misunderstandings."

She left the librarian stammering a response and returned to the cabinets. So, searching for information on artifacts was mostly useless. Time to proceed to some other line of inquiry.

She was deep in contemplation of a very large book filled with fascinating illustrations when she heard Dharan say, "Any luck?"

Lamprophyre closed the book on her finger and sighed. "I'm not very good at this," she admitted. "I think it takes imagination to come up with possibilities to search for. Does it count as success if I'm at least able to quickly discard anything not helpful?"

"Of course," Dharan said. He sat at the chair opposite hers and ran a finger over the spines of the books on her table. The newer ones had the titles embossed on the spines, either painted in black or gilded. Lamprophyre had never seen the point of this, given that covers were much larger and could fit longer titles.

"There are a few I need to read more closely," Lamprophyre said. "Can I borrow them?"

"I'll borrow them, and let you take them," Dharan said. "It's not really encouraged, but no one's going to argue with me, especially if I don't make a fuss about it. You really haven't found anything?"

"I've found *some* things. I know that the shape of an artifact influences the effect it has. Adepts create wands when the artifact has a powerful effect they don't want to linger, or one where all the magic in the stone is intended to discharge at once. So it's possible—" She lowered her voice, though no one was near enough to hear. "It's possible that serpentine artifact wouldn't have worked more than once, or more than a few times. Evart did imply it would turn me back."

Dharan nodded. "So we aren't looking for a ring or a pendant."

"No." Lamprophyre opened her book again. "And this is where a book like the one I want to write would be useful. A compendium of all magical stones. But this one is the best I could find. It's about physical magic—magic to enhance the body—and it lists stones that can be used for different effects, with drawings."

"Interesting." Dharan took the handful of papers where she'd written notes and books to look for. "I think you should focus on the books of stories, since they won't let us take them. I'll see what I can find."

Lamprophyre had been hoping for an excuse to do that. She pushed the other books aside and opened the water-spotted one. This had to be more fun than skimming boring books that had no useful information.

She'd finished the first book and was most of the way through the second before Dharan reappeared, saying, "It's time for a meal. Aren't you hungry?"

As if responding to his words, Lamprophyre's stomach growled. "I guess I am," she said, amused. "I don't suppose we can eat in here—all right, I'm joking, I know your rules. No food where the books are."

"I should think not," Dharan said with mock sternness. "Let's tidy up. We can leave the books here—no one will disturb them."

Lamprophyre gathered her notes and followed Dharan out of the scriptorium, trailed by her soldier guard. This time, the commons was thronged with students in colorful robes, talking loudly enough to disorient Lamprophyre after the peaceful quiet of the library. A handful of lectors in vivid gold robes strolled across the grounds, usually in chatting pairs. The students mostly ignored them, and they paid no attention to the students, though one or two saluted Dharan despite his being in ordinary clothes. "Where's your robe?" Lamprophyre asked.

"I only wear it for lectures. I hate being conspicuous." Dharan put a hand on Lamprophyre's elbow to guide her out of the commons.

"Especially outside the academy. Come, there's a tavern near here I like."

Dharan's tavern lay tucked away on a side street, but it was still doing a brisk trade despite being out of the way. It was open on one side, with small wooden tables scattered in its yard and more tables crowded under its roof. While the guard waited near the entrance, they found seats at a table wedged into the back corner, where the dark, musty smell of mingled human sweat and hot bread nearly overwhelmed Lamprophyre. She waited, breathing shallowly through her mouth, while Dharan negotiated for a meal. That negotiation seemed to require a lot of loud laughter and slapping of backs, something Lamprophyre had noticed only men did.

Dharan returned to their table with some rounds of bread, still warm from the oven, a pot of soft cheese, and a roasted bird on a platter. He handed Lamprophyre the bread and set about carving the bird with his belt knife. Lamprophyre stared at the bread, wondering what to do with it. She knew not to tear it in half, not if she was sharing with someone else, but not what she should do instead.

Dharan pointed at the pot of cheese. "Knife there," he said. "Don't worry. No one's watching."

Somewhat awkwardly, Lamprophyre cut one round of bread in half, then in quarters. The pieces were uneven, but the smell that arose from them made her not care. She accepted a piece of—oh, this was what chicken looked like when it was cut up. She bit off a mouthful, enjoying how the juices burst over her tongue. "I never knew chicken was so delicious."

"I imagine you wouldn't have had it often," Dharan said. "I'm sure it takes a hundred to satisfy you in your usual form."

"One hundred fifty, actually. And I eat them bones and all." She was blocking the sound of the other humans' thoughts, but a sharp, startled awareness of her last words reminded her to be more circumspect. "Anyway," she went on, "this is very good."

"I like this place because the food is good and the company is pleasant, at least during the off hours," Dharan said. "So. Tell me what else you found. Or didn't find."

"Nothing about transformation. There were a couple of books that claimed it was impossible, even. The thing I told you about wands. Some information about how artifacts are created that I didn't understand—I think it was on purpose. As if the author wanted only adepts to be able to use it. That's fairly typical of what I've learned in my other studies."

"I remember. Hang on a minute." Dharan again left the table and returned with a pitcher and two wooden cups. He poured a thin stream of yellowish liquid into each cup. "It's new beer," he said. "Not very alcoholic, though I wonder if you shouldn't try drinking something a little stronger in a safe place. You won't be able to get away with not drinking forever."

Lamprophyre tasted it and managed not to make a face. "I don't think I like alcohol. It's too bitter."

"That's not true of all alcoholic beverages. But you're right that it's an acquired taste." Dharan drank his cup down and refilled it. "I didn't learn much more than you did. I went at it from a historical perspective, looking for records of transformations. All of them are fictional stories, but there was a common thread that suggested some aspect of the stories was true. Namely, that the transformations were all intentional. They never happened by accident."

"So what can we do with that?"

Dharan shrugged. "I don't know yet. But this is going to take more than a little work."

Lamprophyre's discouragement rose. She drank the rest of her beer without noticing the taste. It didn't make her feel strange the way alcohol was supposed to, so Dharan was right about the beverage not being very potent. "We really need to find an adept," she said.

"That's dangerous," Dharan said. "But you already know that."

"I do. I just fell temporarily into despair."

They finished their meal in silence and returned to the library, which was more crowded than before. "Study hour," Dharan said, "which actually takes up an hour and twenty-five minutes. It's so everyone can take advantage of the noon break to get out of the sun and nap."

Lamprophyre examined the room. "They aren't napping."

"Some students actually study."

Dharan moved off to the cabinets while Lamprophyre settled down to finish reading the book. She felt almost guilty at enjoying herself while Dharan was working, but these stories might be important research and not just entertainment. The book still smelled of smoke, and she began to see why; the last third of the pages were scorched along the edges, and some of the beautifully written lines were obliterated by char. But most of it was still legible, and Lamprophyre read on, carefully not touching the brittle sections.

She was halfway through the story before she realized what she was reading. Startled, she turned back to the beginning and read more carefully. The poems in this book had an unfamiliar structure and didn't rhyme at all, making them sound almost as if someone were telling of an event that had happened to them. In this one, a princess found an artifact—the story didn't say what shape—that she used to defend herself from wild beasts by transforming them into harmless creatures.

It was so like the story Hyaloclast had referred to it caught Lamprophyre breathless. She read on, having to extrapolate words and phrases where the long-ago fire had obliterated them. The further she read, the more numb she felt, until she reached the ending and stared sightlessly at the burned spot just beyond it.

"Finished?" Dharan said. He held a stack of books in the crook of his arm and leaned casually against the table.

Lamprophyre blinked. "I think so," she said. She glanced around at the students filling the room. This wasn't something she could say in front of them. "Can we go?"

Dharan's eyebrows went up. "So soon?"

"If we can take the rest of those books, I'm done with these. And I found something."

"Something I see." Dharan nodded as if he understood her reluctance to talk in front of the students. "You return those to the librarian, and we can go."

Lamprophyre handed over the ancient books with no more than a nod for the librarian. She couldn't hear his thoughts over the mental clamor filling the room, but she could guess he wasn't thinking anything complimentary of her. Maybe next time there would be a different librarian.

The streets of Tanajital surged with people as they always did this time of the afternoon, when everyone had risen from their midday rest and was ready to tackle the afternoon with renewed vigor. Lamprophyre had never been aware of this except as a rise in the background hum of the city, mainly because she usually napped longer than humans did.

Now she stayed close to Dharan's side while the guard broke a path for them. She watched the people, some of them moving with purpose along the streets, others stopping to barter and argue with the vendors selling food or cookware or other things Lamprophyre had no name for. None of them paid her any attention. The sense of being invisible filled Lamprophyre with discomfort, as if she were being erased. She shuddered. After what she'd read, that felt like a viable possibility.

When they finally reached the parkland, she breathed out in relief, then inhaled the fresh green scent of the trees and felt her discomfort fade. "Sirrah," she said to the guard, who looked startled to be addressed directly, "would you walk behind us a ways? I wish to speak with Dharan privately."

The soldier cleared his throat. "I'm to guard you," he said, his words slow and deliberate enough that Lamprophyre judged he wasn't very swift of thought.

"And you can do that from back there. Besides, there isn't anyone else here." Lamprophyre smiled at him, and was surprised to see him smile back. She hadn't thought soldiers capable of expressing ordinary emotions while they were on duty.

With the soldier far enough back that he was out of earshot, Lamprophyre drew Dharan close. "That story," she said. "It was near the end of the second book."

"You make it sound ominous," Dharan said. "What about it?"

She drew in another deep breath and exhaled slowly, wishing that delaying talking about it would make it go away. "It was a story about a princess who used an artifact to transform animals. She would be pursued by a bear, for example, and to save herself she'd transform it into a rabbit." She laughed, somewhat shakily. "She must have been doing something wrong if she kept getting chased by things that wanted to eat her."

"So this story says a transformation artifact is possible." Dharan shifted the stack of books he carried. "Does it say what it looks like? Or how to find it?"

Lamprophyre shook her head. "That's not the important part. The last thing that pursues her is a man. She turns him into a squirrel before learning that he was really her betrothed, someone joined to her when they were babies, so she'd never seen him—that's not important. The squirrel ran away and it took time for her to catch it." Her heart was beating rapidly, as if she were the one pursued. "By the time she did, and used the artifact on him, it was too late. He couldn't be restored."

Dharan stopped walking. "It's just a story."

"We don't know that!" Lamprophyre exclaimed. "This one is just like what Hyaloclast told me about. And we've said all along that these stories might have a bit of truth to them. Suppose that's it?" She drew in a breath to calm herself and failed utterly. "What if it's already too late for me?"

CHAPTER EIGHTEEN

"Don't think like that," Dharan said. "There's no reason to believe that part of the story is the true part. Or that any of it is true. We have no way of knowing, and in the absence of proof, we need to focus on what we can control and not worry about what we can't."

"Dharan—"

"No, Lelitha. This isn't false comfort. We have to go on behaving as if there's a solution. Or would you rather give up and learn later that it *wasn't* too late?"

Lamprophyre shook her head. "You're right. It's just that it was so terrifying, and so close to what Hyaloclast discovered. Being trapped forever in a human body is my worst nightmare."

"I understand." Dharan gripped her shoulder reassuringly. "And I choose not to be offended."

His expression was so comical, amusement hidden behind pretended haughtiness, that it made her laugh. "All right," she said. "I won't give up. But I don't think we can afford any delays."

"You need to tell Rokshan what you learned. It may change the direction of his investigation." Dharan continued walking toward the palace doors, his long strides forcing Lamprophyre to trot to keep up.

"And I can't believe I'm saying this, but maybe we need to search the Hall of Visions, too."

"You think some ecclesiast had a prophecy about dragons being transformed?"

"I don't know. But some of those prophecies contained information about the entity. I don't think we should rule them out as a source of knowledge."

Lamprophyre had long been curious about the inside of the Hall of Visions, but she knew from Dharan's earlier visits to the place that it was unlikely she would be able to find anything there. The ecclesiasts who controlled the place kept a tight hold on what non-ecclesiasts were allowed to look at. "You realize you just volunteered yourself, right?"

"What's a little self-torture for a friend?" Dharan said with a smile.

Lamprophyre had wondered, after the previous night's attack, whether the palace might not be more heavily guarded, but there were still only the two soldiers at the door with their deadly-looking polearms. It wasn't until she and Dharan entered the grand entrance hall that she saw anything unusual: more soldiers, these armed with swords and small crossbows, stood at the top of each stair. They surveyed the hall carefully, making note of everyone who entered and left.

Lamprophyre hesitated at the base of the right-hand stair. Those soldiers looked primed to kill anyone who threatened them. But she was a guest of the royal family, and she had the right to enter the palace, yes? Besides, she was accompanied by another soldier, and that was like a symbol of her worthiness to enter. She hoped. She lifted her chin in what in dragons was defiance and marched up the stairs, not so rapidly as to make herself short of breath, but without hesitation.

One of the soldiers at the top of the stairs brought his crossbow to bear on her when she was ten steps away. "No admittance," he said. "Turn around and go back where you came from."

"I'm Le—Lady Lelitha," Lamprophyre said in her haughtiest voice. "I am a guest of the royal family. Please let me pass."

The crossbow didn't waver. "I don't recognize you," the soldier said.

"But I—" She half-turned to look at her soldier escort and Dharan, but when she turned back around, the soldier with the crossbow hadn't flinched. He didn't even seem aware of the men behind her. "Then you should send word for someone who does," Lamprophyre said, "because I assure you the king will be angry if you turn me away." She put her hands behind her back, loosely clasped, so the soldiers wouldn't see them tremble.

Without taking his eyes off Lamprophyre, the soldier jerked his head at his companion, who vanished through the little doorway into the bare, short passage Lamprophyre could barely see. She smiled pleasantly at the soldier, but didn't speak. Rokshan had told her, months ago, that soldiers wouldn't chat while on duty, in case they were fatally distracted. Lamprophyre only hoped his finger wouldn't shake on the trigger. If he shot at her, she'd either die from the bolt or fall to her death getting out of its way. Neither of those prospects appealed to her.

Finally, the second soldier reappeared and said something in a low voice that caused the first soldier to shift his crossbow's aim away from Lamprophyre. "You're allowed," he said. "Not him." He gestured at Dharan.

"It's all right," Dharan said. He handed Lamprophyre his load of books. "Tell Rokshan I'll see him tomorrow as usual. And, good luck, Lelitha." He trotted back down the stairs.

Lamprophyre smiled at the soldiers again and walked past them, leaving behind her escort. The soldiers on guard had already stopped paying attention to her and were once more watching the visitors below, but she didn't stop moving until she was through the passage and into the brightly colored pillared room beyond. She drew in a shaky breath. Suppose they hadn't found anyone to vouch for her?

She suspected the route she took to her room was more round-about than it needed to be, but it was the only one she'd memorized and she didn't feel like exploring. Once there, she barred the door behind her and dumped her load of books on the bed, then collapsed next to them and closed her eyes. Now that she was safe—and she insisted to herself that this room, with its lock and bar, was safe—she could indulge in the fears she'd told Dharan she'd put behind her. Maybe he was right, and the story wasn't true, but if it was, she really couldn't afford to waste time. Especially not in dwelling on how much time she didn't have.

She groaned and rolled over, which put her face to face with the stack of books. It was still several hours until supper, so she might as well read. The answer might be in one of these books. *Or it might be a waste of time*, she told herself, and immediately slapped that thought down. Thinking like that wouldn't get her anywhere, and the only real waste of time was in not acting.

She was soon caught up in her studies enough that time passed without her being aware of it. A knock on her door surprised her into looking up. The light from the windows had a faded look, as if sunset were on the way, and she discovered she'd been squinting for a while, trying to compensate for the growing dimness.

The knock came again. "It's me," Rokshan said.

Lamprophyre unbarred and unlocked the door, and Rokshan slipped through the narrow crack that was all the farther he'd opened the door, as if he were afraid of being followed. "Sorry I'm so late," he said. "It's almost time for supper—why haven't you dressed?"

"I am dressed—oh, you mean there are special clothes for supper?"

Rokshan nodded. He opened her clothespress and rooted around inside. "This will be fine," he said, handing the folded pile of red cloth to her. Lamprophyre held it up and discovered it was a narrow-skirted gown like the one she'd worn to the dragon races, only longer and dyed a rich crimson. Gold embroidery decorated the hem and neckline, rows of trumpet-shaped flowers on twining vines.

Lamprophyre reached for the hem of her shirt. Rokshan made a strangled noise and turned his back on her. "Sorry," Lamprophyre said, "but you did say we're running late, and I want to know what you learned today."

"Not much about the attackers," Rokshan said as she undressed. "None of the witnesses, if you can call them that, saw more than dark shapes fleeing into the night. The attackers didn't leave behind any evidence that might identify them, either. No scraps of fabric conveniently found in only one store in Tanajital, no weapons made only in Fanishkor or Sachetan. They might as well have vanished into the air for all they left traces."

"That's discouraging." Lamprophyre wriggled into the gown. It was one of the things they'd bought at that woman Madhya's store, the store that sold clothes made for anyone to buy. It was too long, the hem dragging on the floor, but otherwise it was comfortable.

"I've set Tekentriya's spies to investigating. They're more likely to discover information than I. I decided to put my efforts toward finding out about your kidnapper, Evart."

Lamprophyre walked around to face Rokshan. "That sounds promising. Was he from Tanajital?"

"He was." Rokshan brushed a long strand of hair over her shoulder. "Evart was a well-known adept specializing in physical magics. His colleagues all spoke highly of his abilities, but everyone I talked to also said he was rather focused on his studies. His wife—"

"He had a wife?"

"Former wife. They were divorced, and I understand from her it was because he was, to paraphrase her rather harsher words, unhealthily obsessed with magic. She didn't have much good to say about him." Rokshan sat on the edge of the bed, shifting books to the side to clear a spot. "He was poor most of the time, and whenever he came into money, he funneled it into magical research. Which would explain why he was vulnerable to the entity's promises."

Lamprophyre sat at the dressing table and ran her fingers through her hair. They caught on a tangle and sent a twinge of pain through her scalp. Scowling at her reflection, she said, "He really does seem like an ideal candidate—obsessed, competent, never has enough money. Did any of his colleagues know anything about the serpentine wand?"

"No one who'd admit to it. I wish I'd had you along to tell if any of them were lying. Even so, none of them were at all shifty when I alluded to Evart maybe having a secret project. One or two of them did seem eager for more details, which tells me they believed he might be capable of working on something clandestinely, but nobody behaved as if they were in on it."

Lamprophyre picked at the tangle. It was going to take forever to unwind all these hairs. Maybe she should cut her hair off. Tekentriya wore her hair short like a man and no one criticized her. "What about his house, or his workshop? Did you get into those?"

"Why, Lelitha, that would be illegal," Rokshan said in a falsely prim voice. "Prince Rokshan has no right to invade private property. *Commander* Rokshan, on the other hand, is within his rights to pursue a threat to the kingdom."

"And did *Commander* Rokshan find anything?"

"Evart's workshop is connected to his home, which was as clean as if no one lived there," Rokshan said in his own voice. "No food, barely any personal belongings. I'm having my men search the farm where you were kept, which was not Evart's property. It belongs to a man named Valinet, or used to—he passed away years ago and his heirs have been squabbling over it since. Stop doing that."

"Doing what?"

Rokshan rose. "Picking at your hair. Here, this is a brush—no, let me demonstrate." Rokshan picked up a silver paddle with hundreds of stiff bristles extending from its surface. He gently applied it to the tangle and coaxed the hairs free. Then he continued stroking her hair with it, disentangling the long strands until her hair hung straight and shining most of the way to her waist. Once the tangles were gone, the sensation of the bristles sliding over her scalp and through her hair was amazing, not quite a tickle and lighter than a touch. She closed her eyes and tilted her head back.

"That feels so good," she murmured. "I have to say this body has benefits. Everything feels so much more intense."

The brush halted. Lamprophyre opened her eyes to see Rokshan set it on the dressing table. "You'll need to brush your hair at least twice a day to keep it from becoming snarled," he said curtly. "Anyway—what was I saying?"

"The farm's heirs were bickering." She didn't understand why he was upset about her hair, unless this was another of those things that might give her secret away, not brushing it properly.

"Right." Rokshan resumed his seat on the bed and let out a deep breath. "I doubt they'll find anything at the farm, but it's worth looking into. The workshop, I had to leave for now. Evart protected it with the same kind of magic Manishi uses on hers. Some of the adepts from the weapons development branch of the Army are breaking them down now."

Lamprophyre perked up. "Adepts?"

"Don't get excited," Rokshan said. "The military doesn't employ high-level adepts because they can't afford to pay as much as the adepts can make in the private sector. These adepts aren't much more than beginners, but working together, they should be able to remove Evart's protections. We will, I hope, be able to enter the workshop day after tomorrow, or at worst the day after that."

"You do mean me as well, right?"

"If you can be spared from your research. How did it go today?"

Lamprophyre had temporarily forgotten her disturbing discovery in the pleasure of talking to Rokshan. "About as successful as your day was," she said, "but…"

When she finished telling him the story of the princess and her transformations, Rokshan said nothing. Lamprophyre said, "I'm trying not to let it worry me, but I'm afraid. What if we really don't have much time?"

"That story could be completely made up," Rokshan said. "It doesn't have to mean anything. And it's not as if we aren't already working as fast as we can. I think we should take it for what it's actually evidence of—that at some point, people knew enough about transformation artifacts that this story seemed plausible."

That cheered Lamprophyre up. "I guess it doesn't make sense to worry about a possible time limit," she said. "We have no way of knowing what that might be."

"Right." Rokshan stood. "And—"

"And what?"

He shook his head. "It was nothing. Just what I said, that it's more important that we now have evidence that more people than Evart have created transformation artifacts." He offered Lamprophyre his arm. "May I escort you, my lady?"

Lamprophyre laughed. "Aren't you afraid someone will believe we're courting?"

"It's just a courtesy. But…" Rokshan opened the door. "It would certainly spare you discomfort if my courting you meant Sanyot left you alone."

Lamprophyre locked the door. "I suppose your parents know I'm not human, and wouldn't believe it was a real courtship, so they wouldn't pester you with questions." She looked at the key. "I don't know where to put this. Why can't I wear a belt pouch with a gown?"

"What's that chain around your neck?" Rokshan asked.

"Oh. It's Evart's chlorite artifact. I forgot I had it." She removed the chain and threaded the key onto it, then hung the chain around her neck again and tucked the pendant and key beneath the neck of her gown. They made a funny lump on her chest, but it wasn't very prominent and Lamprophyre decided she didn't care if they showed or not.

"You're not afraid of having your thoughts overheard, are you?"

"Not really. Mostly I just didn't want to lose it. But if there's a chance someone might have developed the mind-reading artifact, isn't it worth a little extra caution?" Lamprophyre took Rokshan's arm again. "And I don't have to display it openly."

"Very wise," Rokshan said. He rested his hand on Lamprophyre's briefly. "Are you ready for more social interaction? If you want me to dissuade Sanyot, just give me a nod."

"Thank you, but I think I can deal with him myself." But she remembered her confusion of the night before, and wondered if she was right about that.

CHAPTER NINETEEN

I t wasn't until they entered the dining hall that Lamprophyre realized she was about to see the room that had intrigued her imagination ever since Rokshan had first described it. His description had fallen far short of reality.

Candles blazed on every wall and covered metal rings that hung from the ceiling, but what Rokshan hadn't mentioned were the many long, slender mirrors that captured the candlelight and reflected it back into the room until its walls glowed pale gold instead of the white Lamprophyre judged they actually were. It felt like being inside a cave with walls of molten gold, as warm as if it were heated by a dozen drag-ons, and Lamprophyre felt a surprising rush of homesickness. The place looked nothing like her home, so she didn't know why she'd reacted that way. But the warmth, and the way the light made the walls feel comfortably close...maybe she did know, after all.

By comparison to the brilliance of the lights, the white U-shaped table was boring. The chairs lining the outside of the U were all white like the table except for the cushions, which were a pale gold that matched the walls with darker gold patterns sewn all over them. The patterns looked like one of the cloths at Kulat's shop, which amused

Lamprophyre. Anyone wearing that fabric would blend in ridiculously with the chairs. She hoped Kulat hadn't chosen that cloth for her gowns.

The only interesting thing about the table was the many, many silver sticks—no, *utensils*, that was the right word—that shone in the candlelight, and the shapely glass cups with rims of gold. Lamprophyre had heard the stories humans told of dragons' hoards, and the array of silver and glass and gold laid out before her made her think of piles of treasure. How funny that it was humans who actually amassed hoards of precious things.

Rokshan had drawn her along with him as she observed the room and now released her arm and pulled one of the chairs away from the table. "Is this seat acceptable?"

Lamprophyre had no idea what would make one chair better than another. "I'm sure it's fine," she said, sitting on the cushion. It was plump enough that she felt a little unsteady, trying to balance atop it. Then she said in dismay, "You're not sitting with me?"

"The royal family sits at the head table," Rokshan said. He pointed at the base of the U, where part of the table was separated from the U's long sides and raised on a low dais. "I'll see you when the meal is over—there's to be a musical performance. We can sit together then."

Lamprophyre watched him walk away and felt bereft. It was a stupid feeling, she realized almost immediately, and one that only a silly woman would have. Dragons didn't feel maudlin just because they were surrounded by strangers—of course, dragons knew everyone in the flight, so no dragon was ever a stranger, but even if they were, dragons were stronger than that.

She smiled at the older woman seated next to her. "Hello," she said. "I'm—"

"Young Lelitha, yes, I know," the woman said curtly. "The visitor from Adakavi. I am Piya. Tell me, why have I never heard of you before?"

Startled, Lamprophyre replied, "I, well, my family is rather distantly related to Satiya, and we don't see our relations very often."

"That's a very poor excuse for failing to do your duty by your elders. Why did you not show us respect two nights ago, at the gathering? I anticipated you introducing yourself, but you barely spoke to anyone and then fled. I declare, I do not know what this generation is coming to."

"I—"

"And a student at the academy. A girl your age should be contemplating marriage, not wasting her time in useless scholastic pursuits. How many suitors have you?"

Piya's thoughts were as relentless as her words, battering at Lamprophyre like hailstones. Lamprophyre shut them out and said, "I —none, madama, I have no suitors—"

"That can't be true. You must be doing something wrong. You have a duty to your poor parents to present them with grandchildren before they are too old to appreciate them." Piya looked past Lamprophyre and beckoned to someone. "Come, young man, take a seat. Lelitha would like to speak with you."

"How fortunate, because I hoped to speak with Lelitha," Sanyot said. Candlelight gleamed off his bald head and illuminated the regular planes and angles of his face in interesting ways. He was attractive, Lamprophyre decided, but human attractiveness meant nothing to her, and it certainly didn't make his attentions desirable.

Sanyot pulled the chair on Lamprophyre's other side away from the table and seated himself. "Auntie Piya, how nice to see you," he said.

"Don't waste our time, young man, it's Lelitha you should use that flattering tongue on," Piya said.

"Oh, but Lelitha doesn't care for pretty compliments, much as I'd like to tell her how beautiful her dress is." Sanyot smiled at Lamprophyre, and her heart sank, because his expression was that sly, meaningful one that said he intended to flirt with her despite his words.

"Bah, that is foolishness. Lelitha, learn to accept compliments. It's no wonder you've had no suitors." Piya delivered this sentence with the rock-hard certainty of someone who knew better than anyone else how the world should run.

"No suitors? I find that impossible to believe," Sanyot said with another teasing, half-lidded smile.

A resonant, deep sound rang out, making a response impossible. At the open top of the U stood a wooden frame taller than any of the doorways, making Lamprophyre wonder how they'd gotten it into the room. A brass disc almost as large as the frame hung suspended from it by two wrist-thick chains, vibrating from being struck by the oversized mallet a white-clad servant next to it held. The servant raised the mallet to strike the disc yet again, putting her whole body into the swing as if the mallet weighed as much as the disc surely did. The sound echoed through the dining hall and made Lamprophyre wish she could cover her ears. For the first time, she was grateful not to have her draconic hearing.

Men and women in white, long-sleeved shirts and white trousers streamed in from doors behind the base of the U. Some carried piles of golden objects too distant for Lamprophyre to make out, while others carried silver basins almost as big as the cauldron Depik cooked soup for beggars in. She smelled, faintly, the aroma of meat broth, and her hunger stirred.

Across the room, from two doors on either side of the brass disc, brightly-clad women emerged, their clothes decorated with dozens of vividly dyed ribbons that fluttered as they ran. They moved like butterflies, or like bits of colored paper caught by the wind, lightly and delicately into the center of the space surrounded by tables. Lamprophyre watched them in fascination as they took odd poses here and there, their arms arched over their heads or curved low for their hands to brush their feet. Dancers, she thought they might be, and a frisson of excitement shot through her, dispelling some of her discomfort.

Piya picked up a square of white fabric from the table in front of her and draped it over her lap. "I suppose you're one of these modern girls who doesn't know how to cook for her husband," she said. "No understanding of your proper role, no interest in keeping a man's heart won through keeping his stomach fed. I don't know what this generation is coming to."

Someone reached past Lamprophyre and set down a bowl made of solid gold, in color not much darker than the sewing on the cushions. A moment later, someone else ladled a clear brown soup into her bowl before moving on down the row. Sanyot took up his spoon and began eating, so Lamprophyre did the same. At least this was a food she recognized.

"You do plan to attend the dance tomorrow, yes?" Sanyot said between mouthfuls.

Lamprophyre had no idea what he was talking about. "Dance?" she said. She glanced at the colorful women, who moved rhythmically as if they could hear music not audible to anyone else. She'd thought dance was an action, but Sanyot's phrasing suggested a place or maybe an event.

"Of course she'll be there," Piya said. "Dancing is an essential part of courtship. I don't know how you expect to find suitors if you refuse to participate in basic courting activities."

"But I haven't—"

"Yes, I know you haven't, but we'll change all that," Piya interrupted. "Sanyot, you'll see to it Lelitha doesn't avoid the dance. I realize she's shy, but that's no reason to hide."

Again Lamprophyre felt battered. Piya was like a force of nature, implacable and uncaring. Fleeing seemed like an appropriate response, except everyone would see, and want to know why she'd left, and that would draw more attention. Lamprophyre's discomfort gradually turned to anger. Why was she letting this woman browbeat her? And Sanyot did nothing. *Rokshan* would have told this horrible woman to stop.

She looked at Sanyot in mute pleading, but he only smiled at her and said, "I would be happy to be your partner for the dance, Lelitha, if you'll agree."

Lamprophyre wanted nothing less than to be stuck with Sanyot for whatever the Stones a dance was. It didn't sound like anything short and easy to extricate oneself from. "It's a special...dance...as part of the royal wedding, isn't it?" she said. "It must be much grander than any dance I'm familiar with." A dancer swept past, trailing ribbons, but she felt herself caught by Sanyot's gaze, unable to watch the performance.

"It's the largest event in the wedding ceremonies," Sanyot said. "It's to allow those not invited to witness the wedding vows a chance to congratulate the happy couple, and for their parents to show gratitude for all the many gifts those guests have bestowed on Tor and Anchala.

It's the only wedding tradition Gonjiri and Sachetan have in common, so it will be even more elaborate than most."

That was interesting, but it didn't tell Lamprophyre anything about whether she could reasonably not accept Sanyot's invitation. "It sounds beautiful," she said, hoping to sidestep the issue.

Someone removed her half-empty bowl, making her open her mouth to protest that she wasn't finished, but she saw everyone's bowls were being removed, empty or not, and fell silent. Golden plates matching the bowls appeared at each place, and Lamprophyre looked at the head table while she was waiting for her plate to be filled. The king and queen sat at the center, with Lady Risha on the queen's left and a thin, dark-skinned man Lamprophyre guessed was Torannum and Sanyot's father on the king's right. The other members of the two families—

—wait, the two families, but not Sanyot? Lamprophyre scanned the table. Sure enough, there was an empty seat near the right end. Lamprophyre looked for Rokshan and found him midway between Lady Risha and the left end of the table, where Manishi sat. Rokshan's gaze was focused on Sanyot. Even at this distance, Lamprophyre could see his jaw was clenched tight, and he didn't appear to be eating whatever it was they'd served next.

Lamprophyre glanced at Sanyot. His attention was all on her, and when he saw her looking at him, he smiled again. "You never answered my question, my lady," he said in a low, intimate voice. "Dare I hope you'll agree to partner with me for the dance?"

There it was again. "Um," Lamprophyre said, "the whole dance?"

Sanyot raised one eyebrow the way Dharan often did. "I suppose it would be wrong for me to monopolize your time," he said, "despite my desire to banish all your potential suitors to the farthest corners of Gonjiri. But for the processional, surely?"

She wished more than ever that Rokshan was there to guide her. This went far beyond flirting, where she could easily tell Sanyot to leave her alone; she had no idea what the customs or rules were about this dance thing, no idea what a processional was or what else she might be promising if she said yes—and no idea what the repercussions of saying no might be. "I suppose," she said. "For the processional."

"No need to sound so uncertain," Piya said. "Sanyot is a promising young man for all he's a foreigner. I suppose if Anchala intends to set a precedent, there's nothing wrong with the rest of you young people following, yes?"

Lamprophyre cast her gaze back at Rokshan. She didn't know how much of her despair showed on her face, but his expression was truly thunderous. He pushed his chair back, made as if to stand, and Lamprophyre gave the tiniest shake of her head. He couldn't have anything good in mind, and if he was going to assault Sanyot, better it not be in the middle of a formal supper.

Rokshan scowled, but resumed his seat, and Lamprophyre relaxed. Someone leaned past her to scoop bright red chunks of meat in an equally red sauce, garnished with actual sprigs of tiny leaves like a row of minute feathers, onto her golden plate. It probably smelled good, but Lamprophyre's nerves were on edge and prevented her from fully appreciating the aroma.

She watched Piya and Sanyot pick up knife and fork and cut the chunks of meat smaller before eating them, and mimicked their movements. It turned out to be cooked lamb, more tender than any she'd eaten before. The tiny leaves were almost imperceptible to the taste, which meant they were likely there to make the dish look pretty. It was pretty, the bright green leaves against the red sauce, but Lamprophyre was too distressed to appreciate it.

The dancers had stopped their individual flitting about and were gathered at the center of the room, all of them moving identically through the steps of what appeared to be rather complicated dancing. It was a beautiful distraction, and Lamprophyre watched and tried to let their peaceful movements calm her. This ought to be a unique opportunity to see something no dragon could witness, and instead she was plagued by Piya and Sanyot.

"I hope you'll sit with me during the music recital," Sanyot said. "Your reactions are always so charming, I enjoy hearing the music through your ears."

"That would be difficult, don't you think?" Lamprophyre said, wishing Piya wasn't sitting beside her, judging her responses. "Hearing anything but what our own ears tell us."

Sanyot chuckled. "Wise as well as beautiful."

Lamprophyre filled her mouth with lamb to keep from having to respond. She'd never considered how awful dining would be in a situation where she couldn't get away from her dining partner. "Lady Piya," she said, feeling desperate, "how are *you* related to the royal family?" Sanyot had referred to Piya as "Auntie," and maybe this would give her a definition of the unfamiliar word.

"Dear Satiya's sister married my cousin," Piya said. "I'm so pleased to see Anchala so happy. Now if we could just find a match for Rokshan. It's really too bad about the scars, but I'm sure there are many girls who will overlook them."

Unexpected anger rose up in Lamprophyre. "Those scars aren't everything he is," she said hotly, "and you're cruel to suggest that they make him less attractive to women."

Piya's mouth fell open. "Well, I never," she said. "How dare you speak to me that way? I declare I do not know what this generation is coming to."

"This generation doesn't need your pettiness and mean-spirited comments on how they live their lives," Lamprophyre went on, "and I intend to live my life as I choose, not as you seem to think it should go. And Rokshan is handsome, and kind, and he will find a mate in his own time, without the need for your interference."

Piya's complexion was dark with sputtering fury. "Well, I—you insolent girl! Your parents should be ashamed of themselves for not teaching you to respect your elders!"

"My parents taught me to be respectful of those who deserve respect. I don't believe you've ever had a generous, unselfish thought in your life, if this represents how you speak to others." It felt like words were pouring out of her, relieving the tension that had been building ever since she sat down. A tiny voice in the back of her mind was screaming at her to be cautious, but she didn't feel like listening.

"That's an interesting perspective," Sanyot said. "Aren't the dancers talented? Lelitha, this is one of the most famous dance troupes in Tanajital, isn't that interesting?"

"You," Piya spat, "I will have words with Satiya about your behavior. Such rudeness—such disrespect—" She abruptly turned her back on Lamprophyre to speak to the man on her other side.

"I had no idea you were so courageous," Sanyot said in a low voice, all teasing gone. "No one speaks to the aunties that way. She can make your life miserable."

"Only if I let her. And I refuse to listen to her any longer." Lamprophyre sat back as a servant's white-clad body interposed itself between her and Sanyot, removing the plate that, once again, she hadn't finished.

When the servant moved on, Sanyot was looking, not at her, but at the head table. "I didn't realize you and Rokshan were so...close," he said. "My mistake, if I interfered with your courtship."

"We're not courting," Lamprophyre said, alarmed. "He's a very dear friend."

"Forgive me, but if you spoke in my defense that passionately, I would move heaven and earth to make you my wife." Sanyot turned back to face her. "And yet you aren't seated beside him, so your attachment isn't formal."

"No, we really aren't courting. I just feel very strongly about it. He was so badly hurt, and I know his scars used to embarrass him, and that woman was so awful about them..." Lamprophyre listened to herself babble and wondered why she cared so much about proving she and Rokshan weren't intimate. It wasn't as if she wanted Sanyot to court her, and she'd told Rokshan a pretend courtship might not be a terrible idea, but—oh, she felt so confused, and the movement of the dancers dizzied her, and Sanyot's expression was unfamiliar, and she wished with all her heart to have her own body back, even if it meant never seeing things from a human perspective.

Sanyot's brow furrowed slightly. "I would never accuse a lady of lying, and I believe you're telling me the truth," he said, "but I wonder how well you know your own heart."

Lamprophyre looked at Rokshan, who was deep in conversation with Manishi—that was strange—and not paying attention to her. He didn't look any different than he ever did, but for the first time Lamprophyre saw him as she imagined a woman would. He was as attractive as Sanyot in his own way, and any woman would see that. The scars didn't matter. But she wasn't a woman, and Sanyot was wrong; she loved Rokshan because he was her best friend, and things like romantic desire didn't enter into it.

She was saved from answering by a servant who set down a fresh plate before her and piled yellow rice on it, topping the rice with pieces of roasted chicken. It was delicious, and Lamprophyre ate in blessed silence. She'd either finally successfully rebuffed Sanyot, or he enjoyed the chicken as much as she did, because he said nothing more. From the snatches of conversation Lamprophyre overheard coming from her left, Piya was telling her dining companion how rude "Lelitha" was. Let her complain. She couldn't hurt Lamprophyre with her words.

This time, she managed to eat most of her food before the plate was whisked away. It wasn't replaced immediately, and Lamprophyre wiped her mouth with her lap cloth and watched the dancers. They must be strong to go on dancing without pause like that.

"Lelitha," Sanyot said, drawing her attention. "I want to be honest with you." His thoughts were suddenly strong and intent on her, strong enough to hear despite her surroundings, and they were full of an emotion she didn't entirely understand, not love or sexual desire but hope.

Dread reared up inside Lamprophyre. "How so?" she asked, hoping she sounded unconcerned.

"I admit I first spoke to you intending nothing more than a light flirtation. But I soon realized that's not the kind of woman you are. I find you fascinating." Sanyot put a hand over hers where it rested in her lap. "If it's true you and Rokshan are nothing but friends, I would like a closer relationship with you. I know you're not like other women, and I promise I will never do anything to cause you pain. But I would like to know you better."

Stunned, Lamprophyre could do nothing but stare at him. His eyes were large and brown and reminded her of Orthoclase's expressive eyes. In that moment she imagined it was Orthoclase saying those things, asking her to think of him romantically, and guilt and sorrow struck her to her core, as if in rejecting Sanyot, she was rejecting someone she cared for deeply—just not in the way he wanted. It all came back to her deepest fears, even though Sanyot was human and she was a dragon and it was impossible that she could feel desire for him.

"I…" she began. "Sanyot, I don't…I am so sorry, you don't know how sorry—"

"You don't have to say anything else," Sanyot said with a smile that didn't look very happy. His thoughts went from hopeful to despondent in an instant. "I would never pursue a woman who didn't enjoy my attentions."

That made Lamprophyre feel even worse. "I wish I could explain," she began.

Sanyot pressed two fingers to her lips, silencing her. "Don't," he said. "I won't tell you I'm not disappointed. But you have a great capacity for friendship, and I hope we will someday be good friends. Unless you would prefer I not impose on you at all."

"No," Lamprophyre said. "I do like you. I enjoy talking to you." That was true, she realized, so long as they weren't talking about romance. "But that seems hard on you." She knew enough of romance from her stories, and from Depik and Bhakriya's relationship, how painful it could be for two people to share a life, or a friendship, when one of them loved the other and that love wasn't reciprocated. Sanyot didn't love her, but she felt the principle was the same.

"The more I know you, the more I believe your friendship is worth having," Sanyot said. "Don't worry about me. I'm always moving on to the next woman, don't you know?"

He said the last with such wry self-deprecation Lamprophyre was stung into saying, "I don't believe that's true. I think you simply haven't found the right woman, and you're too careful of the other women's feelings to be serious about them when you know *your* feelings aren't truly engaged."

A real smile lit Sanyot's features. "Fierce in defense of your friends," he said as a servant set a plate of beautifully arranged fruit before each of them. "Will you still accompany me for the processional? As a friend? I can't imagine anyone I'd like spending that time with more than you."

"I...all right." The tension and sorrow filling her chest were gone, and she felt such relief she would have promised him almost anything. She'd need to ask Rokshan what the processional was, but she felt sure as she hadn't before that Sanyot would be generous in explaining it if Rokshan didn't.

She ate her fruit with pleasure. Fruit was one of those human foods she'd been surprised by, how many varieties and flavors there were. As a dragon, she'd enjoyed the smell of fruit the way she would a flower: appealing, pleasant, but nothing you'd want to eat. Now it was hard to remember that an orange had meant nothing more to her dragon's nose than something that smelled like pyrite, which was delicious.

The sound of the brass disc startled her into dropping a grape, which bounced off her plate and rolled across the table to Sanyot. He picked it up and ate it, winking at her in a way that made her laugh. "Now it's time for the musical performance," he said, rising from his chair. "I don't want to monopolize your time, but if you haven't agreed to sit with anyone else, may I join you?"

"I told Rokshan I would sit with him, sorry," Lamprophyre said. She let him pull her chair out and stood beside him. Piya shoved back her chair with some force and walked away with no more acknowledgement of Lamprophyre than a vicious glare. Lamprophyre ignored her.

Sanyot smiled and bowed. "Then I will see you at the dance tomorrow, my lady," he said. Swift as thought, he took a step closer and kissed her cheek lightly. "Forgive my impertinence," he added, "and thank you for your generosity of spirit in turning me down kindly."

"Get away from her, Sanyot," a voice said from behind him. Rokshan put a hand on Sanyot's shoulder and spun him around. "She's not interested in your flirtation."

"Rokshan, don't," Lamprophyre said. "I already—"

"According to her, she isn't interested in yours, either," Sanyot said, sounding amused. "For such good friends, it seems the two of you haven't got your stories straight."

Rokshan's lip curled in a snarl, and he shoved Sanyot, catching him enough off-balance that he staggered into Lamprophyre and stepped on her foot. Lamprophyre let out a gasp of pain. "Rokshan, stop," she cried out. "Sanyot and I are friends. That's all. He isn't flirting with me."

"You don't have to put up with him kissing you if you don't like it, Lelitha," Rokshan said.

Sanyot regained his balance and stepped away from the two of them. "You're behaving like a jealous lover, Rokshan," he said. "Lelitha's made it clear she isn't interested in me, and I would never pursue an unwilling woman. But I suggest, if you aren't going to court her, that you leave her free to make her own decisions in that respect." He bowed to Lamprophyre again, said, "Until tomorrow, my lady," and walked away, passing through the small crowd that had stopped to watch the entertainment.

Rokshan's breathing was heavy, and he stared after Sanyot as if he wished he could attack him. Zefira stood behind Rokshan, her eyes not on Rokshan or Sanyot but on Lamprophyre. She looked the way she had at the paraveti tangal when she'd warned Lamprophyre not to lead Sanyot on. Her expression made Lamprophyre uncomfortable, even though she'd done the opposite of leading Sanyot on that evening. She didn't know why she cared so much about what Zefira thought. Maybe it was being human that did it.

Lamprophyre put her hand on Rokshan's arm. "Let's go. I don't know where the performance is held."

Rokshan took her arm absently, his attention on the door through which Sanyot had passed. "Why did he kiss you?" he said in a low voice.

Lamprophyre walked with him out of the dining hall and through the palace corridors. "I don't know. I think it might have been because I turned him down and he was saying goodbye to that possibility, maybe? But you shouldn't have attacked him. I told you I could handle him myself, and I did."

"You turned him down?"

"It was so hard, Rokshan. He had this look I couldn't understand, except I could tell he was sincere in wanting to court me. He isn't a bad man, he's just not anyone I should allow close to me."

Rokshan's hand closed over hers where it rested on his sleeve. "I'm sorry I misunderstood. You looked so miserable earlier, I thought he was imposing on you."

"He was, sort of, but we understand each other better now."

They turned a corner into a room that reminded Lamprophyre of a smaller version of the paraveti tangal hall, without the boxes high above. It smelled strongly of a lot of humans all in one place, overlaid with fruity and musky odors that were the scents humans used to perfume their bodies to disguise their strong, sour scents. It was dark and low-ceilinged, with walls of some brown wood and chairs with dark blue cushions a few shades lighter than the carpets covering the floor. Lamprophyre liked the warm closeness enough that she didn't mind the smell. Much.

Rokshan led Lamprophyre to a seat near the front and sat next to her. "Just so long as he's not flirting anymore."

"He isn't. But I agreed to be his partner for the processional tomorrow. What is that? And are we expected to dance? I know I couldn't do the dancing those women did tonight."

"You *what?*" Rokshan kept his voice down, but it was still intense enough to startle Lamprophyre.

"Was that wrong?" she asked. She should have turned Sanyot down. Agreeing to an unknown activity couldn't be good.

"It's just—" Rokshan shut his mouth in a tight, unhappy line and looked away. Lamprophyre felt sick. If he was angry about this, she didn't know what she'd do.

"I'm sorry," she said in a small voice.

Rokshan looked back at her, and his expression relaxed. "I'm not angry. I'm sorry. It was a stupid reaction and I didn't mean it. It's all right. The processional is just when everyone pairs up and walks around the ballroom. No dancing involved. And you don't have to know any dances. Women choose their partners, and you can get away with not asking anyone to dance." He sighed. "I'd planned to pair with you for the processional, but it doesn't matter."

"Oh." Lamprophyre somehow didn't feel any better hearing this, but she couldn't figure out why.

The lights dimmed, and people around them applauded as a man and woman walked to the front of the room. Lamprophyre clapped along with everyone else, but her mind was still on Rokshan and his strange behavior. If he knew something about Sanyot she didn't, something that would make him unsuitable as a friend—no, that was impossible, because he'd tell her if he did. She settled in to listen to the singing, which was beautiful if limited to what one could hear audibly, unlike dragon singing, which happened on the audible and mental levels. She'd never wanted so desperately to have her own body back.

CHAPTER TWENTY

The library seemed dimmer than it had the previous day, but when Lamprophyre looked closely at the lanterns, she couldn't see any difference. Maybe it was her imagination. Or maybe it was her irritation with the librarian. She'd hoped there were several librarians, and there would be a different one on duty when she returned, but it was the same pinch-faced, smug man as before.

She took her little pile of papers to the window and smiled politely. "I'm back."

"You are indeed," the librarian said with an answering smile. His thoughts said *back again, damn her* and *wish she'd go back to Kolmira.* "But not with Lector Dharan, I see."

Lamprophyre glanced over her shoulder at her stolid guard, who was even more impassive and intimidating than the first. "Dharan is busy elsewhere this morning. That's not a problem, is it?"

"Of course not," the librarian said. *Have to be nice anyway,* his thoughts said.

Lamprophyre waited while he searched the stacks for her requests. Such an odd word to describe a collection of books. It made her imagine tall pillars of books all piled atop one another, though from where she stood, she could see the long rows of wooden shelves—she'd finally thought to ask Rokshan what the fat, wide ladders for holding things were called—with books lined up on them, standing on end with their spines facing out. She had no idea where the word came from. Probably Dharan knew.

The librarian returned with four large books cradled in the crook of his arm. "I'm afraid the Kalivas is still unavailable. We are searching for it, but the collection is quite large and I'm sure you can see how difficult finding one lost book is." He gestured at the shelves behind him. *Maybe she'll stop asking*, he thought.

"Thank you for continuing to look," Lamprophyre said. She enjoyed how his expression became briefly bitter at her words. Taking her books to her desk, she settled in for more research.

She was improving at finding relevant books, she discovered. She still hadn't found anything that contained instructions for creating a transformation artifact, from serpentine or from anything else, but the latest books all touched on transformation magic of some kind or another. One of them suggested that transformation magic might be useful in healing, though it didn't have any concrete examples or stories of that being done, and Lamprophyre decided to take that one with her. Assuming the librarian would allow her to borrow books without Dharan's presence.

Between skimming the books, returning them, and choosing new ones, it was close to noon when she realized how hungry she was. She gathered up her notes and the three books she'd been reading and returned to the window. The librarian regarded her dispassionately. "I would like to take this book with me," she said, pushing the other two toward him to be returned.

"I'm afraid I can't do that," the librarian said. His thoughts were filled with smug pleasure at being able to legitimately turn her down. "You're not a student at the academy, so we have no way of finding you should the book not be returned in a timely fashion."

"But Dharan vouched for me," Lamprophyre said. Irritation rose up within her, but she suppressed it. She was fairly sure, from listening to his thoughts, that nothing she could say would change his mind, but she decided to try politeness. "And you know I'll be responsible. You've seen how I handle the books."

"Actually, I don't know that. Of course I don't think you'd hurt a book intentionally, but accidents happen and, as I said, we have to be able to find you in such an event." He smiled, a nasty expression. "You can always request it another time."

Lamprophyre ground her back teeth together. "Fine." She pushed the third book toward him. "I'll be back later. Thank you."

"Have a nice day," the librarian said in a falsely sweet voice. She'd never wanted to crush someone so badly in her entire life. He was fortunate she was for the moment a weak human.

The guard made her wait while he checked the commons for threats before allowing her to leave. Lamprophyre's first reaction, annoyance, disappeared quickly when she remembered how vulnerable she was. Better to be inconvenienced by a bodyguard than be dead.

Rokshan was waiting for them at the agreed-upon spot near the dragon embassy when they arrived. "Thank you, corporal, you're excused," he said. The guard bowed and walked away.

Lamprophyre observed the sword hanging at Rokshan's hip and said, "I suppose you're better than any guard."

"I'd like to think so," Rokshan said with a grin, "though it's still strange to think of you needing my protection. Let's walk. There's an inn down that way that serves the best saffron rice."

Lamprophyre noticed the people in the street walked wider around them than usual. It was the sword, she concluded. Not many people went armed with more than a long knife, and very few even carried those in this neighborhood. She didn't know if that was due to the presence of a dragon at the end of the street. She'd heard Anamika's father say more than once that crime wasn't as bad these days, not since Lamprophyre had settled there. If her presence could keep humans from hurting one another, she was in favor of that.

Leafy vines twined around the pillars fronting Rokshan's inn and over a lattice sheltering the inn yard, which was filled with little square-topped tables like the tavern Dharan had taken Lamprophyre to the previous day. Rokshan saw Lamprophyre seated at a table under the greenery and disappeared inside. The delicious smells of hot roasted sheep and vegetable soup filled the air, and Lamprophyre drew in a satisfied breath. Dragons didn't eat such varied foods as humans did, and she would miss the many uniquely human foods no dragon could digest.

Rokshan returned and sat next to her. "The food will be out shortly," he said. "Did you have any luck today?"

"Some, except there are a surprising number of books missing. Or misplaced, I suppose. Unavailable to me, at any rate." Lamprophyre eased off her sandal and rubbed her foot where the strap had chafed her skin. "I found a book that has information about transformations being related to healing magic, but the librarian wouldn't let me borrow it. I'll have to get Dharan to do it."

"Healing? That's something we could pursue." Rokshan leaned back in his chair and gazed up at the leaves.

"What about you?" Lamprophyre said. "The attackers?"

Rokshan didn't shift position, but she could feel a sudden tension radiating off him. "I learned nothing good," he said. "I had hoped we might catch one of them, but they all disappeared into Tanajital thoroughly. But investigation turned up information about a gang of extremists interested in overthrowing my father and destroying his government. I think they might be our culprits."

"But that doesn't have anything to do with me, or the entity. Or does it?"

Rokshan shrugged. "They're organized and they have access to weapons, and that's all the entity needs if it wants someone dead. Their political goals don't have to matter."

"You sound as if something else is going on."

Rokshan sat up and rested his elbows on the table. "When I told my father about it, he was very concerned about the political aspect. He wants me to follow up on that. I think he believes their anti-government agenda is the point, and not the existence of our enemy. Who, I have to say, is hard to convince people of if they haven't witnessed it in action."

Lamprophyre blinked. "That's going about it all wrong."

"You and I know that, Lelitha, but my father is used to having his rule challenged one way or another. An anarchist group is something he understands. A mysterious, ancient entity that speaks to people's minds, that's magic, or fantasy, or something equally unknown."

"But you're not going along with it?"

"I am not. But I can't tell my father that. So I'm wasting time with *two* investigations, and when you consider that I also have to fight Tekentriya for the use of her spies, you can see how I might be a little frustrated."

A round-cheeked, middle-aged woman appeared at their table with two bowls of thick red soup and a platter of saffron rice. She gave Lamprophyre a small earthenware plate and smiled. "Have a nice day," she said. It was amazing how much better that sentence sounded when the speaker was sincere.

Rokshan was already filling his own small plate with rice. "And that's before we include Manishi."

Lamprophyre paused in taking her first mouthful of soup. "Manishi? What about her?"

"She behaved very strangely at supper last night. Wanted to know all about you. Where you came from, why you were here, all the way down to your dining preferences." Rokshan took a bite of rice and added, mumbling through his food, "And all in this odd, meaningful way. Like she already knew the answers."

"That's really bad manners, Rokshan. Even I know not to talk with my mouth full."

Rokshan swallowed. "You eat like that all the time, when you're —yourself."

"I do not. I'm very dainty." Lamprophyre patted her lips with her fingertips as emphasis. "But you don't think Manishi knows my secret, or you'd have led with that."

"No, I don't. I think she was pretending to knowledge so I'd get nervous and reveal more than I intended. I acted ignorant, and eventually she backed off, but I saw her watching you with that speculative look in her eye, the one she gets when she's plotting something. I think we should be cautious."

"We're already being cautious. I haven't spoken to her since this happened."

"More cautious, then." He took another bite of rice and followed it with a mouthful of soup.

"Are you in a hurry, Rokshan? You're eating like you have some-where to be," Lamprophyre said.

He looked surprised and lowered his spoon. "I hadn't realized. I think I'm just tense over this investigation. I wish things were as peaceful as they were last week, with neither of us having anything more to do than hear petitioners at the embassy and go swimming."

"I agree." Lamprophyre sighed. "I wonder whether I can still swim."

"I wish we had time to find out."

They ate in silence for a while. Lamprophyre covertly observed Rokshan, but that moment at supper the previous night, the one where she'd seen him from a human perspective, didn't reoccur. It was a relief. She was uncomfortable enough in this body that she didn't need any more confusing moments like that one.

Abruptly, Rokshan said, "You're sure Sanyot didn't impose on you to ask you to pair with him at the processional?"

"Of course I'm sure. He was very polite. I think we might be friends someday. But should I have told him no? I didn't know you wanted me to pair with you."

"No. It's all right. Really, it's not important. I'll find someone."

Lamprophyre refrained from suggesting Zefira as his partner. It was probably unworthy of her, but she didn't like the woman and didn't want Rokshan involved with her. He hadn't seemed interested, but... She decided to take a chance. "You don't want to court with Zefira, do you?"

"It's just 'court,' not 'court with,'" Rokshan said, "and I honestly hadn't thought about it. Why, did it look like I was paying her special attention?"

"No, I was just wondering. I still don't understand most human body language yet." She decided not to reveal that Zefira was inter-ested in Rokshan romantically. It seemed a petty thing to do, if Rokshan didn't care for her, and there was always the chance that Rokshan might see her differently if he knew she cared.

"Zefira's nice enough, and of course she's beautiful, but we've never been more than friends," Rokshan said. "She's almost a clutchmate, if you want to think of it in those terms."

That relieved Lamprophyre's mind. "That's nice."

Rokshan pushed back from the table. "I'm comfortably full, and in a much better frame of mind now I've spent some time with you," he said. "Do you want to return to the library?"

"I need to find Dharan so I can get that book out of the clutches of that smug librarian." Lamprophyre took one last bite of soup and rose. "Will you come with me?"

"I'm your bodyguard, my lady," Rokshan said. "I wouldn't leave you for anything."

A knock on her bedroom door startled Lamprophyre into looking up from her book. It wasn't the special knock she and Rokshan had decided on, just a diffident *taptaptap*. It didn't sound like someone intent on killing her, but she had no idea what that would sound like. So she went to the door and said, "Who's there?"

"It's your gown, my lady," a female voice said.

Lamprophyre slid back the latch and opened the door. She recognized the woman servant as the one who'd brought her breakfast tray that morning. The woman held a paper-wrapped parcel, large and shapeless. "This came for you from Sirrah Kulat. May I put it away for you, my lady?"

"No, I want to look at it, so if you'd put it on the bed?"

The woman obediently laid the parcel on the coverlet. It was tied with string that came free easily when Lamprophyre picked at it. She unfolded the paper and let out an astonished breath. It was the blue-on-blue satiny fabric that had shone like the sun in the lights of Kulat's shop. In Lamprophyre's room, with the late afternoon light indirectly illuminating the walls and the painted ceiling tiles, it shimmered dully, as if it had been dusted with starlight, and the dark blue embroidery looked almost black. It was still a beautiful contrast, and Lamprophyre and the servant stood side by side admiring the fabric, differences of status forgotten in their mutual appreciation.

Finally, the servant cleared her throat and said, "I'm sorry for intruding, my lady, please excuse me."

"No, not at all. Thank you for bringing it."

The woman bowed and let herself out. Lamprophyre looked at the gown for a few beats longer, then picked it up by the shoulders and let it unroll from its packaging. A light silver dust shook out from its folds to drift onto the floor, but most of the shimmer clung to the folds of the gown and to the rougher embroidery. It looked like the silver snow-drifts that huddled in the lee of the stones in her mountain home.

Lamprophyre carefully hung the gown on a peg on the wall. She wasn't sure that was what the peg was for, but the gown was too pretty to put in the clothespress, and that might wrinkle the fabric, anyway. She smoothed the skirt, making it shed more glimmering dust. With the dress spread out like that, it was clear the dust was distributed unevenly, but that only made it more attractive to Lamprophyre's eyes, like a night sky where stars clustered more heavily in places. She coughed and waved away a falling plume of dust. It had better stop shedding soon, or she would spend all her time at the dance trailing a comet's tail of silver. That would be pretty, but the people inhaling it wouldn't appreciate it.

Some of the silver dust clung to her hands as well. She looked around and saw nothing she could clean herself with, so she wiped her hands on her trousers, leaving a grayish smear. She still wasn't used to how sensitive her hands were, how they tingled when she rubbed the coarse weave of her trousers like that. She examined her palms, which were faintly pink from the rubbing. The creases of the skin still had dust ingrained in them, so she rubbed again. It made no difference. She decided if it didn't come off with rubbing, it wasn't likely to come off on anything else.

She eyed the windows, which were too high for her to see out. By the slant of the light, it was...she counted on her fingers and deter-mined if it was just after late afternoon by dragon reckoning, it was nearly five o'clock in human terms. She'd wondered, before her trans-formation, why humans divided their days into twenty-four hours, but only numbered those hours to twelve before starting over, until Rokshan had shown her a clock and explained how much easier they were to read if they only showed twelve hours. That had brought up many more questions, such as what humans had done before clocks were invented, and how they knew how long to make each hour, until Rokshan had flung up his hands and exclaimed, "I should enroll you at the academy, and you can ask unanswerable questions of them for every hour there is in a day!" with a laugh.

Nearly five o'clock meant nearly suppertime, except there was no supper that evening, at least not a typical one. Rokshan had said food would be served at the dance, and that it was traditional to share that meal with one's processional partner. Lamprophyre scratched her palm and wiped silver dust off her fingernail onto her trousers. She wasn't sure when Sanyot intended to call for her, but probably she should put on her gown now. She could read just as easily in a gown as in her shirt and trousers.

The blue satin slipped neatly over her head and settled into place with just a wriggle of her hips. She pulled her hair free of the neckline and let it settle over her shoulders. Tangled again. She sighed and took a seat at the dressing table. A faint dusting of silver touched her face and what was visible of her chest above the neckline, and it shimmered in her dark hair. That was really too much. Lamprophyre set about brushing the silver from her hair, but it clung to the bristles, and after a few minutes she realized she was only moving the dust around.

She laid the brush down and eyed her reflection. People would notice her unusual appearance, but would they find it appealing, or would they think the newcomer was trying too hard for attention? Since there was nothing she could do about it, she decided not to worry.

She reached for a silver clasp to bind her hair with. It twitched sideways, out of her grasp.

Lamprophyre blinked. She reached for it again. The clasp flung itself over the side of the dressing table and made a clinking sound as it hit the floor.

She leaned over to stare at the little metal clasp, which came in two pieces, a silver cuff that wrapped around her hair and a matching pin that slid through two holes in the cuff to secure it. She was sure she hadn't touched it, but maybe she was mistaken. Maybe her sleeve...but no, her sleeves were short, not long enough to have come anywhere near the clasp.

She reached for the clasp—and the pin leaped from the clasp, sprouted a tiny mouth, and said, "Don't put me in your nasty hair!"

Lamprophyre, startled into jerking away, fell off the chair sideways and smacked her elbow painfully against the floor. If she'd fallen into a dream, that pain ought to wake her. But when her eyes finished watering, she saw the pin staring at her—staring, without eyes!—with its mouth curved in a disapproving frown. It had grown arms and legs and was in the process of helping the cuff rise.

"What are you?" she murmured.

"The voice of the future," the cuff said. It stretched like softened wax, then leaped at Lamprophyre's hands, binding her wrists in front of her by wrapping around them twice. Lamprophyre tried to wrench her wrists apart, but the cuff felt like solid iron despite its stretchiness. She staggered to her feet and smashed her wrists against the edge of the dressing table. The cuff parted, freeing her, and she stumbled backwards until she bumped into her bed.

"You can't get away that easily," the pin said, and flung itself at her face. She swatted it away and ran for the door. The need for escape cut through her confusion.

The latch grew a face as she reached for it. "You can't escumbmble," it said, its voice becoming a mumble as she grabbed it with both hands and yanked the door open, or tried to. She struggled with it for half a dozen beats before remembering the bar was in place. Swearing under her breath, she slid it open and finally managed to flee her room. She ran into the hallway and flung herself at the opposite wall, craving the solidity of something real.

Her hands touched a soft, moist surface, and she pulled away, but whatever it was clung to her skin like thick saliva. Gasping, she backed away until she could make sense of what the wall had become. An enormous human face, flat as the wall, stared back at her, its eyes blinking slowly. It looked like a painting come to horrible life. Its mouth was open, and its tongue protruded from it, glistening with spittle. As Lamprophyre watched, the corners of the terrible mouth curved until it was smiling.

At her.

CHAPTER TWENTY-ONE

L amprophyre screamed and turned to flee back into her room, but the door was gone. The wall on that side was of the same embossed gold panels as always, but there were no doors set in it, not hers, not anyone's. Terrified, she ran for the guest wing exit. More living faces stared down at her, their eyes swiveling in their sockets, their lips and tongues moving in a silence so profound she felt she'd gone deaf. The ground moved beneath her feet like slippery, slimy mud, tossing her off balance and slowing her until she wanted to scream.

The hall went on and on. Surely it had never been this long before? She risked a glance behind her and saw the hall extended in that direction only a couple of handspans before it turned into blank nothingness. Lamprophyre's heart thudded so hard it made her whole body shudder with each beat. She couldn't even hear her own breathing, though it was heavy and rapid and made her lungs hurt. Her eyes burned as if they were trying to weep despite the rest of her body feeling dry and achy and exhausted.

Ahead, a spark of light gleamed in the darkness as if the hall were veiled in black and someone had cut a tiny hole to let in sunlight. Gasping in relief, Lamprophyre pushed herself harder, desperate to reach the light. Whatever it might be, whatever lay beyond the black veil, it had to be better than this.

She ran into webs before she reached her goal, moving so fast she entangled herself too deeply to get free. She screamed with fear and frustration. Before she could do more than feel relief that she could still hear, the spiders were on her, their many many thin black legs prickling her skin. It felt the way it did when she sat on one foot for too long and then stretched it out, like a million pinpricks. She could feel their hot, damp breath brushing her skin as their sharp teeth, pointed and black, gnashed near her ears.

She screamed again and breathed fire, setting the webs alight. It was such a relief to be back in her dragon body she didn't care that the webs clung to it. But she wasn't a dragon, she was a human who breathed fire, and it all made so much sense she laughed and hugged one of the spiders, which turned into the servant girl who'd brought the gown. "This way," the servant said, turning a latch that opened a door leading away from the webs. Lamprophyre waved goodbye to the spiders and walked through.

She found herself on the top of a platform so high it brushed the clouds. Their mist caressed her skin, cold and damp the way the spiders' breath had been hot and moist. It had been so long since she'd flown! She spread her wings, and this time she really was herself again, and her heart pounded joyfully at being its right size again. Her wings filled the sky, blue and copper shining in the moonlight—though hadn't it been daytime just beats ago? Lamprophyre didn't care so long as she could fly. She stepped to the edge of the platform, stretching her wings even wider, and—

Someone wrapped their arms around her legs as she was about to take off, bringing her down to earth so her chin smacked against the stone of the platform. "Stop it!" she shouted, kicking her assailant. "Dragons need to fly!"

"Lelitha, why—ow!" It was a male's voice, one she felt she should remember, and it came from the person holding her legs. "Don't kick me!"

"Let me go," Lamprophyre demanded, flapping her wings. She

couldn't take to the skies with this male clinging to her, which made no sense because she was bigger than any male.

The male relaxed his grip on her legs, and Lamprophyre tried to step away, but instead he grabbed her around the waist and, impossibly, lifted her off the ground, holding her close to his body. It wasn't a dragon, it was a human. A human man. Which meant she wasn't a dragon, after all. She sagged helplessly in his arms, weeping tears of discouragement and sorrow.

"Lelitha, are you all right?" the man said. He set her down and turned her to face him. Lamprophyre screamed; his face was like the ones on the wall, flat and distorted and awful with its lolling, dripping tongue. She fought to get away from him, but he held her close again, making her scream more loudly. "Glissene dust," the man said, almost in a whisper. "But how...?"

She heard running footsteps, and deep voices calling out questions. "Stay back," Lamprophyre's captor said. "She's delusional, and—God's breath, it's all over both of us. Damn it."

The man picked Lamprophyre up, ignoring her screams, and ran with her down a passage with walls made of colored glass, only the pictures the glass made moved like real people and animals, and all of them laughed and pointed at Lamprophyre as she was carried help-lessly past. Her throat hurt from screaming, her body ached, and she couldn't stop tears from leaking out of her eyes, not even proper tears, just a constant endless trickle of salty water.

They left the colored glass walls behind to step into a silver bubble, perfectly round and with its walls rippling like water when the wind blows over it. The man spun her in his arms and leaped, higher and higher until they were almost flying, and then falling, falling, falling beneath the rippling silver, and then—

Water slapped Lamprophyre as if she'd been thrown into it, and she hit the bottom of a pool, not a natural one by the flat feel of the surface beneath her rear end. Hands pushed her down until she was completely submerged, and she choked and sputtered because she hadn't taken a breath before being dunked. She struck out at the hands on her shoulders, clawing at them, but they wouldn't let go. She kicked, thrashed, and suddenly the hands were gone. She shot up through the surface of the water, gasping for air. Everything was blurry. She wiped water from her eyes and squinted.

Human-sized figures filled the room, blurry and indistinct despite her eyes being mostly clear. They weren't humans, though; they had human bodies, but their heads were animal heads, horses and cows and sheep and a couple of pigs. They were carrying on conversations she couldn't understand in animal languages, oinking and snorting and snuffling. Lamprophyre discovered she was kneeling on the bottom of the pool, which was only chest deep to her in that position. She tried to stand, but her legs and arms shook too hard to support her.

"We need rice. Or bread. Potatoes would work, too," said the vaguely familiar voice. Lamprophyre turned and discovered the speaker was beside her, soaking wet as she was. He, too, had an animal head, but his was that of a fox. He climbed over the stone ledge surrounding the pool and helped Lamprophyre out, then lifted her into his arms and carried her through the crowd of animal-men to a tussock of green grass shaped like a cupped hand. Lamprophyre curled up in the hand's curve, shaking with cold as well as fear and confusion now.

"Someone bring us dry clothes," the fox-man said. Really, his voice was so familiar, and yet she simply could not recognize it. "And food. Move! She's still in danger."

"Who is in danger?" Lamprophyre said, or tried to; it came out as a hoarse whistling cough that rattled her lungs and made her lips feel numb.

"It's all right, Lelitha, everything will be all right," the fox-man said. He knelt beside her and took her hand, and in that gesture she finally recognized Sanyot. But he wasn't a fox, he was a human—Lamprophyre clutched his hand tightly and closed her eyes. With her eyes closed, the world settled in around her, and she found she could breathe properly. She still hurt everywhere, and her throat felt raw, but the murmuring conversations no longer sounded like animal noises. She shivered, and then couldn't stop shivering.

Arms went around her, and Sanyot held onto her, steadying her as she shivered. She'd never been so grateful to anyone in her life. His body gave off a nice steady heat she welcomed, and gradually the shivering subsided to the occasional tremble.

When he released her, she protested. "You have to get out of those wet clothes," he told her. She opened her eyes and had to look away quickly because hearing Sanyot's voice come out of the fox's head made her feel achier. Some of the people in the room now were women, and they surrounded her, rubbing her with soft blankets. A few of them helped her take her ruined gown off. That was two of Kulat's creations destroyed. She hoped the haughty tailor never found out. He might blame their destruction on her.

Lamprophyre briefly thought about whether she ought to be naked in front of men, and then decided she didn't care so long as she could be dry and warm. Soon one of the women pulled a soft, shapeless robe over her head and helped her find the armholes, and one of the other women brushed out her wet hair, squeezing water from it, and if everyone would stop having animal heads she felt she would be perfectly fine.

The fox-man returned to her side. He was also in dry clothes and his fur—but Sanyot was bald, so how did that make any sense? Lamprophyre closed her eyes again, but Sanyot prodded her. "You have to eat now," he said, and raised a spoonful of golden rice to her lips.

"I'm not hungry."

"It will make you well, Lelitha. Eat. Please."

Lamprophyre made a face, but obediently ate the rice. The first few bites tasted awful and made her stomach roil, but by the fifth bite, her hunger was roused, and she devoured everything in the large bowl, eating until her stomach was distended and she felt she could never eat again.

As she ate, the world shimmered around her like heat haze bleeding off the white bricks of Tanajital's streets. She watched in fascination as the animal heads flickered and then disappeared, revealing perfectly normal human heads. All of them watched her eat so intently it made her uncomfortable. She looked at Sanyot, who had his own bowl of rice that wasn't as large as hers. "What happened to me?" she asked when her bowl was empty.

Sanyot's gaze flicked to the watching servants. "I don't—" He shook his head. "You were poisoned, Lelitha."

A muted gasp ran round the room, which Lamprophyre discovered was the talking chamber from her first night in the palace, down to the pool Sanyot had dumped her in. "Poisoned?" she said. "But I haven't eaten anything that could have been poisoned."

Sanyot shook his head again. "Contact poison. Glissene dust. It makes you hallucinate and..." He looked at the servants again. "We should speak privately."

Lamprophyre looked around. The servants weren't even pretending not to be listening. "Will you help me back to my room?" she asked.

Sanyot nodded and helped her stand, handing off their bowls to a woman who looked like she wished she could follow them. Lamprophyre still ached all over and found she needed Sanyot's help to keep a straight line. She eyed the walls, but no spiders or grotesque faces appeared, and the ground was steady beneath her feet.

"How did you know what the poison was?" she asked when they were alone in the hall to the guest chambers.

"It comes from Sachetan," Sanyot said. "It's from a rare type of jellyfish. Contact with them when they're alive produces a kind of euphoric state, but dried and ground up they make a silver dust that causes hallucinations. The more dust, the more intense the hallucinations. There were traces of it all over your gown, but it must have been bathed in the stuff for you to react the way you did. Where did it come from?"

"I thought it was supposed to look like that," Lamprophyre said. "It was so pretty...Sanyot, it was in my hair and on my hands and all over—" She stopped and swallowed to keep from throwing up. "Why would Kulat have done that? Or, you said it was from Sachetan. Maybe he didn't know what it was?"

"Maybe," Sanyot said grimly. "Or maybe someone wanted to play a very nasty trick on you."

They reached Lamprophyre's door. It hung slightly ajar, something that worried Lamprophyre until she remembered her flight from the room. "Come in," she said. "There's still something you're not telling me."

Sanyot stopped in front of her bed, which sparkled. "You can't sleep here," he said. "This room needs to be thoroughly cleaned, and that blanket ought to be burned."

"All right, but—what else happened?"

Sanyot's expression was unfamiliar, hard and cold and not the least bit flirtatious. "You passed me with no sign you even knew I was there," he said. "When I caught up to you, you were at the top of the stairs in the great hall. Preparing to leap to your death."

Lamprophyre's joints went weak. She lowered herself into the chair and closed her hands on her knees to stop both of them from shaking. "You think someone wanted that?"

"I don't know. It's impossible to predict what someone under the influence of glissene dust will do. So it's not ideal as an assassin's tool. But it's perfect if someone doesn't care what happens to their victim. Humiliation, or injury, or even death." Sanyot looked capable of strangling whoever had poisoned her. That made her remember—

"Rokshan," she said. "I need to tell him about this."

Sanyot raised an eyebrow. "You think this is a matter of military significance? Or are you still unwilling...no, never mind."

"Never mind what?"

He shook his head. "This can't be related to the attack on Anchala. It's a completely different kind of assault."

Lamprophyre considered telling Sanyot the truth. He'd saved her life, after all, and now that he wasn't trying to flirt with her, she found him a reassuring presence. But the more people who knew what was really going on, the more possible it was that someone would reveal it to the wrong person. "Yes, but suppose this is a new, um, means of attack? Rokshan needs to know."

"Let's see if the servants can find you a new room, and I'll send someone to fetch Rokshan." Sanyot offered his hand and pulled Lamprophyre to her feet. "It will be all right. I really do think this was a prank that got out of hand." He left the room, leaving the door hanging ajar.

He'd sounded certain, but Lamprophyre wasn't so sure. She still had so many questions. Her mind buzzed dully with them as she waited for him to return. Sanyot was gone for several minutes, but finally he slipped through the door and shut it behind him. "How easy would it be for someone in Gonjiri to get glissene dust?" she asked.

"I'm not sure. It's an illegal substance in Sachetan, which of course means there's a brisk trade in it among black marketeers. And *that* means it's sold here as well. But that's as much as I know. I'm not even sure what the going rate is, but I'm guessing, with as much as there still is on your floor and bed, somebody spent a pile of rupyas on it."

"But it's illegal."

"Right. That doesn't mean it's unavailable."

"I mean that Kulat wouldn't have bought an illegal substance just to make my gown pretty, and he couldn't have bought it thinking it was something innocuous. Which means he wasn't responsible."

"That makes sense," Sanyot said. "So someone tampered with your gown, though I don't know how they managed to do it. Did someone get into this room while you were out?"

"I don't think so. And the gown was wrapped in paper when it arrived, with the dust inside the package. So I think...I think someone must have opened the package and put—"

The door slammed open. "La—Lelitha!"

Lamprophyre jerked, startled, and Sanyot held her hand more tightly. Rokshan stood in the doorway, clutching its side with one hand as if he needed its support. His hair was disordered, as if he'd been running, and he was breathing heavily. He took two steps toward her and then stopped, his eyes on Sanyot. "What is *he* doing here?"

"He saved my life," Lamprophyre said, just as Sanyot said, "Still the jealous lover, eh?"

Rokshan's gaze darted from Lamprophyre to Sanyot and back. "Saved your life?"

It comforted Lamprophyre to have Rokshan there, even if he was irrationally upset about Sanyot's presence. But her aching body longed to lie down somewhere, and the idea of telling him everything that had happened wearied her further. "I was poisoned," she said. "By a Sachetanese poison that works through skin contact. And the poison is all over this room. So can we find somewhere for me to sleep? Because I feel as if I've been beaten."

Rokshan put his arm around her shoulders, steadying her. "What did it do to you?"

"It causes hallucinations," Sanyot said. "Such as the one where

Lelitha apparently believed she was a dragon and intended to fly off the steps of the great hall."

Rokshan's arm tightened convulsively on Lamprophyre's shoulders. "A dragon," he said, not making it a question. "I take it you stopped her. Thank you."

"I couldn't allow her to plummet to her death," Sanyot said with a smile. "But if your gratitude will extend to you not looking daggers at me all the time, I accept."

To Lamprophyre's surprise, Rokshan smiled. "I'm afraid I'm not always rational where my friends are concerned," he said. "You're a good friend to my cousin."

"It's my pleasure." Sanyot opened the door. "I'll find someone to clean this room. I know how to do it safely, but I'll need some assistance."

"You shouldn't have to do that, Sanyot," Lamprophyre protested.

"My lady, I would be negligent if I did anything else," Sanyot said with a slight bow.

"But weren't you poisoned too? You should rest."

"It was a very light dose, and I feel well." Sanyot gestured for Rokshan and Lamprophyre to precede him. "Don't worry about me."

"But—"

"Lelitha, he's right," Rokshan said. "Sanyot, are there any side effects from this poison? Since you seem to know all about it."

"I don't, really, at least not more than any Sachetanese does. It should leave you very sore, Lelitha, and your appetite for meat may diminish for a day or two. But you won't have any more hallucinations now that we've washed the residue off and you've gotten some starch into your system." Sanyot shrugged. "Though if you find the culprit, I'd like to know who it is. Our government takes the sale of illegal substances very seriously."

"Thank you again, Sanyot. I'm sorry we missed our processional," Lamprophyre said.

Sanyot's eyes widened in mock alarm. "We did! That's one more thing I owe your poisoner for. Now I *really* need to know who did it so I can pummel him to my satisfaction." He smiled and hurried off down the corridor.

Rokshan didn't let go of Lamprophyre until they reached the glass-walled sitting room. He helped her sit and then pulled a rope hanging from one corner of the ceiling. Nothing happened, but Rokshan returned and sat heavily on a chair opposite hers. "Lelitha, I am so sorry," he said.

"Why are *you* sorry? It's not your fault."

"No, but I'm supposed to protect you while you're...you know. I doubt a contact poison could hurt you when you're yourself."

Lamprophyre put a hand on his knee. "Let's not worry about blaming ourselves, all right? Let's find out who did this. Sanyot said it's not an assassin's poison, in the sense of being an efficient killer, but that doesn't mean the poisoner didn't want me dead."

Rokshan bowed his head. "Tell me what happened."

Lamprophyre didn't want to do anything but sleep, but she explained about the delivery of the gown, about the effects of the poison and how Sanyot had stopped from her leaping to her death, down to being dunked in the pool and fed a huge bowl of rice. "I don't think Kulat is responsible," she said, "which means it was someone who had access to the gown *and* wanted me hurt or humiliated."

As she said the last three words, a horrible thought entered her mind. It must have showed on her face, because Rokshan said, "You've thought of someone."

"It's probably not true. I have no evidence."

"So who is it?"

Lamprophyre let out a deep breath. "Zefira."

Rokshan looked bewildered. "Zefira? She hardly knows you!"

"I know, but...never mind. It can't be true. You're right, why would she do that?"

"Lelitha, what made you suspect her?"

Lamprophyre tried to come up with a lie and realized she never wanted to lie to her best friend. "She's attracted to you," she said bluntly. "She thinks I stand in the way of her being with you. She also thinks I led Sanyot to believe I was attracted to him when I actually wasn't. And I suspect she believes I toyed with both you and Sanyot at supper last night so you'd fight over me."

Rokshan blinked. "Well," he said. "That certainly sounds like a reasonable supposition, if not actual evidence. I would have paired with you for the processional if Sanyot hadn't gotten there first, and poisoning you would have opened the way for her to pair with me."

"It's not evidence, though, right?"

"No. Evidence would be if she had a jar of this glissene dust in her rooms, or if she'd written a note saying how she meant to deal with you once and for all." Rokshan looked ill. "I thought Zefira was a friend."

"It might not be her," Lamprophyre said. "It's just a guess."

"I know. So I won't accuse her immediately. But I will talk to the servants to see if any of them remember someone tampering with your gown. Who brought it to you?"

"I don't know her name. She brought my breakfast this morning. So maybe she is assigned to my rooms."

"That's Haleta. I'll talk to her first." Rokshan rose and pulled the rope again, harder this time. "Where the devil is everyone?"

"I don't know what the rope is for."

"It's a bell rope. It rings in the servants' quarters to let them know someone is in need of help." Rokshan sat across from her again. "I can't believe this happened when I wasn't here to stop it."

"You're being irrational again, Rokshan."

"I know. I'm sorry." His eyes met hers. "Lelitha—Lamprophyre."

"Yes?"

He looked away and sighed heavily. "Nothing. I'm just having trouble not feeling guilty."

Footsteps sounded down the hall, and a servant in green and yellow appeared. "I apologize for the delay," he said. "How may I serve you?"

"Lady Lelitha needs a new room while her old one is being cleaned," Rokshan said.

The servant bowed. "If you'll follow me, my lady?"

Rokshan kept pace with her the whole way back through the guest wing and into her new room. This one didn't have a bar to lock it securely, and Rokshan said, "We'll need the key. Both keys."

"I don't know where those are, your highness," the servant said.

Rokshan's hand clenched into a fist. "Then *find them*," he said in a low, terrible voice. The servant paled, bowed very deeply, and fled.

"Lie down," Rokshan said.

"I can't undress while you're here," Lamprophyre said.

"Just rest, all right? I'll wait with you until the keys arrive. Then you're to lock yourself in. Do you mind if I keep the second key?"

Lamprophyre lay down on the bed. Her still-damp hair immediately chilled her shoulders, and she swiped it out from beneath her so it fanned out on her pillow. "I hate this hair," she said. "Can I cut it off?"

"I suppose," Rokshan said. "But it's beautiful hair."

"Says the man who keeps his even shorter than is customary," Lamprophyre shot back.

He chuckled. "True. It's up to you, Lelitha."

Lamprophyre wiggled until the blanket slid out from under her, then cuddled up beneath it. It was almost as comforting as sleeping in a pile with the rest of her clutch when they were all dragonets, warm and cozy and soft. "I hope it's not Zefira," she murmured.

"I hope whoever it is has a clear connection to our enemy," Rokshan said. "A connection we can use to gain more information. Or even strike back."

Lamprophyre heard his words in a haze. Her aches weren't fading, but it felt as if they were muffled by fluffy down pillows, a pleasure that had almost reconciled her to her human body. "Fight back," she agreed, and then she was asleep.

CHAPTER TWENTY-TWO

The noise of the key in the lock woke Lamprophyre like a jab with a pointed stick. She scrambled out of bed and cast about for a weapon. Nothing. Why hadn't she insisted on being armed?

The door swung open, and Rokshan walked in carrying a tray. "Are you all right?" he asked, taking in her wild-eyed appearance.

Lamprophyre nodded. "I was just sleeping deeply, and I forgot you had the key. I thought—no, it's nothing." Her heart was slowing back to its normal too-fast rate, too fast for a dragon, at least. She sat on the edge of the bed and clawed hair out of her eyes. "What time is it?"

"Nine-thirty. Nearly mid-morning. I thought you should be allowed to sleep a little longer than usual, in case that helps your recovery." The new room had a table next to the soft chair, and Rokshan set the tray on it. "Eggs, rice, and this new thing Akarshan's invented by frying shredded cooked potato. After what Sanyot said, I thought I wouldn't bother with meat."

Lamprophyre scowled. She'd become fond of sausage. But she sat at the table and ate. The fried cooked potatoes were surprisingly good, buttery and a little salty, and she gobbled them down as if it had been years since she'd eaten. She didn't like eggs any better than she ever did, but they were filling, as was the rice. She washed it down with water from a plain wooden cup, so much better than gold or silver, which gave the water a funny tang. Rokshan sat on the edge of her bed and silently watched her eat. When she was finished, he said, "I found out what happened to your gown."

The food turned to lead in her stomach. "It doesn't sound like it's good news."

"It's not. Apparently the gown arrived at the servants' entrance yesterday afternoon, and it sat in the servants' hall for about half an hour while Mirendi—that's the chatelaine, the woman in charge of running the household—tracked down Haleta to take it to you. I don't know why it had to be Haleta, but I don't interfere with Mirendi's work. At any rate, one of the servants saw someone untie the wrapping and look at the gown. He didn't think anything of it because he assumed anyone tampering with a guest's belongings had permission."

"That's reasonable."

"I'm not sure I agree. But he's not the most intelligent person, so I didn't rip into him for not reporting it immediately. He was able to identify the woman." Rokshan took a deep breath. "It was Colshi. Zefira's personal maid."

That made Lamprophyre feel numb, even though it was what she'd suspected. "Did you talk to Colshi?"

"I did. She confessed to pouring 'a lot of silver dust' into the parcel and tying it up again. She also said it was a joke Zefira wanted to play on you, and was terrified at being interrogated. I found the empty jar where she said it would be, so that's something. I've had her confined while I work out what to do."

"So you don't think she knew it was a poison?"

Rokshan stood and walked to the dressing table. It had a couple of hairbrushes and a hand mirror on it, and he shifted the brushes until they were lined up parallel to the mirror. "I don't. I think Zefira didn't tell her any more than she had to. But this is a complicated situation. Right now it looks like Colshi is the guilty one. And Zefira is heir to a principality."

Lamprophyre shot to her feet. "You can't mean she's immune to punishment?"

"No, Lelitha, I don't mean that. But I have to proceed cautiously.

We can't make wild accusations." He nudged the mirror with his fore-finger. "I want you to come with me when I question her. We need to know her thoughts."

"Those can't be considered evidence, even if I was free to reveal I could do that."

"Colshi's testimony will help. But what I want to know is where Zefira got the idea. If she was influenced by our enemy—"

Lamprophyre's mouth fell open. She said, "I thought it was just jealousy."

"Jealousy would have been a dusting of the poison. A whole jar is serious malice. And I know Zefira. I can believe jealousy of her, but she's not a malicious person. So either I'm wrong, and someone I've known well for years has suddenly changed her behavior, or someone else got to her."

"So she could be the one in the palace the entity has corrupted. But she was there when those assassins attacked. Would she really have put herself in danger if she was the one who told the entity where to find me?"

"Nobody shot at her. I think it's a strong possibility. But we need to prove it."

Lamprophyre lowered herself into her seat and rubbed her fore-head, which ached a little. "I'm not sure how we can. I haven't detected anything out of the ordinary in the thoughts of those who've been influenced by the entity. Evart, or the Third Ecclesiast."

Rokshan picked up one of the hairbrushes and spun it in his fingers. "I know. But we have to keep trying. I can't believe this crea-ture can speak to humans or dragons and leave no trace of itself." He handed Lamprophyre the hairbrush. "You should brush your hair, and then we'll go back to your room so you can put on your own clothes. Then we'll talk to Zefira. It needs to be soon, before she finds out Colshi's been imprisoned."

"You do it. You're better at managing this awful hair than I am."

Rokshan scowled. He pressed the brush into her hand. "Stop being lazy. We don't have time."

"All right," Lamprophyre said, taken aback by his abruptness. She dragged the brush through the tangles until it looked straight enough for good grooming. She set the brush on the dressing table, slightly appalled at how many strands of hair clung to its bristles, and followed Rokshan out the door.

She hadn't been in the palace at this hour before, having always left early to go to the academy, and it surprised her how many people there were, busily going about their work, their thoughts focused on cleaning or running errands. She glanced over her shoulder to see whoever was at the far end of the corridor thinking about getting into the room now that she and Rokshan had left it, but the servant was slow to appear around the corner, and she left the hall without seeing who would clean the room she'd barely used.

The guest wing was enormous, far bigger than Lamprophyre had realized, with long halls intersecting with other halls and doors that hung open as servants passed between rooms. Rokshan walked rapidly, forcing Lamprophyre to trot to keep up with him. She thought about protesting, but guessed there was a chance Zefira might leave, and she didn't want to chase her all over Tanajital.

Rokshan's steps slowed as he neared a door that, unlike the others, was closed. "I'll do the talking," he said. "You just listen."

Lamprophyre nodded.

Rokshan knocked lightly on the door. Lamprophyre didn't hear a response, thanks to her weak human ears, but Rokshan either had better hearing or didn't care about politeness, because he opened the door and walked inside. Lamprophyre followed, feeling unaccountably nervous. It wasn't as if Zefira could hurt her, not in public, anyway, but she still felt as if she was doing something…maybe not something wrong, but something underhanded in listening to Zefira's thoughts with the intent of convicting her.

Lamprophyre shook her head to dispel those ridiculous thoughts. She would have died from Zefira's "prank" if Sanyot hadn't been there. She owed the woman no consideration.

Zefira sat at her dressing table, arranging her hair. A flash of embarrassment stung Lamprophyre at how casually perfect Zefira's movements were, how nice her hair looked compared to Lamprophyre's, and then she felt stupid at caring about anything so ridiculously human as hair. Zefira didn't turn away from the mirror, just regarded Rokshan in its reflection. "Good morning," she said with a cheerful smile. "How are you, Lelitha? We all heard you were taken ill." *Can't possibly know,* she thought.

Rokshan didn't smile back. "It will go easier for you," he said quietly, "if you tell me the truth now."

Zefira lowered her hands, but still didn't turn around. "Truth about what?" She sounded so innocent, but her thoughts were in turmoil.

Standing behind him, Lamprophyre could see Rokshan's reflection, and he looked impassive, as if this were any ordinary conversation. "Please, Zefira," he said. "Don't play games with me."

Suddenly Zefira's thoughts untangled, and a new voice echoed through the woman's head. ***It was a joke,*** the voice thought. Lamprophyre clenched her fists to keep her reaction from showing on her face. She knew that voice. It had spoken to her in the darkness, threatened to overwhelm her until Lamprophyre had called on a God not her own to stop it.

"Oh, Rokshan, it was a joke," Zefira said, thinking *all this fuss over some silver dust, how stupid is he? And over a fat girl like that.* "Nothing terrible happened." It was clear to Lamprophyre that she didn't realize the second voice was anything but her own thoughts.

"Lelitha almost died," Rokshan said. "Your little joke was criminally negligent."

That frightened Zefira, but she maintained her cool, laughing demeanor. "Criminal? Of course not. And it's not my fault if she wandered into danger."

"Not your fault?" Rokshan shouted. "You think you're entitled to hurt people for your amusement? Don't think your rank will protect you, Zefira. I intend to bring this before the king. We'll see if you're still laughing when you're disinherited."

Zefira flinched, her eyes wide with fear. "Rokshan," she said in a trembling voice, "we're friends. You would never hurt a friend." *It was a joke,* she thought, and the evil voice said ***yes, it was a joke, he's being unreasonable because he cares about the fat girl. I didn't do anything wrong.***

"Funny, that's what I thought about you," Rokshan said. "Or did it not matter to you that you were hurting me indirectly by trying to humiliate my cousin?"

"It was just a little dust. It shouldn't have taken her like that," Zefira said, thinking *I thought more was better! I didn't want her dead!*

I wanted her gone. I did what I had to. Should have used even more, the entity thought, masking its own thoughts in Zefira's.

Zefira suddenly focused on Lamprophyre. "I'm sorry," she said, thinking *how do I fix this? Can still get rid of her.*

"So you admit it," Lamprophyre said, taking a step forward so she wasn't behind Rokshan. "Why did you do it? I've never done anything to you."

"I…" Zefira looked at Rokshan. *Can't admit it,* she thought.

Lamprophyre heard the entity stir within Zefira's thoughts. **He'll hate me if I admit to loving him,** it said. Then it went very still. **You,** it said, its voice more malevolent than before. **Listening in like a snoop. You think you have the upper hand? I have more power than you ever dreamed of.**

Lamprophyre gasped and shut out her awareness of Zefira's thoughts. "Rokshan, it knows," she whispered, grabbing his hand.

Zefira's eyes widened again. Then they rolled up in her head, and she collapsed in a thrashing, twitching heap on the floor.

Rokshan dropped to his knees beside her, holding her so she couldn't bash her head against the floor or the edge of the dressing table. "Go get help," he said curtly. "Find a healer, or send someone for a healer, but go *now*."

Lamprophyre ran from the room. She listened for thoughts, hoping madly to get some direction, but she was still too close to Zefira, whose thoughts had become a formless mess threaded through with vicious hatred as the entity attacked her. Blocking her out again, she ran blindly down the hall, shouting, "Help me! Someone help!"

She came around a corner and collided with a tall man carrying a bundle of folded cloths. "I need a healer to come to Lady Zefira's room immediately," she gasped. "Please—I don't know where the healer is—"

"I'll do it, my lady," the man said, and ran back the way he'd come. Lamprophyre turned and hurried back to Zefira's room, hoping it wasn't too late. Stones, how stupid did you have to be not to recognize thoughts not your own? She was furious with Zefira even as her heart ached for the woman.

Zefira had stopped convulsing when Lamprophyre returned. "I sent someone for the healer," Lamprophyre told Rokshan. "Is she..."

"She's alive, but unconscious," Rokshan said. "What happened to her?"

"I heard it. The entity spoke within her. Then it somehow realized I was listening in and it attacked her." Lamprophyre knelt beside Rokshan and Zefira, brushing the woman's ruined hair out of her face. How ridiculous Lamprophyre's envy seemed now. "But it definitely told her to poison me. What's more, Zefira really did intend it to be a joke, and she meant to use only a little of the dust, but the entity told her she should use more. Zefira didn't want me dead—the entity did."

"That's not much comfort." But Rokshan's bleak expression softened.

They sat in silence until the door opened, and a crowd of people pressed in, including a man in a sleeveless black healer's tunic Lamprophyre recognized as the man who'd healed Anchala. She got to her feet and retreated to the far wall as Rokshan lifted Zefira and laid her on the bed for the healer to examine.

The healer carried a leather bag about as long as Lamprophyre's human arm that he set on the floor beside the bed. He opened it, dug around in it for a bit, and came up with a strand of moonstone beads long enough to circle Zefira's head, which was what he did with them. The beads were translucent white with a blue glow where the sunlight struck them. Nothing happened when they touched Zefira's skin, and the healer ignored them, searching his bag until he found a couple of carved pieces of jade.

"What happened?" he asked Rokshan.

"She had a seizure of some kind," Rokshan said. "It lasted for about a minute. Then she fell unconscious, and I couldn't rouse her."

The healer nodded. "Hold this," he said, handing one piece of jade to Rokshan. "Warm it in your hands and give it to me when I ask." He breathed on the other piece of jade, which was a flattened oval disc, and placed it in the hollow of Zefira's throat.

Lamprophyre realized her fists were clenched tight and made

herself relax. Carefully, wary of how many people were in the room, she listened for Zefira's thoughts. Even an unconscious person had thoughts, though they were never coherent. There were now seven people in the room, all of them intent on the healer, who was thinking *never good when the moonstone doesn't light*. Zefira's mind, however, was empty, without even the background hum people generated when they weren't thinking of anything in particular.

Lamprophyre felt tears sting her eyes. "Rokshan," she whispered. He didn't respond, and she didn't think he'd heard her. That was just as well. There wasn't anything he could do. Nothing any of them could do, unless the healer could work a miracle.

"Now," the healer said, holding out his hand to Rokshan. Rokshan gave him the jade. It had a triangular shape, with the points of the triangle rounded. The healer pressed one point gently to Zefira's skin beneath her left eye and traced invisible lines all over her face, then on her hands and wrists. Nothing happened. Lamprophyre found her gaze focused on the strand of moonstones, willing them to light up or catch fire or do *something* that would show the healing was working. They remained inert.

Finally, the healer sat back. "Her body is perfectly healthy," he said, addressing the room in general. "But her consciousness is deeply dormant. I think some of the structures of her brain were damaged, which caused the seizure."

"Will she recover?" Rokshan asked.

Not likely, the healer thought. Aloud, he said, "It's possible. There is a healing center in the city that specializes in treating illnesses of the brain. They'd know more than I. But she should be taken there immediately."

"We'll see to it. Thank you." Rokshan turned and looked surprised to see Lamprophyre still there. "You three, arrange for transportation for Lady Zefira. Lelitha and I will go ahead, if you'll tell us where to go?"

Lamprophyre didn't pay attention to the healer's directions. Her whole self was focused on Zefira. She hadn't liked the woman, and maybe in some hard, calculating way Zefira had gotten what she deserved for plotting with the entity, but Lamprophyre still cared more about people than about that evil, ancient enemy. In her heart, she wanted vengeance for Zefira and everyone else the entity had hurt.

"Lelitha. Let's go," Rokshan said.

She followed him through the halls and into the streets of Tanajital, blocking out her awareness of everyone else's thoughts so she could be alone inside her own head. Rokshan walked slowly, as if despite what the healer had said, he felt no urgency. Lamprophyre suddenly felt a surge of compassion. Zefira was his friend, or had been before she'd turned on Lamprophyre, and how awful to discover a clutchmate was capable of such evil.

She cast about for something to talk about, something that might distract him, and said, "Rokshan. Am I fat?"

Rokshan jerked. "What?"

"Both Zefira and the entity said I was a fat girl, like it was a bad thing. Am I fat?"

To her surprise, Rokshan laughed. "That's the one question asked by a woman no man is ever allowed to answer. If he says no, she won't believe him, and if he says yes, she'll never speak to him again."

"I don't understand. Plenty of humans are fat. Is that an unattractive thing?"

Rokshan shrugged. "Some people think so. Sometimes being fat is unattractive just like being thin can be unattractive. Like, for example, Manishi."

Lamprophyre didn't like Manishi, so learning her skinny frame was unattractive obscurely satisfied her. "But you said this body was beautiful, so why would Zefira think it was the bad kind of fat?"

With a sigh, Rokshan said, "Zefira was jealous of you, and people who are jealous often exaggerate and criticize their enemy's physical characteristics to make themselves feel better. And I wouldn't call you fat. Women your size are usually referred to as 'well-rounded.'"

"So you think fat is a bad thing, too."

"Of course not!"

"Then why do you have a special word for it to avoid saying I'm fat?"

Rokshan stopped in the middle of the street, making someone else swerve to avoid him and his sword. He pressed his fingers over his closed eyes and said, "I don't know, Lelitha. Maybe I'm not as generous of thought as I should be. Maybe there's a part of me that believes being fat is bad. All I can tell you is that you are beautiful, and anyone who thinks you're not just because you're heavier than some women is a fool."

Lamprophyre stared at him. She was struck once more by that odd, dissociative feeling of seeing him as a human woman sees a man, tall and dark-skinned with powerful, elegant hands, and then the moment passed and he was Rokshan again. "I suppose it doesn't really matter if I'm attractive in this form," she said. "What matters is that I'm able to find a solution to my problem."

"That's true. Since it really is just the two of us searching. Well, and Dharan and the clutch."

Lamprophyre frowned. "What makes you say that?"

Rokshan took her hand to keep her close as they turned onto one of Tanajital's main streets, thronged with pedestrians and mule-drawn carts. "I forgot because of learning what Zefira did. There was another attack by those extremists, the group that shot at you. Only it was aimed at some of the royal holdings here in the city. Arson."

"That's terrible. Was anyone hurt?"

"Three people died. Which is awful, but it's not what concerns me. The problem is that Father has decided the attack on you after the paraveti tangal really was aimed at Anchala instead. He believes the attackers are interested in hurting his government, and are maybe working their way up to trying to assassinate him." Rokshan drew her closer to avoid a group of men who weren't inclined to move out of anyone's way, not even someone armed as Rokshan was. "It means he doesn't believe you're in need of special protection."

Lamprophyre stopped, and Rokshan tugged on her hand to get her moving again. "But what about Zefira's little prank?"

"That convinced him even more that it was all coincidence, since it's unlikely anyone in the palace has a connection with the extremists. I tried to tell him what we suspected, but it's like I said before—he isn't likely to believe in anything he can't see."

A shaky breath escaped her. "I suppose it doesn't matter," she said, "given that there's nothing soldiers can do to stop an invisible, possibly immaterial enemy."

"They can stop anyone it coerces. Lelitha, we still have to be careful."

Lamprophyre gazed at the crowds surrounding her. They all seemed completely uninterested in her. That was a terrible, dangerous illusion. "We need to find a solution, fast," she said.

CHAPTER TWENTY-THREE

Lamprophyre scribbled another title on a slip of paper and stacked it atop the others. She was having trouble staying focused on research. She kept seeing Zefira as they'd left her at the healing center, her blank, empty face, her eyes opening and closing so slowly it couldn't be called a blink, and felt oddly guilty, as if she were responsible for Zefira's condition. That was ridiculous, and probably her guilt was more because she wasn't sorrier that Zefira had been hurt.

She shook her head and ran her finger down the page of her current book. It was the strangest thing she'd ever seen—it wasn't an ordinary book, full of information or stories, but a book containing nothing but lists of other books. Each book listed included a couple of paragraphs explaining what it was about. It was the fastest way she could imagine to skim through a lot of books, but how anyone had ever thought to compile that information in the first place, she had no idea.

There. That was five titles. Scowling inwardly at the library's restrictions, she carried her papers to the window. To her surprise, the sour, pinch-faced librarian wasn't there. In his place stood a younger man who smiled at her pleasantly as she approached. *Pretty girl, wonder who she is*, he thought.

"I would like to look at these books, if I can," Lamprophyre said.

"Are you a student?" the man asked, but his thoughts didn't contain any hidden hostility.

"I'm Lelitha. I'm a student at the academy in Kolmira and I'm studying with Lector Dharan for a few days. While the wedding festivities are going on," Lamprophyre said.

The man nodded. "So Dharan vouches for you? Lucky you. He doesn't take on many students." The man accepted her slips of paper and turned to go—and bumped into the librarian, whose expression was unusually forbidding.

The librarian took the papers from the man's hand so swiftly he didn't have time to react. "I will see to these," he said, "and you, Narahar, should return to your duties."

That is *my duty,* Narahar thought in some annoyance, but he nodded respectfully and walked away into the stacks. Lamprophyre watched him go. It was too bad *he* couldn't help her, but clearly he was her nemesis's subordinate and not in a position to fight back.

The librarian looked down his broad nose at Lamprophyre. "I see you still have one book," he said. "You may have four more, not five." He took a slip of paper and handed it back to her. Lamprophyre made herself smile politely. If only Dharan were here—but he was busy, and it wasn't as if she didn't understand the principles of research now. She was sure the mean librarian wouldn't be so dismissive of Dharan.

She glanced at the paper in her hand. Kalivas. Now, had that been coincidence, or something else? She hadn't been listening to the librarian's thoughts to know which it was. All she knew was that for three days now, he'd refused to bring the book to her, and while he might have been telling the truth the first time, that it was misplaced, she felt certain he now knew where it was and for some reason didn't want her to have it.

She wished she could remember what the book was about. The author, Kalivas, had written some two hundred and fifty years earlier, and she recalled that it had been indexed under the "Artifacts" subject, but she'd read so many books in the past three days the ones she'd only skimmed through, or hadn't been able to read at all, blurred in memory. By now, she probably didn't need it, having found so much more information about artifacts elsewhere, but the librarian's continued stubborn refusals had made her curious.

The librarian returned with a stack of three books. "I'm afraid this one has been damaged and is out of circulation while it's being repaired," he said, handing her another piece of paper. *She'll believe that*, he thought.

So he *was* deliberately getting in her way, but why? "It's too bad there's no way to know if a book is unavailable short of looking for it," she said, keeping a tight hold on her anger. "So I don't waste your time."

"Yes, that is unfortunate, isn't it?" the librarian said with a forbidding frown.

Lamprophyre took her books back to her table, thought about slamming them down to relieve her frustration, decided they didn't deserve such treatment, and set them down gently. She flipped through the topmost one without seeing its contents. The librarian didn't want her looking at certain books, books that were actually available but that he chose to lie about being unavailable. Why might he do that?

She realized she was drawing neat little circles on one of the scraps of paper and made herself stop. He might have decided she didn't deserve to look at certain books because she wasn't a student there. Or maybe he simply picked books at random to frustrate her. Or— Lamprophyre's hand froze. Or maybe someone else told him which books she wasn't allowed to see. Someone ancient and evil.

But how likely was that? Was it plausible that the entity had found an entry to the mind of someone perfectly positioned to block her efforts to find a solution? Given that they still didn't know how the entity chose its victims, it was all too plausible. It had the ability to hear thoughts, and all it needed was to touch hundreds of minds until it found ones who recognized her, or had spoken to her.

She dropped the pencil and buried her face in her hands. The entity could be everywhere—maybe not all at once, but if it was nothing but a voice in people's heads, it could slip from one to another faster than Lamprophyre could follow. It could destroy people's minds.

It didn't seem to have a physical presence. In the face of all of that, despair seemed the only rational option.

She breathed in and out, slowly, and let her mind drift until she felt calmer. She was being ridiculous. The entity had power, true, but it wasn't omnipotent or it would have killed her itself already. Maybe they hadn't seen its physical body, but it seemed unlikely that it didn't have one. And she was sure their suppositions about the entity's other limitation, how it likely could only corrupt people who were vulnerable to its promises, were correct. So if the entity did have this librarian under its control, Lamprophyre ought to be able to make use of that.

She skimmed through the three new books absently, her mind now focused on outwitting the entity. Only one of them was useful, and she set it aside to read later. She took the others back with no more than a glance at the librarian, whose thoughts were gloating. He thought he'd thwarted her. He was in for a nasty surprise.

She spent the next couple of hundred beats—the next ten minutes, she was in a human body and could use human measurements— flicking through the cards and reading her book of lists carefully. What else had Kalivas written, and what was he known for? And who else wrote on those topics?

Finally, she had a handful of papers and a heart bursting with righteous indignation. Carefully maintaining an expression of calm indifference, she approached the librarian. Now to test her theory.

"These three, please," she said. "And I'm sure Dharan will want to borrow those other two, but I won't ask you to ignore the rules and not count them against my total."

"Thank you for being respectful," the librarian said with a smile that stopped just short of being a sneer.

When he vanished into the stacks, Lamprophyre leaned on the shelf, pulling herself up on it so she could see beyond the window and past the first few rows of shelves. Sure enough, there was the junior librarian Narahar, carefully sliding books into spaces on one of the shelves.

"Thank you for helping me earlier," she called out, not too loudly in case the mean librarian's hearing was keener than it should be. "You're

Narahar, right? What are your duties, if they don't include finding books for students?"

Narahar had looked up at her first words and smiled. He put away a final book and came back to the window. "My duties are whatever Lector Ilhan decides they are," he said. "He likes having control over retrieving the books." Narahar lowered his voice. "Just between us, I think he resents Lector Dharan's catalog system because it lets everyone be a librarian, more or less."

Lamprophyre thumped to the ground. "Is that Lector Ilhan? The, um, stern librarian?"

Narahar's smile broadened. "How politic of you not to use the word I'm sure was actually in your mind. Yes, Lector Ilhan became head librarian almost two years ago. Lector Karuna decided she was tired of academia and went into retirement. She was responsible for seeing the catalog project through to the end. She would have liked you."

"Really?" Lamprophyre hadn't expected that. "Why?"

"Oh, she was always fond of Lector Dharan's proteges. Said he had a gift for spotting intellectual talent." Narahar glanced over his shoulder. "I should get back to work. But it was nice to meet you, Lelitha."

Lamprophyre leaned against the shelf to watch Narahar retreat hastily into the stacks as Ilhan approached, empty-handed. Hah. She'd been right.

"These two are missing," Ilhan said as he handed back her requests, "and this one is in the restricted section. I'm so sorry." He didn't sound even a little bit sorry, but Lamprophyre didn't care.

"What's the restricted section?" she asked.

"It contains books only accessible to lectors, and then only under certain circumstances." Ilhan was thinking *she'll get Lector Dharan in to get past me, even he won't succeed.* "Most of them are very old and fragile, and frequent handling would damage them."

"So—if you don't mind my asking—why do you still have them, if no one can read them?" Lamprophyre asked in her sweetest, most innocent voice.

Little liar, Ilhan thought, and said, "We must protect knowledge in all its forms. Many of those books are awaiting funds to copy them, and then they will be made public again."

"I know how expensive that can be," Lamprophyre said. "Will you search for the other two?"

"Of course," Ilhan said. *She'll never know, keep her from guessing*, he thought. "Feel free to request them again in a day or so."

"Thank you. Here are my next requests," Lamprophyre said, holding out more pieces of paper.

The smug smile faltered. "One moment," Ilhan said, and walked away.

Lamprophyre leaned against the shelf and flicked through her remaining requests. Now she would see how committed Ilhan was to thwarting her, or to obeying the little voice in his head. Though after hearing the entity speak to Zefira, Lamprophyre was convinced the entity didn't always identify itself as its own creature. Zefira clearly hadn't been able to distinguish between its thoughts and her own. Either way, Lamprophyre had nearly a dozen requests, all connected to the Kalivas book in some way, and Ilhan would either have to allow her to read some of them or look very suspicious in not giving her access to any of them.

Soon Ilhan approached, once more empty-handed. "This is very strange," he said. "I'm afraid all three of those are missing. One of them was stolen, I believe." *Something going on here, she can't possibly know the truth,* he thought, and *keep stalling, can't let her see them.*

"That *is* strange," Lamprophyre said, sounding as innocently perplexed as he did. "You don't suppose someone took all the books related to that topic?"

Ilhan's expression didn't change, but his thoughts became sharper and almost panicked: *she knows, how can she know, why does she care about those old histories?* "That's unlikely," he said. "We do not censor knowledge at the academy."

Lamprophyre forbore to comment. "Well, I have three more requests," she said, handing them over. "I'm sure they can't *all* be missing." She smiled at Ilhan, whose face was a dispassionate mask like a statue and whose thoughts were in turmoil. It cheered her immensely.

As soon as Ilhan disappeared between the shelves, Narahar strolled up and rested his arms on the shelf. "What are you playing at?" he asked. *Something odd about her*, he thought.

Lamprophyre controlled an impulse to babble something that might convince him she was an ordinary human woman. He could have no idea of her true identity. "No game," she said. "I'm just curious."

"I should tell you off for wasting the librarian's time, but I admit to being curious myself." Narahar lowered his head so he could speak more privately. "Have you requested a lot of books that are missing?"

"I don't know many would be a lot. Several, certainly. But I'm sure Lector Ilhan wouldn't deceive anyone."

Lamprophyre eyed Narahar carefully, and sure enough, he thought *not sure about that, he likes power and he'd do almost anything to get it, what power from denying this woman, though?* "Of course he wouldn't," he said. "I'm sure it's just coincidence."

Ilhan reappeared just at that moment, carrying a single book. "Narahar, don't you have duties to attend to?"

"Of course, sir. I was just answering this young lady's question about library policy." Narahar gave Lamprophyre a meaningful look, but Lamprophyre had already decided she wouldn't give Narahar away no matter what he said.

Ilhan handed Lamprophyre the book. "The other two are in the restricted section. I hope this one will be useful to you."

"I'm sure it will," Lamprophyre said, not really paying attention to her words because she was so preoccupied with listening to Ilhan's thoughts: *throw her a bone* and *can't possible help her without the others.* What others? He might mean the other books, in which case he'd probably given this one to her because it was useless. But that raised the question of what, exactly, he was trying to stop her learning. He didn't know she was a dragon or she'd have heard it in his thoughts, so if he knew she wanted information about transformation magic, he couldn't know why.

She sat once more at her desk and opened the book, not seeing the words on the page. She wasn't even sure what she was looking for, at least in terms of the books related to the Kalivas book, because she didn't know what that one contained. So either Ilhan wanted to stop her learning anything, or there was something in the Kalivas book that the entity didn't want her finding out. Lamprophyre smiled. Finally, the entity had slipped up. Lamprophyre wouldn't have known there was anything important in that book if the entity hadn't had Ilhan block her access to it. Therefore, it was now urgent that she track down that book and the ones related to it.

Conscious of having won a small victory, she read the new book Ilhan had grudgingly parted with cover to cover. As she'd guessed, she didn't learn anything new. It was a history rather than a book on magic or artifacts, a history that touched on events following the Cataclysm that had nearly destroyed human civilization and had separated dragons from humans for more than a millennium. After finishing it, Lamprophyre copied down its title and author and a note to herself: *connection to other books*. She didn't really need a note to remember, but it was something she could give to Dharan in case he needed to read it himself.

"Ready to go?" Dharan said, startling her.

"I was just thinking about you," she said. "It's a good thing thinking of people doesn't really summon them to your side. Imagine if that happened with people you disliked."

Dharan chuckled. "I hadn't thought of that, but you're right. Do you need me to borrow these?"

"Yes, please."

Lamprophyre waited at the table while Dharan took the books back to the shelf and negotiated to borrow the ones Lamprophyre wanted. She caught snatches of his thoughts as she listened in on Ilhan; Dharan was thinking about supper and how well she'd taken to research, Ilhan's mind was a tangle of irritation over helping Lamprophyre indirectly and a sort of fawning respect for Dharan.

The commons was once more full of students and lectors, all of them intent on their suppers. Their singleness of purpose made it easy to listen to their thoughts, but Lamprophyre blocked them anyway. Human appetites for food were all more or less the same, and very boring.

Lamprophyre's guard trailed them all the way to Rokshan's favorite inn, where Rokshan waited for them, and then he walked away at Rokshan's thanks and dismissal. "Why do I still have a bodyguard if your father thinks the danger is aimed at him?" Lamprophyre asked.

"Because I'm still a commander in the Army and can make that decision independently of what my father believes," Rokshan said. "I ordered food already, so let's sit and discuss. I want to know if you've learned anything."

Lamprophyre scooted her chair close to the table and leaned forward, inviting Rokshan and Dharan to lean in as well. "I think that head librarian, Ilhan, is under a certain someone's influence."

Dharan's eyes widened. "I wish I could say that's impossible, but in truth, Ilhan is exactly the sort of personality the entity could easily corrupt, if we're right about who's vulnerable to it."

"How did you find out?" Rokshan asked. "Not the way we learned about Zefira, I assume."

Lamprophyre shook her head. "He's deliberately steering me away from a certain line of research. I pushed the boundaries of what he's done to see what I could prove, and I'm convinced the entity is controlling him. As convinced as I can be without actually hearing its thoughts in his head."

"What research?" Dharan said. "Is it something I can do?"

"I don't know. I think he'd give you the same runaround he did me." Lamprophyre let out a deep breath. "And I don't even know what it is the entity doesn't want me to learn. It's a lot of books I would never have thought to look at. I don't suppose you know anything about a scholar named Kalivas?"

"Historian and collector of folklore," Dharan said promptly. "He was born about three hundred years ago, lived in Suwedhi most of his life when he wasn't traveling. About a third of the most popular folktales, meaning the ones the average person knows, were first written down by him."

"That seems completely unrelated to transformation artifacts," Rokshan said, "unless he wrote down a story about them."

"That's possible. I'm sure I could find a copy of his folktale collection at a bookseller." Dharan leaned back for a serving girl to set a plate full of rice and steak in front of him. Lamprophyre inhaled the delicious aroma and eagerly picked up her fork and knife to eat her own delicious steak. "But Kalivas wrote a lot more than just folktales, including several histories that aren't in vogue now. His approach was counter to modern thought, so not a lot of people have heard of them. What Kalivas book were you after, Lelitha?"

Lamprophyre swallowed a bite of steak, juicy and hot and incredible. If the glissene dust had killed her appetite for meat, the effect hadn't lasted long. "It was called *The Last Days of Hamadri*."

"Huh. Sounds like pre-catastrophe history. No one's ever found evidence of a city called Hamadri." Dharan lowered his fork. "Which likely makes the book full of speculation. So much was lost in the catastrophe, anyone writing about it in our time has to make more guesses that I personally believe are appropriate in a history."

"But if Hyaloclast's story about the transformation artifact is true," Rokshan said through a mouthful of meat, "it might have come from that time. And given that this Kalivas collected folklore as well as history, why couldn't he have written that story down?" He took another bite. "That makes it very reasonable that the entity wouldn't want you to know about it."

"That makes sense, because I found a related book that was also a history of the Great Cataclysm," Lamprophyre said. "Or, I should say, I forced Ilhan to give me a related book."

"Forced? That's interesting," Dharan said.

Lamprophyre told them what she'd done that afternoon, making Dharan laugh. "That was clever," he said. "You cornered him so he couldn't not give you *something*. But you say he thought it was useless without the other books?"

"Yes, and I read it and I agree." Lamprophyre pushed what was left of her rice around on her plate. "But I wrote the title and author down in case we need to find it again."

Dharan accepted the paper from her and tucked it away in his belt pouch. "I'll see if I can make time to look at it," he said. "This is a bad time of year, what with final recitations and people turning in their theses. I'm afraid I haven't been much help."

"We're making progress, though," Rokshan said. "We know of one person who has contact with the entity, and I think we can make use of that. If you don't mind having your actions known to our enemy, Lelitha."

A chill passed through Lamprophyre. It hadn't occurred to her that if the entity could speak to Ilhan, it knew his thoughts, which meant it could know anything Lamprophyre did or said in front of Ilhan. "That's unsettling," she said, trying for a light tone.

It didn't deceive Rokshan, who squeezed her hand briefly in reassurance. "We are confident the entity doesn't know everything—that it has to use human or dragon minds to perceive the world. That means we can feed it disinformation by speaking in front of Ilhan."

"That's interesting," Dharan said. "Like what?"

"I don't know yet," Rokshan said, chewing his lower lip in thought. "But it's something to keep in mind." He stood. "Lelitha, are you ready to go?"

"I'll join you at the library in the morning," Dharan said. "We'll see if I can't get Ilhan to disgorge a few of those supposedly missing books." He saluted Rokshan with one of those wrist-gripping gestures that were also something only men did, squeezed Lamprophyre's shoulder companionably, and headed off toward his lodgings.

Lamprophyre and Rokshan strolled through the streets, which were coming alive again as day turned into evening and the nighttime city awoke. "There's another private family gathering tonight, but you could claim lingering illness if you want to get out of it," Rokshan said.

"I think I'd just like to sleep, if you're sure that's all right," Lamprophyre said. She wasn't terribly tired, but the idea of socializing and pretending to be human, even if Sanyot was a friend now, made her uncomfortable.

"It's fine. Though I'm sure Auntie Piya will be disappointed. I heard her say something this morning about needing to teach you good manners." Rokshan grinned. "What did you say to her?"

"I yelled at her for insulting you."

The grin fell away. "Lelitha, you didn't have to put yourself on her bad side for my sake. I can take care of myself."

"I don't like hearing my friends insulted. She's a horrible person and if I really were human, I would hate to be related to her."

"Nobody talks to the aunties that way. They're all stubborn and self-righteous and have an iron-clad certainty that they know what's best for everyone."

"That's what Sanyot said. But I don't care." Lamprophyre took Rokshan's hand as they passed through a particularly dense crowd of revelers.

"You're the bravest person I know. Though I shouldn't say that, because you probably don't realize how brave it is to stand up to Auntie Piya." Rokshan tugged her closer. "But I know you well enough to know you'd have done it anyway."

"What is an auntie, anyway?"

Rokshan laughed. "It's like cousin. An aunt is the sister of your mother or father, but we call any older female relative aunt, as a sign of respect. Or fear."

He made such a comical face as he said this Lamprophyre had to laugh herself. "Well, if all the aunties are like Piya, I'm not sure why anyone would respect them."

"I did say fear, too, right? The aunties are convinced the world would spin backwards if they weren't in control. They have advice about courting and marriage and childbearing, all of it delivered in no-nonsense demands they believe are simply rational good sense."

They passed through the parkland and approached the side door, where Rokshan finally let go of Lamprophyre's hand to salute the guards. "Go on to your room, and I'll make your excuses," he said. "Your original room, which has been thoroughly cleaned. I'll see you tomorrow morning. I—" He paused.

"What is it?"

"I—nothing. I'll tell you tomorrow. Good night."

They parted ways in the glass-walled sitting room, and Lamprophyre walked to her bedroom alone. Now that she was safely in the palace, she discovered she was tired, after all. She shifted her books on her hip and smiled at how much that position resembled carrying a baby. She'd seen any number of women walking through the streets with babies perched on their hips. A baby would object to the rough handling she gave the books, though.

She fumbled the key on its chain over her head and unlocked the door. The room was dimly lit by the moonlight filtering in from the high, round windows, but it smelled freshly cleaned. Lamprophyre dropped the books on the bed and lit the lamp. Such a clever invention, these matchlighters.

She turned around and sucked in a startled breath. Manishi sat in the soft chair, leaning slightly forward. "Good evening, Lamprophyre," she said.

CHAPTER TWENTY-FOUR

Lamprophyre's jaw went slack with astonishment. "What—"

"Let's not waste time pretending you aren't who you are," Manishi said. Her mouth curved in a wicked smile. "And no, I'm not going to tell you how I figured it out. A lady needs a few secrets, after all."

Lamprophyre found she was sitting on the edge of the bed with the books pressed against her left leg. "Then I don't know if we have anything to talk about," she said.

"Of course we do. Or am I wrong, and you want to stay in that body forever?" Manishi looked her up and down. "Not that I'd blame you. Who gave you that body, anyway?"

"A lady needs a few secrets."

Manishi laughed. "Well said. All right. You want to regain your own body. I can make that happen."

Lamprophyre's heart thudded painfully in her chest, and it was suddenly hard to breathe. "I don't believe you," she said. "And even if you could, you wouldn't do it out of the goodness of your heart."

"Of course I wouldn't. See, we do understand each other." Manishi leaned back and rested her hands on the chair's arms, loosely gripping their ends, for all the world like Ekanath on his throne. "You give me what I want, and I give you what you want."

Lamprophyre's mouth was dry. She tried to swallow, but her throat felt tight and breathing was still difficult. "I'm not giving you anything until you prove you can do what you say."

"You don't really think I'd transform you without some guarantee of payment?" Manishi propped her feet on the footstool, crossing her legs at the ankles. She looked perfectly relaxed, which irritated Lamprophyre. That irritation banished some of her anxiety. Manishi had to be lying. This was just another one of her deceptions.

"I think you're capable of pretending to have the ability to transform me for your own benefit," she said. "Which again leaves us with nothing to talk about."

Manishi rolled her eyes and made a dramatic face. "You know," she said, "you really shouldn't be so paranoid. Suspicion is healthy, but at some point, you have to trust."

"You've betrayed me and my clutchmates in the past, and we've ruined your plans. How can that lead to trust?"

"Because now we each need something the other can provide." Manishi lowered her feet and leaned forward with her elbows on her knees and her hands clasped under her chin. "I know we haven't had the best relationship in the past—"

"That's an understatement!"

"But I should point out I haven't told anyone your secret. So I've already proven myself. And think what you like of me, but every magic I've performed on your behalf has succeeded. So if I say I can transform you back, you can believe it."

Lamprophyre said nothing. She wished desperately that Rokshan were there, because he knew his sister well and was better than Lamprophyre at telling when Manishi was lying. In this case, the problem wasn't so much that Manishi might be lying—she was right about her magical skill—as that whatever Manishi wanted in return might be dangerous to promise. She was sneaky and amoral and self-centered, and her magical experiments were always aimed at providing her more power.

But this might be Lamprophyre's only hope.

Lamprophyre let out a deep breath and wished she hadn't, because it might have made her look uncertain, and she needed to be as calm as Manishi. "All right," she said. "What do you want?"

Manishi's wicked smile reappeared. "I want a dragon egg."

Lamprophyre shot off the bed, her fists clenched. "No. Impossible. There's no way."

"Of course there is. You promise me your first egg, and I'll turn you back." The smile deepened. "You see how that binds me to my promise? If I can't transform you, I get no payment."

"You want me to hand over *my child* to an amoral, selfish—"

"Now, now, let's not get personal," Manishi chided. "Besides, what would I want with a baby dragon? I just want the egg. You can provide me with an unfertilized one, yes?"

Anger made Lamprophyre tremble. She clenched her fists harder to stop the shaking. "It doesn't work like that," she said. "Dragons don't produce eggs monthly the way humans do. It's every three to five years for us. And if an egg isn't fertilized, it's reabsorbed. So what you want is impossible as well as morally repugnant."

"Hmm. That does make things difficult." Manishi tapped her lips with her forefinger. "I suppose I could make do with the shell, once the baby dragon hatches."

"The shell?" Lamprophyre thought that over, looking for ways in which Manishi might benefit too much. The shell wasn't worth anything once the dragonet hatched. Most dragons pulverized the shell and used the golden dust to decorate the walls of their caves. It was a cheap exchange for her dragon body, especially since she wasn't sure she would ever have an egg. "All right. The shell of my first egg."

"Excellent," Manishi said, her smile returning. "I'll perform the transformation spell, and you will give me the shell of your first egg."

Lamprophyre immediately felt uneasy. She'd bargained Manishi down from a terrible demand, so why did she feel this was what Manishi had actually wanted all along?

"It will take some preparation," Manishi was saying, "and obviously we can't do it in here. I'll have to rearrange my workshop so there's enough room for you in your usual form. Having access to my tools will help."

Lamprophyre nodded. "How soon?"

"Tomorrow evening. And let's keep this between ourselves, shall we? I don't want a lot of nosy dragons crowding the streets around my workshop."

"I won't let them come, but I'm not going to conceal this from my friends. And Rokshan will be with me."

Manishi made a face. "My brother has nothing to do with this. It's not like you'll need him for protection."

"He's my best friend, and he's coming with me."

Manishi shrugged. "All right. If you insist." She rose from the chair as lazily as a cat stretching out its long, curved back. "Don't eat anything after noon tomorrow, and be at my workshop by seven o'clock. Rokshan can tell you when that is."

"After sunset. I'll be there. Wait!"

Manishi had her hand on the door latch. "Wait for what? You haven't changed your mind already, have you?"

"No. How did you get in here?"

Another smile touched Manishi's lips, this one mischievous. It made her look like a child—a gaunt, hollow-eyed child. "Secrets, remember?" she said. "You shouldn't underestimate what magic is capable of." She let herself out and closed the door behind her.

Lamprophyre sagged onto the bed, making the books slide further. She had to talk to Rokshan immediately. But he was with his family, and getting him free of them might be difficult. Worse, she might be drawn into conversation. She closed her eyes and said as many human curse words as she could think of. Darsha had taught her the meanings of ones Rokshan used and wouldn't tell her. Swearing made her feel slightly better.

She changed into her red gown with the gold embroidery. There was a chance this might indicate her interest in being part of the gathering, but she was sure wearing her shirt and trousers when everyone else wore more formal garb would draw the kind of attention she wanted to avoid. Golden sandals went with the gown, which was still too long, and between the sandals and her gown's hem brushing the tops of her feet with every step she felt she might go mad from the constant touching. But there was nothing she could do about it but endure.

She made her way to the talking room easily, her steps slowing as she began to hear voices raised in conversation. This was a bad idea, but it would be worse not to be able to tell Rokshan her news. The realization that at this time tomorrow she might be herself again had taken hold of her, and she found she was shaking again, this time with excitement.

She stopped in the doorway and scanned the room. Of course Rokshan would be on the far side, talking to Sanyot as if they were friends. Maybe they were now. She drew in a deep breath and began making her way around knots of chattering humans toward Rokshan. He had his back to her, so she couldn't even signal him. She resolutely didn't do more than nod and smile at people who looked like they wanted to draw her into conversation, even though she felt guilty at ignoring them. That was a human feeling. She couldn't wait to be in a dragon body again.

"Lelitha! Come here, girl, I want a word with you."

A hand grasped her wrist and tugged her toward the speaker. Piya's expression was sour, as if she'd bitten into a lemon and found it rotten as well as bitter. "You shouldn't ignore your elders, girl, it's rude," she said. "Now, show some respect and introduce yourself."

"I don't—" Lamprophyre began.

"Oh, she's such a pretty girl, you must be mistaken about her character," another woman said. She had the same beginnings of wrinkles Piya had, but was shorter and slimmer and wore her black hair coiled atop her head. "Lelitha, is it? I think I know your mother. Belema, or Balrina."

"Balmina." Lamprophyre came out with Lelitha's fictional mother's name without thinking. "But I don't think—"

"Did you say Lelitha?" said the third woman, leaning forward and cupping her hand behind her left ear. Her hair was pure white and her face was a mass of wrinkles. "I thought she was dead. Wasn't she poisoned?"

"It was just a brief illness, Rejuta," the second woman said, or rather shouted. "Lelitha is fine. You are fine, aren't you, child?"

"I—"

"Lelitha doesn't think she needs to do anything special to attract a man, Minuri," Piya said, her expression still sour. "I say, even if Rokshan ought to be grateful any girl will give him the time of day, Lelitha should have enough self-respect to behave properly."

Lamprophyre tried to free herself from Piya's grip, but the woman almost had a dragon's strength. "I'm not—"

"Rokshan?" Minuri smiled pleasantly at Lamprophyre. "Oh, dear child, that's setting your sights rather high, don't you think? Rokshan may not be the most important of the royal children, but he's still far above you. Now, young Sanyot really is more appropriate, and so handsome, too."

Lamprophyre was beginning to feel as if she were caught in a windstorm, battered about by powerful, random gusts. "I'm not interested in Sanyot," she began, "and—"

"Girls these days think they can flirt with anyone they like and not have to bear the consequences," Piya said.

"Bear *what*?" Rejuta said. Her elderly voice creaked like a door caught in the same wind that buffeted Lamprophyre.

"*Consequences*, Rejuta," Minuri shouted. "I'm sure Lelitha didn't mean it," she told Piya. She took Lamprophyre's free hand and patted it. "You seem like such a nice girl."

"*I don't want to court with anyone*," Lamprophyre said through gritted teeth. That was the wrong phrasing, but she didn't care. "I need to speak with Rokshan now. Please let go." She wrenched at her hand and was still unable to free it.

Minuri's smile faded. "Well, I never," she said. "We have your best interests at heart, and this is how you repay us? This hostility and disrespect?"

"I told you what she was like, Minuri," Piya said triumphantly. "Lelitha needs lessons in good manners. You're never going to catch a husband if you go on like this," she told Lamprophyre. "He'll see how you behave to his mother and will cast you off like *that*." She released Lamprophyre to snap her fingers for emphasis. Lamprophyre backed away immediately.

"Don't walk away from us, child," Minuri said, waggling a finger in Lamprophyre's face. "You should listen to your elders—"

"Lelitha, welcome," Rokshan said from behind Lamprophyre. Her knees went weak with relief. "My apologies, ladies, but I need to speak with Lelitha privately." He put a hand on her shoulder and steered her away.

"We are not finished, Rokshan," Piya said. "Rokshan! You return here this instant! I have a few words for you."

Rokshan ignored Piya and continued walking Lamprophyre in the direction of the door. "Just pretend you don't hear them," he murmured. "Auntie Piya's not as fast as she used to be, and we can outrun her."

Out the door, down the hall, and safely into the glass-walled waiting room, Rokshan released Lamprophyre's shoulder and sat on one of the sofas. "What's wrong?"

"How do you know something's wrong?"

"You were exhausted when we parted ways. If you're here and not asleep in your bed, something must have happened."

Lamprophyre paced a tight circle in front of him. She was too agitated to sit. "Rokshan, Manishi can turn me back."

Rokshan's head snapped up. "She *what*? How does she—God's breath, Lelitha, what happened?"

Lamprophyre summed up her interaction with Manishi, ending with, "I'm not sure I made a safe bargain, but I can't bear this much longer. If Manishi really can do it—"

"I don't see how giving away something you don't use, something with no intrinsic value, is a mistake." Rokshan looked up at Lamprophyre. "This is it."

"You don't look pleased," Lamprophyre said. His expression was remote, closed-off, as if they were discussing the boring weather of a fine, clear day.

"I suppose I'm cautiously optimistic. Manishi is good at magic, but this is beyond anything anyone's heard of in centuries. It might still fail."

His words brought Lamprophyre back down to earth. She sat beside Rokshan and clasped her hands in her lap. "You're right. I shouldn't be so excited. Failure will be so much worse if I'm overly optimistic."

"Don't be too discouraged, either," Rokshan said. He closed his hand over her joined ones. "We'll just see what happens. And if it's a failure, we'll try something else."

Lamprophyre nodded. "But it won't fail. I'm confident of that."

"I hope you're right," Rokshan said.

CHAPTER TWENTY-FIVE

Clouds blackened the eastern skies when Lamprophyre and Rokshan left the palace for the warehouses where Lamprophyre's clutch lived. Wind made the trees lining the parkland bend and shake, their leaves hissing and rattling louder than the wind. Lamprophyre was glad to have Rokshan's hand to hold; she felt she might be blown away by the force of the gale. Loose strands of hair lashed her face, though most of it was bound away tightly at the nape of her neck. She remembered other nights, other storms, and racing the wind despite her mother's forbiddance. If this was over soon enough, she promised herself she would race the wind again tonight in celebration.

Their only company on the streets of Tanajital were windblown handbills torn from the walls and sent scattering across the city. Almost everyone was indoors now, waiting for the storm to pass. Lamprophyre sniffed the air, but smelled only the faint scent of distant rain and the sharp smell that lingered after a lightning strike. She hadn't seen any lightning yet, but there was still plenty of time.

It had been a long day, and research hadn't made it shorter despite how well it distracted her. It hadn't helped that even Dharan couldn't get Ilhan to disgorge the books she wanted. She'd watched Dharan and Ilhan have a superficially civil conversation in which Ilhan had repeatedly deflected Dharan's requests. Finally, Ilhan had said, "I'm sorry, Lector Dharan, but some books are too fragile for anyone to handle, even you," and Dharan had had to retreat.

The memory of Ilhan's smug thoughts irritated Lamprophyre even hours after her encounter with the librarian. There had to be a way around him.

"What was that?" Rokshan said.

She hadn't realized she'd spoken aloud. "Just thinking about Ilhan and how if I had my own body back, I could terrify him into giving me what I want."

Rokshan chuckled. "I wouldn't count on that. If he wasn't willing to help Dharan, I doubt he's afraid of a dragon."

"Probably. It was just a nice daydream."

They turned the corner onto the warehouses' street. It was almost full dark now, and the only light came from the lanterns firmly fixed to poles at wide intervals along the street. They made pools of light illuminating the white bricks paving the road, but their light didn't go much farther than that, leaving stretches of shadow deep enough to hide even a dragon. Lamprophyre listened for thoughts and heard only her clutchmates, which relieved her mind even as she mocked herself for feeling relieved. It wasn't as if anyone was out and about to attack them, certainly not in this storm.

She poked her head inside the first warehouse. "I have news," she said. "Where is everyone?"

Bromargyrite emerged from the shadows. "Flint and Coquina are at the embassy, and Porphyry went home this morning. What did you learn?"

The sounds of movement came from warehouses farther up the street. "Lamprophyre!" Dolomite said. "I was hoping you'd be a dragon again."

"She wouldn't do that without us knowing, Dolomite," Orthoclase said. "What brings you out on a night like this?"

Facing her clutchmates, Lamprophyre felt unexpectedly nervous, as if she were about to confess to a crime or admit to having fallen in love. "Manishi says she knows how to turn me back," she said.

The three dragons all spread their wings at once in a restless, star-tled motion. "Is this true?" Bromargyrite said. "Just like that?"

"Just like that," Rokshan said, "though we don't know the details. Manishi does."

Bromargyrite shook his head. "It can't possibly work."

"It has to work," Orthoclase said. "Manishi may be a horrible human, but she's gifted in magic."

"But we don't like her. Do we?" Dolomite asked. "And she doesn't like us."

"It doesn't matter. We have to take this chance," Lamprophyre said.

Bromargyrite sighed. "Don't take this the wrong way, Lamprophyre, but it's almost a bad thing, having you back in dragon form."

"How is it a bad thing?" Lamprophyre looked up and further up at the vividly orange dragon, whose expression was pensive.

"I didn't mean a bad thing for me personally, or even for you," Bromargyrite said. "I mean we made progress on finding out about the entity because you were in a body that gave you access to all those books. We're so close to a breakthrough, I can't help but think, maybe—"

"Don't say I have to wait!" Lamprophyre shouted. "You don't know what it's like being trapped in this soft, fragile body. We'll figure some-thing out with the research. Besides, that awful librarian has us in his power, so it's not like I was really making progress."

"I'm sorry," Bromargyrite said. He leaned down so his face was level with Lamprophyre's. "You're right. You shouldn't have to endure this one beat longer than necessary."

Lamprophyre wiped tears from her eyes, feeling stupid about her human body's unnecessary reaction. "I'll be back as soon as it's done," she said. "And we'll figure out what to do about the entity then."

"Good luck," Dolomite said. "I hope it works."

Lamprophyre nodded. She put her small hand on Bromargyrite's nose. "Thanks," she said.

"Thanks for what? Being insensitive?" Bromargyrite said with a smile.

"For looking for the positive in this situation. If it doesn't work—"

"Which it will."

"If it doesn't work, at least there are still things I can do, right?"

Bromargyrite nodded. "Good luck," he said.

Lamprophyre took Rokshan's hand again as they walked through the streets and into the slums. This time, it was for comfort. His firm, warm hand, larger than hers, felt like a tether preventing her from being swept away not only by the wind, but by the darkness that was so much deeper in this rundown part of Tanajital. Very few lanterns here were lit, and the ones that were blew wildly in the oncoming storm rather than being fastened tightly to poles.

Lamprophyre eyed the tiny flames and wondered what would happen if a lantern blew off its chain and smashed, spreading burning oil everywhere. The slums were crowded enough that fire would spread rapidly. She hoped the chains were strong.

Manishi's workshop looked more dour and forbidding than ever. Windowless, with its roof sagging on one side and the paint peeling from the corners, it looked abandoned—not only abandoned, but forbidden, something parents warned their children to stay away from. Lamprophyre chided her imagination for summoning such thoughts. If she was going to avoid Manishi's workshop, it would be because it truly was dangerous, if only because Manishi herself could be a danger. Tonight, this was where she wanted to be.

Rokshan let go her hand to knock on the door. After a few beats, Manishi shoved it open with some effort. "It's about time," she said. "Hurry before the rain follows you inside." She wore her usual worker's clothing, scruffy and poorly made, but had added an incongruous copper necklace to the ensemble. The necklace looked like a tangle of lace woven by a drunken spider. Lamprophyre remembered the spiders of her hallucination and shuddered. Spiders weren't anything dragons feared, and the fact that Lamprophyre's confused mind had thrown up that particular nightmare made her worry that she'd been human for too long.

The lighting inside was better than Lamprophyre remembered, with milky glass globes glowing with a steady white light Lamprophyre suspected was magical. Manishi's workshop was normally big enough to fit Lamprophyre's dragon body, if snugly. Now Manishi had shoved her work table against the wall opposite the door and somehow winched her obsidian mirror, a human-sized slab of black volcanic glass, up to lie flat against the ceiling, widening the available space. She had also drawn an intricate chalk circle on the floor, outlined with tiny pictures too crude to be intelligible. Lamprophyre walked wide around it.

She regarded the changes and tried to calculate how much space they left for her as a dragon. A sudden jolt of fear shot through her as she realized she couldn't remember what the room looked like from her draconic perspective. It had only been six days—she couldn't have forgotten that in only six days?

She made herself breathe normally and rested her hand on one of the many-drawered cabinets lining the walls. Its grainy, unvarnished surface reassured her. She remembered brushing up against it on one visit and being yelled at by Manishi for clumsiness. That was real, and this was real, and the memory anchored Lamprophyre in the present.

"What do we do?" she asked.

Manishi was rummaging in a large drawer near the base of a cabinet. "*You* do nothing," she said absently. "Rokshan, stand in the corner, unless you want your friend smashing you when she's restored."

"You think that's a possibility?" Rokshan asked, sounding dubious, but he went to stand in the indicated corner.

"I'm not sure what kind of interim transformation she might go through. It could be dramatic." Manishi stood, holding a calcium carbonate crystal the size of her fist. Its fat orange-red hexagonal crystals extended from the central node in all directions, making it look like some weirdly uniform sea creature. Manishi shoved the drawer shut with her foot and laid the crystal atop the cabinet, where it rocked slightly. "Where did I...oh, yes."

"What do you mean, interim transformation?" Lamprophyre asked, feeling slightly alarmed. Interim anything did not sound good.

Manishi had opened another, smaller drawer, and the clicking sound of stones tapping against stones was barely audible over the roar of the wind outside. "My research indicates that your body may settle on some other form while it searches for the correct one. Why do I never have the right size topaz?"

"Some other form?" The alarm became genuine fear. She didn't want to be stuck in some other human body—or did Manishi mean *any* form? Becoming an animal would be worse than being human.

"Or forms," Manishi said, as casually as if she were commenting on the worsening weather. "It's a transitory effect. Don't worry about it."

She turned away from the cabinet with a handful of something clutched in her left hand. "I could have sworn I had a large topaz in that cabinet," she muttered. "Don't worry, it will still work. It will just use up more of my resources. Now, sit there in the middle of the floor. Inside the chalk circle."

Lamprophyre carefully stepped over the chalk outline and settled herself on the floor in that odd legs-crossed position Rokshan always used. It was surprisingly comfortable, though the earthen floor felt damp and bits of it clung to her palms when she steadied herself.

Manishi began placing small yellow topazes, faceted to catch the light, along the curve of the circle, on the inside. She positioned one opposite each of the tiny drawings. Once or twice she used a blue topaz instead of a yellow one. Lamprophyre couldn't see any significance to that difference, but she was afraid of disrupting Manishi's concentration to ask.

When Manishi had completed her circle, she set the remaining stones atop the nearest cabinet, where they caught the white light from the lamps and sparkled like chips of yellow ice. Manishi removed the copper necklace and disentangled it, revealing that it wasn't a necklace, it was a coil of thin copper wire. She retrieved the red crystal lump and wound copper wire around it in what to Lamprophyre looked like randomness. But it was also beautiful, the copper a rich complement to the rust-red crystals, and when Manishi made a loop at the top and wrapped more wire around the loop to secure it, Lamprophyre could see it was a pendant, if a large one. It was more suited to a dragon's size than a human's.

Manishi took a pair of wire snips off the wall beneath the obsidian mirror and cut the pendant free. Then she bent what was left of the wire into a large hoop, slid the pendant onto the hoop, and twisted the ends together to make an oddly stiff necklace. She handed it to Lamprophyre. "Put that on, and hold the crystal in your left hand," she said.

The "necklace" was large enough that the pendant hung to the middle of Lamprophyre's chest, resting between her breasts. That wasn't uncomfortable, but the stiff wire around her neck kept shifting, and Lamprophyre feared it might slip down over her shoulders. She wasn't sure it was big enough to fit her when she was restored, but at worst, her neck would break the wire rather than the wire strangling her. Her hand was too small to wrap entirely around the pendant, but she gripped it as tightly as she could, tightly enough it would probably leave marks in her soft skin.

Manishi walked past Lamprophyre, stepping over the chalk lines, and Lamprophyre twisted to watch her open yet another drawer, this one larger than the others. After a moment's rooting around, Manishi took out a fat rod of selenite the length of her forearm. It was six-sided like a natural crystal, but looked as if it had been shaped that way. Its translucent surface was marked by hundreds of parallel striations that made it look milky.

"All right," she said. "Hold as still as you can, and don't let go of the crystal. This shouldn't take long."

Lamprophyre nodded, then froze as Manishi glared at her. The pendant in her hand was a strange combination of rough and smooth, the protruding shafts of the crystal poking her hand, the copper wire smooth and slick between the shafts. Her heart beat rapidly enough she was sure its movement was visible, though she didn't dare look down to find out. In the corner, Rokshan watched, his face expressionless. It was amazing he could stay so calm—or maybe he wasn't calm and was just good at hiding his agitation. She thought about smiling to reassure him and decided not to risk another glare.

Manishi took a slow step to the left, then another, gradually curving to pace the circumference of the chalk circle. Lamprophyre focused on breathing calmly, one deep breath after another, as she listened to the sound of Manishi's bare feet on the hard earth. Her footsteps should have been barely perceptible, but they thudded as if Manishi were made of stone.

Eventually she came within Lamprophyre's sight again, and Lamprophyre managed not to twitch in surprise. The selenite rod glowed now, a bright white glow as if Manishi had captured whatever stone made the globes on the wall emit light. It made the brown skin of Manishi's hands look darker by contrast.

At the top of the circle, or at least the point directly opposite where Lamprophyre faced, Manishi stopped. She extended the rod to touch the nearest topaz, bending a little at the waist to do so. Light sparked as the two stones met, and Manishi withdrew, not seeming at all startled by the flash. She moved on to the next stone, and Lamprophyre looked at the one she'd touched. It was still topaz, but all the color had leached out of it, leaving it looking like a faceted lump of clear glass.

Another flash of light drew Lamprophyre's attention. Once more, the topaz had become colorless, but this time she realized the selenite rod was very faintly yellow, a color that intensified every time it touched a stone. Manishi moved out of sight, and Lamprophyre glanced at Rokshan again. His gaze was still fixed on her, his features expressionless, and she suddenly wished he would smile or grimace or do something that showed he cared about what was happening. She closed her eyes briefly to calm herself. She was being ridiculous. Of course Rokshan cared. He was staying calm for her sake. She needed to do the same for him.

Manishi once more returned to the top of the circle. The selenite rod still glowed, but now it was a rich amber color, with the striations on its long sides more visible. Lamprophyre focused on Manishi and was surprised to see her tremble. She'd never seen Manishi affected physically by working magic. The rod shivered as if Manishi couldn't control the tremors running through her. Lamprophyre opened her mouth to ask if the adept was all right, and Manishi said, "Don't speak, you fool."

She raised the rod to a vertical position in front of her face, bisecting it so she looked like someone had sliced her in half down the middle. It was an unsettling image, and an unsettling thought, and a prickle of unease set up shop at the base of Lamprophyre's neck. It suddenly occurred to her that this might be a plot by Manishi to get revenge on Lamprophyre for refusing to sell her any more stone. That didn't seem to Lamprophyre to be a revenge-worthy action, but Manishi was strange and thought in strange ways.

She shifted, and Manishi glared at her again just before waving the rod at Lamprophyre's forehead like swinging a sword. Lamprophyre couldn't help flinching slightly before her conscious mind made her freeze in place. The rod didn't strike her, though; its tip grazed her skin and settled against the center of her forehead, pressing so lightly even her sensitive skin barely felt it.

She swallowed her nervousness and tried to focus on the rod, but that made her eyes ache. So instead she looked at Manishi, who was sweating and trembling harder now. Manishi raised the rod to the vertical position again, then swung it at Lamprophyre's left shoulder. This time, the pressure was greater, but still not enough to be painful. The glow intensified. Now the rod was brighter than the globes and its color was deeper than before.

Swing. The rod touched Lamprophyre's right shoulder. *Swing.* *Swing.* The upper curve of her left breast, and then the right. Manishi's hand shook so hard Lamprophyre didn't know how she managed to hang onto the rod. The rod touched Lamprophyre's stomach, right where the strange hole in her belly was, then her left knee and her right. With every touch, the glow intensified, until it was too bright to look at and the color, now almost brown, faded behind that glow. Lamprophyre's heart beat so hard it hurt, and her hand felt numb from clutching the pendant.

Manishi paused, lowering her head and breathing as heavily as if she'd run around Tanajital's wall rather than pacing slowly in this little circle. Drops of sweat fell from her forehead to darken the earth. "Almost...there," she panted. Lamprophyre held so still she was sure she would ache when this was all over.

"Hold out...the pendant," Manishi whispered. "Arm's...length."

Lamprophyre held the pendant with her arm extended as straight in front of her as she could manage. The wire gave and distorted until the circle became an oval. Manishi nodded and stood upright. "Here it comes," she said. Slowly, as if moving through thick tar, her hand rose, and the tip of the painfully glowing rod extended until it touched the bottom of the pendant in Lamprophyre's outstretched hand.

Nothing happened.

Lamprophyre, who had tensed all over waiting for an explosion, relaxed slightly. She peered at the rod and the crystal, still in contact, and felt such despair she wanted to curl up and weep. Rokshan pushed off from the wall and walked toward them. "Is it—"

A tremendous crack split the air. An invisible force struck Lamprophyre, sending her flying backward to crash into one of the cabinets. Her head smacked into the hard surface and pain shot through it, briefly blinding her and making her eyes water. She lay still for a moment, stunned by the impact and the explosion. All she heard was a high-pitched whine that seemed to come from inside her skull. Blinking away tears, she sat up and pushed hair out of her face. The workshop didn't look as if it had experienced an explosion. Cabinets, table, even the stones perched precariously atop the cabinets hadn't moved or been destroyed.

Rokshan knelt beside the limp shape of Manishi. "We need to get her to a healer immediately," he said. "Maybe they can save her."

Lamprophyre realized she was still clutching the crystal and released it, shaking out her hand to get the blood flowing. "She's not dead?"

Rokshan shook his head. He looked around as if searching for something. His gaze fell on Lamprophyre. "I need your sleeve."

"My sleeve?"

He drew his belt knife and advanced on her. "Just hold still." With a few deft strokes, he cut her left sleeve away and knotted the pieces into one long strip. "Now, run to—God's breath, I can't think—there's a healing center just past the slums. We passed it on the way here, remember?"

Lamprophyre barely remembered noticing the jade-green door; she'd had her head down against the wind. "I'll hurry," she said. Then she looked at Manishi fully and had to stifle a scream. The woman's right arm below the elbow was as black as if a dragon had burned her. Blood flowed from a dozen deep lacerations, pumping as if her heart wanted it expelled from her body. And her hand, and the rod she'd held in it, were entirely gone.

Rokshan was knotting the strip of Lamprophyre's shirt around Manishi's arm just below the elbow. "Run, Lamprophyre," he said, his voice grim. Lamprophyre ran.

CHAPTER TWENTY-SIX

Lamprophyre huddled in the corner of the workshop, beneath the obsidian mirror, as two healers and their assistants crouched over Manishi. Beside her, Rokshan leaned against the wall, his gaze fixed on the little group. "I hope I did the right thing," he murmured.

"In calling for the healers?" Lamprophyre asked, startled. He couldn't mean he wished his sister dead. Certainly not because Manishi's magic had failed to restore her.

"Stopping the bleeding that way," Rokshan said. "A tourniquet can be dangerous. But I thought, there's no way they could restore her arm, no matter what I did." His voice sounded distant, coming from some faraway land.

"You kept her from bleeding to death. That explosion—I don't even know if it was a real explosion. Whatever it was might have killed her." Lamprophyre fingered the pendant she still wore around her neck. It was undamaged.

"You're sure you weren't hurt?"

Lamprophyre touched the lump on the back of her head. "I don't feel injured. Maybe sore from hitting the cabinets. I'm fine."

Rokshan squeezed her shoulder. "That explosion could have killed all of us. I wonder why it didn't."

"I don't know. I don't care." The despair Lamprophyre had held at bay all through her run to the healing center and all through the trip back surged within her. "It didn't work."

Rokshan's grip tightened. "La—Lelitha, it's all—"

"Don't you *dare* say it's all right," Lamprophyre snarled. She wrenched away from him and slid down the wall to sit at its base, hugging her knees. "Nothing about this is all right."

Rokshan had the good sense to say nothing.

One of the healers' assistants rose and approached them. "Her highness will live," she said. "But her arm...I'm sorry, Prince Rokshan, but there was nothing they could do for her arm."

"I understand," Rokshan said. "We're grateful her life was spared. Do I need to summon a litter for her?"

"We arranged for one to follow us when we left the healing center. It should be outside now." The assistant, an older woman with short hair that curled around her face, hesitated, then added, "The healers would like to know what caused the injury."

"A magic working that went wrong," Rokshan said curtly. "Not their business."

The woman nodded rapidly and bowed. "Of course," she said, but Lamprophyre saw the woman look speculatively at her and wondered if not giving the healers an answer was the best idea. They couldn't help guessing, and suppose they came up with some theory that had the three of them doing something illegal? But Lamprophyre couldn't think of a clever lie, so she said nothing.

The assistant crossed the room to the door and heaved it open with some effort. The wind had died down, but rain had taken its place and poured down in sheets. Lamprophyre felt awful for the bearers, who had to be miserable. She hoped they were waiting somewhere out of the rain.

The female healer stood and joined the assistant at the door. The sound of the rain beating down on the roof drowned out the woman's voice, but Lamprophyre saw her lips move in speech. Shortly after that, a couple of well-built men, not terribly wet, entered. They gently picked Manishi up and carried her out. Lamprophyre stared at the stump of her arm, fleshy and brown rather than blackened as it had been after the explosion. Manishi would have a lot to deal with when she woke up.

It worried Lamprophyre that Manishi was still unconscious, but the healers didn't seem to think it was a problem. There was so much about this Lamprophyre didn't understand. Not understanding things made her feel stupid, which made her irritable, which made her want to act, do something, anything that would make a situation make sense.

"We should go," Rokshan said. "I'm sorry there's no litter for you. You shouldn't have to get soaked."

"It's no problem," Lamprophyre said, irritably, then cursed herself for letting her bad mood spill over onto Rokshan. "I'm sorry. I didn't mean to snap. But I don't want to wait for a litter. I'd rather get wet than stay here." She shivered and wrapped her arms around herself. "It feels like death touched this place and it's only good luck it didn't hang around."

"Poetic," Rokshan said. "But I take your meaning."

The storm was worse even than Lamprophyre had thought, listening to its howl and the pounding rain. She was soaked before she took a dozen steps. Almost she wished she hadn't insisted on leaving immediately. The rain was colder than it was when it deluged the city in the summer, and it deepened the chill she'd felt ever since sitting in that chalk circle. She wrapped her arms around herself again and stumbled after Rokshan, ducking her head against the rain.

They had just reached the parkland when the rain began to taper off, and by the time they left the strip of trees behind, it had stopped entirely. Lamprophyre squeezed water out of her thick hair and tossed the long horse's tail over her shoulder. It didn't disturb her as wet hair usually did because the rest of her was too wet to care. Ahead, Rokshan shook his head vigorously and sent drops of water flying. That was it. She was cutting the damn hair off and never mind what anyone said about styles for women.

At the side door, the palace guards, who were remarkably dry, stepped forward to investigate the litter. "There's been an accident," Rokshan said, putting himself between them and his unconscious sister. "Princess Manishi has been badly injured and needs to be carried. I vouch for these men—unless you think you should leave your posts?"

The two guards exchanged glances, then shook their heads. Rokshan turned to Lamprophyre. "Go get dried off," he said. "I'll see to Manishi, and inform my parents, but then I'll join you. We need to talk."

That got Lamprophyre a curious look from the guards, but they were well-trained, and Lamprophyre suspected they weren't comfortable challenging their commander. She waited for Rokshan and the two bearers carrying Manishi to enter, then followed them. Manishi was thin enough she really only needed one person to carry her, but it looked as if the bearers were used to carrying unconscious people and knew how best to manage it.

Feeling lost and unnecessary, she continued through the halls at the end of the procession, turning off to the guest wing at the east waiting room. Its colorful glass walls were the same as always, but Lamprophyre, having watched first Anchala and then Manishi pass through them injured, didn't think she'd look at them with a casual eye ever again.

Safely in her room, she leaned against her locked and barred door and closed her eyes. It hadn't worked. She'd been so hopeful—Manishi was so gifted—and it hadn't worked. Worse, it had nearly killed Manishi. Lamprophyre didn't like the adept and hated dealing with her, but she wasn't so bloodthirsty as to wish the woman dead. Though now she wouldn't have to worry about what clever and possibly evil use Manishi might have for a dragon's egg shell.

She shivered again and opened her eyes. She needed to get dry and put on warm clothes. Quickly she stripped out of her shirt and trousers and kicked off her sandals, which were cold and clammy and whose leather straps clung unpleasantly to her feet. Her skin was still damp, and *now* the wet hair stuck to her skin and made her wish she could crawl out of it. Putting on dry clothes would be stupid, because her wet body would just dampen them.

She remembered being pulled out of the pool in the talking room and the servants rubbing her with cloths. She didn't have anything that was meant for drying people, at least she didn't think so, but her blanket might work. She got to work rubbing herself. The blanket was soft and thick and soaked up the remaining water readily, and in only a few dozen beats everything but her annoying hair was dry. Sighing in relief, she put on a shapeless soft robe dyed a deep blue. She didn't know what it was really for, because she hadn't seen any women wearing one like it, but it comforted her.

She curled up in the padded chair and pulled her knees to her chin. This position comforted her, too, like snuggling up in her father's arms when she was a dragonet. Thinking of Aegirine and her dragonet days made her heart ache. How glad she was her father couldn't see her now. Though knowing him, he would have comforted her without any comment on how different she was in a human body. He probably wouldn't have seen a difference at all. The thoughts made her aching heart hurt more, and she discovered she was crying. It was stupid. Crying couldn't solve this problem. She cried anyway.

She heard Rokshan's familiar knock and then the rattle of the door. She'd forgotten she'd barred it. Wearily, she rose and slid the latch back. Rokshan slipped inside the way he always did, as if there were something furtive about his being in her room. His face was set and hard and became harder when he looked at her. "Lamprophyre," he said.

Lamprophyre wiped away tears. "I'm sorry. I know it's stupid. I should never have let my hopes rise. I should have known it was too good to be true."

Rokshan gripped her shoulders briefly. "We couldn't have known."

"Why not?" Lamprophyre said. "It was too easy. Manishi just *happens* to have a solution and it just *happens* to require things she has on hand? And it wasn't serpentine."

"We don't know that serpentine is the only thing that will work. This was just bad luck. Lamprophyre. Look at me."

Lamprophyre had turned away from Rokshan, and now she turned her head just enough to meet his eyes. "We'll find a solution," he said. "And if not..."

"If not, what?"

Rokshan walked to the dressing table and leaned on it. "Nothing. Forget I said anything."

Unexpected anger surged through Lamprophyre. "You *didn't* say anything," she said. "And this isn't the first time. What were you going to say, Rokshan?"

Rokshan was silent. He bowed his head so Lamprophyre could see his face reflected in the dressing table mirror. It was as expressionless as it had been in Manishi's workshop, and seeing it infuriated her, made her feel as if none of this mattered to him and he thought her suffering was nothing.

"What is *wrong* with you?" she shouted. "You were going to say it wouldn't be so bad if I never regained my body, weren't you? How the Stones is that supposed to make me feel better, Rokshan? You think, if it lasts long enough, I'll get used to this squishy body and the awful hair and the fact that I'm helpless against every possible threat the entity might throw at me?"

Rokshan whirled and took a few steps toward her until he was half a handspan away. "You're dead set on humans being inferior to dragons, aren't you?" he shouted back. "It never occurs to you that maybe there are some advantages to being a squishy human. But no, you've got no problem being arrogant and smug and denigrating my species like I'm supposed to smile and nod and take it!"

Lamprophyre sucked in an outraged breath. "I've never said anything like that!"

"You didn't have to. It's implied in every word that comes out of your mouth." Rokshan loomed over her. "Maybe we never find a solution. Maybe this is what you'll be for the rest of your life. What are you going to do if that's so? Bitch and whine for the next sixty years about how awful your lot is? Or come to terms with this body?"

His words shook her to her core. Never to fly again. Never to feel strength coursing through her as she broke stone with her claws. Never to know the joy of carrying an egg or seeing her dragonet born. "How dare you," she whispered, hearing her voice shake. "You sound like you want me to fail. Some friend you are. Was I only ever interesting to you because I could fly?"

Rokshan's whole body tensed with anger. "I never wanted you to fail," he said. "What I want is for you to face reality. So what if you're never a dragon again?"

"I *am* a dragon!" Lamprophyre shouted. "Just because I'm in this body—"

"Call it what you want. You have a human body, and you need to deal with the possibility—"

"Stop it!" Lamprophyre dashed tears from her stupid eyes. "Stop saying that! Why won't you stop reminding me I'm human?"

"Because I've fallen in love with you!" Rokshan shouted.

His words struck her like flying face first into Mother Stone's snow-covered slopes. The silence that followed them rang in her ears, a distant high-pitched droning like a dozen dragons singing the same note at once. Rokshan still loomed over her, his expression furious, his chest rising and falling rapidly with his heavy breathing. Her own chest ached as if she'd forgotten how to breathe. Tears still spilled over her cheeks, but she was afraid to wipe them away, afraid to be the first to break the tension between them.

Rokshan's shoulders sagged. He closed his eyes and turned away from her. "You're my best friend," he said. "It never occurred to me..." He stopped, stood with his back to her. "I didn't know what that friendship would feel like when you were a beautiful woman. What it would mean to see you in a body I could be attracted to."

Lamprophyre moistened her dry lips. "Rokshan," she began.

He waved a quelling hand in her direction without turning around. "Don't say anything. I know it's an illusion. And I do believe we'll find a way to restore you, and these irrational feelings I have will go away. I'm sorry. I shouldn't have said anything, but I lost my temper. I'm *sorry*."

Things she hadn't understood before were starting to make sense. "You were jealous of Sanyot," she said.

Rokshan nodded.

"And you didn't...you weren't just worried about my safety, you wanted to be the one who protected me. Because you cared for me the way a man does for a woman."

Rokshan nodded again. "I should have...damn it. I don't know what I could have done differently aside from staying away from you entirely. And I couldn't do that. What a betrayal of our friendship."

"I'm glad you didn't. It would have hurt terribly." Lamprophyre took a few steps toward him, stopping short of touching him. "Rokshan. Look at me."

He hesitated before turning around, and Lamprophyre felt numb again, because his expression was as bleak and hopeless as she'd ever seen on anyone, dragon or human. In that moment, her perspective changed, and she once more saw him the way a woman would, the angles and curves of his face, the faint shadow of stubble on his chin, the dark eyes fixed on hers. It made her catch her breath in stunned surprise.

"I wished you were a dragon," she blurted out.

His expression stopped being quite so bleak. "You did?"

"I told my clutchmates I thought you would be a good dragon if you were one. I've thought about what it would be like to fly with you, not you riding my shoulders, but flying together." She swallowed. Her throat was as dry as her lips. "I think it's something I've thought about without realizing ever since we became friends."

Rokshan's puzzlement deepened. "I don't understand what you're getting at."

"I mean," Lamprophyre said, "if things were the other way around —if you'd been the one transformed so we were both dragons—I would have fallen in love with you, too."

Rokshan said nothing. His expression was once more becoming that blank, horrible look it had been when he entered her room. Miserably, Lamprophyre ducked her head and said, "I mean, I'm saying I understand if you feel that way about me, because..." In a rush, she went on, "Rokshan, I never thought I'd fall in love with anyone, and maybe it's strange—maybe there's something wrong with me that I'm so attached to someone not even of my species, or maybe it's wrong to think friendship between a male and a female has to turn into romantic love. I don't know."

Slowly, as if she were a skittish animal, Rokshan touched her face, tilting her chin so she had to look at him. "You mean you care about me, too," he said quietly.

More tears rose in her eyes. This ridiculous body really did have an endless supply of them. "I don't know what I feel," she exclaimed, "except that if we were both dragons, I think I'd love you with all my heart, and maybe...maybe it doesn't matter which body I have, so long as yours matches mine."

Rokshan let his hand fall. "I don't know if that makes it better, or worse," he said. "Lamprophyre, you're still a dragon where it counts. Forget what I said about getting used to being human. I love you, and I don't want you to be miserable for the rest of your life because you're in the wrong body."

Lamprophyre looked at him again. This time, she willed herself into that strange otherness of perception. She looked at his height and the breadth of his shoulders and the curve of his chin and thought of all the other men she'd seen, of what she knew of human beauty. She thought of the times she'd imagined Rokshan as a dragon and how satisfying those imaginings had been for no reason she understood—or was willing to pursue.

"You said this was an illusion," she said. "That your feelings would pass."

He shook his head. "That was a lie I've been telling myself for the past week. It's only been seven days, Lamprophyre. Nobody falls in love that fast unless those feelings were already there. I loved you before because you are my best friend. This new body of yours just let those feelings change."

He looked so serious Lamprophyre's heart ached again. She turned away and sat on the edge of her bed, gripping the wrinkled linen bedclothes so the soft fabric gave her something else to feel. "I can't stay human," she said. "The entity knows who I am, and it's just a matter of time before it gets me."

"I know," Rokshan said. "We'll find a way."

She was wrong. Her body had finally run out of tears. His words should have devastated her, but she felt so overwhelmed she was past crying. "All right," she said. "But what happens then?"

Rokshan walked to her side and rested his hand on her shoulder. "You should sleep," he said. "This terrible night has to end sometime. Sleep, and we'll figure things out in the morning. Starting with getting that book away from the librarian."

Lamprophyre looked up at him. "How are we going to do that?"

"I have an idea," Rokshan said. He smiled, and it so transformed his face Lamprophyre felt as if he'd knocked all the air from her body. She put her hand over his where it lay on her shoulder, and his smile faded. "Lamprophyre," he began.

"It's remarkable, don't you think?" Lamprophyre said, overriding him. "You love me. I love you. It should be impossible." She held his hand more tightly. "Can we pretend, just for a moment, that it isn't? That we are just two people who care deeply for one another? Because —" Her throat closed up briefly. "Because I have been afraid for so long that I was broken, that I would never love anyone, and now I don't care that I'm a dragon in love with a human, because it is so much better than no love at all."

Swiftly Rokshan sat beside her on the bed and drew her into his arms. "You do realize I'm the only man in the world who wouldn't take that as an insult," he said with a laugh.

"I know," Lamprophyre said. Tentatively, she put her arms around his waist. Hugging, that was one thing, but this was so different, this consciousness of his body against hers, how his was hard and muscular and hers was soft and squishy. She wondered how it felt to him, whether he liked her softness or wished her body was more like his. Every time she thought she understood humanity, she came up against something new.

Rokshan ran his hand down the length of her damp hair. "Don't cut it," he said.

"But I hate it."

"It's beautiful. As a favor to me. Please. I love it."

His light touch made her tingle all over. "All right," she said. "But only for you."

He squeezed her gently, then released her. "Sleep," he said. "I'll be back in the morning. We'll need to meet with Dharan to make this plan work."

"You have a plan?"

"I have most of a plan." Rokshan went to the door and paused with his hand on the latch. "Whatever happens," he added, "we will face it together. Just like everything else."

His confidence, his calm certainty, reassured her even more than his touch had. "I'll hold you to that," she said with a smile.

She locked and barred the door behind him, turned out the light, and settled in under the thin sheet that was all that was left of the bedclothes now that her blanket was wet. The room wasn't cold, but she found the soft blue robe comforting. Maybe it was intended for sleeping in, maybe not, but in the darkness of her room, she could afford not to care about passing for human.

She curled up on her side and stared at the dim gray moons that were the row of windows. In love with a human. This was not something she could share with the flight, not even her clutch, and not because they wouldn't understand, which they wouldn't; it was a feeling so close and dear to her heart she couldn't bear to expose it to public scrutiny. Maybe everyone in love felt this way, and she just didn't know about it, but she couldn't imagine how to explain the complex tangle of feelings that filled her. Hyaloclast—

She covered her face with her hands and groaned. What the Stones would Hyaloclast say if Lamprophyre told her she was in love with Rokshan? The dragon queen was as hard and unsentimental as Mother Stone herself. Lamprophyre assumed her mother had loved her father, but it wasn't something they ever talked about, and when she pictured herself telling Hyaloclast she was in love, her thoughts stuttered into a white nothingness.

It didn't matter. Right now, it only mattered that Lamprophyre be restored. And maybe Rokshan was right, after all, and his feelings for her wouldn't stay romantic once she was herself again. A dragon and a human had no future together. She buried her head under her pillow and hoped sleep would claim her soon.

CHAPTER TWENTY-SEVEN

The academy library was practically empty at ten o'clock the next morning. Only a handful of students, and one woman wearing a gold lector's robe, occupied the tables. They had spread out throughout the scriptorium like a grazing herd of wild horses, not wanting to encroach on each other's territory but unwilling to get too far from the herd. Lamprophyre's usual table was unoccupied, which cheered her. It didn't matter which table she used, but she'd become accustomed to this one.

Ilhan pretended not to notice her as she approached the window. "Good morning," she said politely. "I only have one request."

"How unusual," Ilhan said with a sneering smile. Lamprophyre returned it with a smile she was sure looked more genuine than his. She noticed Narahar shelving books a few rows away and felt even more cheerful. Rokshan's plan would fail without him.

Narahar saw her and gave her a little wave, but didn't approach. That was all right. In fact, it might be better if he wasn't too friendly with her right away. Lamprophyre leaned against the shelf and surveyed the room. Four women, three men, not counting the lector. She wondered what studies they were pursuing, and if Ilhan was more forthcoming with them than he was with her. Surely very few of them threatened his intellectual self-image.

Ilhan returned holding a book. "I'm so glad it's available," Lamprophyre said, then wished she hadn't sounded so perky. The librarian wasn't stupid and he might figure out something was up if she was too enthusiastic. Or, worse, suppose he interpreted her cheerful comment as veiled sarcasm?

But he only eyed her narrowly and turned back to his work. Lamprophyre took the book to her table and opened it at random. She flicked a glance at Rokshan, doing duty as her guard today and standing patiently near the door. He nodded and left the room.

The book was a rather complex tome of magical theory, far beyond Lamprophyre's comprehension. It was also about five hundred pages long, and was clearly a book that even the fastest reader would be occupied with for at least an hour. Lamprophyre flipped through it slowly, covertly regarding Ilhan and Narahar. Both the librarian and his assistant returned to the window every few hundred beats. No one else approached them. Dharan needed to act soon, though, because they couldn't guarantee that state of affairs would continue.

The door opened. Dharan entered, followed by Rokshan, who once more took up his station by the door. Dharan went immediately to the window, which was empty. Lamprophyre held her breath. If Ilhan wasn't the one to return first, the whole plan would have to start over.

Footsteps sounded off the distant bookcases, and in a moment, Ilhan appeared. Lamprophyre busily pretended to read. She heard Ilhan say, "Lector Dharan. What a pleasure. How can I help you?"

"I'm preparing an introduction to a history of Kolmira," Dharan said. "I need these books."

Paper rustled. "I'm happy to help," Ilhan said. "Wait here, please."

Lamprophyre waited just long enough for the footsteps to fade into silence. Then she leaped from her chair and rushed to the window, carrying the heavy book. She glanced at Dharan, but said nothing. So far, everything was going according to plan. Dharan's requests would, he'd assured her and Rokshan, take Ilhan all over the stacks and keep him occupied for several minutes. They just needed Narahar to be as diligent as Lamprophyre believed he was.

Beats passed. Lamprophyre pulled herself up on the shelf to peer beyond the window and was glared at by Dharan. She made a face at him, but returned to standing. Narahar, where was Narahar? Lamprophyre wiped her damp palms on her trousers and made herself breathe calmly. At worst, they'd just have to start over, but she wasn't sure her palms could take the strain.

Someone approached through the aisles made by the bookcases. "Lector Dharan," Narahar said with a smile. "And Lelitha. Who was here first?"

Dharan waved a hand at Lamprophyre. She held out a slip of paper. "I just need this one," she said.

Narahar glanced over the title. He looked at Lamprophyre. "One minute," he said, and disappeared into the stacks.

Lamprophyre and Dharan once more exchanged glances. That was step three accomplished. Now all they could do was wait. Lamprophyre turned her back on the window and looked at Rokshan. He'd assumed a parade rest stance near the door that put him out of the way of anyone entering, while still giving him freedom to stop anyone who tried to attack her. At the moment, he was examining a young man who'd just entered the scriptorium. The young man seemed nervous to be confronted by Rokshan and walked wide around him and his deadly-looking sword. Rokshan seemed uninterested in the young man's peace of mind; he glowered at the newcomer until the man found a chair and almost fell into it.

Too soon, Lamprophyre heard footsteps returning. "Here are your books, lector," Ilhan said. He set a stack of five volumes on the shelf. Lamprophyre swore inwardly. Ilhan couldn't be present when Narahar returned, not if they wanted this plan to work. Bad enough that she was obviously waiting on a book; Ilhan was suspicious enough to realize what she intended.

"Thank you, lector," Dharan said. "You've been to Kolmira, yes?"

"I have, lector," Ilhan said. He'd been looking at Lamprophyre, but Dharan's polite question drew his attention away from her. Lamprophyre carefully didn't meet Ilhan's eyes. *Hurry, Narahar, hurry...*

"In your opinion, what is the most notable architectural feature of the city?" Dharan asked. "I'd like to begin with an overview of the city as it's appeared to visitors across the centuries. Some would say the Vigilance, but I think that's rather too obvious a landmark, don't you agree?"

"You're so right, lector, the Vigilance is what everyone thinks of," Ilhan said. Lamprophyre could almost hear him preening with pride at being consulted on an academic matter by Dharan. "No, for my money the Almoner House is far more interesting. It's less dramatic, of course, but it's much older and has played so many different parts over time."

Dharan shifted position to draw Ilhan's attention even more away from Lamprophyre. "I hadn't thought of that," he said in a tone of surprise. "I had my first religious instruction there, did you know? I suppose it's so much a part of my childhood—"

"Lelitha," Narahar said. Lamprophyre spun around, startled. At the other end of the shelf, Dharan kept talking, and to her relief, Ilhan continued to pay close attention to his reminiscences. "Here's the book you wanted."

Lamprophyre let out a deep breath. The book was old, its leather worn, but after several months of handling books of all ages and conditions, she was a good judge of just how old a book really was. "This doesn't look two hundred and fifty years old," she said without thinking.

"What was that?" Ilhan said, interrupting Dharan. He took a few quick paces until he was standing beside Narahar. "What book is this?"

Narahar looked confused at Ilhan's abruptness. "It's *The Last Days of Hamadri*," he said. "Is there a problem?"

"This book is not for circulation," Ilhan said. He held out his hand and gestured for Narahar to give him the book. "You should know better."

Lamprophyre grabbed the book before Ilhan could touch it. "It's in perfectly good shape," she said, "not at all in need of mending. And I'm so glad it's not lost. I don't see why I shouldn't read it."

"Yes, Ilhan, why not?" Dharan said, his words pleasant, his gaze steely cold.

"You trick—" Ilhan snapped his mouth closed on more words. He glanced at Narahar, whose expression was now impassive. "Very well," Ilhan said. "But you study it here. It doesn't leave these premises."

"And why not?" Dharan said.

Lamprophyre's heart sank. The plan had worked, they had their prize, and it was time to retreat. But Dharan clearly had something else in mind. Lamprophyre wished she dared listen to the librarian's thoughts, but her memory of hearing the entity think in Zefira's head, and what had happened to Zefira when the entity realized Lamprophyre knew of its presence, made her afraid of seeing Ilhan attacked and injured in the same way.

Ilhan drew himself up to his full height, which was still shorter than Dharan. "I am the head librarian," he said, "and I am responsible for the books. I appreciate your reputation, lector, but unless you wish to undergo the years of training it takes to fill this position, you should not question my rules."

"That's an interesting interpretation of your remit," Dharan said. "I happen to know your responsibility is not only to the books, but to the academy and its presidency, and like all officers of the academy, you and your rules may be called into question by any lector in good standing. I put five years of my life into transforming this library into a place of learning and not a locked repository of knowledge, guarded by privilege-blinded autocrats like you."

Lamprophyre heard Rokshan let out a low whistle. She cast a quick glance over her shoulder at the rest of the students, who were all listening to this conversation with avid attention. The woman lector had her chin propped on her hand like someone enjoying a performance. "Um, Dharan," Lamprophyre said, "I think—"

"Autocrat? I?" Ilhan ignored Lamprophyre. "I suppose someone like you would see it that way. Genius is all very well in its place, but it's no substitute for breeding."

Lamprophyre gasped. She wasn't sure why Ilhan thought attacking Dharan for having been born poor was a good idea, but she knew an insult when she heard it.

Dharan didn't flinch. "You've been obstructing my colleague since the day she entered this library. I have to wonder how many other people's research you've interfered with. Is it a game to you, or do you feel you have some higher calling?"

Ilhan sputtered, "Why, you upstart, I should—"

"Don't finish that sentence, Lector Ilhan," the woman lector said. She rose from her seat and approached the window. "Sirrahs, this seems to call for an intervention. Lector Dharan, am I right that you wish to make a formal complaint?"

"I do," Dharan said. Lamprophyre clutched her hard-won book close to her chest and wondered if she was about to faint.

"Then I suggest you do so. Lector Ilhan, I'll be happy to attest to the legality of the complaint." The woman smiled at Dharan and Ilhan. "Now, Lector Dharan, I think you should leave to prepare your complaint. And to preserve the peace of the library. Your mutual animosity makes quiet research impossible."

"My colleague will remain," Dharan said, sounding impassive, as if he hadn't nearly started a fistfight.

The woman lector sized up Lamprophyre. "I think, on the whole, it's better she leaves too," she said. "But I don't think she should be deprived of her book. Lector Ilhan, make note of a five-day loan for this young woman."

"Absolutely not," Ilhan said, drawing himself up again. "I have declared that it is not to leave this room."

"Come now, lector, I don't see the problem," the woman said. "It's in good condition, and Lector Dharan is her sponsor—you don't think *he* would destroy or lose a book, even if you disagree with him?" She leaned forward, and the cheerful pleasantness fell away from her face. "I am a witness, Ilhan. You might want to consider what kind of witness I will bear before the academy. How irrational do you want to appear?"

Ilhan swallowed. "Record the loan, Narahar," he said.

"Thank you," Lamprophyre said. She hurried to the door, not looking to see if Dharan was following. Rokshan's eyes were wide, and he looked to be stifling laughter. She brushed past him and was brought up short by his hand on her shoulder.

"Take care," he murmured in her ear, and stepped through the door. She waited close behind him until he gestured her forward. The commons was as empty as the scriptorium, and none of the few students hurrying to cross it paid them any attention, but she felt as if a million eyes watched her from the trees. Her and her book. It was too thin to be a burden, but she felt its weight regardless.

Rokshan put his arm around her shoulders and steered her away. She heard someone following them and glanced over her shoulder at Dharan. "What the St—I mean, what was that about?" she demanded. "We had a plan, Dharan. You nearly ruined it."

"I know, but when I saw Megari was there, I decided to try for the high-hanging fruit," Dharan said. "Hurry, before anything else happens."

None of Rokshan or Dharan's favorite eateries were open this early, so they walked a few dozen dragonlengths to Dharan's lodgings. They were in an unexpectedly busy part of town, three rooms over a tavern that was quiet enough at the moment, but which Lamprophyre was sure would become intolerably noisy by nightfall. The door opened on a small sitting room overlooking the street, comfortably crowded with cushioned chairs in bright colors and two bookcases crammed full of books, some of which Lamprophyre recognized. The thick rug covering the floor reminded Lamprophyre of a sunset, its colors bands of red and gold and yellow, plush enough to tickle her toes despite her sandals. It was too bad the embassy didn't have rugs like this—and with that thought, her perspective shifted alarmingly, and for a panicked moment she couldn't remember how the street had looked to her dragon's eyes.

She sank into a soft chair near the entrance, the book still clutched to her chest, and watched Dharan cross the room to open the window. Street noises filtered through the gap, too distant for conversations to be intelligible. Rokshan ducked beneath the low-hanging lantern hooked to the ceiling and took a seat near Lamprophyre. "Please tell me you had a reason for nearly getting us thrown out, without the book," he said.

Dharan twitched the curtains closed over the open window. They didn't block the sounds, but they did diffuse the sunlight, making the room feel even warmer and cozier than before. "Lector Megari is one of the presidency of the academy," he said. "She detests authoritarianism despite herself being an authority, and I know she doesn't respect Ilhan. I took a chance on goading Ilhan into doing or saying something that would force her hand." He dropped onto the blue bench extending beneath the window and gripped it with both hands. "And as a result, we were able to walk away with that book."

"But I could have read it there," Lamprophyre protested.

"You could. I couldn't. And I like taking notes," Dharan said. "Now we have plenty of time to examine it."

"And with the way our luck is running, it will turn out to be useless," Rokshan said. "Look, someone has to be realistic," he added, throwing up his hands to defend himself against their glares. "I'm just saying we should prepare for disappointment, just in case."

"But we did more than just get the book," Lamprophyre said. "The entity knows we're on its trail. We've struck it a blow, in a sense."

"Yes, and that may be more important in the long run," Rokshan agreed.

"Isn't anyone going to thank me?" Dharan said. "Or did you want to prop up the library wall all morning, Rokshan, while Lamprophyre read the book?"

"Well, I'm going to read it now, and the two of you can find something else to do," Lamprophyre said. "I should be done around noon."

"I never felt the least bit of intellectual inferiority to anyone until you dragons came to town," Dharan said with a grin. "Rokshan, a game of spindles?"

"Are you sure about that?" Rokshan said with an answering grin. "Adding a guaranteed losing streak to your intellectual inferiority?"

"You only say that because you always win. I can feel my luck changing. It's in the air." Dharan stood and retrieved a long, flat wooden box from the top of one of the bookcases.

Lamprophyre had already opened the book. Though its paper was brown and spotted with age, and the leather binding worn nearly bald along the spine, she was certain it wasn't as old as it ought to be. "Are we sure this is the right book?"

Dharan handed the box to Rokshan and picked up the book. He flipped through the pages carefully and sniffed the binding. "I think this must be a later copy. Or it might be an original that was mended sometime in the last, oh, seventy years, but the pages would be unevenly worn if that were the case. It's all right. If it wasn't important, the entity wouldn't have worked so hard at keeping it out of our hands. It doesn't have to be the original."

Lamprophyre accepted the book back from Dharan and turned to the first page. It might not have been the original, but it was old enough to be handwritten rather than printed. The handwriting was clear and bold, easy to read, and Lamprophyre silently thanked the unknown scribe who had taken such care with it.

Dharan never had given her Kalivas's collection of folktales, so she had never read anything by the author. It was a surprise to find his style was almost modern, conversational rather than stilted as most of her other research books were. She drew her legs up beneath her and settled in comfortably. True, this book might be an important key to turning her back, but it was also an interesting story, and Lamprophyre loved a good story.

This one was so good she reached its end with no idea of how long it had taken, or what time it was now. With the curtains shrouding the window, she couldn't check the length and direction of the shadows. A feeling of floating in a timeless space descended on her, and she closed the book and let her shoulders, which had tensed up while she read, relax.

"I'm finished," she called out.

She heard movement in the next room, and soon Rokshan appeared in the doorway. "What did you learn?"

Lamprophyre looked down at the book's smooth, worn cover. "I don't know," she said. "There's no obvious reason the entity might have wanted us not to have this book. It doesn't mention magic at all."

Dharan followed Rokshan through the doorway and resumed his seat on the bench. "So what does it mention?"

"It's more or less what the title says. The history of a city that was destroyed during the Cataclysm. It's really interesting, too—he starts by establishing the city's everyday life, and introduces some people who lived there—"

"Almost certainly fictional," Dharan said. "No actual records from that time exist."

"Well, he makes them seem real. Anyway, it moves on from those first chapters to how the city's doom overtook it. The city's defenders, human and dragon, fought against—what's wrong?"

Both Rokshan and Dharan had abruptly sat up and were staring at her more intently. "Human and dragon?" Rokshan said. "I've never heard any stories about the catastrophe that had humans and dragons fighting as one."

"Well, this one does. And it says they fought against an unstoppable foe that swept over Hamadri like a great fiery wind. Specifically, it says, 'The banded desert overcame them, and their destruction was in the wind and the fire. It consumed the defenders and swept over Hamadri until only bones were left.'"

"Very magical. That's an idea that is a product of Kalivas's time," Dharan said. "Modern historians believe the catastrophe was a natural disaster of some kind, possibly a skystone falling to earth and causing widespread destruction. Nobody today thinks there was something magical about it."

"I don't think we should assume modern thinkers know any more than their ancient counterparts," Lamprophyre said. "No offense to them, but if there are no records from that time, everyone writing about the Cataclysm is equally ignorant."

"Yes, but..." Dharan's voice trailed off. "All right, I suppose if this book is important to the entity in some way, we shouldn't make assumptions."

"But I don't see how," Lamprophyre said. "If the entity wants to keep me in a human body, there's nothing in this book that has anything to do with that."

"So maybe we've stumbled on something else," Rokshan said. "Some other secret the entity is worried about."

Lamprophyre handed the book to Dharan and stretched out her legs. "A secret buried so deep we wouldn't have even known about it if the entity hadn't tried to conceal it. That's reassuring."

"It certainly implies our enemy isn't all-knowing," Dharan said. "I hope we can figure the secret out, because I don't think Ilhan will be fooled twice."

"Let's have something to eat, and then we'll leave you to investigate, Dharan. Lamprophyre and I have to visit Evart's workshop," Rokshan said.

He offered his hand to Lamprophyre to help her rise and held onto it for a few beats after she was on her feet. She felt strangely excited by the touch of his hand, so familiar now after a week of being human. By the way he looked at her, the curve of his smile saying more than a thousand words could, it felt different to him, too. They hadn't spoken about the previous night, which both relieved Lamprophyre's mind and filled her heart with confusion. Feeling love was complicated, but talking about it was even worse. She didn't know what she should say or if she should say it in front of Dharan, didn't know what came next. Darsha's information didn't cover a situation like hers.

"You go on ahead," Dharan said. "I'm not very hungry, and I'm eager to begin."

Rokshan shrugged. "Then, tomorrow morning? An early start?"

Dharan nodded. He was already deep in contemplation of the book.

CHAPTER TWENTY-EIGHT

They stopped at a street vendor to buy skewers of roasted meat and chunks of potato and ate as they walked. The potatoes were too dry, the meat dripping with juice as if to compensate, and Lamprophyre was content to walk in silence, letting the sounds of the city wash over her. Without her draconic hearing, the noise was simply confusion, lacking the deeper thrum she thought of as the city's heartbeat, and she wished she could block it out the way she blocked the thousands of thoughts surging around her.

Rokshan dropped his empty bamboo skewer on the street and took Lamprophyre's hand. "This is so different now," he said with that same sideways smile.

Lamprophyre tossed aside her own skewer. "I don't know why," she said. "Rokshan, is this a good idea?"

"Is what a good idea?"

She raised their joined hands. "Even I know this means more than keeping us from becoming separated."

The smile fell away from his face. "I don't know what happens next," he said. "Every time I convince myself that we don't have a future together, you look at me with those eyes that are still so familiar, and I can't bear the thought of letting you go. And then I hate myself for my selfishness in wishing you could stay this way."

"But you're still doing everything you can to change me back. You're not selfish."

Rokshan let out a low chuckle. "If you didn't do me the courtesy of not listening to my thoughts, you'd know that's not true."

Lamprophyre stepped closer to him to avoid a couple of children racing past. "I think actions are more important than thoughts. I think about scaring petitioners all the time, the ones who are rude or demanding, but I never do. Isn't that what matters?"

They'd entered a quieter neighborhood, one where the crowds weren't quite so overwhelming, but Rokshan didn't let go of her hand. "A reverend would say Jiwanyil judges our hearts," he said, "which implies he considers both actions and thoughts. Maybe humans are blessed for not entertaining the random impulses everyone has."

"Well, dragons care more about actions, probably because we hear each other's thoughts and know when those thoughts are at odds with our actions. And we believe Mother Stone doesn't reject anyone just for thinking or wishing something evil." A passing woman, her hair gray and her face deeply lined, eyed Lamprophyre and Rokshan, her gaze lingering on their joined hands. She caught Lamprophyre's eye and smiled, a conspiratorial, merry expression that made Lamprophyre blush as if she'd been caught doing something inappropriate. But she didn't let go of Rokshan's hand.

"Either way, I think we should both focus on finding the transformation magic, and not worry about what will happen when you're restored," Rokshan said. "And until then..." He gently squeezed her hand. "Until then, I will be a fool, and let myself believe our love is possible."

"Why does that make you a fool?"

He sighed. "Because there is nothing but heartbreak at the end of this path, and if I were wise, I wouldn't be holding your hand right now."

His words left a hollow feeling inside her. "I don't care about heartbreak," she exclaimed. "This may be the only love I ever feel, and I don't want to lose it."

"You said that last night. I didn't know it bothered you so much that you weren't in love with anyone."

"Dragons have to pair-bond. There are so few of us, we can't afford not to bear children. I'm the only dragon I know who's never felt an attraction to at least one member of the flight." The memory brought tears to her eyes that she blinked away. "I have always felt so ashamed of that."

"Maybe that makes you different, but I don't think it makes you broken," Rokshan said. "Some humans aren't interested in sex or marriage at all. That's just how they are. And there's nothing wrong with that. Just like there would be nothing wrong with you if you never fell in love with anyone." He stopped and turned her to face him, ignoring the passersby who dodged around them. "I'm glad you're the way you are, and I guess I really am selfish, because I am fiercely, deeply joyful that I'm the one you fell in love with and not some dragon. It shows you have good taste."

The smile that lit his eyes as he spoke made Lamprophyre laugh, it was such a funny mixture of pride and amusement. "So you think I was waiting my whole life for you?" she said.

Rokshan shrugged. "It's a theory. And maybe that means there's hope for us, after all." He tugged on her hand. "Evart's workshop is a few streets away this way."

"It took them a while to remove the wards. Is that because Evart was powerful, or because the Army's adepts aren't very good?"

"A little of both. What matters is that they didn't blow themselves and the workshop all the way to Nirinatan to scare the dragons."

Lamprophyre pictured a handful of screaming humans flying through the air and stifled a smile. Good thing Mother Stone really didn't care whether dragons thought virtuous thoughts, because that one was unworthy, even though it was also funny.

Most of the buildings they now passed looked more like individual homes than shops, low, one-story buildings with tiled roofs that would be proof against fire. That was fortunate, because the houses stood close together, some of them sharing walls with one another, and Lamprophyre had seen fire spread faster than water pouring downhill through neighborhoods much like this one. The air was rich with the scents of midday meals, roasting meats and vegetables seasoned with spices Depik had told her the names of, cumin and cardamom and cinnamon and spicy pepper. The skewer of meat had filled her, but the spices roused her hunger again.

They turned a corner, and ahead Lamprophyre saw a couple of soldiers standing in front of one of the houses. "Evart worked here?" she asked. "Isn't that dangerous?"

"I've come to the conclusion that Evart didn't care about the safety of others," Rokshan said. "This was his home as well as his workshop. He wasn't wealthy enough to have a separate one somewhere away from where people live."

That made Lamprophyre think of Manishi. "Is Manishi...I don't want to say 'well,' but did she wake?"

"Early this morning," Rokshan said. "And you'd think she hadn't lost most of her arm at all. She rose from her bed and insisted on returning to her workshop immediately. I don't understand her, I really don't."

"Neither do I," Lamprophyre said, but she wasn't sure that was true. Manishi was a horrible person, but she was also smart and driven, and it made an odd kind of sense that the adept wouldn't allow anything like being maimed stop her doing what she was passionate about.

Rokshan slowed as they approached the soldiers and let go of Lamprophyre's hand to salute them. The soldiers returned the salute, theirs more formal than Rokshan's, and lowered their weapons fractionally as if acknowledging their commander's presence. Both of them eyed Lamprophyre, but made no move to stop her.

She chose not to listen to their thoughts, in case they were thinking about whether or not she was attractive. Now that she knew what love felt like, she didn't like the idea of being the subject of some man's lascivious thoughts, even though she knew from Darsha that men often thought of women in a sexual way when they would never dream of approaching those women for an actual physical relationship. "It's just how men are," Darsha had said, "and to be honest, I've built a career around that."

Lamprophyre thought of what she and Rokshan had just discussed, the differences between thoughts and actions, and felt a little guilty at disliking those men for thinking of her sexually when they had behaved with perfect propriety. And she didn't even know they'd had those thoughts at all. Still, she felt better when they were inside the house and out of those soldiers' line of sight.

Evart's home was as small on the inside as it had appeared from the street. The one window, which was next to the door, let in just enough sunlight that Lamprophyre had to squint for her eyes to adjust to the low light. Blinking, she began to make out shapes: a chair pulled slightly away from a table, as if someone had just stood to answer the door; a pallet bed raised only a few inches off the ground; a wash table with a basin and pitcher of chipped ceramic. A doorway hung with a curtain faced the front door. The room was tidier than Lamprophyre had envisioned, though that was because there weren't enough furnishings to make a mess.

She circled the room, examining the furnishings. A battered iron lantern with cracked glass stood on the table, unlit and, by the lack of smell, unlit for a while. The water in the pitcher smelled stale and had tiny insects floating in it. "This isn't much more elaborate than the servants' houses at the embassy," she said. "Maybe I should provide better amenities for Depik and Bhakriya."

"Something to worry about another time," Rokshan said. He lit the lamp, which gave off a wan glow not much brighter than the sunlight, and pulled the curtain aside to enter the next room. Lamprophyre followed him.

The second room was barer than the first. It didn't look anything like Manishi's workshop, which was the only other adept's workshop Lamprophyre knew to compare it to. There were no many-drawered cabinets, no glossy obsidian mirror-table—well, Evart was unlikely to be able to afford one—no loose chunks of stone. Instead, two sagging wooden bookcases along the far wall held dozens of small wooden boxes that reminded her of the catalog drawers in the library, but unfinished and without paper labels. A shorter shelf, not even as tall as Lamprophyre, stood beside the doorway. It held paper, ink, chalk, and a couple of items she didn't know names for, as well as a coil of hairy, fibrous rope and a stubby belt knife with an amber hilt.

A painted white circle filled most of the available floor space. It was a little like the chalk circle Manishi had drawn for that ill-fated magic, but only in the sense that both were perfectly round. Evart's lacked any of the flourishes and drawings Manishi had used. "This is the basis for a lot of different workings," she said, pointing at it.

"Yes," Rokshan said. He was rooting through the boxes. "The adepts said it's common for people to make a permanent circle they then add to for specific magic. Saves time. What kind of stone is this?" He held up a chunk of smoothly polished stone, mostly white but with streaks and spots of black mottling its surface. "It looks like white serpentine."

"Wyklite. It's a kind of borocalcite," Lamprophyre said. "It must be a long way from home. Are you sure it's a good idea to handle those? What if they're magically imbued?"

"The adepts said everything in here was inert. No chance of me blasting myself with pyrite." Rokshan dropped the wyklite into its box and turned away from the shelves. "I'm not sure what we're looking for. Something we can use. Serpentine, if we're lucky."

"Then I suppose we have to go through the boxes," Lamprophyre said. "What happens to all this? Inert or not, it represents a lot of raw resources."

"I've claimed it for my father's government. Though I think maybe we should give some of it to Manishi. It can't replace her arm, but...I don't know. I'm feeling inappropriately guilty about what happened." Rokshan took a box off the highest shelf and handed it to Lamprophyre. "Though it's not our fault the working failed."

Lamprophyre stirred the contents of the box with her finger. Citrines, not very high quality. They were all faceted, but irregularly, as if the lapidary had been drunk when she did the work. "I know what you mean. I can identify the rarer stones, and maybe we could give a handful of those to her."

Rokshan continued hauling boxes off the shelves. "For now, why don't you sort those according to how common they are. Damn. That proposed book of yours would be so handy right now. I would really like to know what else Evart was working on."

"I know what *some* of these are for," Lamprophyre said. "Citrines are for vision when they're polished and good fortune when they're faceted. Apparently Evart failed to use them properly." She looked into another box. "Agates are for strength, but different agates have different effects. This is lace agate, and I'm not sure what it does."

Rokshan came to look over her shoulder at the box full of stones, their stripes irregularly curved as if insects had bitten scallops out of them. "Pretty. Are all agates like that?"

"The stripes? Yes. It's what makes it agate and not chalcedony. The banding—" She stopped as a memory stirred. "Banded desert."

"Wasn't that in the Kalivas book?" Rokshan asked.

"Yes. But..." She shook her head. "There was also some old dragon story about a stone with banding, and the desert...I can't remember."

"There's a first," Rokshan teased.

Lamprophyre elbowed him in the stomach, not very hard. "I can't remember *everything*, Rokshan. I'm sure it will come to me later. What other stones are there?"

She examined each box as Rokshan handed them down. A few were empty of anything but stone dust, which annoyed Lamprophyre. If she were in her own body, she could have identified the missing stone by smell. The best she could do was bring the boxes close to the lantern to see the color of what was left. None of it was dark green.

"Amethyst, turquoise, garnet," she said, setting three boxes aside. "He couldn't have been that poor if he could afford turquoise. All of that except what we dragons harvest comes from beyond Fanishkor."

Rokshan said nothing. Lamprophyre glanced up from where she sat on the floor, sorting boxes, to see him staring into a box, his face perfectly still. "Did you find something?" she asked.

Rokshan handed the box to her without a word. It rattled when Lamprophyre took it, as if it were mostly empty. She looked inside and saw three nuggets of polished stone, dark green with black mottled markings.

Serpentine.

She fumbled the box in her surprise, then clutched it close to her chest. "I don't—" She didn't know how to finish the sentence, had no idea what she'd meant to say. Her heart had sped up until it was thumping faster than a deer fleeing a dragon.

"It might not be enough," Rokshan said. His voice sounded distant, as if he were at the far end of the street instead of a couple of handspans away. "They're such small pieces."

"Maybe an adept can combine them into...I don't know. Set them in metal as part of a single piece?"

Rokshan nodded. "At the very least, it will give an adept something to work from. If we had an adept."

Lamprophyre picked up the largest nugget. It was the size of a walnut and closer to cubical than round. She didn't have to say it, because she knew what Rokshan was thinking: they couldn't take this to Manishi, not after what had happened. "Maybe Sabarna..."

"Maybe," Rokshan agreed. "Though I wonder how trustworthy she is. She *was* one of the adepts involved in the mind-reading artifact race. She might not be the best person to reveal your identity to."

"She helped me before without asking for anything," Lamprophyre said. "At least she might direct us to someone who can create a trans-formation artifact, if she can't."

"It's worth trying." Rokshan squatted next to Lamprophyre. "Let's finish going through this stuff, just in case, and then we'll approach Sabarna."

There turned out to be forty-three wooden boxes. Most of them contained commonplace stones, easy for anyone to buy, but there was a chunk of pyrite the size of Rokshan's fist in one and a double handful of polished, perfectly ovoid sodalite stones in another, a rich blue the color of her own body with lovely white striations. Lamprophyre ran her fingers through those longingly. Sodalite had been—no, still was, she was a dragon even if her human body couldn't consume stone—one of her favorite flavors and was rare enough she almost never had any. She sighed and pushed the box away. "I wish I knew what he used to put me to sleep that night," she said.

"I wish he hadn't killed himself so we could ask him," Rokshan said with a grimace. "Let's leave these where they are, since you've sorted them so nicely, and I'll arrange for the adepts to take custody of them tomorrow. Though if we're going to give some to Manishi, better choose now."

Lamprophyre put the little chunks of serpentine in her belt pouch and considered the rest of the stones. She scooped several of the sodalites into her belt pouch, added a couple of hematite spheres that gleamed silver-black in the lamplight and two of the wyklite lumps, and after some reflection took a chunk of uncut emerald and an orange-red calcium carbonate crystal as well. The red crystal was the same as the one Manishi had made into a pendant for Lamprophyre as part of the failed transformation, if smaller, and although Lamprophyre had left the pendant in Manishi's workshop, she didn't know if it could be used for magic again. This crystal felt like balancing the scales between them.

Back on the street, Rokshan gave instructions to the soldiers on guard. Lamprophyre scanned the street in both directions, not listening. Their explorations had taken longer than Lamprophyre had realized, and the sun was now low in the sky and the street was busy with pedestrians returning home from their day jobs or setting out for their nighttime work. She carefully didn't listen to their thoughts. None of them appeared intent on attacking her; few of them paid her any attention at all.

"I didn't realize how late it was," Rokshan said. "Sabarna will be abed by the time we reach the academy. We'll have to go tomorrow."

Disappointment and frustration filled Lamprophyre. "Tomorrow?"

"It's just a few hours, Lelitha. I know how you must feel, but we have to be patient."

Lamprophyre scowled. Patience. She felt she'd exercised enough patience this week to use up a lifetime's supply of it—a dragon's lifetime. "I hope there are no mandatory wedding activities tonight. I don't feel sociable."

"Not for you. The immediate families of the happy couple have an evening purification service to witness. It sanctifies the man and woman before Jiwanyil, preparing them to make oath before God's representatives." Rokshan's scowl matched hers. "I remember the one for Manishi's wedding, and Tekentriya's before that. It takes at least two hours and all the witnesses do is sit and watch."

"At least you get to sit."

"Optimistic as ever." Rokshan took her hand and kissed the back of it. "We'll have to hurry back if I'm to be there on time. Much as I'd like to share a meal with you."

"So would I. I'm so used to eating my supper with you. It's uncomplicated, because it's something we did when I was myself—" She lowered her voice, conscious of how near the soldiers were. "And it's something we'll go on doing after...you know."

"True." Rokshan tugged on her hand, and they headed off down the street. This time, Lamprophyre stayed close beside him, not wanting to be jostled by the increasing crowds. The noise was great enough to prevent casual conversation, and Lamprophyre stepped closer, holding Rokshan's arm with her other hand.

She watched him instead of the street occasionally, trusting him to keep her from being swept away. It was increasingly easy to see him as a woman sees a man, as someone she was attracted to. She ignored the tiny voice within her that was appalled that she might find someone not of her species attractive and desirable. This human body had changed her perspective in so many ways, and this was just another one of them.

From this side, the scars that ran up Rokshan's neck and across his cheek were visible. Lamprophyre understood now how someone might view the scars as marring his body, the rough ridging interrupting the smooth brown skin. To her, knowing how he'd come by them, they were a mark of triumph, of having survived what should have killed him. She remembered how the rest of his body looked and was struck by a sudden desire to touch the scars, to see how they felt. It wasn't something she could do here in the street, and probably shouldn't do without his permission, but the idea of being in intimate contact with his body gave her an unexpected tingling feeling.

Rokshan's attention shifted to her briefly before he went back to watching the street. "You're staring at me," he said.

That made Lamprophyre blush, as if she'd actually touched his scars in public. "I like the way you look," she said, feeling shy about saying it.

Rokshan smiled, but his gaze roved the crowds restlessly. "That fills me with happiness."

"What are you looking for?"

He glanced swiftly at her again. "Threats. Anyone who might intend you harm. I almost wish someone would attack. I feel in the mood to deliver a good thrashing."

"Why is that?"

Rokshan's lips thinned in a straight, hard line, and for a moment he didn't say anything. Finally, when Lamprophyre was about to repeat her question, he said, "Finding the serpentine reminded me what our ultimate goal is, and, I'm sorry, Lelitha, but my instincts are at war with each other. I want you restored and I want you to stay human, and whatever happens, whichever way this falls out, it's going to hurt both of us."

His words struck her to the heart. All day, she'd been able to think solely of the moment—of Rokshan's hand holding hers, of that light kiss he'd brushed against the back of her hand—and forget that none of this could last. Now, for the first time since her transformation, she allowed herself to consider the possibility that she would never be restored. Setting aside the threat the entity was to her, being human, truly human, for the rest of a short human lifespan would be...not entirely awful. Not if Rokshan was with her.

Then the moment passed, and horror struck her—horror that she'd let herself even think that way. She was a dragon. She couldn't abide staying human, not even for— She made herself breathe calmly. "What happened to us figuring it out together?" she said, trying for a light, cheerful tone.

Rokshan laughed. His hand tightened on hers. "You're right, we will," he said. "Though I'd still like to pummel something. It would relieve the tension that's weighing on the back of my neck like a millstone."

"What's a millstone?"

"A very heavy rock for grinding grain into flour." Rokshan released her hand only to put his arm around her and hold her close for a few steps. "I love you, Lelitha, and whether that's as your friend or as something more, nothing will change that."

Lamprophyre relaxed. "That's how I feel."

CHAPTER TWENTY-NINE

They walked in silence the rest of the way to the palace, where the soldiers at the side door saluted them. Lamprophyre, remembering the wicked little crossbow the soldier on the stairs had pointed at her, once again felt grateful to be in Rokshan's company.

Rokshan didn't let go of her hand once they were within. "I don't care what people think," he said when Lamprophyre asked if their attachment should be made public. "If I'm only going to have a few days with you in this form, I intend to make the most of every one of those days."

She liked it when he spoke so firmly of his feelings for her. It made the excited tingle stronger. "Will you come to my room when the ceremony is over?" she asked.

Rokshan's smile disappeared. "Lelitha," he began.

"Excuse me, Lady Lelitha?" A servant hurried toward them down the hall from the guest wing. "I have a message for you."

Lamprophyre accepted the folded, sealed paper and read its contents as the servant hurried away. "Kulat needs to see me for a fitting," she said. "I don't know what that is."

"It means trying on clothing to make sure they're the right size." Rokshan read the note over her shoulder. "I'm surprised he needs a fitting. He seemed to think he could get your gowns right the first time."

"It's late. Maybe I should go in the morning." The idea of going straight to her room and summoning Haleta to bring her a meal was so appealing she felt physical pain at the thought of crossing the city again.

Rokshan shrugged. "I don't know. Kulat is eccentric. If he wants you to come today, he means today. And I don't think you want to risk ending up on his bad side. Not with how beautiful his gowns are."

"I'm afraid he'll know the first two were ruined and will think I don't deserve his genius," Lamprophyre said.

"Or he'll realize you'll need to replace them, and that will mean more custom for him," Rokshan pointed out. "I'll find you a body-guard. It won't take long, and then you can spend a nice quiet evening in."

That sounded comforting. "And we can talk later."

"Come with me," Rokshan said, heading back the way they'd come. "I don't think it's a good idea for me to visit you in your room at night."

"Why not?"

Rokshan was silent for a few moments. Finally, he said, "I love you, and I have desires for you the way a man does for a woman. But I promised myself I wouldn't act on those desires again until I'm married."

"Oh. You mean sex," Lamprophyre said, enlightenment dawning. "But we don't have to do that."

"You don't know how powerful those desires can be," Rokshan said. "It's better not to put ourselves in the way of temptation."

That irritated Lamprophyre a little. She had tremendous willpower, and she knew sex with Rokshan was a bad idea, even if humans could be sexually active without being pair-bonded, so it was unlikely she would be tempted. Maybe Rokshan wasn't as strong-willed as a dragon. Well, she loved him anyway, even if he was a slave to his passions. So she said, "I understand. Thank you."

"It's not that I don't find you desirable," he assured her.

"Of course you do."

Rokshan burst out laughing. "I'm sorry," he said when his laughter died away. "You just sounded so certain of your attractiveness just then. It's not at all what a human woman would have said."

Lamprophyre blushed. "I'll try to be more careful to sound human."

"I don't care how you sound. Just go on being yourself," Rokshan said.

They left the palace and crossed the training grounds to the military compound at the far side. Lamprophyre had never been inside, though she was familiar with the red roofs from having flown over the buildings so often on her approach to the palace. Now she stood beside Rokshan as he chatted with a soldier seated at a desk about trivialities and examined the room. It wasn't very big, and from what she'd observed of the many windows dotting the single-story building's sides, she guessed there were a lot of small rooms filling this otherwise sizable building.

Many lanterns lit the room, making it brighter than day, though as the sun was setting that wasn't a very hard bar to meet. There were five doors, all of them closed, that must open on more of those small rooms. This one had three other desks in addition to the one the soldier sat at, but none of the others were occupied. Lamprophyre guessed everyone else had gone off to their suppers. Wherever that was, it wasn't in this building, because Lamprophyre smelled no food, just damp plaster and leather and, faintly, the smell of paper.

"...your very best," Rokshan was saying as Lamprophyre's attention turned once more to the desk. "Lady Lelitha's safety is of the highest concern."

"Of course, Commander," the soldier said. *Commander's light o' love, likely*, he thought, and *don't blame him, she's a sweet little armful and no mistake.* Could *everyone* tell how they felt about each other?

"If you'll wait a minute, I'll be right back," the soldier went on, and pushed away from his desk to exit through the nearest door. The scent of roasted pig wafted through the opening.

"I'm taking someone away from his supper," Lamprophyre said.

"A soldier's job is to be ready for action at any time," Rokshan said, "which includes interrupting supper. And speaking of interrupting things, I really have to hurry to be ready for the ceremony. Are you all right if I leave you?"

"I know the way to Kulat's. I'll be fine."

Rokshan squeezed her hand reassuringly. "I'll see you in the morning," he said, and hesitated for a beat or two. Lamprophyre watched him, wondering what else he wanted to say, but after those few beats, he smiled and let himself out.

Lamprophyre waited. Time slipped past slowly, boring her. She hated waiting for things. She eyed the soldier's desk, which had several papers covered with writing on it, and thought about reading the papers to entertain herself. It wasn't as if she weren't trustworthy, and likely nothing in those papers would matter to her. She decided she was too noble to snoop and resolutely didn't look at them, even though she could read upside-down writing almost as easily as writing that was right ways up.

Finally, the door swung open. The smell of pig was stronger, rousing Lamprophyre's hunger. Maybe she should eat first—no, she'd already disrupted some soldier's supper, and she liked the idea of getting her errand out of the way before settling in for a quiet evening.

The desk soldier returned, accompanied by a younger soldier who gazed at Lamprophyre curiously. He was short and slender, and his uniform hung off him as if it had been made for someone else. Lamprophyre thought he might be as young as her human body appeared to be.

"Corporal Ahladh, you'll escort Lady Lelitha on her errand and back to the palace," the desk soldier said.

Corporal Ahladh saluted the soldier, then Lamprophyre. He looked so earnest Lamprophyre had to conceal a smile for fear he'd think she was laughing at him. It was just the way his tunic shifted when he raised his arm, like the cloth was trying to smother him, that amused her, and that wasn't his fault.

"I have to go to Kulat, the tailor," she said when they were outside. "Do you know where that is?"

"No, madama, I'm sorry," Ahladh said. "I mean, my lady. No."

"That's all right, I do." Lamprophyre examined him closely. He didn't look like anyone capable of giving an assailant a good fight, and for a moment she felt trepidation at entrusting her safety to him. But he was armed, and the desk soldier had said he would choose someone competent, and she knew none of Rokshan's subordinates would disregard his instructions.

The evening city had come fully awake, and in the light of the setting sun, the streets seemed busier, more cheerful. Lamprophyre heard men and women greeting each other with shouts and laughter, saw groups of people walking past with their arms linked together, and relaxed. It was hard to stay tense when everyone around you was so happy.

She glanced at Ahladh. He wasn't relaxed; his gaze swept the street before them, never lingering long anywhere, and his hand hovered near the hilt of his sword, not quite touching it, but clearly ready to use it. He so reminded her of Rokshan that she relaxed further. Clearly he was more competent than his thin frame suggested.

Someone bumped into her, and she heard a muffled apology. Quickly she shifted her weight to feel the brush of her belt pouch, hidden beneath the tail of her shirt. Rokshan had taught her never to make a grab for her belt pouch if she thought someone had tried to steal it. "You're just giving away its location to some other thief," he'd said. This had been an ordinary street encounter, not an attempted theft, but it made her uncomfortable. Walking with Rokshan meant people stepped wide around her, and Ahladh might be competent, but he wasn't physically intimidating. She moved closer to him anyway.

"It's this way," she said, pointing at an upcoming intersection of a very wide street crossing the one they were on, which was equally wide. "To the right."

Ahladh nodded, but didn't say anything. She remembered what Rokshan had said about soldiers on duty and didn't try to strike up a conversation.

Music drifted toward her on the air, gradually growing louder as they turned the corner. The new street felt more crowded than the first, and after a few beats, Lamprophyre realized why: some sort of celebration was going on, and the street was filled with dancers in pairs, whirling and hopping and leaping to the sound of pipes and drums and stringed instruments. Observers ringed the impromptu dancing space, and Lamprophyre slowed to find a way past them.

Ahladh put a hand on her shoulder. "We should walk wide around them," he said. "Is the tailor's shop far?"

"It's just a few places down. This way." Lamprophyre pointed.

Ahladh nodded. Then his eyes went wide, and he grunted and stumbled into Lamprophyre, forcing her back into one of the watchers. "Hey!" the man said, turning.

Lamprophyre tried to step away from the man, but Ahladh kept advancing on her. "Stop!" she exclaimed, pushing Ahladh away. The young soldier put his hands on her shoulders and then sagged, dragging her down with him. Lamprophyre struggled to free herself. He weighed more than he appeared to, or—

She registered the spreading bloodstain on the back of his uniform shirt just as Ahladh's grip on her shoulders loosened and he collapsed on top of her. Shocked, Lamprophyre screamed and shoved at Ahladh's inert body, which pinned her legs. The same man she'd bumped into said, "God's breath, you idiot, stop—" and then let out a shout of astonishment at seeing Ahladh.

Lamprophyre freed herself and stood, breathing heavily with fear. The world had slowed to a crawl, and everyone around her moved as if they were swimming through warm honey. Her eyes met those of a dark-clad man standing nearby. He held a short knife whose blade was dark with blood. The crowd around them had started to move, responding to the screaming and shouting, but no one seemed aware of this man or his knife. He watched Lamprophyre impassively, as if none of this mattered to him. Then he shifted his grip on the knife, and the illusion of slowness vanished as he leaped at her.

Lamprophyre screamed again and ducked. The knife scored a line across her nearest neighbor's back, making the woman cry out in pain and turn to see who had attacked her. Lamprophyre didn't wait to see what she might do. She turned and fled.

The crowd might as well have been an impassable bramble for all she made headway against it. Shoving and kicking, she pressed forward, hoping the assassin was having as much trouble as she was. She saw the second assassin just beats before she would have run into her arms, only just recognizing the sharp blade and dark clothes that made the woman stand out in the crowd. Stupid, stupid for an assassin to be so recognizable, but Lamprophyre was grateful for their stupidity.

She veered left and kept running. She didn't know where to go. Kulat's might be safe, except why had the assassins known to attack her in this place, at exactly this time? If Kulat were a tool of the entity —no, not Kulat's store. She was already out of breath, Stones take Evart and how he'd given her a weak human body. She would never make it to the palace. The warehouses where her clutch lived were on the other side of the city. She might try to reach the city guard headquarters, but how could she explain her peril? Most people weren't pursued by assassins for no reason, and she couldn't tell anyone the reason these were after her.

That left the embassy. It was—she frantically took in her surroundings—it was several streets away, but closer than any other refuge, and she could make it that far.

She reached another intersection and fled down the new street. In her mind, she pictured her route the only way she knew, from the air, and converted the image into a reflection of the route from her street-level position. Seven more streets. Maybe she'd outrun the assassins. She didn't slow or turn to see if this were true. She'd rather look stupid and go racing into the embassy courtyard pursued by no one than let a moment's pause get her killed.

She weaved around pedestrians. None of them paid her any attention. Terror sharpened her senses, drove her through the smallest gaps between people who walked the streets oblivious to the death that pursued her. Her heart pounded, making her feel sick and dizzy, her lungs wheezed, and her sandals sent up sharp pains through her legs every time her feet hit the ground.

Someone grabbed her, spun her around, and shoved her to fall hard to the ground. She screamed as the assassin's blade swept toward her heart.

With a last, desperate effort, she rolled to one side and felt the knife tug at her sleeve. She kept rolling until she was on hands and knees, then thrust herself to her feet and took off running again. That hadn't been one of the assassins she'd seen before. If there were more even than those three—she made herself focus on running and not on entertaining terrible fears she could do nothing about.

Four more streets. She was staggering now, unable to run and unwilling to lie down and be killed. She no longer had the energy to avoid people, and cries of anger followed her down the street as she caromed off anyone in her path. Her vision was gray at the edges. In her lightheaded breathlessness, she felt as if she were flying through a forest, trees grabbing at her scales and her wings and trying to bring her into their tangled embrace. That was wrong, but she couldn't clear her head to know what was right.

A tree grabbed her shoulder, dragging her to a halt. Then there was pain, a hot stabbing pain through her lower back, another shooting through her spine, and she collapsed. She was human again, because no dragon could be hurt that way, and she tried to drag herself away from the pain. That just made it worse. Someone rolled her onto her back, and the knife plunged into her stomach, thrusting upward toward her heart. The gray edges to her vision spread, filling more of her sight, and she had one clear thought, *Why is everything so quiet?* before the gray became black and she knew nothing more.

CHAPTER THIRTY

Lamprophyre lay on her back beside a river that mumbled and chuckled its way to the sea. Weariness filled every part of her, numbing her limbs and her shoulders and neck so she couldn't move, but she didn't care, because she didn't want to move. The river's voice grew quieter, then louder, then diminished until it was nearly silent. That was strange. She was sure she hadn't moved, but she'd never heard of a river that could leap its banks and run away from someone.

She stared up at the dark gray sky, which blended with the gray mountains and the gray hills—no, that was wrong, the world wasn't that uniformly gray. She blinked, or thought she blinked, but saw no motion as her eyelids fluttered open. Unless her eyelids hadn't opened, and she was looking at the insides of them. That made sense—her eyes were closed, and nothing was visible. Opening her eyes seemed as wearying as moving any other part of her body.

So instead she lay and listened for the river's return. There was something touching her skin, something soft and scratchy at the same time. It brushed against her legs and stomach and breasts—but that was wrong, too. Since when had she had breasts? Or— Horror jabbed her in the middle of her chest, a short panicky jolt that shot through her. She was lying on her back and her wings didn't protest.

Frightened, she tried to move and discovered her body wouldn't respond, not from weariness but from a true numbness that said her nerves weren't connected to any part of her. She couldn't even open her mouth to scream. A keening wail vibrated in her throat and leaked from her lips, thin and high-pitched. Her face was wet, though it wasn't raining, but suppose she was wrong about that and she couldn't feel the rain on her face any more than she could move her body?

The river's quiet rumbling grew louder until it was less of a rumble and more of a sharp, staccato beat against its banks. It almost sounded like words—and with that thought, something clicked inside her head, and the river's voice *was* words: "...no pain, I hope?"

Her jaw was still locked shut. She struggled harder to shape the sounds coming out of her throat. Someone put a cold hand on her wrist. "Lie still. The healing isn't over yet." The cold hand moved from her wrist to clasp her hand. It felt even colder that way. "Squeeze once if you understand me."

Lamprophyre focused all her attention on her hand, chilled by the speaker's grasp. Making it move felt like swimming through mud, pushing and pushing and making no progress. She realized her jaw was tenser than before, and she seized on that knowledge. If she could clench her jaw, she could squeeze her hand. She pictured her fingers moving, one by one, and with a final tremendous effort made her hand close, so slightly, on the cold hand holding it.

"Excellent," the voice said. Lamprophyre didn't know why she'd ever mistaken it for a river; it was sharp and precise and put Lamprophyre in mind of a bird pecking the ground in search of a worm. "Just a few more questions. Do you remember your name? Squeeze once for yes and twice for no."

Squeezing was easier the second time. The question frightened her again—was there a chance she'd have forgotten her own name? More questions arose, bubbling up around her unstoppably. Why was she in this state? Why couldn't she move? Where was this place?

"Good," the voice said. "Do you remember what happened to you?"

Lamprophyre squeezed twice as hard as she could. It wasn't very hard. More water trickled over her face, leaking down into her ears. Someone dabbed the water away with a soft cloth.

"It's all right, you don't have to remember right now," the voice said soothingly. "Last question. Are you in any pain?"

Again she squeezed twice. The voice didn't respond right away, which unnerved her. "Don't be afraid," the voice finally said. "You're at the Northeast district healing center, and we'll take good care of you. But you need to sleep now so the healing can proceed. When you wake, you'll be more alert and we can talk further. Rest now." The cold hand withdrew, and before Lamprophyre could protest that she didn't want to sleep, something cold touched the center of her forehead. It was familiar, but she had no time to recall the last time she'd experienced this before falling deeply into sleep.

It felt like no time had passed when she woke again. This time, she had no confusion over talking rivers and gray landscapes. She still lay on her back, but her eyes blinked open normally, and in the dim light she could nevertheless clearly see a ceiling of white plaster crossed by dark brown beams. The light had the cold, sharp quality of a magical light rather than sunlight, and despite the dimness it made her eyes ache a little. But she could see. She couldn't hear anything, but the room was still enough that might just be because the walls and door were thick. Nothing to panic about. Yet.

She lay still and sorted through memories. Walking through the city to Kulat's shop. Ahladh stabbed in the back, knocking her down. Her flight from the assassins. Falling, sharp pains, and—she pushed that memory aside so it wasn't more than a shadow.

Her mind was much clearer now. She was a dragon in a human body, which was why she could be injured by human weapons. Why she could lie painlessly on her back, for that matter. She had left the palace to go to Kulat's shop, accompanied by the soldier Rokshan had—

Her eyes flew open, and she tried to sit up. Rokshan. If the people at the healing center didn't know who she was, they couldn't have sent word to the palace, and Rokshan would have no idea where she was. She had no idea how long the healings had taken, but even if Rokshan hadn't expected to see her again before morning, if it had taken longer than a night, he would be going mad now with trying to find her.

"Is someone there?" she shouted, or tried to; the shout came out as a whisper, as if her throat was still numb. The sound wouldn't go farther than the thick door. She tried once more to sit. This time, she didn't feel numb, she felt achy and tremulous, as if she'd already exerted herself beyond her capacity and her body had no more reserves for motion. Fear threatened to overwhelm her, and she crushed it into the space where she'd banished her worst memories. This was a healing center. They wouldn't weaken her. This condition was only temporary.

Focusing on her right hand, she pictured the fingers moving and was thrilled to feel them twitch. They brushed against the soft blanket covering her, and the touch relieved her mind further. She hadn't lost all her tactile senses.

She went on trying to make parts of her move, her fingers, her hands, her wrists, and had just reached her right elbow when the door opened and a woman in a healer's black tunic walked in. "You're awake sooner than we expected," she said. "That's very good news."

"I can't move," Lamprophyre whispered.

"I'm afraid that's a side effect of the healing." The healer shut the door behind her. Lamprophyre recognized her as the woman who'd taken Rokshan's payment for healing Lamprophyre's broken arm. Mareet, that was her name.

"I remember you," Lamprophyre said.

Mareet peered at her. "I don't...yes, I remember, you're the young princess with the broken arm Prince Rokshan brought to us!" She laughed, a bit self-consciously. "I apologize for not recognizing you sooner. I'm afraid you were badly injured enough you didn't look much like yourself."

"I'm not—" Lamprophyre decided not to confuse things further by insisting she wasn't a princess. "How badly injured?"

The woman took Lamprophyre's hand in hers, and Lamprophyre recognized the cold hand from earlier. "Just relax while I examine you." In her other hand, she held a palm-sized jade sphere she placed over Lamprophyre's heart. She rolled the sphere across Lamprophyre's torso and then up to her shoulders and down her arms. Then she removed the blanket and ran the sphere from Lamprophyre's hips to her ankles. Lamprophyre discovered she was wearing a shapeless pale green tunic that came to the middle of her thighs, softer than the blanket and very thin.

Finally, after rolling the sphere over the soles of Lamprophyre's feet, which tickled, the healer put it away into the front of her tunic and smiled. "The stab wounds are entirely healed. You will need rest for a while, but you should make a full recovery."

"So why can't I move?"

Mareet's smile faded. "One of the blows nicked your spine, and we immobilized you to treat that wound. But soon you'll have your body entirely restored. It's just important you not wrench your spine before it's healed."

Lamprophyre listened to her thoughts and heard nothing to indicate she was lying. "How long have I been here?"

"You were brought in around half past seven last night, and it's nearly noon now." Mareet smiled again. "Can we send word to anyone? The palace?"

Nearly noon. Rokshan must be out of his mind with worry. "Please have someone tell Prince Rokshan where I am?"

"Of course. And I'll have someone bring you a meal soon. You won't feel hungry right away, but you should eat to keep your strength up." Mareet squeezed Lamprophyre's hand gently, then released her. "You were very lucky, princess. Whoever your attackers were, they intended...no, I'm sorry, I shouldn't distress you."

"They intended my death," Lamprophyre said.

Mareet hesitated, then nodded. "I don't know all the details, but one of the people who stopped to help you was a healer on his way to work here. He was carrying enough moonstone to keep you from bleeding to death. Jiwanyil must value your life, to send such a miracle your way."

Lamprophyre felt numb from more than the healing. "A miracle," she agreed.

When the woman was gone, Lamprophyre closed her eyes and relaxed into her immobility, not straining to move anymore. She didn't think Jiwanyil cared about the fate of a dragon, and Mother Stone never reached into the mortal realm, but divine intervention aside, she had been incredibly lucky. Though Jiwanyil had intervened at her plea twice before, so maybe...

She let out a deep breath. It didn't matter. She wouldn't be any less alive if it was pure luck. The entity had struck at her again, and she'd survived against the odds. And Corporal Ahladh had not.

She tried to feel anger at him for failing in his duties, but she couldn't help seeing his startled face in memory, the spreading blood-stain, and that made it hard for her to resent his failure. Maybe there was nothing he could have done. She was the one who'd walked into the middle of the crowd, allowing the assassin to get close enough to stab Ahladh, so maybe the whole thing was her fault.

The door opened, and a man in healer's black entered. "Let's get you moving, my lady," he said with a cheery grin. He carried a stack of pillows and arranged them beneath Lamprophyre so her shoulders were propped up. It was a more comfortable position than lying flat, and she told him so.

"We do what we can to ease your recovery," he said. He reached into a square of black fabric stitched to the front of his tunic and with-drew a thin gold chain and a handful of lace agates carved into thumb-sized flat discs with holes in their centers. Whistling, he threaded three discs onto the chain, weighed them in one hand, then added a fourth and dropped the rest back into the pouch. Lamprophyre exam-ined the fabric pouch closely. How useful, to have a pouch sewn into your clothes and not swinging free where any thief might snatch it!

The healer reached around behind Lamprophyre's neck with the chain and fastened the clasp so the four discs rested on her chest above her breasts, just above the chlorite artifact and her room key. She craned her head as best she could to watch him brush each disc gently with his left forefinger. As he touched each one, it glowed with a pale light that set the lacy bands of the stones into sharp relief. Instantly the aches in her shoulders and arms and neck lessened, and she moved her fingers and then her arms gingerly, feeling as though she needed to be careful or she might break something. Which was ridicu-lous, but being paralyzed, even temporarily, had shaken her.

"Take my hand, my lady, and squeeze as hard as you can." The healer extended his hand, and Lamprophyre took it easily and did her best to crush it. She could tell it was a weak grip, but the healer's smile broadened, and he said, "Careful now, I'll need that hand later." He withdrew from her grasp and patted her hand lightly. "Practice moving your hands and arms, and someone will bring food shortly. Then as soon as your spine is all right, we'll restore the rest of your movement. You'll be able to walk out of here under your own power in a couple of hours."

His brisk certainty reassured Lamprophyre more than Mareet's calmness. When he left, she flexed her arms and opened and closed her hands, then ran her fingers over her stomach and upper legs, which was all she could reach because she couldn't bend at the waist. She reminded herself that this was temporary and folded her hands across her stomach.

She felt alert enough, and calm enough, to worry about Rokshan and why he wasn't here yet. Yes, it took time to send a message, and suppose he wasn't at the palace to receive it? But she felt irrationally upset that he hadn't arrived yet.

Food arrived, a bowl of clear chicken broth and a stack of small round flatbreads, with berry preserves to spread on them. It smelled good, but Lamprophyre only managed half the bowl and a few rounds of bread before her stomach insisted it was full. Eating nearly lying flat was awkward, and she spilled more than a few drops on the cloth they spread beneath her chin, but she managed. Still Rokshan didn't come.

She lay quietly in bed and amused herself by listening to the thoughts of anyone who came within range. There weren't many of those, and almost all of them were preoccupied with healing matters. One person Lamprophyre thought must be very close, possibly next door, thought only of pain in slow, aching waves that kept him or her from coherent thought. She wished she had a book to read. She wished Rokshan were there.

When the door opened, she tried to sit up and managed to lift her shoulders from the pillows. "Try not to move too much," Mareet said. Lamprophyre, disappointed that she wasn't Rokshan, sank back into the pillows.

Mareet didn't react as if she'd noticed Lamprophyre's disappointment. She was accompanied by the healer who'd used the agates on her and another man, this one wearing a red tunic. Both men were considerably taller than Mareet, which made them a lot taller than Lamprophyre.

Mareet removed the blanket covering Lamprophyre and tugged the soft gown up until her belly was exposed. The air was cool against Lamprophyre's bare skin. She noticed the men had turned their backs —well, her female parts were exposed now, and it was polite of them not to stare, but she had thought healers, who had to see all sorts of human bodies, wouldn't have the same modesty reaction that always flustered Rokshan.

Mareet felt along Lamprophyre's belly, pressing gently as she moved her hands from the strange hole in her stomach across to her hips and then to just above her female parts. "Can you feel that?"

"Of course."

Mareet's hands moved back up, still pressing, around the curves of her hips and to her bottom. Then she went back to touching Lamprophyre's hip bones, this time on her back near her spine. "Feel that?"

Lamprophyre nodded. The touch was a little painful from Mareet pressing harder now.

"Now I'm going to finish the healing," Mareet said. "You'll feel a tug on your spine, but it won't hurt."

She reached into the pouch sewn into her clothes—really, it was so clever—and moved her hand as if finding something by touch. "There," she said, withdrawing a slender spindle-shaped stone the length of her middle finger. Its mottled green and black polished surface gleamed dully in the white magical light. Lamprophyre gasped.

It was serpentine.

CHAPTER THIRTY-ONE

W ithout thinking, Lamprophyre grabbed Mareet's hand, gripping it hard enough that the spindle cut into Mareet's flesh. Mareet gasped in pain and surprise. "What are you—"

"Where did you get that?" Lamprophyre demanded. "Where?"

"Let go of me," Mareet said. Her voice wasn't pleasant anymore. Despite her plump, rosy cheeks, she had the look of someone whose confusion was rapidly giving way to anger.

"Tell me!" Lamprophyre exclaimed. "This is important!"

Mareet wrenched her hand away from Lamprophyre's grasp. "This stone is extremely powerful. Grabbing it like that could have seriously injured both of us."

Lamprophyre closed her eyes and drew in a deep breath, which she let out slowly, willing herself calm. "I know it's powerful," she said. "I'm sorry. I was surprised to see it. I didn't know..." That wasn't true, though. She'd read that some adepts believed serpentine could be used in healing. But to see it here, wielded so casually—it was an even less likely coincidence than the one that had saved Lamprophyre's life. "What is it for?"

Mareet's expression softened. "It produces a change," she said. "Spine and nerve injuries don't heal the way the rest of the body does.

302

They can't be convinced to repair themselves. So this stone instead transforms the injured part back to the way it was before it was injured. It's not healing the way we understand it, really, but it still repairs you. There's no need for fear."

"I'm not afraid. But—" Lamprophyre bit her lip, feeling torn by indecision. Transformation. So it was possible. The question was, could someone here use serpentine to transform her whole body?

"I'm sorry I interrupted," she said. "Please continue. But I'd like to know more about the transformation afterward."

Mareet tugged on Lamprophyre's gown to cover her. "Let's get her on her side," she said to the men. With no effort, the two men lifted Lamprophyre and turned her so she lay on her side facing the door. One of them positioned himself at her head, the other at her feet, and both held her securely in place so she didn't rock forward or backward. Lamprophyre held still anyway. She felt tense again, wondering what it would be like to have her body altered. She hoped the magic wouldn't reach too far into the past for a restoration. It might kill her to have part of her body become draconic again.

Mareet walked around behind Lamprophyre and rucked up the gown again, exposing her from the waist down. "This won't hurt," she reassured Lamprophyre. Lamprophyre felt cool stone touch the base of her spine. A warm trickle spread upward and downward from the spot. Then she felt something tug gently on her spine, as if someone had wrapped her fingers around the bones and pulled them into a new, better arrangement. The warmth ceased, and Mareet removed the stone and pulled the gown down over Lamprophyre's bottom.

"Just one more thing," the healer murmured, and Lamprophyre again felt cold stone touch her back, though the coldness was damped by the cloth between the stone and her skin. Mareet rolled the stone orb over Lamprophyre's spine, from her hips to the base of her skull. "Perfect," Mareet said, removing the stone. "You're as good as new."

Lamprophyre let out a deep breath. "Thank you," she said.

The men laid her on her back again, and the one who had given her the agate necklace removed it from around her neck and threaded four more discs onto it before returning it. When he'd made the stones glow with the touch of his finger, the mild aches in her legs and hips vanished, and she was able to move her lower joints with ease.

"You're healed now," Mareet said, "but we'll let the lace agate work on you for a while, restoring your strength so you won't need to be carried."

"Thank you. All of you," Lamprophyre said. "Now, about the serpentine—"

Mareet examined the stone spindle as if she'd forgotten she held it. "I'd be happy to answer your questions, but they'll have to wait. I have three more patients to treat. I'll speak with you before you leave, is that all right?"

Lamprophyre thought curiosity might kill her before then, but there was no help for it. "That's fine, just please don't forget?"

Now Mareet turned her inquiring gaze on Lamprophyre. "No one's ever been this curious about this stone. I admit I'd like to know why. But I really do have to leave." She dropped the serpentine into her pouch. "I promise I'll be back."

The three left the room, the male healer giving her a friendly smile before shutting the door behind him. The moment they were gone, Lamprophyre sat up and swung her legs over the side of the bed. It was tall enough that her feet dangled, unable to reach the floor. She felt no dizziness, no aches, but her legs and arms felt as weak as if she were recovering from cave sickness. She started to stand, but changed her mind when her foot touched the floor and she wobbled. Standing and walking could wait.

She tucked her legs back under the blanket and rearranged the pillows so she could sit more upright. Now she wasn't just bored, she was impatient. She made herself concentrate on her breathing, on filling her lungs with air and letting it stream out of her again. She felt the steady thrum of her heart as it sent blood coursing through her body. She listened to nearby thoughts until the nearby person who was still in pain threatened to drive her mad with impatience, then she blocked the thoughts and cast about for something else to do. Review the stones whose magical effects she knew, she could do that. Bloodstone, good against disease. Emerald, wealth. Agate—well, now she knew lace agate restored strength. She could add that to her book.

The door flung open hard enough to slam into the wall. Rokshan burst through the doorway and came to an abrupt halt at the foot of her bed. Behind him, Lamprophyre heard voices raised in complaint before the door swung shut, blocking them out. Rokshan's chest heaved as if he'd been running, and his eyes were wild and his hair disordered. He looked like a madman.

"Finally," Lamprophyre said, feeling her impatience grow even as she was relieved to see him. Irrationally, she added, "Where have you been? I—"

It was all she managed before Rokshan took two swift steps to her side, swept her into his arms, and pressed his lips to hers.

A thrill of sensation that had nothing to do with magic shot through her. His lips on hers were hard and insistent, but this close, she couldn't help hearing his thoughts, which were a mad jumble of fear and pain and relief and a warm, urgent passion she knew was desire, and his roughness broke her heart. She put her arms around him and returned his kiss, not caring that she didn't know how because she could feel Rokshan's unhappiness melting into joyful pleasure at having her in his arms, kissing him.

His kiss became more gentle, still firm, but not as uncomfortable as at first. He threaded his fingers through her hair, sending another thrill through her. Now she could appreciate the amazing sensation of his lips touching hers, how sensitive the skin was, how that smallest touch warmed her whole body. No one had ever told her how miraculous kissing felt, though maybe it was impossible to describe.

She gently ran her fingers over his cheek, brushing past the smooth skin and over the burn scars. They were even smoother than his unburned skin, slippery narrow ridges that felt almost as nice under her fingers as the rest of his face. No woman would reject him for his scars if she knew what they felt like—and then she remembered *she* was the woman in his life, and a powerful surge of emotion thrilled through her, warming her body in unexpected ways.

His hands had strayed from her hair to her back, and he put his hands low on her hips and pulled her closer so her body pressed against his. Again desire shot through her, and she realized she was breathing heavily and her heart beat too rapidly. His skin felt so warm and smooth she wanted to touch more of it, to feel his skin against hers. She groped for the hem of his shirt and pulled on it, exposing his stomach. Here, too, the scars felt natural, a part of him she wanted to know more of. "Rokshan," she murmured, "what's happening?"

Rokshan kissed her deeply and then withdrew. Lamprophyre, her lips ready for another kiss, drew in a sharp breath and reached for him again. He took her hands and held them clasped in his, preventing her removing his shirt. "And that," he said with a smile, "is why I shouldn't come to your room at night."

Still breathing heavily, Lamprophyre realized her gown was rucked up around her waist beneath the blankets. Her whole body ached with longing for his touch. "That was being ready for sex?"

"That was very much being ready for sex, and I'm glad we only have the illusion of privacy here, because I'm starting to reconsider my promise." Rokshan sat on the edge of the bed, her hands still clasped in his, and Lamprophyre shifted to make room for him. "Knowing you nearly died is the sort of thing that makes humans want to celebrate life, and sex is an important part of that celebration."

"I didn't understand how powerful that desire was." Lamprophyre leaned back against the pillows and willed herself calm. "I don't know if it's like that for dragons. For the first time, I think there's something about humanity that is truly wonderful."

"How generous of you," Rokshan teased. Then the smile fell away from his face. "I only know you were attacked. Why didn't your guard protect you? I assume you didn't disregard my instructions not to go out alone."

"Of course not. Corporal Ahladh...I don't know if he was at fault or not. We were pressed closely in the crowd, and I think those attackers were very good..." The memory she'd been suppressing, of knives plunging into her body, took her off guard, and she closed her eyes and let out a shuddering breath. "I think Kulat arranged it. Rokshan, how could he do that?"

Rokshan's hands tightened on hers. "Tell me everything," he said in a flat, emotionless voice.

She managed to tell the whole story without crying or gagging on the memories, including waking up twice in the healing center and what happened afterward. Rokshan listened in silence until she was finished, then said, "You were luckier than we deserve, I think. That someone capable of healing you came to your rescue...Lamprophyre, that was a close escape."

"Close twice over. I might have been paralyzed if—" She gasped. "Rokshan, the healers use serpentine. She—Mareet—said it was for transformation. I think they might be able to restore me!"

Rokshan scooted closer and helped support her as she sat upright. "You didn't tell her the truth?"

"No." Lamprophyre leaned against his shoulder. "But I think I have to. The transformation she worked on my spine was perfect and painless. This has to be the solution."

Rokshan said nothing. His thoughts drifted in and out of hearing: *solution* and *lose her*. She put her arms around his waist and held him, not knowing what to say. The memory of kissing him still made her tingle. If she returned to her dragon body, she would never have that again. Twenty-four hours ago she would have scoffed at the idea that sex might be important enough to make her change her mind about being restored. Now...but it wasn't just about the physical pleasure, was it? It was how she'd felt peaceful and happy with Rokshan's arms around her, how she'd felt closer to him than she'd ever felt to anyone in her life. Losing that would be almost as bad as losing her true body had been.

"I have to try," she said. "You know I do."

"I know. And I want you restored." Rokshan's warm breath stirred the hair that fell over her forehead. She was almost resigned to the hair. "Let's talk to Mareet. Maybe it's not something she can do, but we have to try."

Lamprophyre nodded. "But I have to know if Kulat was involved."

"I was going to pay him a visit when word arrived that you'd been injured. Then everything else seemed unimportant."

"I understand. But if the entity reached him, and he doesn't know we know, maybe that's something we can use."

"I'm not sure how. The last time you eavesdropped on the entity, someone nearly died."

Lamprophyre hadn't thought about Zefira at all since taking her to the healing center for treatment. "Has she recovered?"

"I asked them to send word every day with news of her condition, and she's started to respond to stimuli, like bright lights or being poked. But she hasn't spoken, and they aren't sure how much of their speech she understands. I don't know how hopeful to be." Rokshan released her and stood. "I think I should investigate Kulat sooner rather than later. When will Mareet be available?"

"She said, later, but I don't know how much later she meant."

Rokshan nodded. "I'll be back as soon as possible. Hopefully with good news." He bent and kissed her, gently. "I love you. I hope Mareet has a solution."

He wasn't fully in contact with her anymore, so his thoughts were inaudible, but she almost broke her rule about listening to him because she desperately wanted to know which of those last two statements, so incompatible, were true.

She lay back against the pillows after he left and stared at the ceiling. She was starting to feel disoriented by the magical lights and longed to see the sun again. Based on what Mareet had said, it was probably midafternoon by now, maybe a little later. With luck, she'd be able to go home by sunset. She caught herself. Back to the palace, not home. The palace couldn't possibly be home. She didn't even think of her comfortable embassy as home. The mental slip embarrassed her.

She curled on her side, enjoying how easily her body moved now that it wasn't paralyzed, and closed her eyes. Sleep might help, though she didn't feel tired. It would pass the time, anyway. She went back to running through stones in her head, but kept being distracted by memories of kissing Rokshan and feeling his skin against her hands. Had she really been dismissive of him for fearing what might happen if they were alone in the privacy of her room? That, too, embarrassed her.

The sound of the door opening startled her. She wiped drool from her open mouth and realized she'd fallen asleep without knowing. Mareet entered, nudging the door wide with her foot as her hands busied themselves putting her hair up. "Sorry, did I wake you?" she asked.

"It's all right, I didn't want to sleep long. What time is it?"

"Almost five in the evening. How do you feel? If you're strong enough, you're free to leave."

Lamprophyre sat up and stretched. "I feel just as I always do, though maybe a little achy."

Mareet nodded. "That's normal." She approached Lamprophyre and withdrew the serpentine spindle from her pouch. "You wanted to know about this?"

"Sort of," Lamprophyre said. "What kinds of transformation is serpentine capable of?"

"Serpentine? Why do you call it that?" Mareet brought the spindle close to her eyes to examine it. She looked as though she expected it to transform in front of her. Her thoughts said *yes, the name fits, wonder why no one told us.*

"That's its name. It looks like snakeskin, I suppose—I don't know much about snakes." Most snakes were too small to register with dragons.

"We just call it alteration stone. It comes from southern Sachetan. Very rare." Mareet lowered the stone and said, "How do you know anything about it? We use it rarely."

"Before I answer that, can you answer my question?" Lamprophyre said. "What can serpentine transform?"

Mareet frowned. *Hard to explain*, she thought. "I'm not sure I understand. An alteration stone—serpentine—changes something from its current state to an earlier state. You could say it taps into the body's memory of itself, though of course there's no such thing. It's just a useful metaphor. At any rate, serpentine can replace broken parts with whole ones, provided you take action quickly. The longer you wait, the harder the transformation is."

That sent a chill of fear through Lamprophyre, but she refused to dwell on it. "How long?"

"We're not sure. Days, maybe weeks. Half a year is far too long, we know that."

"And is it only parts?"

"Only living tissue or bone, certainly. It works on animals as well as humans, if that's what you're asking."

"No. I mean, could you transform an entire person? Like, if someone were burned over most of their body, could serpentine transform them into their earlier, unburned self?"

Mareet pursed her lips in thought. "I don't know. No one's tried that before. It would require...or maybe not. I'm not sure. Theoretically? Yes, I'd say it's possible." She dropped the serpentine into her pouch, frowning. "I should warn you that it would almost certainly be too late for Prince Rokshan. His injuries were sustained far too long ago."

Lamprophyre hadn't even considered suggesting that. To her surprise, Mareet's thoughts about Rokshan were affectionate, admiring even. Lamprophyre felt a stab of irrational jealousy she had to contain. "Why didn't someone do that when he was first injured? They told us —him—even postponing treatment by days would limit its effectiveness."

"Like I said, no one's ever tried such a whole-body procedure before. And serpentine has only been available here for a few months." Mareet blushed slightly and ducked her head. "I didn't tell you the healing I performed on you is not common. In fact, it's rather experimental. Maybe I should have told you, but there's no drawbacks to the treatment—if it fails, it simply does nothing. I judged it safe."

"I don't mind," Lamprophyre said, impatient with the woman's diffidence. "That's not important. It's not Rokshan who needs transformation. It's me."

Startled, Mareet raised her head and said, "You, your highness? But there's nothing wrong with you. If you...that is, if you're not satisfied with your weight, I can't perform such a drastic healing on you simply so you can lose a few pounds."

The idea was so ridiculous Lamprophyre laughed. "It's not that," she said. Mareet's thoughts when she looked at Lamprophyre were all admiring: *so pretty* and *wonder if Prince Rokshan cares for her, what a sweet romance.* They made Lamprophyre ashamed of her momentary jealousy.

She made a decision. She'd hoped Rokshan would be there for this, but she didn't want to wait and possibly lose Mareet's attention. "I have a secret I want to share with you," she said. "It's going to be hard for you to believe, but I need you to trust me, because you may be the only one who can help me."

Cryptic, Mareet thought. "How is that?" she said. She sounded calm, but her thoughts were agitated, wondering what secret the princess might have and whether it might be something Mareet would be honor bound to reveal.

Lamprophyre hesitated, going over possibilities in her head, looking for the most convincing way to tell this woman the truth. Finally, realizing there was no good way to reveal this, she let out a deep breath and said, "I'm not human. I'm a dragon in human form. My name is Lamprophyre."

CHAPTER THIRTY-TWO

Mareet blinked. Her forehead wrinkled, making her eyebrows come close to meeting in the center. "You're what?"

Lamprophyre kept her gaze locked on Mareet's eyes. If she looked away, she might lose the woman entirely. "I'm a dragon. The dragon ambassador Lamprophyre. Someone transformed me into a human, and I need to find a way to change back."

Mareet took a step backward, fumbling with one hand for the wall and then leaning against it as if her legs wouldn't support her. "But you're a princess," she said. "You have a family. If this is some kind of joke—"

"It's no joke." Lamprophyre kept her voice calm and certain, willing the sound to convince Mareet. "Everything about my human life was made up by Rokshan and me. When he returns, he'll tell you the same thing I just did. I swear it's true."

"It can't be true. It's impossible." Mareet's gaze swept over Lamprophyre's body, clearly looking for physical evidence of what Lamprophyre had told her. "No one can do anything like that, no matter how much magic they have."

"How sure are you of that?"

Mareet looked startled. "Well, it's obvious, isn't it? Or else we'd have heard about it before."

Now Lamprophyre had a dilemma. The reason it had never been done before, she was sure, was because no one but Evart had had a malign ancient entity whispering to them in darkness, instructing them in creating such an artifact. But Mareet didn't need to know this—or did she? Lamprophyre decided to hang on to that knowledge as a last resort. "The man who transformed me wanted to coerce me to do something," she said, clinging as close to truth as she could, "and knew that coercion would work better if I was a vulnerable human. I imagine no one's ever thought such a transformation was necessary. That doesn't mean it's impossible."

"Even so..." Mareet's voice trailed off. "Isn't there any part of you that is still dragon? Because as far as I can see, you're a disturbed young woman who wants to abuse a magical artifact that's still mostly experimental."

Lamprophyre ground her teeth. "Why would anyone do that? Isn't that as unlikely as the possibility that I'm really a dragon? And in that case, why would you believe that instead of what I'm telling you?"

The door opened. Rokshan said, "I found—oh." He entered the room and quietly shut the door behind him. "Did you tell her?"

Lamprophyre nodded. "We're discussing whether I'm a dragon or a madwoman."

"She's telling the truth," Rokshan said to Mareet. "She was transformed by an adept who wanted her fortune in exchange for turning her back. But he was killed, and his serpentine artifact was destroyed, and now we need someone who knows how to reverse the transformation."

Mareet's mouth, which had fallen slightly open, shut abruptly. "So both of you are in on it."

"Mareet, Lamprophyre is my best friend," Rokshan said. "I've done everything I can to protect her while she's in this vulnerable state, including keeping her identity a secret. I swear what we've told you is true. Lamprophyre only revealed the truth because you appear to be the only person who might be capable of restoring her. Please believe we're not trying to trick you or make a fool of you."

Mareet's thoughts raced like mad, circling between *dragon* and *if they're lying*. Impulsively, Lamprophyre said, "We're not lying, and if you knew anything about dragons, I could prove it. But I don't think there's anything I can tell you that will convince you. I have to hope you'll trust us."

She knew the instant Mareet made up her mind because her thoughts suddenly cleared, and Lamprophyre heard *what point in lying?* Mareet pushed off the wall to stand up straight and said, "All right. I believe you. But I don't know what you think I can do. I told Princess Lel—I mean, I told Lamprophyre no one's ever performed a full-body transformation. And to restore you to something the size of a dragon —I don't even know if we have enough alteration stone."

"She said it comes from southern Sachetan," Lamprophyre said. "The clutch could fly south for some. How much do you need, Mareet?"

Mareet eyed Lamprophyre again. This time, she was calculating in her head, words and numbers that made no sense to Lamprophyre. "I'm not sure," she said. She withdrew the serpentine spindle from her pouch and showed it to Lamprophyre and Rokshan. "Something this size contains enough magical power to perform as many as twenty restorations like the one I did on your spine. If it doesn't scale up, that would mean to transform you into a dragon we'd need a quantity of serpentine half your current weight."

"But Evart—the adept who turned me human—he used a wand with a stone only three times the size of that one," Lamprophyre said.

"I'll have to experiment, do some calculations," Mareet said. "Let's just assume for now that it won't require more than seventy pounds of serpentine. It's good to know what that other adept was capable of. It will give me something to aim for. But we need to act fast. How long ago was the transformation?"

"It was the day I brought her in with a broken arm," Rokshan said. "Eight days."

Mareet frowned. "It might already be too late. I don't want to give you false hope."

"I'd rather try and fail than not try at all," Lamprophyre said. "How soon will you know what it will take?"

"A few hours." Mareet's frown lightened. "I have an idea of how to make it work, but it might not be pleasant. Though I'm sure that doesn't matter to you."

Lamprophyre shook her head. "I just want my body back."

Mareet glanced from Lamprophyre to Rokshan, thinking *hard for them to be in love if they're different species* and *wonder if I'm doing them a favor or not*. But she only said, "Come back around eight tonight and I'll be able to tell you if it's even possible."

"Thank you," Lamprophyre said. "I owe you my life. Anything you want, if it's within my power, I'll do it for you."

"We can worry about that when you're a dragon again," Mareet said.

The sun was low on the horizon when Lamprophyre and Rokshan left the healing center. After so long isolated in the timeless silence of her artificially lit room, Lamprophyre felt as disoriented as she'd expected. She'd expected it to be earlier in the day despite what Mareet had told her. She blinked in the late afternoon light and said, "What do we do until eight?"

"Food," Rokshan said. "And then we deal with what I learned from Kulat."

"I almost forgot. Did you speak to him?"

Rokshan twined his fingers with hers and headed off down the street. "It's fortunate I found out where you were before I did. I might have ruined our chance at learning what he knows."

"I don't understand."

Rokshan's hand closed on hers more tightly, not enough to hurt, but enough that Lamprophyre could hear a whisper of thought: *almost lost you*. "There was an early morning ceremony today. Mother convinced me I should attend, though it wasn't compulsory. But it meant I didn't realize you weren't in your room until nearly nine. I spent some time looking for you in the palace and learned Dharan hadn't been there, which meant you hadn't gone to the library."

"I wonder what Dharan thinks happened to me?"

Rokshan shrugged. "He had lectures today, so he might not have realized you were gone, either. Anyway, after I couldn't find you in the palace, I went to the barracks to ask your escort whether anything had happened last night, only to discover the man hadn't returned. Captain Rogat had sent soldiers to investigate, but it was as if Corporal Ahladh and you had simply disappeared. Which is when I started to panic."

It was Lamprophyre's turn to squeeze his hand in reassurance. "Then what?"

"The soldiers returned while I was there, bringing the news that Ahladh was dead and you were missing. I'm afraid I tore into them with undeserved fury. They said the attack had been planned, as far as they could tell, and that made me fear you'd been captured rather than killed. So I was about to accost Kulat, given that it was in response to his summons that you'd gone into the city, but then word came from the healing center and I went there instead."

The thought of how Rokshan must have felt all morning made Lamprophyre's eyes prickle with tears. She blinked them away and said, "So you didn't speak with Kulat."

"Not this morning. I went there just an hour ago, and as I said, it's good I didn't storm his shop, ranting and accusing him of complicity with the assassins. When I arrived, *he* accosted *me*, very angry that you hadn't obeyed his summons and why didn't anyone respect his genius, things like that. He wasn't at all afraid the way he would have been if he'd planned the attack, or been coerced into helping with it."

Lamprophyre looked ahead to where the red sandstone of the coliseum rose to dominate the skyline. The view sent a pang of sadness through her as she remembered flying through its arches, followed by a pang of fear at how distant that memory was, as if her identity as a dragon was slowly fading. "But that doesn't make sense," she said. "How could the assassins have known where to attack me if Kulat didn't give them the information? Nobody else saw that note."

"There's a small chance someone passed them the information," Rokshan said, "and an even smaller one that they just got lucky. But I think it's easier than that. I think the entity encouraged Kulat to send for you, and told whoever is behind the assassins about his message."

For a moment, the world went hazy, and Lamprophyre needed Rokshan's hand to keep herself from falling. "Behind the assassins," she repeated. "That would mean someone who is conscious of the entity's presence. Someone like the Third Ecclesiast, or Evart."

"It's not impossible, and it's a good deal more probable than any of the other possibilities." Rokshan turned to enter a low-roofed inn from which delicious smells of meat and tomatoes and hot bread emanated. "And it's something we can attack directly. I have Tekentriya's spies working on finding the people behind these supposed extremist attacks."

"I thought you said that was a waste of time." The interior of the inn was dimly lit, and along with the low ceiling, it felt comfortable, as if no assassins could fit inside. Lamprophyre sat at the table Rokshan found for them, and tension fell away from her shoulders.

Rokshan waved at the young man wandering between the tables, apparently seeing to the patrons' needs. "I said it was a waste of time to look for a group of political extremists because that's not what our enemy is. But it doesn't matter what the spies think they're looking for so long as they find the right group, and the only good thing that came out of you nearly being killed is that Tekentriya's people now have strong evidence to further their investigation. They'll track down the assassins, we'll capture their leader, and then..." He paused to ask the young man to bring two of whatever was being served that day and a couple of mugs of ale. "I'm not sure what happens after that, but we'll figure something out."

"And I might be restored by then," Lamprophyre said.

"Which would make it easier, because you wouldn't be vulnerable anymore."

Lamprophyre nodded. The young man returned with two mugs, and she raised hers to her nose and sniffed. It didn't smell terrible, and that frightened her again, bringing back the fear that she was losing her true self. No dragon would find alcohol appealing. She sniffed again, then took a sip. It wasn't as disgusting as she remembered her first taste being.

"So what do you intend us to do with Kulat?" she asked. "Given that my listening to his thoughts could hurt him if the entity finds out."

"Nothing except be very wary of any requests he sends," Rokshan said. "If you could listen to his thoughts, it could prove whether he's been influenced by the entity, but I feel confident enough in my guess that I don't think it's necessary."

"That's so sad. I didn't think Kulat was evil, but I suppose he doesn't have to be evil to give in to the entity's promises, just vain or selfish."

"He nearly got you killed, so I'm not inclined to waste my sympathy on him." Rokshan drained his mug and signaled for another. Around them, whispers of conversation both audible and mental threaded through the air. Lamprophyre blocked out the mental murmurings so she could focus better on Rokshan's words.

"Then what is it we're going to do?" she asked.

"Talk to the spies and find out what they've learned." Rokshan fell silent as the young man placed first a mug of ale, then a flattened bowl containing yellow lamb stew in the center of the table. He followed it with two plates laden with rice and a shallow basket filled with bread triangles. "It might not be much yet, but I don't want to waste any time," he added when the young man was gone.

Lamprophyre poured stew over her rice and scooped some of the resulting mess into her mouth with a piece of bread. She would definitely miss this dish when she was a dragon again. "Do you think we'll be able to attack the entity through its victim, or whatever you want to call this leader?"

"I hope so. I'm tired of always reacting instead of acting. Whatever this entity is, it must have weaknesses, ones we never see because it's always hiding behind its victims. If we can get our hands on someone who's actively working with the creature, I think I can do something with that."

Lamprophyre nodded. Her mouth was too full to speak, but she didn't have anything to add. The two of them ate in silence until the bowl was empty and Lamprophyre felt comfortably full. She watched Rokshan as she ate. His mind was clearly elsewhere because he never focused on her, just on the walls or the stew bowl or his plate. She hoped he was coming up with a clever plan. She'd never realized before how many of her plans involved using her draconic body or abilities to overwhelm weak humans. The thought made her angry. Surely there was more to her than her ability to fly or breathe fire?

"Are you done?" she asked when Rokshan had sat for several minutes, not eating, just staring at nothing.

He startled, then smiled at her as if he knew he'd been caught daydreaming. "Sorry. I was thinking of ways to make our enemy—our human enemy—reveal the truth about his or her master."

"I wondered. Shall we go?"

Rokshan rose and extended his hand to Lamprophyre. "Only another hour or so, and then..."

Lamprophyre didn't have to ask what he meant. "And then," she agreed.

CHAPTER THIRTY-THREE

At nearly noon the next day, the coliseum walls cast almost no shadows, and Lamprophyre was grateful they weren't doing this in the heart of summer, when the sun's rays beat down mercilessly on the dark red earth and broiled the brains of anyone foolish enough not to seek shelter. She couldn't help remembering her first days in Tanajital, when she'd temporarily lived in the coliseum. How different it looked now that it was familiar. Paraveti tangal performances, Coquina's games, the races...she'd seen the coliseum from so many perspectives it was as comfortable as the embassy.

She sat with her back against the interior wall and crossed her legs under her. It felt natural enough a gesture she shuddered and almost uncrossed them. But that would be giving in to the fear that it was already too late for her, that she was more human than dragon, and she refused to be afraid. So she gripped her knees and told herself it would all be over soon.

In the center of the coliseum floor, Mareet directed Porphyry, Dolomite, and Orthoclase in drawing lines and curves in the earth. Somebody would likely be upset about them marring the smooth floor, but Lamprophyre didn't care. They'd trample it down afterward—no, *she* would trample it down, her first act in her restored body.

It was a large design, whatever it was. For the first time, she thought to wonder what the point of the designs adepts used was. Manishi always used a ritual circle. Evart had had one painted on his workshop floor. But if it was the stone that held the magic, why use a circle?

She yawned and stretched. If she didn't count the nap she'd had before revealing her secret to Mareet, she'd been awake nearly a full twenty-four hours. A very busy twenty-four hours.

She and Rokshan had met with Tekentriya's spies, which had been discouraging. It wasn't so much that they hadn't found anything yet as that the chief spy, or at least the one in charge of the spies working on this problem, was overtly dismissive of Rokshan and ignored Lamprophyre entirely. Chaita clearly shared Tekentriya's low opinion of her little brother despite Rokshan's experience as a military leader and his position as liaison to the dragon ambassador. In the end, Lamprophyre and Rokshan had left with the barest promise that the spies would tell Rokshan if they learned anything. Lamprophyre didn't think much of the likelihood that the chief spy would follow through.

"Don't fall asleep," Coquina said. "If I can't sleep, neither can you." The big grass-green dragon sat surrounded by piles of serpentine chunks of varying sizes and shapes. She held an oblong piece the length of her middle finger in the claws of her left hand and with her right first claw delicately shaved off flakes of stone thin enough to be translucent. It had already taken on most of a spindle shape, fat at the top and coming to a blunt point at the bottom.

"You had a decent night's sleep," Lamprophyre pointed out.

To her surprise, Coquina blushed. "Not really. Flint and I were awake for most of it."

"What, talking all night? You must really be attached."

Coquina blushed so hard her scales were pale brown. "We didn't do much talking."

Lamprophyre's tired brain finally figured it out. "Coquina!" she exclaimed.

Coquina shushed her, glancing around as if watching for eavesdroppers. "With everything being so confused, you being restored and all that, we didn't want to make a fuss about becoming pair-bonded. But it sort of just happened."

"It—but that's wonderful!" Lamprophyre got up and hugged Coquina's leg, which was all she could manage. Coquina put the spindle down and patted Lamprophyre's back gently enough it didn't hurt. "You shouldn't feel you need to keep it a secret. I think we could all use a boost."

"Time enough for that when you're you again, and I can turn the diplomatic duties back over to you." Coquina sighed and went back to shaping the rock. "Flint and I are ready to go home for a while."

"I hope we can make that happen."

A shadow passed low over them, and Flint alighted a few paces away. "I hope these are the right ones," he said. "There's very little jade to be had anywhere, and I paid more than it's worth for the moonstone." He dropped a little sack that barely clinked at Lamprophyre's feet and handed her a larger one, its surface knobby.

Lamprophyre rummaged through the large sack. "Mareet will have to confirm it, but I think this is right. She did say large moonstone beads, and I think these are the right size."

Flint took a seat beside Coquina, well away from her piles of stone. "Can I help?"

"Those need to be carved into ovals," Coquina said, pointing.

Flint captured her pointing hand in both of his and squeezed it lightly before letting go. "Happy to oblige."

"Congratulations," Lamprophyre said, and enjoyed how Flint's scales darkened briefly. He always was quick to blush.

"You told her? I thought we were keeping it a secret," he told Coquina.

"Female clutchmates don't keep secrets like that one," Lamprophyre said, "and can't you see she's bursting with happiness?"

Flint eyed his mate speculatively. "I don't suppose I look any different," he said, "but if anyone can tell—"

"In a little while, Lamprophyre will be restored, and we can tell everyone." Coquina set the completed spindle in a pile with several others about the same size and picked up a new oblong stone.

Flint settled on his haunches and began shaping a fist-sized knob of serpentine into a smooth oval. "I wonder why they need the design," he mused, jerking his chin in Mareet's direction. Dolomite had left the group to hover some thirty feet above the pattern. Mareet gestured for the other two to move back, exposing the full design to Dolomite's view.

"I was thinking the same thing," Lamprophyre said. Dolomite drifted downward, and Lamprophyre realized he held a long, pointed stick in one hand. Carefully maintaining his altitude just above the circle, he extended the stick to make a few lines. From her position, Lamprophyre couldn't tell what the design looked like, but Dolomite certainly seemed intent on making it perfect. Lamprophyre trusted his artist's eye to execute Mareet's vision.

Her curiosity roused, she rose and walked to the design as Dolomite rolled in midair and flew to one side, alighting well away from the carved lines. The pattern was large enough that even standing next to it, she couldn't make out the details. It was the sort of thing that would only make sense from above. Soon enough, she'd be able to fly over it.

"It has to be big enough to fit your dragon form," Mareet said, coming to her side.

"It's really happening," Lamprophyre said.

"Don't get too excited. This has never been done before, and it could still fail."

That warning was too late, but it didn't matter. Lamprophyre felt in her bones it would work. "Flint brought the rest of the stone. I hope it's the right kind."

Mareet followed her to the knobby sack and upended it, sending moonstone beads and carved jade roundels rolling everywhere. She knelt to gather them into one place. "Prince Rokshan isn't back yet?"

"No. That's not a problem, is it?" Lamprophyre raised her head to look at the sky, hoping Rokshan and Bromargyrite would appear.

"We're not in a hurry, at least no more than before. If it's too late for you, an hour's delay won't change that." Mareet separated moon-stone from jade and moved her lips as if silently counting. "More than enough. Now we need the gold wire, and then it's time."

Lamprophyre glanced at the sky again. She didn't want to point out that if it *wasn't* too late for her, they had no idea when it would become too late, and an hour might make all the difference in the world. Better not to embrace pessimistic thoughts.

Mareet was picking over the piles of shaped stone, selecting some and putting them in her tunic pouch. "You dragons are so much faster than a human lapidary," she said, "and much more precise."

"It's because we know stone on a fundamental level," Coquina said. "We feel its shape, and carving it properly is just a matter of freeing that shape."

Flint set down an oval and picked up another hunk of serpentine. "Orthoclase and Porphyry look done in." He gestured at the two dragons, who had retreated to the far wall and collapsed in boneless, exhausted piles. "I don't know if any dragon has made a flight like theirs before."

Lamprophyre looked at her clutchmates and felt a fierce love for both of her friends. "I can't repay them for that. All the way to southern Sachetan and back before dawn."

"We don't repay each other," Flint said. "You'd do it for them, and they know it."

"Even so..." Lamprophyre sighed and sat next to Coquina. "I guess it's being in this body that makes me feel obligated."

She heard the flap of enormous wings and looked up to see giant orange Bromargyrite descending over the western wall. Rokshan was off his shoulders almost before he'd landed. "I'm sorry that took so long," he said, waving a spool that gleamed gold at them. "The palace blacksmith was resistant to melting down that much gold and then drawing it as wire, but I couldn't exactly go to someone outside the palace and risk having to argue with them about whether I had a right to melt things from the treasury."

"You didn't steal from the king, did you?" Lamprophyre said, aghast.

"I had his permission, Lamprophyre." Rokshan saluted her with the coil of wire, then handed it to Mareet. "He wants it back if we can manage it. And he sent his best wishes for our success."

That warmed Lamprophyre's heart. Probably the king was motivated by politics, but it was still a nice sentiment.

Mareet was already threading moonstones onto the wire, pausing to twist intricate shapes between each bead. She patted her pouch and her hips and said, "I forgot to bring wire cutters."

"Let me," Coquina said. She slipped a claw over the length of wire Mareet held out to her and delicately cut it in two.

They all watched as Mareet made two dozen wirework and bead patterns the size of her two palms, flat and intricately woven with a long tail of gold wire extending from each. Lamprophyre picked one up to examine it. The wire wove in and out between the moonstone and jade beads, making pictures: abstract, barely recognizable pictures of animals like bears and cats. It reminded Lamprophyre of a medallion, though it was far too big for a human to wear as jewelry and too small to look good on a dragon. They might work as wall hangings.

Finally, Mareet set aside the spool of gold wire, much diminished, and gathered the wire medallions in her arms. "Everyone needs to stay away from the design now. Not Lamprophyre. Stand here—don't touch the lines."

Lamprophyre didn't need that warning. She made her way through the maze of grooves to where Mareet pointed, a large open area that would fit her when she was restored. At the center, she hesitated. "What do I do? Stand?"

"It doesn't matter. Whatever is most comfortable." Mareet's bird-like voice was sharper, more intent, but Lamprophyre could tell the adept wasn't really paying attention to her. She decided to sit. It might take time to complete the magic, and as sleepy as she was, standing made her even more tired.

Mareet pivoted, stepped wide, and made another turn, then bent to lay one of the medallions across two intersecting lines. Lamprophyre watched her take a few more steps before placing another one. It was like a dance, if dances had strange asymmetrical rhythms and pauses. Maybe some dances did. Ten days in a human body wasn't enough to teach her everything about humanity.

Mareet moved around the design until she was behind Lamprophyre. Lamprophyre didn't turn to continue watching her. Instead, she looked at Rokshan, who'd taken a position directly facing her. He stood with his hands loosely clasped behind his back—parade rest, he called it, some military thing or other. "It has the advantage of concealing your hands so no one can see if they're shaking," he'd told her with a grin.

Now he watched her, his expression impassive as if none of this meant anything to him. With no remorse, she listened for his thoughts. For a moment, the thoughts of everyone present barraged her, the dragons in varying states of thinking about their roles in the magic, Mareet focused on wiring serpentine ovals into each medallion, and then Rokshan's thoughts struck her like a blow to the face. *Maybe it won't work*, he thought, then *has to work* and *I can't bear this* before coming back to the start. His thoughts were awash in pain and sorrow and longing that made Lamprophyre want to leap from her position and throw her arms around him.

She couldn't, though, could she? There was no point in revealing her love for Rokshan just as that love became impossible. The clutch wouldn't be cruel or critical of her, but she was sure they would be horrified, just as she would have been if, say, Orthoclase had fallen in love with Anchala. And their reaction would make this a dozen times worse.

She deliberately blocked out all the thoughts surrounding her and smiled at Rokshan. He didn't smile back, and her mouth trembled and then fell in a still line. He wouldn't be attracted to her anymore when she was herself again, and her own heart felt as if someone had clawed it in two, because she had to admit what she'd known all along but refused to acknowledge: she would love Rokshan regardless of her shape, and she didn't care if that made her strange, or wrong, or broken. She would go on loving him, and he would go back to being her best friend. And she didn't know if she could take it.

"All right," Mareet said, startling her out of her reverie. "Lie back, Lamprophyre, with your legs straight and your arms by your side."

Lamprophyre drew in a deep breath and let it out slowly. "This will work," she told Rokshan.

Rokshan nodded once. "I know." His face was set and tense the way it got when he was suppressing a strong emotion. She wondered if he knew how much that expression gave away.

She lay back in the center of the design as instructed. The sun, almost directly overhead, burned her eyes, and she closed them and hoped that wasn't a problem. Sounds intensified: the scraping of Mareet's sandals against the ground, the rumbling of Bromargyrite saying something too quietly for her human ears to perceive, the thrumming of her heart that was already accelerating even though nothing had happened yet.

She concentrated on her breathing, in through the nose, out through the mouth, and as she did so, she gradually became aware of her body as if the air surrounding her were millions of tiny blades of grass, brushing against her skin. It wasn't painful, but it did make her feel as big as a dragon, every sensation magnified, every movement exaggerated.

Mareet stopped moving. Lamprophyre heard one of the dragons, she didn't know who, shift position with their wings scraping lightly together. Then there was silence. In her strangely enlarged state, the moments felt stretched thin, as if each beat extended longer than a dragon could hold her breath. And yet she felt no impatience. This was what she had waited for, and in that timeless space she felt she could wait forever and she felt she would die if something didn't happen soon, and those two things didn't feel at all incompatible.

Then she heard Mareet say, "This is it. Stay well back, everyone. I have no idea what this will look like, but you can't interfere no matter what you see, or it could kill her."

Lamprophyre was glad Mareet had explained that to her the previous night, when she and Mareet and Rokshan had discussed the plan. She didn't think she could hold on to her placidity if she'd learned about the possibility of death for the first time right now. Again she focused on breathing, slowly, trying to make her breathing match her heartbeats.

She became aware of heat, not the heat of the sun but something warmer and much closer—or maybe it was warmer because it was closer. It felt like a steady fire burning just a handspan from her left knee. She'd almost dismissed it as illusion when another little fire ignited beside her right shoulder. Gradually, more fires arose, all of them near her joints, until her whole body except for her head felt as warm as if it were the summer day she'd imagined.

Mareet moved again, this time rapidly pattering around Lamprophyre, sometimes coming close enough that Lamprophyre could hear her labored breathing. This, too, Mareet had explained: after laying out the serpentine spindles at key points near Lamprophyre's body, she had to spin each one rapidly enough that the first was still moving by the time she reached the last. Lamprophyre had been skeptical of this part, but Mareet had been confident, and really, what could Lamprophyre do if Mareet wasn't fast enough?

More breathing, though her heart beat faster and her breathing kept time with it. Dampness rose up beneath her arms and behind her knees and dotted her scalp with moisture. She heard a sigh from several throats, a disappointed sound. Mareet said, "It's all right. I'll try again. We have time."

"Should some of us help?" That was Orthoclase.

"It has to be activated by a single hand," Mareet said. "Don't worry. I'll be faster this time."

Once more Lamprophyre heard the pattering of Mareet's footsteps. Despite herself, Lamprophyre's tension increased, all her muscles tightening. She thought of Rokshan, who alone had been silent this whole time. She didn't need to hear his thoughts to know how he felt, but she wished she could hold his hand for comfort. His comfort, or hers, or both, she didn't know.

The pattering stopped. "Stand up, Lamprophyre!" Mareet shouted. "Stand up out of your body now!"

Fear and excitement propelled Lamprophyre into a sitting position, and then to her feet. This was the moment when it all came together, the medallions and the spindles reaching into the past to remind her body what it ought to be. As she rose up, she pictured herself stepping out of her human form like a butterfly shedding its chrysalis. She felt as light as goose down, as if she might fly away if she weren't careful. She flexed her wings, stretched her arms, and rose to the tips of her toes.

Then she opened her eyes. All around her, serpentine spindles spun, wobbling, and as she watched, they began to topple. Lamprophyre looked down at her body.

She was still human.

CHAPTER THIRTY-FOUR

She squeezed her eyes closed again and flexed her wings. This was an illusion, this body. She'd just seen what she feared seeing. But muscles shifted without the added weight of wings, just a shrug of the shoulders. She clenched her fists and strained with all her might, willing her body to burst out of its human prison, shredding flesh and snapping bone. All her joints burned with exertion. Realizing she was holding her breath, she let it loose with an explosive *pah* and opened her eyes.

This time, she didn't look at herself, but at the people surrounding her. Their expressions of sorrow and despair told her everything she needed to know. She turned to Mareet, who looked unusually pale and was sweating as much as Lamprophyre had. "Try again," Lamprophyre said. "We have plenty of stone. Try again."

Mareet's heavy breathing made her chest move in and out. "It won't work. You've been human for too long. The magic has nothing to catch—"

"*Try again!*" Lamprophyre screamed. She wound her fingers in her long, tangled hair and pulled, welcoming the sharp pain that shot through her scalp. "It *will* work! You did it wrong—fix this!"

"Lamprophyre," Rokshan said from behind her. She spun around to face him. He looked impassive again, his features unnaturally still. "It's too late. Trying again won't make a difference."

"Shut up!" she shouted. She stormed toward him, not trying to avoid the grooves. "You wanted this, didn't you? You wanted me to stay human! You made this happen!"

His expression didn't change aside from his lips tightening. Lamprophyre let go of her hair and shoved him, making him take a step back. "You got your wish," she said in a low, vicious voice, "and now I'm trapped forever, you...you..." Her eyes ached with unshed tears and her throat felt like it was closing up. "I thought you were my friend," she whispered, and burst into tears.

Arms went around her, and Rokshan drew her close, holding her tightly. She pressed her forehead against his chest and sobbed. How stupid she'd been to let herself believe Mareet's magic would work on her. It had been such a good idea—and that should have warned her. It was far too wonderful a possibility to be true. Just as the story in the burned book had implied. Every clue had pointed to this outcome.

Rokshan stroked her hair and whispered, "I'm sorry. I'm so sorry."

She nodded, unable to speak for crying. He ran his hand down the length of her hair again, sending a pleasant tingle through her she resented. She didn't want to feel good in any way, because nothing would ever be all right again.

"I'm sorry," Mareet said. Lamprophyre could barely hear her over the sound of her crying. "The magic did work. I mean, it did something, it didn't just fail. It's just been too long since you were transformed. We couldn't have known that without trying."

Lamprophyre wished Mareet would stop talking even as she appreciated what she was saying. It was the right magic, but it was too late. And they'd moved as fast as they could once they knew the magic was possible. Lamprophyre still couldn't help going over possibilities. If they'd told Mareet the truth the first day they'd met...if Lamprophyre hadn't wasted all that time pretending to be human...if she'd immediately pursued the information she learned about serpentine possibly being used in healing...but none of that made a difference. It had still failed.

Her tears were drying up, turning into shaking, tearless sobs. "It wasn't your fault," she whispered to Rokshan. "I didn't mean any of that."

"I understand," Rokshan said.

Peace, unexpected and welcome, threaded its way into her heart. As miserable and despairing as she was, it still meant something to be held by her love and to feel the warmth of his love for her. His thoughts drifted in and out, audible because she was standing in the circle of his arms: *love* and *not at this cost* and *can't stay like this forever*, and her heart ached with joy to know he didn't feel happiness at her plight.

She wiped her eyes and stepped away from him, aware of the clutch's misery. "All right," she said. "That didn't work. I don't know what to try next."

"Is there anything else?" Dolomite said. "I thought this was the last chance."

Lamprophyre winced inwardly. Trust Dolomite to come out with the most tactless comment possible. But he was too sweet and guileless to hate. "We still don't know how Evart did it," she said. "He used serpentine, so it wasn't whatever Manishi tried, and I wasn't human before this, so his magic didn't reach into the past to turn me into an earlier self. I think there's still a possibility out there."

"I'm sorry, Lamprophyre, but I'm discouraged," Coquina said. "You've been searching those books for half a dozen days with no success. You might be right about there being a solution, but how are we going to find it?"

"I think we need to set this aside for the rest of the day," Rokshan said. "Orthoclase and Porphyry are exhausted, and so am I, and Lamprophyre hasn't slept either. If there's a solution, we're more likely to find it if we're not sleep-deprived."

Lamprophyre hated that idea. She felt more driven than ever to find a true solution. But Rokshan was right, and now that her misery and disappointment weren't so immediate, weariness crept over her, seeping into her bones and muscles.

"Mareet, I want you to take the serpentine," she said.

Mareet looked startled. "That's a fortune. I can't. Besides, we have no use for that much stone."

"Then take as much as you can use. With my thanks. You very nearly pulled off a miracle."

"I don't know if I deserve thanks," Mareet said. "I should never have given you false hope."

Lamprophyre bent to pick up the nearest medallion. "It wasn't, though. It's nobody's fault that we waited too long. I'm sorry I lost my temper—I was just—"

"Horribly disappointed," Mareet said with a smile. She held out her hand for the medallion. "Perfectly understandable."

The other dragons were busy gathering the medallions and the remaining stone. Mareet filled a small sack with stone spindles and dropped the medallions atop it. "Good luck, Lamprophyre," she said. "I don't know how appropriate this is, but I'll pray to Jiwanyil on your behalf."

"Thank you," Lamprophyre said. Probably Mareet shouldn't propitiate the human god for a dragon's sake, but Jiwanyil had intervened in Lamprophyre's life before, and Lamprophyre wasn't so proud as to reject someone's well-meant wishes.

When Mareet was gone, Porphyry said, "I'm sorry to leave so abruptly, but I really am exhausted. Why don't you come to the warehouses in the morning, Lamprophyre, and we can talk about a new strategy."

"Good idea," Bromargyrite said. He was gathering the rest of the serpentine. "I'll keep an eye on this stuff. If we do find Evart's solution, we'll need it."

"Do you want a ride back to the palace?" Coquina asked.

Lamprophyre shook her head. "I want to walk. Clear my head." Adding the terror of flying to the burden of failure was more than she could bear.

She looked around at the coliseum again as the dragons took off into the sky. Everything was so colorful, the deep sandy red of the coliseum stones, the brightness of Bromargyrite and Porphyry contrasting with the darker colors of Dolomite and Flint like bits of paper blowing in the wind. It was irrational to think everything should be somber and dark like the city was in mourning with her, draped in black the way humans did for a death.

"Lamprophyre," Rokshan said. She turned to see his outstretched hand. "Let's go."

She trudged through the streets beside him, barely noticing the crowds. They, too, were as cheerful as if they didn't know her life had ended. She knew she was being overly dramatic, she knew this wasn't really the end, but she wanted to indulge herself in misery for a while. It was something dragons did when they lost a loved one to Mother Stone, curl up and let anger and sorrow overcome them for a few thousand beats. She didn't know if it was the same for humans, but right now she didn't care. She was going to cling to her draconic identity for as long as she could.

When they passed the parkland and were crossing the grassy area toward the palace's grand front entrance, Rokshan said, "There's a ceremony tonight. Part of the wedding festivities. I think you should go."

Dread swept away her anger and sorrow for a few beats. "I don't want to go," she said, knowing she sounded whiny. "And I don't see why I should. I'm not actually Lady Lelitha."

"You do still need to protect your identity," Rokshan pointed out. "And you're not helping yourself if you sit in your room and mope."

His advice irritated her, the more so because she felt deep down he was right. She didn't want to give him the satisfaction. Not yet. "It's probably boring," she said. "I'd rather stay in and read."

"And miss seeing Auntie Piya's monstrosity of a house?" Rokshan said. He smiled at her, a wicked, amused smile. "She has the most extensive collection of atrocious art objects in all of Gonjiri. You know how much you love looking down on humans and their appalling artistic taste."

"I do not!" Lamprophyre exclaimed. "Humans have pretty art, too. It's just that you also have horrible things no intelligent creature should give space to in their caves. Or houses. You know what I mean."

"Well, this is your chance to see a lot of them all in one place. Auntie Piya is hosting a dedication for the happy couple. Anchala and Torannum each select something symbolic of themselves to dedicate to their marriage—something they're willing to give up to make their marriage stronger. It's usually interesting and doesn't take more than an hour." Rokshan stopped and swung her around to face him. "We'll go together and make fun of Auntie Piya's horrible taste, all right?"

She could hear scraps of his thoughts, enough to know how hard he was trying to cheer her up. So she smiled, and said, "All right. But they had better be more awful than I can imagine."

"She has a half-scale statue of the god Meyari plated with gold, with leaves carved from gemstones the size of walnuts," Rokshan said. "It's so gaudy the Archprelate's palace refused to take it when she donated it to them five years ago. I'd never heard Khadar be so tactful in my life."

Lamprophyre shuddered. "Now I won't be happy until I've seen it."

Lamprophyre stood beside the drooping golden willow boughs and stared in rapt astonishment. "Your description was totally inadequate," she breathed.

"Words don't capture it," Rokshan agreed.

Lamprophyre's gaze followed the line of the branches to where they emerged from the golden trunk. The artist—if you could dignify the thing's creator with the title—had captured the god's form as if she were in late autumn, with only a few leaves clinging to her branches. But... "Rokshan, I don't know much about trees," she said, "but aren't those oak leaves?"

Rokshan smirked. "You noticed that. So did the High Ecclesiasts. If Auntie Piya wasn't such a devout supporter of the faith, there would have been an eruption that she'd dared offer such a flawed rendition of the God. Like I said, Khadar rose to new heights of tact in refusing."

Lamprophyre shuffled sideways to get a new perspective on the thing. "What exactly did Khadar say to keep Piya happy? Or does he have to avoid her at gatherings the way I do?"

That made Rokshan chuckle. "He praised her for her generosity and said the piece would receive far more attention, and therefore bring greater glory to Meyari, if it stayed in her house rather than being shut away in the Archprelate's palace. I'll say this for Auntie

Piya, she's very generous in opening her home to visitors interested in art. If she had better taste, imagine what a gift that would be."

Lamprophyre glanced around. "You're so right."

She had never been inside a private home before and hadn't known what to expect, aside from how Piya's home would likely be vividly colorful on the inside where its outsides were a bland beige color. As with the art, her imagination hadn't come close.

Piya's house was unexpectedly lovely to Lamprophyre's eyes, with arched doorways leading visitors through a series of wide, high-ceilinged corridors lined with statuary and paintings. The art was gaudy—Rokshan had been right about that—but someone with a real eye for beauty, likely not Piya, had laid it all out in a pleasant, sensible way in which different styles and artistic visions met harmoniously. The walls were all stark white, but that only drew the eye to the extraordinary colors and shapes. Lamprophyre inhaled, and smelled again a hint of cinnamon sweetness. She wouldn't be surprised to learn the unknown designer had included fragrances in her presentation.

The corridors let out in this large, round room where the statue of Meyari occupied the center. The room was tall enough, rising more than a dragonlength to its domed ceiling, that the insane artist might have created a full-sized statue and still had room beneath the dome. Lamprophyre tried to estimate how much gold it would take to cover such a statue and failed.

The dome wasn't plaster, but an iron framework fitted with ten curved glass panes off which light from many dozen magical lamps reflected, making the night sky invisible. Lamprophyre tilted her head to look at the glass more directly. It imperfectly reflected the people and art objects beneath like so many golden mirrors. She resisted the urge to straighten her impossible hair. Too bad she'd promised Rokshan she wouldn't cut it, because it was unusually unmanageable tonight.

Rokshan took her hand, startling her out of her distraction. "Come look at this," he said.

The room was more crowded than it had been when they arrived, filling up with nicely-clothed men and women who strolled around the perimeter of the room admiring the wall art, or stood beside the

Meyari statue in silent...well, probably not admiration. Appalled astonishment, maybe?

Rokshan led her to where two short staircases faced each other, curving along the wall to rise to a semicircular platform about as tall as Lamprophyre. A man wearing a knee-length pink robe the color of a rosebud that bared one shoulder swept past carrying a tray of glasses, most of which contained a dark red liquid. Lamprophyre stared after him. All right, she didn't know any more about human clothing than she did trees, but that had looked like a woman's robe, what with the gold floral pattern along the hem and neckline. "Rokshan," she began.

"Auntie Piya's late husband," Rokshan said, not appearing to notice the pink man. He gestured at a framed portrait hanging on the wall beneath the platform. "Observe and be awed."

Lamprophyre looked. It took her a moment to realize what she was looking at. Then she covered her mouth to hold in a laugh. "He looks like one of those birds with long thin legs," she choked. "Only purple."

"The portrait painter forgot to add in background," Rokshan said, "which is why it looks like he's standing on one leg. There's supposed to be a stool under his raised foot." He glanced around. "God's breath, she sneaked up on us," he whispered. "Pretend you're impressed."

"Rokshan, I'd like a word with you," Piya said from behind them. "Isn't this painting marvelous? The artist really captured my late husband's essence." She glared at Lamprophyre. "Young Lelitha. Come to apologize?"

"Auntie Piya, thank you for the invitation," Rokshan said, overriding Lamprophyre's retort. "Lelitha has never seen a dedication before. I'm sure it will make an impression."

"I wonder," Piya said darkly, eyeing Lamprophyre as if she expected her to spout heresies any moment. "Rokshan, if you intend to court this young woman, you should realize what you are letting yourself in for. Disrespectful, without good manners, willful. Your parents should not approve of such a match."

"I don't think—" Lamprophyre said hotly.

"Thank you for your opinion, Auntie, you know how I respect it," Rokshan said, cutting Lamprophyre off again. "Don't you think Lelitha can only benefit from the good examples of others? Particularly ones with your experience and wisdom."

Lamprophyre rolled her eyes. She couldn't tell if Rokshan was serious or if he was subtly making fun of Piya. But Piya took his words at face value. She preened. "That's very true, Rokshan. Your parents must be proud of having raised such a respectful son. Lelitha, see that you are deserving of this young man. You are clearly misguided rather than inherently bad, and that is something you may yet improve upon. I declare, I do not know what this generation is coming to."

Lamprophyre opened her mouth to protest, and Rokshan squeezed her hand painfully hard, making her gasp. "I believe it's almost time for the dedication, Auntie, and we shouldn't keep you from your guests," he said, and dragged Lamprophyre away past two more men in pink robes.

"She's *awful*," Lamprophyre said when they were well away from Piya.

"I know, but she can't hurt us." Rokshan gestured to one of the pink-robed men and took a glass off the tray. "You don't want this. Red wine is particularly strong-tasting."

"Is that what they do, serve drinks? Why do they wear women's clothes?"

Rokshan choked on his sip of wine. "Those are traditional servants' clothes, maybe a little outdated, but...all right, they do look like dresses." He sipped again. "Auntie Piya only hires men servants, and they all have to be handsome. She definitely appreciates the male form, and those uniforms show it off."

Lamprophyre looked at the nearest servant. "I suppose," she said, trying to slip into a woman's perspective. "They are certainly pleasingly muscular. I think—"

"Prince Rokshan?"

The speaker was a woman, dressed unlike the rest of the guests in plain dark trousers and a green shirt the same color as Dolomite. She also wore her hair cut short like a man, or like Tekentriya. "Chaita asks that you join her at the barracks. She's made a discovery."

"About the assassins?" Rokshan asked in a low voice.

The woman responded with a curt nod. "She asks for military assistance in bringing them down."

Rokshan turned to Lamprophyre. "Stay here. If I'm not back in time, don't leave alone. In fact, once Anchala is done with the ceremony, stick close to her and go back to the palace when she does."

Lamprophyre nodded. Rokshan squeezed her hand, lightly this time, and followed Tekentriya's spy through the increasing crowd to disappear through the nearest arched doorway.

Sighing, Lamprophyre went back to looking at the art and tried not to feel abandoned. It was a good thing Dolomite couldn't fit into Piya's house, because he would be appalled at Piya's taste. She passed by a series of paintings all by the same artist—no, upon closer inspection she realized they were cleverly sewn pictures formed by thousands of tiny colored stitches. The idea was interesting, even if the subject matter—dogs in human clothes—baffled her.

Another servant swept by and paused to offer her the tray. She waved him away politely. Maybe that was a mistake. Everyone else held glasses, and suppose she stood out? And it wasn't as if she had to drink the wine. Well, she wasn't going to chase down a servant. She'd just wait until one came past again.

She stopped in front of a carved wooden statue of a man maybe two handspans tall, holding a long, crooked staff with his other hand resting on an improbably fluffy sheep. It wasn't nearly as horrible as the rest of the collection, and she wished she could touch the smooth, warm wood. But even she knew that was uncivilized.

"So Piya's taste isn't entirely execrable," a voice beside her said. Lamprophyre turned and regarded an elderly man with white hair and a thick white beard. He had his attention on the statue, but said to her, "The subject matter is cloying, but the execution isn't bad. Though I admit I'm fond of rosewood, aren't you?"

"I don't know much about hu—about art," Lamprophyre said. "I'm not familiar with the differences between woods."

"See the dark grain against the rich brown of the wood?" the man said, extending a finger to follow the lines of the statue without touching it. "It's a characteristic of rosewood."

"I'll remember that," Lamprophyre said. "I think the sheep is very lifelike."

The old man chuckled. "A true master would capture the essence of the sheep and its master without resorting to facile representation." He turned his head and looked directly at her. "You can't escape me, Lamprophyre," he said in the same calm voice.

Lamprophyre stepped back, startled, and put out a hand to steady herself. It missed the statue by pure luck and landed on the plinth. "What did you say?"

"I said facile representation is the mark of the amateur," the man said. "Are you well?"

"I'm fine. Please excuse me," Lamprophyre said, and hurried away, not really knowing where she was going. Belatedly she tried to listen to the old man's thoughts, but the crowd's noise deafened her, and she blocked all thoughts from her hearing. Pausing near the stitched dog pictures, she calmed her breathing. That hadn't been her imagination, and it hadn't been the old man speaking. Somehow, the entity had reached out to her through him.

"...and I really don't see that it's any of her business," a passing woman said to her companion. She paused and turned her head to look at Lamprophyre, slowly enough to make Lamprophyre's skin crawl.

"I'm coming for you, Lamprophyre," the woman said.

Her companion's head turned as well. "Don't bother trying to escape," she said.

Lamprophyre gasped. The woman turned back to her companion and said, "I don't care if she is his mother, she's got no right to speak to me that way," and the two of them moved off into the crowd.

Lamprophyre bolted for the doorway and fled through the corridors. She made it almost halfway to the exit before common sense halted her flight. She couldn't leave alone. That might even be what the entity wanted, to scare her into going someplace where she had no defense against assassins with cruel knives. She made herself calm down, putting her hands on either side of a plaster statue of Katayan painted in colors too gaudy even for a real dragon. She needed to return to the room, wait for Anchala to be finished, then attach herself to the princess until she was safely back in the palace.

Unless the entity didn't care who Lamprophyre was with. Unless the entity was willing to kill everyone around her to get at her.

Lamprophyre let out one last deep breath and trudged back through the halls, not seeing any of the delightfully garish art. What she should do was get a message to Rokshan. She just didn't know how. Well, she knew who the servants were; maybe one of them could take a message. At the very least, they'd know someone who could.

She hurried back to the domed room to discover the ceremony had begun. At least, she assumed so from how Piya stood on the semicircular platform, flanked by Anchala and Torannum. Torannum held a fabric-wrapped bundle the size of his hand, and Anchala had a covered basket looped over her arm. "...great pleasure to host this dedication," Piya was saying. "The tradition dates back to the founding of Gonjiri, when..."

"Drink, madama?" a servant asked.

"No, thank you—wait!" Lamprophyre lowered her voice when the people nearest her gave her dirty looks for interrupting Piya's speech. "Can you get a message to someone for me?"

The servant bowed his head. "If you think it will make a difference, Lelitha," he said.

Lamprophyre froze. Across the room, Torannum had unwrapped his bundle and was displaying it to the crowd, but she didn't dare take her eyes off the servant to see what it was. "What did you say?" she asked, going for calculated ignorance.

The servant's smile twitched faintly wider. "So this is what you look like," he said. "I pictured you taller and more slender. You escaped my men once, but I don't think you'll manage it a second time."

Light dawned. "You're him," Lamprophyre breathed. "The entity's tool. The master of the assassins."

The smile flickered, then faded away. "I'm no one's tool," the man said. "But that won't make a difference to you. Tool or free man, I have sworn to see you dead."

CHAPTER THIRTY-FIVE

Lamprophyre didn't move. "You can't hurt me here. Unless your cunning plan involves you being taken and killed as well."

"Don't be so sure. I've evaded your friend's searchers this long." The man's smile returned. It reminded Lamprophyre of a creature from one of Dharan's books, a long scaly animal with a toothy, mirthless smile. "And I notice my men have drawn him off. He'll be devastated to know he failed to protect you."

"Shh," a nearby person said, half-turning to reprimand Lamprophyre. She ignored the woman.

"So this was on purpose?" she said in a low voice. "Your men let themselves be noticed as a distraction?"

The man shrugged. "They're used to moving in shadow. Striking from shadow. The fools in the military don't have a hope—"

"Will you be silent!" the same nearby person whispered.

The man who was certainly not a real servant turned on the whisperer, snarling. He overtopped the woman by half a handspan, and she recoiled and sidled away. "As I said, the military hasn't a chance of finding them," he said, as pleasantly as if he hadn't been beats away from violence just then. "Now you're going to come with me."

Lamprophyre glared at him. "I will not. I'm not a fool."

The smile returned, toothy and vicious. "You will," he said, "or I'll kill the princess and take you by force. It makes no difference to me, but I admit I like the idea of you walking out of here under your own power."

"You can't kill Anchala."

The man shifted his ridiculous robe, revealing a glint of steel along one thigh. "No one here is armed. No one will stop me. Your choice, Lelitha."

Lamprophyre looked past him to where Anchala stood at the top of the stairs, laughing with the rest of the crowd at something Torannum had said. Her life, or Anchala's. It wasn't even a choice. "Where?" she asked.

The man put a hand low on her back and gave her a gentle nudge. "Just walk."

Lamprophyre walked as slowly as she dared to the doorway. Having this man at her back made her skin crawl, even without knowing he had a knife. Rokshan had said he would return, and if she moved slowly enough—but that was stupid, wasn't it, because if the man was right about the skill of his subordinates, Rokshan might spend all night chasing them. There was no way he could come to her rescue.

The man didn't react as if her slowness bothered him. He just kept his hand on her back and exerted a gentle pressure to keep her moving forward. They passed through halls filled with terrible art, and Lamprophyre's gaze darted everywhere, searching for a possible weapon. Those little statues might work, if they were heavy enough. She sped up, stepping away from his hand, but the man matched her pace. "Don't bother attacking me," he said. "I'm stronger and faster. All you'd do is make me angry, and I don't think you want me dealing with you in anger."

"Why don't you just kill me now?" Lamprophyre said.

The man laughed. "You're not alone in wondering that. Let's just say I want to get to know you better. After all, I've pursued you for days—we ought to recognize the bond that makes between two people, yes?"

That made no sense. Desperate, Lamprophyre listened for his thoughts. They were far enough away from the domed room that all she heard from the crowd were distant, drifting scraps of sound, not enough to overwhelm her. To her surprise, the man's thoughts were more coherent than any she'd heard before, full sentences rather than fragments. It was as if he were talking to himself inside his head. A flash of memory, of the entity destroying Zefira's mind, made her hesitate for less than a beat. But this evil man intended her death, and she didn't give a damn what happened to him if the entity decided it was done with him.

She listened, slowing her steps further. *I'll take her back to the house and question her,* he was thinking. *Whatever the dark lady wants with her, I wonder if the girl will pay double to prevent it? Could mean a triumph for me.*

"Who hired you?" Lamprophyre asked. It was a bad idea to reveal that she could hear his thoughts, but if she could shift the conversation correctly, she could use the information she heard from him. If he could be bought, so much the better. Dark lady? If that meant the entity, Lamprophyre now knew twice as much about the creature as she had before. Though knowing the entity was female probably wouldn't help her.

"I'm surprised you don't know," the man said, thinking *It's hard to believe this tiny fat girl has enough enemies that she doesn't know which one wants her dead.* "You have that many enemies?"

"I have a large fortune," Lamprophyre lied. "Some people would like to get their hands on it. I can give it to you if you let me go." He wouldn't go for that, but it might be a good idea to make him think she was stupid.

And then Lamprophyre felt a sickly, pulsing sensation in her head. **Kill her now,** an unpleasantly familiar voice said.

"Your fortune means nothing to me," the man said. *Not now,* he thought.

You are playing a dangerous game. Kill her now.

You don't control me, dark lady. She dies on my terms or not at all, the man thought.

I have given you everything you wished for. You will obey, Terelok, or suffer.

"Are you sure?" Lamprophyre said, responding to his last spoken words though she dearly wanted to challenge one or both of her enemies. "It's a very large fortune."

You see? You could be outbid, Terelok thought.

The entity said nothing, but Lamprophyre could feel it seething in the back of Terelok's mind. Why it didn't kill him for his defiance, she had no idea, but if the two of them were at odds, she could do something with that.

"Prince Rokshan is my betrothed," she said, inspired. "If I'm killed, he will bring the full might of the military down on my murderer. I don't know how long you can go on escaping, but do you really want to spend the rest of your life on the run?"

"You underestimate my skills," Terelok said. *Well?* he thought.

"But if you take my offer, accept the money I'll give you, you won't have to use those skills *and* you'll be a rich man," Lamprophyre said. They were in the hall that ended at the front door, and she was sure if she couldn't convince him soon, when they stepped outside, she would lose him forever.

*I gave you power. **Wealth is nothing beside that**,* the entity said.

Lamprophyre held her breath. If the entity discovered her listening in, anything might happen.

Wealth can breed power, Terelok said.

They were almost to the door. "I swear I'll deliver my fortune to you, and I won't try to capture you," Lamprophyre said.

She lies. She— The sickly pulse of power grew stronger. ***You hear!*** The entity shrieked. ***Kill her now, Terelok, she must die!***

Lamprophyre spun around to face Terelok, who for the first time looked confused. "Are you a tool, or a man?" she demanded.

"How can you..." Terelok whispered. *She can hear me? My thoughts?*

The entity's attention focused again on Lamprophyre. ***It doesn't matter,*** it said. ***You will die.***

Lamprophyre turned and ran for the door.

She made it only a few steps before Terelok threw himself at her, bringing her down. She kicked at his face and struck his shoulder instead. Terelok let out a grunt and shoved himself up. Lamprophyre crawled to her hands and knees and scrambled away, only to feel his hard hands grabbing her ankles and dragging her backward. She screamed, putting her whole heart into it, then screamed again as loudly as she could.

Terelok's thoughts were fragmented now, but she didn't need to hear them to guess what he was thinking. A hand went over her mouth, silencing her. She kicked and fought and tried to bite, but he outweighed her. He lifted her in his arms and headed for the door.

Better, the entity thought. Malicious glee echoed from the word. **Kill her, Terelok, and you will have everything you desire.**

You evil, disgusting creature! Lamprophyre thought. *Kill me yourself if that's what you want!*

She didn't expect a response, but the entity's voice echoed in her head. **I don't care how you die, just that you do.**

But why? I don't even know who you are!

Terelok shoved the door open with his foot and tightened his grip on Lamprophyre. She heard a nasty chuckle. **I am the doom of humanity. I am the death of dragons. I am coming. The skies will burn.**

You're a person. A female person. You can hear thoughts and speak to people's minds. It was growing harder to carry on a mental conversation while thrashing to get away from Terelok. He gave no sign that he could hear the conversation. *Why me?*

You think I give my secrets away for the asking? Again Lamprophyre heard the chuckle. **You don't even know what you know. That amuses me.**

The skies were bright with stars, and cool air brushed over Lamprophyre's skin. It was such a strange contrast to the violence with which Terelok held her she choked back a hysterical giggle. He would take her somewhere dark and secret, and he would kill her, and Rokshan might not ever find her body. And no one would stop the entity when it came, whatever that meant.

She could think of only one more possibility. It was unlikely, but she was helpless and this was the only way she could strike. *Terelok,* she thought, *put me down.*

Terelok stopped. He looked at her with that same puzzled expression.

Put me down, she repeated. *You don't want to find out what I'm capable of.* She didn't know how she was doing this, whether she'd put thoughts into Terelok's head or the entity had made him capable of hearing thoughts like a dragon, but she pushed those worries aside for fear she'd lose the ability.

"Are you...you're speaking to me," Terelok whispered.

Don't listen to her, the entity said. ***Kill her now before she destroys you.***

Lamprophyre wanted to laugh again, but this time it was a laugh of relief. The entity had just planted suspicions in Terelok's mind that Lamprophyre had only hoped for. *She's right, Terelok, I can destroy you. Put me down.*

Terelok's breathing became heavy. His gaze flicked in all directions, as if he was looking for guidance. In that moment, Lamprophyre understood. The entity had no physical body, at least not one anywhere close by. It was nothing but a series of thoughts. And if Lamprophyre could speak to it...

You will never win, Lamprophyre said, *and I won't let you manipulate anyone else.* And then she struck.

She had never done anything like it before. No one had. But she had felt the entity's presence in Zefira's mind just as it had felt hers. The entity had been able to shred Zefira's mind. Without letting herself think about how impossible it was, she opened her mind the way she did when she was listening for a very distant thought and embraced the entity's awareness.

It felt like dropping into a pool of black oil, clinging to every bit of her. She wanted to scream at how the oil tried to seep into the rest of her thoughts, but that would be a mistake that would give the entity power over her. So instead she focused on listening to the entity, hearing past its surface thoughts and the words it spat at her into the depths of its consciousness and memory. It howled in pain, but Lamprophyre was in, she had encompassed her enemy, and the two of them entwined so that Lamprophyre was no longer conscious of Terelok or of her physical body and what he might be doing to it.

The entity's memories were fuddled by distance, as if it had been alive for centuries and those earliest thoughts were murky with time. Lamprophyre saw flashes of coherent thought that brushed past too quickly for her to make more sense of them than that they were places, high mountaintops, vast flatlands, river valleys, forests of trees Lamprophyre didn't recognize. The entity fought for control, but Lamprophyre held on and forced it to remember, hoping that somewhere in those memories was the key to its identity and purpose.

Now there were people, dragons and humans alike, and human cities and dragon caves. Those memories enraged the entity, which surprised Lamprophyre; it behaved as if its own thoughts were an affront, and that made no sense. Then one final image appeared in memory, and Lamprophyre couldn't help herself—she gasped in shock as the image of Mother Stone in all her snowy glory filled her vision.

You know Mother Stone, she said. *You're a dragon.*

The entity screamed, shaking Lamprophyre to the core. Then, horribly, it laughed. **But which one?** it said. **Which one, which one... You will never trust your flight again, will you?**

For a moment, Lamprophyre froze. It couldn't be one of the flight, and yet, who else was there? There were no other dragons. But she would have known—

The entity struck back.

It burned like fire, something Lamprophyre had never understood until she was human. Pain radiated through her, throwing her back into her body. Her mind was still entangled with the entity's, and the shock of being both physical and immaterial made her convulse, nearly tearing her out of Terelok's arms. His hand wasn't over her mouth anymore, but there seemed no point in screaming. Instead, she pictured knives, tiny blades the size of her thumb and great big weapons almost the size of Rokshan's sword. She pictured her mind threaded through with them, and as the entity tore itself free of her, she envisioned them tearing deep into her enemy, imaginary knives that cut like true steel.

The entity screamed again and fled, lashing out one last time but missing Lamprophyre. Another sharp pain shot through her, and she realized she'd hit the ground, cracking her head and bottom against the small white bricks of the street. She lay, stunned and dizzy, for a few beats before realizing Terelok didn't have her captive anymore. With a tremendous effort, she turned her head.

Terelok lay beside her, his legs and arms flung at strange angles no living, conscious human could sustain. His eyes were closed, and he didn't seem to be breathing. So that last attack hadn't been meant for her. Lamprophyre rolled onto hands and knees and crawled to Terelok's side. No warm breath brushed her cheek when she laid it against his mouth. Satisfied, she lay on her back and stared up at the stars. She felt as if her every muscle had been wrung by giant hands, leaving her too weak to move. She'd get up soon. Just not now.

"Hey!"

Lamprophyre closed her eyes. This was Tanajital. It was too much to expect that even this quiet side street in the quiet neighborhood where Piya lived would be completely empty at night. She heard running footsteps, and then a boy's excited voice saying, "There's two deaders lying right here! C'mon, look!"

"I'm not dead," she managed. "You need to send to the—" The palace, or get Piya involved? Piya would be outraged at being made part of this disaster.

"Go knock on that door and tell them one of Piya's guests was assaulted," she said. "She'll be so happy to help."

CHAPTER THIRTY-SIX

By the time Piya came storming out of her house, demanding to know what the interruption was, Lamprophyre had regained her strength and was standing well away from Terelok's body and the guards milling around it. She knew the city guards were a division of the military, and presumably had the same martial training as the regular soldiers, but it was hard to reconcile their bumbling, uncertain movements with the sharp attentiveness of the soldiers she'd watched drill on the training grounds.

"Lady Lelitha," the guard at her side said, "you can't tell us anything else about why a stranger would want to attack you?"

He'd asked this question half a dozen times in half a dozen different ways since arriving. Lamprophyre shot him an annoyed look. "I have no idea," she said. "It's rumored that I have a large fortune. Maybe he wanted to force me to give it to him."

"Rumored?"

Lamprophyre sighed. Beyond them, Piya appeared to be haranguing the guards surrounding Terelok's body. It wasn't as funny as she'd imagined. "I don't think my personal wealth is any of your business, sirrah."

"It's Captain, actually." The captain stiffened as if she'd insulted him. She didn't really care what he thought of her. "And you'd never seen him before tonight?"

That question, he'd asked eight times. "No." She'd elaborated on that answer the first few times, but now she hoped if she gave him monosyllabic answers, he'd allow her to return to the palace. Though come to think of it, did this man have the power to keep her against her will? It wasn't as if she'd broken any laws or killed Terelok herself.

"I think that's all the information I can give you, Captain," she said, managing not to sound irritated. He might be stupid, but he did have a job to do. "You can report to Commander Rokshan anything you learn about my kidnapper."

The captain's body became even more rigid. "I beg your pardon, Lady Lelitha, but you're not in a position to give orders."

The tension and fear and frustration she felt surged within her, overflowing the bounds of patience. "That is not an order, Captain," she said in a low, hard voice. "That is a statement of obvious fact that even you should realize. Commander Rokshan is responsible for investigating attempts on my life. I am in no position to know the extent of your responsibilities. I *do* know that if you *don't* tell Rokshan what you learn, when he discovers you concealed information from him he will very likely destroy you. And you will deserve it." She turned on her heel and strode away.

She realized immediately that in her desire to make a grand, dramatic exit, she hadn't thought about where she should go. The crowd outside Piya's house had grown substantially in the time she had been interrogated by the idiot captain, and most of them were the finely-dressed attendees of the dedication. Lamprophyre scanned the crowd. To her relief, she found Anchala and Torannum standing just inside the door. Torannum had his arm around Anchala, and both of them regarded her with looks of concern.

"You were kidnapped right out of Auntie Piya's house!" Anchala exclaimed, putting her arms around Lamprophyre. "How terrifying!"

"And how humiliating for Auntie Piya that she hired the man." Torannum looked past the two to where the guards were bundling Terelok's body into a litter. Piya still looked like she was chastising the guards. "Did he say why he did it?"

"He didn't say anything," Lamprophyre lied. "But he threatened to kill Anchala if I didn't come with him."

"Oh!" Anchala squeezed tighter. "You are so brave, Lelitha. But you shouldn't have given in. Someone would have stopped him."

"I don't think any of Auntie Piya's guests were armed, love," Torannum said. "Lelitha, we owe you a great debt."

"It's all right," Lamprophyre said, feeling uncomfortable at Anchala's unavoidable thoughts of *could have been killed* and *what would Rokshan have done, clearly he cares for her*. She gently extricated herself from Anchala's embrace and said, "Can we go back to the palace now? I want to sleep and forget all about this."

"Of course," Anchala said. "Tor, will you arrange for litters for the two of us? Lelitha, you should come back inside and have some wine. I'm sure you need something to steady your nerves."

Lamprophyre nodded. She didn't like the idea of wine, but she knew it did help humans feel better after a shock, so she could think of it as medicine.

Anchala guided her to a small room with a single couch and chair and two tiny tables barely big enough to hold a wine glass. "Lie down for now," she said. Lamprophyre lay down and rubbed the back of her head where it had struck the bricks. It was still sore and there was a lump beneath her hair. Touching it was painful, so she stopped doing that and closed her eyes.

In the peaceful quiet of this little room, which had been spared the excesses of Piya's artistic taste, she could let herself shake with fear at how narrow an escape that had been. She wished she knew how much it mattered that the entity's tool was dead. It—she—was capable of talking to many different people, but not all at the same time, or so Lamprophyre guessed. And very few of the people the entity spoke to knew she was a separate creature from their own dark thoughts. Lamprophyre suspected the people who'd spoken to her during the dedication ceremony didn't have any idea they'd been temporarily coerced by—

Lamprophyre's shaking stopped. By a dragon.

Now that she wasn't fighting for her life, she could be rational. It was simply impossible that the entity was a member of the flight. A dragon's surface thoughts were audible to the rest of the flight, but those surface thoughts were always a reflection of their deeper thoughts and desires. No dragon could pretend to be one thing and really be something else, which was what it would take for the entity to conceal itself among the flight. So its taunt about Lamprophyre never trusting the flight again was an empty one.

But what else was there? There were no other dragons. No stories even hinted at the possibility of other flights. The chances of there being a lone dragon—an *evil* lone dragon—somewhere in the world were so low as to be nonexistent. And yet Lamprophyre knew her guess was correct. Their enemy was a dragon who wanted the world to burn, humans and dragons alike. And she had abilities no dragon had ever known.

Lamprophyre's eyes flew open. Except that wasn't true, was it? She, Lamprophyre, had spoken to the evil dragon and she'd spoken to Terelok, both using mental communication. And the evil dragon spoke mind-to-mind with her victims. It hadn't felt like hearing thoughts the way Lamprophyre always did, where you thought words or had feelings in the privacy of your own mind and another dragon overheard them. This had been more like silently speaking thoughts that anyone could hear.

Maybe she was wrong, and that was an illusion, but it didn't explain how Terelok had heard her thoughts. Perhaps the artifact the adepts were trying to create, the one that would let them hear thoughts—but no, Terelok hadn't worn any artifacts, and she was sure such a thing was still hypothetical.

The other possibility, that speaking thoughts was something made possible by the evil dragon's presence, made little more sense and raised the question, again, of why this dragon was capable of things no other dragon could do. It made Lamprophyre's head ache worse to contemplate it.

Anchala entered the room bearing a glass filled with ruby-dark liquid. "Sorry that took so long. Everything's in disarray." She helped Lamprophyre sit and waited for her to drink the wine. Lamprophyre managed not to make a face at the strong flavor. Rokshan had been right about red wine.

"We'll leave as soon as the litters get here," Anchala went on. "I'm so glad you're not injured. And..." She looked away from Lamprophyre. "You and Rokshan, you're courting, aren't you?"

"Um," Lamprophyre said, confusion tangling her thoughts. It wasn't a bad thing to admit to being in love with Rokshan, right? Or was it better to lie for his sake, so he wouldn't have to explain why his romance with the mysterious stranger from Adakavi had ended? "We didn't want to make it public."

"During the wedding festivities. I understand." Anchala nodded as if she'd solved a clever riddle. Then she put her arms around Lamprophyre and hugged her. "I'm so happy for both of you," she whispered. Her thoughts said *finally Rokshan* and *still such a mystery*, but they weren't suspicious, and Lamprophyre relaxed and hugged Anchala back.

"Don't worry, I won't say a word, not even to Tor," Anchala said when she released Lamprophyre. "You won't be able to maintain your privacy for long, though. Rokshan may not be as much a public figure as the rest of us, but people still watch him, and any hint of romance will be pounced on by the citizens of Tanajital like a cat stalking a mouse."

"We'll do what we can, but I know it can't last forever," Lamprophyre said. That was true of so many things.

The litter arrived only a few minutes later. Lamprophyre hurried from the door to climb into it, hunching in on herself to avoid the stares and whispered comments from those remaining outside Piya's house. It felt like fleeing from a violent storm, only with a whirlwind of battering thoughts beating down on her instead of raindrops. She shut the thoughts out and curled up in the litter. She'd never been so grateful for the closed-off feeling the draperies gave.

It was tempting to believe she was safe now that Terelok was dead. Even Tanajital couldn't have hundreds or even dozens of men and women whose greed and selfishness perfectly suited them to the entity's needs and were capable of perceiving her as separate from their own thoughts. But that wasn't sensible thinking. The entity—Lamprophyre shied away from thinking of her as a dragon, though that was more foolishness—only needed one person she could convince to serve her, one person in a position to attack and kill Lamprophyre, and then it would be over. Lamprophyre would never be able to rest so long as the entity was alive.

She also wasn't foolish enough to believe she'd destroyed the entity with that attack. Maybe the entity had unusual mental abilities, but she also had a physical body, and unless Lamprophyre had done to her what the entity had done to Zefira and Terelok, which she didn't believe she had, the entity was wounded but not dead.

The litter moved smoothly through the streets, as smoothly as if the street were perfectly even and the bearers capable of gliding along over it. Lamprophyre twitched one curtain aside to see where they were. It was pitch-black outside and smelled of damp wood and living green leaves. So, not on the streets, then. She closed the curtain on the parkland and tried to relax. No one would attack her here, she was almost to the palace...where there might be other victims of the entity waiting to kill her. Lamprophyre curled up on herself and hugged her knees to her chest, hoping she would stop shaking before the litter reached the palace. How humiliating if she couldn't walk through the door under her own power!

Soon, the litter touched the ground with a light bump, and hands parted the curtains to help her out. She shook herself free of their aid. It was rude, but after Terelok's assault she didn't want to be touched by strange men.

Anchala had alit nearby, assisted by Torannum. She linked her arm with his and said, "You should go to bed, Lelitha. I'll leave a message for Rokshan that you're well and you're not to be disturbed until morning."

"It's all right," Lamprophyre said. "If he finds out anything about the attack, I'd like to know."

Anchala gave her a skeptical look, but said nothing. Lamprophyre blushed. She could hear Anchala's thoughts, which were all speculations about whether "Lelitha" and Rokshan were sexually intimate. There wasn't anything Lamprophyre could do about that short of revealing her identity to Anchala, so she pretended nothing was wrong and hurried inside.

She reached her room without encountering anyone who might be a threat and locked and barred her door behind her. She caught a glimpse of her reflection in the full-length mirror and sighed. Her dress was wrinkled and smeared with dirt in places, her awful hair was tangled, and she had a vivid scrape along one cheek that she didn't remember acquiring. She smoothed the wrinkles, or tried to; the gown seemed to want to hang onto them and the dirt. That was three beautiful gowns the entity had ruined.

She removed the gown and hung it on one of the wall pegs. Maybe Haleta could do something about it, assuming that was one of her duties as Lamprophyre's maid. Then she put on the shapeless blue robe and sat at the dressing table to brush the tangles out of her hair. The activity was surprisingly soothing, once she'd worked through the worst of the mess. The bristles tickled her scalp pleasantly. The human body was so much more sensitive than a dragon's body, at least where the sense of touch was concerned. Only that odd spot on the back of a dragon's head was as sensitive as the entire human body seemed to be.

She laid the brush down and contemplated her bed. This was the problem with hair. You got it brushed out properly and then immediately you had to do things, like sleep, that would simply tangle it again. Hair was stupid. She wished she knew why Rokshan liked hers so much, given that he didn't love hair in general enough to grow his own hair as long as hers.

She ran her fingers through her long, straight black hair once, then gave up. She was too tired to care about hair, or evil dragons, or the possibility that someone in the palace might be manipulated into killing her. She turned down the lamp and climbed into bed. In the warm darkness, her fears retreated enough that she no longer felt tense, just exhausted from the evening's ordeal. Her eyelids drooped, and almost immediately she was asleep.

Pounding on the door woke her out of a vivid dream of flying with Rokshan, who in the dream was a dragon, propelling her upright with her heart pounding as hard as the fists on the door. By how dark the room was, it was the middle of the night, possibly as late as the dreaming hour. She made herself relax. Anyone interested in killing her wouldn't announce himself to the world.

The person pounded again. "Lelitha, wake up," Rokshan said.

Lamprophyre turned up the lamp and hurried to unlock and unbar the door. Rokshan let himself in as furtively as he always did. She braced herself for him to take her roughly in his arms and kiss her the way he had at the healing center, but he only shut the door behind him and looked at her, his face impassive.

"Did you find them?" she asked.

"It was like chasing phantoms," Rokshan said. "We only knew they were real because they left, not a trail, obviously, but signs of their passing. Broken windows or carts, graffiti gouged into walls. Chaita is in a foul mood. She's embarrassed at her people's complete inability to locate the enemy, and she blamed me and my soldiers for the failure. Which so obviously wasn't our fault it just embarrassed her further."

Lamprophyre waited for him to say something about her attacker, but he just fell silent. He looked as exhausted as she had felt before a few hours of sleep refreshed her. She realized he was silent because he didn't know about Terelok or any of what had happened at Piya's. The thought of telling him, of facing his anger over the situation, even if he wasn't angry at her, made her feel sick and uncomfortable inside.

"I think you should sit," she told him. "I learned something tonight."

Rokshan's expression became curious. "Learned something?" he said, sitting in the padded chair. "At Auntie Piya's? You surprise me."

"Yes, and you won't be happy about it, so please don't start shouting or kissing me until I've told you everything."

Rokshan's eyebrows went up. "I can't imagine what you could possibly say that would make me want to both shout and kiss you at the same time."

Lamprophyre managed a weak smile. She sat on the edge of her bed. "You'll understand soon."

She told him everything, starting with the entity addressing her through the minds of Piya's guests and ending with Terelok dead and the entity temporarily thwarted. Rokshan's face went so still when she told him she'd encountered the leader of the assassins he looked like a statue, one carved by a genius who understood human emotion so well she made it clear Rokshan was beats away from exploding. His expression made Lamprophyre so nervous she started talking faster, wishing the story was over and he could go back to looking like himself again.

When she finished, Rokshan closed his eyes and shuddered, then drew in a deep breath and let it out slowly. "You were right," he said. "I can't believe I left you vulnerable to that man."

"Rokshan, I didn't mean for you to blame yourself."

"I love you, Lamprophyre. Your safety means everything to me. I'm not saying it's rational, I'm saying I have a deep-seated need to protect you." He let out another slow breath. "So the entity killed Terelok."

"Yes. I assume. I'm sure I didn't."

"And the entity is a dragon." Rokshan shook his head. "It's impossible to believe. It really is."

"I know."

Rokshan stood and walked to the dressing table, where he leaned heavily on it with his head bowed. "But you hurt it."

"I did. I don't know how badly, or how permanently. But I think we have to assume she's not dead and will go on trying to kill me."

"Why you?" Rokshan shouted, startling Lamprophyre. "Why the devil do you matter so much to her?"

It was a question that hadn't occurred to Lamprophyre in a while. She wasn't anything special so far as dragons went. Yes, she had a better memory than most, but there were plenty of dragons who were faster, smarter, prettier, wittier...she was the dragon queen's daughter, but dragons didn't care about that...she was the first dragon to make contact with humans and the first to care about dragons and humans getting along...

"She wants humans and dragons destroyed," she said, feeling the idea creep over her like morning mist. "I must be key to that somehow. We already said that was something unique to me. She must believe killing me will allow her to succeed at her plan. Whatever it is."

"So we need to learn what that plan is," Rokshan said. "And we need to discover her identity and location. And then we will destroy her."

"If we—" Lamprophyre shut her mouth. This was not the time to point out how hard it was to kill a dragon, not while Rokshan still looked like he wanted to tear someone apart.

In the mirror, she saw Rokshan close his eyes again. His hands gripped the edge of the dressing table so hard the knuckles paled. "I don't know how much more of this I can bear," he said. "Knowing your life is in danger—Lamprophyre, I can't be with you all the time. I can't lock you in this room away from any assassin."

Lamprophyre stood and crossed the room to his side, laying one hand on his wrist. He was so tense it felt like stone beneath her fingers. "We only have to endure until we discover the entity. Then it won't matter whether I'm human or dragon, because I won't be in danger anymore."

Rokshan looked at her. His eyes looked bruised and tired. "I think we have to face reality," he said. "There's no cure for you."

It felt like a punch to the chest. Lamprophyre closed her hand over his wrist and squeezed, though she wasn't strong enough to hurt him. She wanted to scream at him that he was being overly pessimistic, that they had to keep trying, but the morning's failure had hurt her more than she realized. "But there's still whatever Evart did," she protested, and hated how weak and uncertain she sounded. "Somebody must...it can be replicated..."

Rokshan shook his head. "We haven't found a single person who knows anything about what Evart was doing. He didn't leave any records, and if he consulted books, we can't find them. Lamprophyre. There's no cure."

His straightforward, unadorned words cut straight to her heart. All her other protests died on her lips. "There's no cure," she admitted, and was surprised at how relieved she felt in saying it.

"You're going to be in that body for the rest of your life," Rokshan went on. "We can't afford to pretend otherwise."

"I know. I can't...but I know it's true." She felt she should be crying, because humans always wept for a death, and this was the death of her hopes. But her aching eyes stayed dry.

Rokshan brushed hair back from her face, trailing his fingers down its length. "It's not so awful, is it?" he said. It sounded like a plea, something wrung out of his heart by force. "Tell me this is something you can live with."

She looked up at him. *He* was crying, or at least looked on the verge of it. She put her arms around his waist and laid her head on his shoulder, not sure if she was comforting him or asking him for comfort. His thoughts washed unbidden over her: *wanted this didn't want she will never forgive me.*

"I'll never forgive you for what?" she asked without thinking.

He jerked, startled. "You were listening to my thoughts."

"It happens when we're this close. I'm sorry. I should have tried harder—"

"It's all right." He let out a sigh. "I was thinking you would never forgive me for being happy about this."

Once more she felt as if he'd struck her. Her first instinct was to pull free of his embrace and run away from him. But this was the palace, and there wasn't anywhere she could go to escape him forever. So she controlled her impulse and tried to think logically. She loved him, and she didn't want to hurt him even if he deserved it for celebrating her loss. "You're happy because you don't have to give me up," she said.

"Yes. I'm sorry."

"It's all right. I understand. You mean, so long as this is inevitable, we might as well look for the good."

"Yes," Rokshan repeated. His thoughts cheered up slightly and became tinged with relief that she didn't hate him.

Lamprophyre closed her eyes and tried to block Rokshan's thoughts. She was so close to him the best she could do was make them quiet and distant so she could ignore them. She didn't want to think about this now. She wanted to go back to sleep and pretend this was all a nightmare she would wake from soon, or at the very least get some sleep before having to face the truth in the morning.

Rokshan's arms tightened around her. "Lamprophyre," he said, "I want you to marry me."

Lamprophyre jerked away from him, so badly startled she couldn't speak. "You what?" she finally managed.

"I want the right to be by your side every day and every night." Rokshan took her hands in his. "I want to be able to protect you—to never have to leave you."

A chill passed through her. "So you can be my...my caretaker?" she said. "Isn't that a long way to go to keep me safe?"

She'd meant it as an attack, words to wound him for his ridiculous assumptions, but he smiled and shook his head. "That sounded bad, didn't it?" He changed his loose grip on her hands and went to his knees before her. "You are my best friend," he said, "and you are the love of my life. However it happened, whatever evil the entity intended in making you human, I can't help but feel grateful for the good that came out of it. I want to spend the rest of my life with you. Please, Lamprophyre. Marry me."

The ringing in her ears made it hard for her to hear him, but she still felt she would remember his words until the day she died. "I... Rokshan, I..." She closed her eyes for a few beats. When she opened them again, Rokshan was still looking up at her with an expression of such hope it finally brought tears to her eyes. She'd never felt so confused in her life. Marry Rokshan. She'd imagined herself pair-bonded to him if he was a dragon, so what made marriage to him as a human any different?

She leaned down and kissed him, welcoming again the soft, marvelously sensitive touch. "I don't want to say no," she said, "but I can't say yes. Rokshan, I'm still not used to the idea that this is what I'll be for the rest of my life. If I marry you, that's like the final admission that there's no hope that I'll be restored. So give me time, please."

Rokshan nodded. "I understand," he said. He sounded disappointed, but not heartbroken, not as if she'd hurt him irreparably by her refusal. He got to his feet and held her again. "You know how I feel. When you're ready, tell me. And take as long as you need."

It reassured her that his thoughts echoed his words almost perfectly, though they were tinged with sadness. She also heard the distant whisperings of desire that made her wonder what would have happened if she'd said yes, with the two of them alone in her dimly-lit room with the bed so very convenient. He kissed her, lightly, then kissed her again before releasing her. "I have to go," he said.

"I know."

"I'll be back after dawn. We'll need to tackle the library again.

Somebody must have written about an evil ancient dragon who can speak to people's minds."

Lamprophyre wasn't sure this was true, but his kisses had fogged her brain and sent warmth spreading through her, and she didn't want to argue with him. "If it's there, we'll find it," she said, and hoped with all her heart it was true.

CHAPTER THIRTY-SEVEN

Dharan met them in the academy commons the following morning, dressed for once in his lector's gold robe. "I have a lecture to give in a few minutes," he said, gesturing at himself, "but I wanted to tell you what I learned in the Hall of Visions yesterday."

Lamprophyre had almost forgotten he'd said another visit there might be necessary. "You need to hear what we learned first," she said. There was no time to give him the full story. "The entity is a dragon."

Dharan had opened his mouth to begin speaking. Now it fell open a little wider. "A dr...are you sure?"

"Very sure."

Dharan closed his eyes and swore. "That changes my entire theory about the 'skies will burn' prophecies. I found two more of them, and... God's breath, things are starting to make sense." He cast a glance over his shoulder at three students hurrying to enter one of the larger buildings. "Never mind. We'll talk later. The important thing is that I didn't find any prophecies relating to transformations, so that's a dead end. But a dragon..." He shook his head and turned to follow the students, his long legs striding rapidly enough almost to be running.

Lamprophyre watched him go. "So Jiwanyil never told any ecclesiasts about transformations," she said.

"It was always a long shot," Rokshan said.

"I know. And I'm not even terribly disappointed. This isn't a religious problem." She didn't feel much of anything except a leaden weight where her heart was. She'd woken that morning to the realization that Rokshan was right, and there likely wasn't a solution for her. Now she felt the way she had in the days after her father had rejoined Mother Stone, heavy and dull and unable to see a future in which she would feel herself again. This would pass, she knew, but her heart didn't believe it.

Narahar was at the window when Lamprophyre and Rokshan entered. He greeted her with a smile. "It's been a few days," he said. "I hope you haven't decided an academic life isn't for you."

"I've been busy with wedding celebrations," Lamprophyre said, which was mostly true. It was amazing how easy lying was when you didn't have to worry about someone hearing your thoughts. No wonder humans were addicted to it. "I would like to look at these two books," she added, handing over the last of her requests from the earlier research session. It was probably pointless, but maybe if she continued to find no information about serpentine or transformations, she could convince herself to let go of the fantasy.

Narahar nodded and walked away. Lamprophyre leaned on the shelf and watched Rokshan, whose attention roved across the students occupying the desks. There were more of them than usual, which reminded Lamprophyre of what Dharan had said about this being a busy time of year for him, all those students handing in assignments. Maybe she should enroll at the academy for real. If she was doomed to be human, she would need something to occupy herself, and it might as well be something she loved.

"Here you are," Narahar said, and Lamprophyre turned around to accept the two books. One of them was rather battered, and she said so. "I know, but you'll treat it carefully, right?" he said. "I'm not worried."

"I'm not sure Lector Ilhan would agree," Lamprophyre said.

Narahar leaned forward. "Lector Ilhan isn't in a position to argue," he said in a low, conspiratorial voice. "He didn't come in this morning. Sent word that he was ill."

"Ill?" And Lamprophyre had struck a blow to the entity the night before. She was sure it was no coincidence. "I hope it's nothing serious."

"I'm sure he'll be fine," Narahar said, but he still looked as if there were something shameful about Ilhan's illness. "He's never been ill a day in his life, so maybe he's due."

"Maybe," Lamprophyre said.

She took her books to her desk and leafed through them half-heartedly. The first contained nothing she hadn't read before—no mention of serpentine, no claims of transformations. The second was the battered book, which smelled strongly of mildew and whose pages were loose in the binding. She turned pages carefully, not wanting to be responsible for destroying a book even though this one desperately needed to be repaired or recopied.

She almost missed the word 'serpentine' halfway down a page and had to scrabble back through the pages to find it again. One page came loose from the binding, and she nudged it back into place, impatient with the stupid book. There. She traced down the page with a shaking finger, hope rising in her despite her efforts to restrain it. Being disappointed again would be devastating.

The book was a history of famous uses of magic, some of them well-known because of their historic importance, others that were the first recorded use of an important magic artifact. The passage on serpentine... Lamprophyre read on in growing excitement. It went into great detail about the "semi-mythical" stone and its transformative powers, including stories of its use. If only they'd found this book a week ago!

Then, abruptly, the section came to an end with a few lines: *While many records attest to the above, no serpentine still exists in our day, making it impossible to prove their veracity. The adept Ostela (874-930 CY) was the last to claim to have performed a serpentine transformation, and her records were lost in the fire that took her life. It is therefore necessary to place serpentine in the category of 'legendary' artifacts rather than anything extant.*

The hope filling her burned to ash. She stared blindly at the page for a few dozen beats before slowly closing the book and setting it aside. So it wouldn't have mattered when they found the book, because it was as useless as all the others. On the one hand, it was the clearest evidence they had that serpentine did what they believed it would, but the book didn't tell her anything she hadn't learned from observing Evart. And it had no instructions, no records of *how* serpentine transformed someone. Useless.

She took the books back to Narahar, who looked at her in concern. "Is everything all right?"

"Just discouraged. I'm going to try another approach."

She returned to her desk with a blank sheet of paper and a charcoal pencil, but instead of tackling the little drawers, she stared at the cream-colored paper, thick and rough-textured, with her mind numbly circling what she already knew. No transformation. Evil dragon entity. *Ancient* evil dragon entity. Evart dead, Zefira maybe permanently injured, Terelok dead, Ilhan ill. Speaking thoughts instead of overhearing them. None of it made any sense.

She remembered speaking with the evil dragon the night before, how desperately it had wanted Terelok to kill her. *You don't even know what you know*, the dragon had said. Suddenly impatient with herself, she pushed back from the desk and strode to the cabinets. The one thing she was certain of was that the evil dragon considered her a threat. She could either give up and mope like a whiny dragonet, or she could fight.

Now, what to look for... She searched on every subject related to dragons she could think of. Maybe that was a mistake, because humans had known so little of dragons for centuries that their knowledge was flawed and incomplete, but she had to start somewhere.

"These," she said to Narahar when she had a fat stack of book requests. Narahar took the five papers with a smile. She wondered how she looked to him: determined, assertive, or just mad?

"I hope *The Last Days of Hamadri* was useful," he said when he returned with a stack of four books. "I can't find this one by Surat, sorry."

At least she knew Narahar wasn't lying to her; she could hear his thoughts, and they were amused and curious about what exactly the Kolmiran student was trying to find. "That's all right," she said. "*The*

Last Days of Hamadri?" She'd left it with Dharan after reading it, and it had slipped her mind entirely.

"Yes. You were so determined to read it, I'd hate to think it wasn't valuable, after all."

"It was excellent. And—"

Memory struck. *The banded desert overcame them, and their destruction was in the wind and the fire. It consumed the defenders and swept over Hamadri until only bones were left.* Banded desert. Wind and fire. "It gave me some ideas," she said, and snatched up her books and returned to her desk.

So, what did she already know? There had been an event, a thousand or more years ago, called the catastrophe by humans and the Great Cataclysm by dragons. Neither remembered what had caused it, but both agreed it had nearly wiped their civilizations out. Humans believed it had killed all the dragons, and dragons remembered that they had retreated from humanity because of it. But Kalivas had written both humans and dragons had worked together to fight the destruction, and that the destruction had been caused by...what? It sounded like a natural force, but who could fight a whirlwind or fire? It had to have been some creature or creatures. Wind and fire.

Or dragons.

Lamprophyre felt sick. Dragons wouldn't attack defenseless creatures, and humans were soft and fragile and vulnerable. But dragons were creatures of air and fire, everyone knew that, and if Kalivas had been writing metaphorically, he might well have meant Hamadri had been overrun by dragons.

So why would dragons do such a thing? And why would other dragons resist them? The idea of the flight being in conflict with itself, dragons fighting dragons, was almost inconceivable. But if you assumed such a thing was possible, it made sense that some dragons would believe protecting humans was essential. And if dragons and humans had been friends before the Cataclysm...

Lamprophyre put her face in her hands and massaged her temples. She was making far too many assumptions. Time to find some proof.

She read passages, discarded books, requested others. She heard the thoughts of the students watching her: *can't possibly read that fast* and *whose student is she?* and *must have a deadline.* Distantly, she was aware of Rokshan watching her as well, but he didn't move from his position by the door. She hoped he wasn't bored. She felt alive for the first time in days, her mind buzzing along as fast as those tiny birds that hovered the way dragons did.

At some point, she realized she had no more book requests, and an untidy stack of paper covered in dusty charcoal writing lay under her left arm, which was smudged with more charcoal. She closed the book in front of her and let out a deep breath, stretching out aching muscles and shaking out her cramped hand. Her mind quivered as if knowledge were tangible and it had been poured into her brain like wine into a glass, slopping over the edges. She was almost certainly the first person in centuries who knew what had happened in the Great Cataclysm. It was an exhilarating feeling.

She returned her books to Narahar, who took them with a smile. "So, what did you discover?" he asked. "I'm dying to know. I've never seen anyone work like that."

Knowledge shifted inside her mind. "It's a work in progress," she said, "but someday, everyone will know."

Rokshan stood upright from where he'd been lounging near the door as she approached. "You look as if you were successful," he said. "You found out about serpentine, after all." He didn't look upset about the possibility, and she felt a surge of love for him that surprised her. Whatever his personal desires, he loved her enough to want the best for her—even if it meant losing her.

"Not serpentine," she said. "We need to find Dharan. You should both hear this."

They tracked Dharan down in one of the lecture halls, where he was speaking to a student. Lamprophyre found she was bouncing on the balls of her feet and made herself stop. The knowledge would still be there in an hour. Though if Dharan took an hour to deal with this student, whose thoughts revealed that she had a sexual interest in the lector and had made up a question to get him to talk to her, Lampro-phyre might explode with impatience.

Finally, *finally* the student left, and Dharan gathered up a couple of books and walked toward them. "You found something," he said, seeing Lamprophyre's expression.

"I know what the Great Cataclysm—the catastrophe—was," she said, feeling the words burst uncontrollably out of her. "I know what caused it and I have a suspicion of how it relates to the entity."

"*That's* what you learned?" Rokshan exclaimed. "What does that have to do with anything?"

"But that's what I was going to tell you," Dharan said. "I'm certain the 'skies will burn' prophecies are confusing because they refer to *two* catastrophes. Not just one to come, but the one that happened a thousand years ago."

"Just listen," Lamprophyre said, impatient with the interruptions. "It's all in the books if you know what you're looking for. Before the Cataclysm, humans and dragons lived together. Not literally, because human cities don't fit dragons, and dragon caves aren't hospitable to humans, just like now. But they did things together, and helped each other, and I'm sure there were even humans who flew with dragons—there was one book that talked about partnerships."

"That prophecy about two acting as one," Dharan said. "We knew this."

Lamprophyre waved him to silence. "We *suspected* this. The important thing is that those stories humans tell about dragons attacking—those are true. Somehow, a group of dragons decided to attack humans. Other dragons, probably the ones partnered with humans, fought back. And there was destruction. Tremendous destruction that nearly wiped out civilization. It wasn't a natural disaster, or a magical illness. It was dragons."

The two men stared at her in silence. Finally, Rokshan said, "So what does that have to do with the entity? Because you can't mean what I think you mean. It's impossible."

"I know. But I'm sure it's true. The entity, that dragon—we all agreed it was an ancient force before we knew the details. Whoever she is, she's one of the dragons that caused the Cataclysm."

Dharan shook his head. "Not even a dragon lives that long. And what proof do you have? Couldn't it just as likely be a modern dragon who wants to accomplish what those earlier dragons failed to do?"

Lamprophyre hesitated. "This isn't from research," she said. "It's based on a feeling I had when I spoke to her. She said she was coming, that she was the doom of humanity and the death of dragons. Only the way she said it felt as if she meant she was coming *back*. That this was something she'd done before and intended to do again."

"But that would make her over a thousand years old. That makes her more than twice as old as the longest-lived dragon you've told us about," Rokshan said.

"I don't have all the answers. Worse, there's nothing in the records that tells how she was stopped before, not in any detail. We only know she was because civilization is still around." Lamprophyre shook her head. "Maybe whatever happened allowed her to live so long. I guess this isn't as exciting as I thought."

Rokshan gripped her hand. "It's important," he said, "because now we know for sure we're fighting a living creature, and one that isn't invulnerable. We just have to find her."

"She could be anywhere," Lamprophyre said. "We'd have noticed if there were a strange dragon hanging around Tanajital, which means her range for mental communication is tremendous. And she's capable of things I didn't know were possible."

"Things that are possible for all dragons," Rokshan pointed out. "You learned how to attack her the way she attacked Zefira and Terelok."

"Wait, what was that? You attacked the entity?" Dharan said.

Lamprophyre had forgotten he didn't know about the previous night's events. She summed up Terelok's attack and her encounter with the evil dragon for him. Dharan's expression grew grimmer as she spoke. When she finished, he said, "That was dangerous. The entity might have killed you."

"I think, if it could kill me directly, it wouldn't have needed Terelok," Lamprophyre said. "Whatever Jiwanyil did when I called on him to protect me the first time the entity spoke to me, I think it had lasting effects."

Dharan scowled. "You're making it damned hard for me to be an atheist."

Rokshan clapped him on the shoulder. "Try not to take it too hard," he said. "Let's get something to eat, and then we can work out how to locate this ancient evil dragon bent on the destruction of everything good."

Lamprophyre hadn't realized she was hungry until Rokshan mentioned food. She still felt more excited than she had in days. Maybe she was stuck in this human body, but she could still fight her enemy. And with Rokshan by her side...

She walked with Rokshan behind Dharan, who'd said he knew a tavern whose oven-roasted chicken he wanted to try, and marveled at how right his hand felt in hers. All her fears had melted away in the face of this new evidence. She wasn't sure why learning the truth behind the Cataclysm had done that, since it wasn't exactly encouraging; it wouldn't restore her, didn't even hint at the possibility. And yet the thought of being human for the rest of her short human life didn't hurt the way it had the night before.

She looked at Rokshan, who was saying something to Dharan, and that surge of love swept over her again. True, if she'd been able to choose, she'd have wanted them both to be dragons, but he was her dearest love, and marrying him felt good and right. "Rokshan," she said.

A large shadow swept over the street, provoking cries of surprise from the humans thronging it but no fear. Lamprophyre looked up at the large, dark shape backlit by the bright noon sun. Bromargyrite. Fear shot through her. Bromargyrite wouldn't disrupt a public street unless it was an emergency.

People scattered as the dragon descended, filling the street almost completely. It took Lamprophyre a moment to realize the dragon wasn't Bromargyrite, who was large, but not that large. Then shock rooted her to her place. It was Hyaloclast.

She and Rokshan and Dharan were now the only people left in that part of the street. Everyone else had retreated to a safe distance, well out of the way of Hyaloclast's tail and wings. Lamprophyre walked forward to greet the dragon queen. Nervous tension made her shoulders ache. If Bromargyrite would have heralded an emergency, Hyaloclast's presence had to mean disaster.

She halted half a dragonlength from Hyaloclast and looked up into the dragon queen's blood-red eyes. Hyaloclast was breathing heavily from exertion, and that frightened Lamprophyre more, because she'd never seen her physically at the edge of her reserves. Both Hyaloclast's fists were clenched, and her shoulders heaved with her breathing.

"What's wrong?" Lamprophyre said, terrified of what the answer might be.

Hyaloclast said nothing. She crouched low so her head was on a level with Lamprophyre's and extended her right fist like an offering. Lamprophyre held out both hands, and Hyaloclast dropped something into them. It was the size of her two fists, heavy and smooth and solid, carved all over with deep grooves in no pattern Lamprophyre recognized. Its mottled green and black surface spoke to Lamprophyre. Serpentine.

Hyaloclast said, "I found it."

CHAPTER THIRTY-EIGHT

Lamprophyre's hands instinctively closed around the chunk of serpentine. She stared at Hyaloclast. "Found what?"

"The story," Hyaloclast said. She drew in air and held it for a few beats to calm her breathing. "I told you I remembered a story in which a carving blessed by Mother Stone transformed creatures. Scoria knew more of the legend. She gave me direction, and I hunted until I found it."

"But..." Questions bubbled up in Lamprophyre's chest until she was choked with them. She groped for something to say. "We thought it had to be a wand."

Hyaloclast shrugged. "When it comes to artifacts, I know almost nothing. But I insisted the man who gave me this prove that it works. This is the solution, Lamprophyre."

"How does it work?" Rokshan said, startling Lamprophyre. She'd been so intent on her inner turmoil she hadn't noticed his approach at her left side.

Hyaloclast paused before answering Rokshan. "It's not easy," she finally said. "The person performing the transformation must have a deep understanding of the form they want. Otherwise it would be as simple as touching the thing and willing it to change you. Which obviously hasn't happened."

Lamprophyre shook her head. The object in her hands suddenly felt ten times heavier. "Who can do that?" she asked, knowing the answer but hoping irrationally that there was no one who understood her that well.

"I will," Hyaloclast said. "You think I don't know you better than I know myself? I rocked you to sleep when you were a dragonet and I nursed you through the sickness that claimed your father. I remember your body, and I'm confident I can restore you."

"But not here in the street, surely," Dharan said. Him, she'd heard approaching, and he stood to her right, bracketing her. She had a sudden image of how they must look, two tall men flanking a small, plump woman, facing down the biggest dragon anyone had ever seen.

"No," Hyaloclast said. "In the field outside the city. Climb up."

"No," Lamprophyre said, stepping backward. "I mean—I hate flying. And I want..." Hyaloclast would be appalled if she confessed to loving Rokshan. "I'll meet you there. It's not much of a walk."

Hyaloclast's eyes narrowed. Lamprophyre resolutely shut out her mother's thoughts. If Hyaloclast knew the truth and was repulsed by it, Lamprophyre didn't want to know. It wouldn't change what both of them had to do.

She held out her hands. "You keep it. It will be safer with you."

Hyaloclast took the carving. "I'll be waiting," she said, and leaped into the sky, filling the street with a vast wind that knocked Lamprophyre into Rokshan's arms. Lamprophyre watched her go until she was a black speck over the northern wall of the city.

Rokshan didn't release her when the street was still again. The three of them stood silent as the rest of the people trickled back to fill the space where Hyaloclast had been, watching the skies as if expecting her to return. Lamprophyre felt dull and numb again. Restored to her dragon form. Twelve hours earlier she would have welcomed the news. Now it made her feel downcast, as if she'd been denied her heart's desire only minutes after discovering what it was.

"We should go," she said, stepping away from Rokshan.

"We?" Rokshan said.

Lamprophyre didn't look at him. "I don't want to do this alone."

"Maybe I—" Dharan began. Lamprophyre glanced up when he didn't finish that sentence immediately and saw him looking at her and then at Rokshan. "I see," he said. "You don't need me along for this. Lamprophyre, I'm sorry."

Lamprophyre nodded. His compassionate words brought tears to her eyes. Dharan gripped Rokshan's shoulder without saying another word and turned and walked away.

Rokshan sighed heavily. "It's what you wanted," he said. He took her hand as a couple of large men brushed past her, making her wobble. "You won't be trapped like this forever."

"I don't feel trapped!" Lamprophyre exclaimed. "I wanted— Rokshan, we can't be together, and I wanted that more than anything. Let's—" She swallowed against the lump in her throat. "Let's run away."

"Excuse me?" Rokshan said.

"We can go to Kolmira, or Sunital, and I'll stay human and we can be married, and nothing will have to change." The idea had taken hold of her with such force she almost couldn't hear the little voice in her head screaming at how stupid she was being.

Rokshan closed his eyes. Then he pulled her toward him and put his arms around her, ignoring the passing crowd. "You know Hyaloclast won't make you do this," he said. "We don't have to run. But it's not her you'd be fleeing, is it? It's yourself."

Tears flowed down her cheeks unchecked. She buried her face in Rokshan's shirt and cried, trying to drown out the voice that kept getting louder. She couldn't stay human. It wasn't in her nature. But being a dragon while her love was a human wasn't something anyone would understand, and she cried harder, this time out of pain and grief at being so utterly different from every other dragon she knew.

She cried until Rokshan's shirt was wet and her throat and eyes ached and she ran out of tears. Then she dried her face and said, "I'm sorry."

"There's nothing to be sorry for," Rokshan said. His eyes shone with unshed tears the way they had last night. She wished with all her heart that she'd told him yes then. That they'd had sex while they had the chance. Now it didn't matter.

Rokshan touched her cheek lightly, and a little half-smile curved his lips. "I love you," he said, "and I don't care what form you're in so long as it's still you."

That made her heart ache worse. She was almost positive Rokshan wouldn't love her when she was a dragon, at least not the way he did now, and she regretted even more the lost opportunity to have that physical intimacy. "I'll always love you," she said, "and maybe it's worse for you to know this, but I would have married you if things hadn't worked out this way."

His smile broadened. "Much better," he said, and kissed her, long and sweet. Lamprophyre heard someone making a hooting noise she didn't understand, but all that mattered was the moment.

They walked in silence, hand in hand, toward the city gate. Lamprophyre had never used it, though it was large enough to admit a dragon. What was the point if you had wings? A tiny spark lit within her, reminding her of the joy of flying, and the pain in her heart eased a little. She was behaving like this was a death sentence instead of what she'd hoped for for nearly a twelveday. Had it really only been that long? It felt like forever.

The fields north of the city were green with winter's growth, short, fine grasses that covered the fields as they lay fallow before the next planting. Lamprophyre thought about all the humans who would toil to make these fields ready, and then to plant seeds and cultivate the little plants. She didn't know what crops grew here. It had never mattered to her before. Now that she was human, or would be for a few thousand more beats, she felt connected to the crops as food she could eat. It felt strange, seeing plants through human eyes. Returning to her own form might be a difficult adjustment.

The air smelled fresh and warm and comfortable, not at all like the sweltering heat of summer. Another dozen twelvedays and the weather would shift again. Maybe she would return home for the summer. Tana-jital didn't really need her constant ambassadorial presence, and it would take her away from Rokshan. The thought escaped her before she could stop it, and then she couldn't stop thinking about it. She didn't want to leave Rokshan, and she couldn't bear the thought of being near him when he was human and she wasn't. It burned inside her, filling her with guilt.

Abruptly Rokshan stopped and turned her to face him. "This is ridiculous," he said. "We're behaving like a couple of condemned crimi-nals on the way to the gallows. We should be celebrating. Lampro-phyre, what do you miss most about being in dragon form?"

"Flying," Lamprophyre said without hesitation.

"I agree," Rokshan said. "So as soon as you're restored, we'll go flying. And soon everything will be as it was before."

Lamprophyre didn't think this was likely, but she could hear Rokshan's pain in his thoughts because she had broken her rule again. So she nodded and smiled. If it made things easier for him, she could pretend this was something she wanted.

Hyaloclast sat in one of the fallow fields, a dark blotch visible for a hundred dragonlengths against the fresh green grass. She sat as if she'd been waiting much longer than the thousand-plus beats it had taken Rokshan and Lamprophyre to arrive. She eyed their joined hands in silence. "Lamprophyre, stand here," she said, pointing to a spot half a dragonlength from her. Lamprophyre squeezed Rokshan's hand once and walked to the indicated spot.

Hyaloclast handed Lamprophyre the carving. Lamprophyre turned it over in her hands, examining it. It wasn't representational art, didn't look like any animal or tree or mountain Lamprophyre recognized; it was a heavy egg-shaped lump carved with deep grooves in an abstract pattern. The surface between the grooves was smoothly polished and shone in the sunlight. It had a flat base that would let it sit upright on a shelf. If it hadn't been attractive, it might have joined Piya's collection.

Hyaloclast edged closer and took both of Lamprophyre's hands in one of hers. The dragon queen's warm, almost hot hand engulfed Lamprophyre's as well as the artifact. "Just stand still," Hyaloclast murmured. "This will hurt, though I'm not sure how much. The adept who demonstrated used a bird, not a human."

Lamprophyre made herself relax. Pain would pass.

Hyaloclast closed her eyes, and the ridges above them contracted in deep thought. Nothing else happened. Lamprophyre wished she'd thought to ask how long it would take. Obviously it didn't matter whether it happened immediately or not, but it would have been nice—

Pain struck her, making her scream at the unexpected agony. Something huge and invisible grabbed her and *twisted*, hard, making muscles tear and bones grate against bones. Rokshan shouted. She screamed again, then cried out, "Don't interfere!" and hoped Rokshan's good sense would prevail.

She smelled blood, a lot of blood, mingling with the scent of the green grass in a sickening, stomach-churning odor that felt as if it was attacking her, forcing its way into her nostrils and between her lips. She gagged, then convulsed, but brought nothing up. The hand twisted her again, making her scream once more, and then it was gone. She fell to her knees and then flat on her face, still clutching the serpentine artifact, and sucked in air as desperately as if she'd nearly drowned.

Gradually, she became aware of sounds, the chirping of birds, the wind blowing through the grasses, and the heavy slow thump of her own heart, echoing in her ears. She felt as heavy as if she were made of stone, something solid and eternal like granite. Carefully, she straightened to a kneeling position and waited for her breathing to calm. The smell of blood was gone.

Hyaloclast stood a short distance away. She didn't look at all out of breath. Lamprophyre didn't know why she looked different until she said, "Can you stand?"

"Not yet," Lamprophyre said, and froze. That hadn't been her voice, or at least not Lelitha's voice. It was deep and rich and resonant. She looked at Hyaloclast again and realized she was looking at the dragon queen not from below, but from beside. Trembling, she extended her arms and looked at them.

They were blue.

Lamprophyre dropped the serpentine artifact and closed her eyes.

She flexed her wings and felt them lift and rise. They were as heavy as the rest of her—well, she'd become used to her human weight, which was a fraction of her dragon's form. She spun around and heard Rokshan exclaim as if he'd had to avoid being knocked over by her tail. "Sorry," she said, opening her eyes.

"You've been human for a twelveday. It makes sense that you'd forget things," Rokshan said.

Human. Lamprophyre's happiness evaporated. She looked down at Rokshan, who was his usual tiny self again. His expression was impassive, and she cringed inside to imagine what feeling that expression hid. She settled down on her haunches and reached for his hand. Her body felt almost numb by comparison to that marvelously sensitive human form, but the touch of his hand was exactly the same.

Rokshan held her hand for a moment, then pulled away. "It worked," he said. It was inane, but Lamprophyre couldn't think of anything important to say, either.

She looked over her shoulder at Hyaloclast. She could feel Rokshan's presence beside her, a sense like being near a burning brand. It was a pleasant sensation. "Thank you," she said. "I know there isn't any way I can repay you, but thank you."

"I didn't do it to be repaid, Lamprophyre," Hyaloclast said. Her eyes were still narrowed as she regarded Lamprophyre and Rokshan. Abruptly, she said, "Stand up."

Puzzled, Lamprophyre stood. Hyaloclast loomed over her and tilted her head back, looking first into one eye and then the other. She ran her hand over Lamprophyre's head, gently pressing down on the sensitive spot at the back. Lamprophyre's eyes crossed involuntarily at the feeling, not painful but not quite pleasurable. She couldn't remember if it had been that sensitive before.

"*Stones,*" Hyaloclast swore. Lamprophyre had never heard her mother swear before. "Did you have sex with him?"

Lamprophyre blushed. "No," she said, feeling both puzzled and afraid now.

"You must have done something," Hyaloclast said. "You're pairbonded."

Lamprophyre whipped around to stare at Rokshan and stepped

back too late when she realized she'd knocked him over. He looked as stunned as she felt. "That's impossible," Lamprophyre said. "Impossible. We didn't do anything but kiss."

The look her mother gave her made her wish she could sink into the ground. "I don't know what kind of attachment he has to you," Hyaloclast said, "but you are clearly pair-bonded to him. There's a physiological change—"

"But I didn't feel anything! Aren't dragons supposed to feel when it happens?"

Hyaloclast sighed. "If it happened when you were in human form, you likely wouldn't have. Humans lack the physiology to sense a pair-bond. Which to me suggests they lack the physiology to *form* a pair-bond. Clearly I'm wrong." She sighed again. "He'll have to die."

"*What?*" Lamprophyre exclaimed. A sharp, hot flash like a burning blade shot through her.

"You can't be pair-bonded to more than one person at a time, and a dragon and a human have no future, no way to produce offspring," Hyaloclast said. "He has to die so you can fulfil your potential as a dragon."

She made a move toward Rokshan, who'd just gotten to his feet. Lamprophyre put herself between him and the dragon queen. "Try it," she snarled. "You'll have to kill me to get to him, and I swear I won't make it easy."

Hyaloclast stopped. Her lips compressed in a thin, hard line. "I wasn't serious," she said. "That was to prove my supposition correct. How did you feel when I threatened the prince?"

Lamprophyre, still crouched and snarling, said nothing. But she remembered the feeling that had struck her when Hyaloclast had threatened Rokshan. It was gone now, but she still felt the brand that was Rokshan somewhere close behind her.

"There's a connection, isn't there," Hyaloclast said. "You know where he is as if you're attached in some way. That connection will grow stronger over time. It must mean...I don't know. I can only guess. You were still a dragon while you were in human form, or you couldn't have heard thoughts. You must not have lost your capacity to form a pair-bond." She smiled, a bitter, mirthless expression. "I should be happy that we have another curiosity to investigate, but I am parent enough only to see years of sorrow ahead for my daughter."

Rokshan came forward and put his hand on Lamprophyre's flank. "She was my best friend before she was my dearest love," he said, "and I refuse to believe that shared love will make us miserable."

"You are optimistic, little prince," Hyaloclast said.

"No. Daring. I want you to turn me into a dragon," Rokshan said.

Lamprophyre gasped.

"I can't do that," Hyaloclast said.

Rokshan's gaze didn't waver. "Evart figured it out. That artifact clearly has the power. It's the only way to give us both the life we want, together."

"But you've never been a dragon. You have no dragon body to return to. And no one is capable of imagining you as something you've never been." Hyaloclast sat back on her haunches. "You don't understand the tremendous willpower it takes, the amount of concentration, and the capacity of memory. Only a dragon could accomplish it, and no dragon has the knowledge."

"Then I'll find someone who can." Rokshan looked up at Lamprophyre. "It's what you want, isn't it?"

Lamprophyre nodded. She'd forgotten how to speak.

"Then I'll do it. However long it takes." Rokshan bent to pick up the serpentine artifact. "But now we have something to tell you."

"I shudder to imagine what more surprises you have in store for me," Hyaloclast said with a wry smile.

Lamprophyre blinked. She'd forgotten about the entity. If anyone needed to know about her, it was Hyaloclast. "It's a long story," she said, "and it starts a thousand years ago. Where it ends..." She drew in a breath and released it slowly along with a puff of smoke. "Where it ends, we don't yet know."

CHAPTER THIRTY-NINE

Lamprophyre slowed her descent to land lightly on the edge of the parkland, well away from the grand pavilion erected in the center of the training ground. In the three days since her restoration, she'd flown as much as she could without exhausting herself, accustoming herself to her body. That hadn't been as much flying as she'd hoped. She felt as tired and breathless after even a short flight as she had those first few days in her human body. But it was getting easier. She'd stopped knocking things over accidentally with her tail two days ago.

She walked forward to the edge of the space where the guests would stand, wishing the ground wasn't still squishy from yesterday's storm. It was roped off by lengths of silk circling the pavilion, with gaps for humans to pass through. None of the gaps would admit a dragon, but Lamprophyre didn't like the idea of being pressed so closely by people. She was content to sit outside the roped-off space and witness from a distance.

She was the first to arrive, which also contented her. She liked the feeling of being alone, without the press of thoughts or bodies that characterized even the embassy these days. It had been a surprise when dozens of people had showed up at the embassy when she'd "returned from the mountains," most of them only interested in greeting her and telling her how she'd been missed. Maybe she'd been wrong about how Tanajital felt about its dragon ambassador.

Settling on her haunches, she surveyed the pavilion. It was the biggest tent she'd ever seen, covered with a swath of canvas painted gaily in swirls of rose and green. Of course, it had to be large to fit both families, all of whom would stand witness to the ceremony, as well as the Archprelate and all five High Ecclesiasts. She crouched low to see beneath the canvas. The space was empty except for two low, padded stools whose tops were barely slanted so someone could kneel comfortably on them. Rokshan had said the ceremony included lots of standing and kneeling, and nobody wanted the bride or groom to pass out.

Rokshan. Wherever he was, it was far enough away for her attachment to him to be imperceptible. Though Hyaloclast had been right that its strength would increase. The heat of it was never overpowering, but she could sense him at greater distances every day.

She hadn't told her clutch about her unusual pair-bonding. She wouldn't be able to conceal it much longer, but finding the right way to bring it up had proved difficult. It was cowardly, she knew, but the thought of them being appalled or disgusted—of hearing those emotions in their thoughts—made her wish...no. She would never wish things different. And maybe that was the answer: she loved Rokshan, she wasn't ashamed of him or their love, and she should trust her clutchmates to understand.

She heard the flap of wings behind her, and shortly Coquina joined her. "That is an enormous tent," she said. "And how lucky that the day is pleasant. I'm sure the storm had them all worried."

"I did tell Rokshan it wouldn't last, but that was probably hard for Anchala to believe," Lamprophyre said.

"Humans put so much of themselves into their ceremonies, it makes sense that she'd worry." Coquina settled back and furled her wings. "Not like dragons. Pair-bonding, for example. It's so simple. One beat, you're the closest of friends, and the next, everything's different."

"So much simpler," Lamprophyre agreed, willing herself not to blush.

"And then it's like you can't remember how you felt about your mate before he was your mate," Coquina said. "It's marvelous."

"So you're happy. You and Flint."

"Of course. That deep connection, knowing where he is all the time like this tingling down my spine..." Coquina sighed. "I'm glad we stayed for the wedding, but I'm looking forward to going home. I love winter in the mountains."

"So do I." She wished Rokshan were close enough for her to feel his nearness.

Coquina suddenly let out an exasperated noise. "Lamprophyre," she said irritably, "I can only be patient for so long. Either you can tell me on your own, or I can drag it out of you."

Lamprophyre looked at her, startled. "Tell you what?"

"That you're pair-bonded. To Rokshan."

Lamprophyre sucked in a breath. "What?"

Coquina rolled her eyes. "I didn't believe it at first, because it's impossible. But when you're pair-bonded, you can sense the presence of a pair-bond in someone else. Obviously it's not one of our clutch-mates, and you haven't been home in a dozen twelvedays." She extended her tiny sixth claw and began delicately cleaning around the base of her other claws. "How did it happen?"

Relief at no longer keeping the secret made the tension ebb from Lamprophyre's shoulders. "We—Hyaloclast and I—we don't know. A human isn't supposed to be capable of forming a pair-bond, but I was a dragon in human form...anyway. But I love him," she said, feeling defiant in saying it aloud.

"Maybe that was inevitable," Coquina said with a shrug. "He *is* your best friend, and that's really how it works for dragons—you grow up having your clutchmates as your closest friends, and then one of them becomes closer than that." She smiled. "And Rokshan is practically a dragon in human form."

"He's what?"

Coquina shrugged again. "He's generous, and protective, and nurturing of others, and good at making others their best selves. Those are all male dragon characteristics. Maybe you saw something in him you didn't realize was there."

A warm, glowing sensation swelled within Lamprophyre, something that filled her the way a new idea she'd never thought to consider did. "Maybe you're right," she murmured. If she had recognized something in Rokshan that spoke to her as a dragon, maybe she wasn't so strange, after all. "And he wants to be a dragon," she blurted out, then felt stupid. Rokshan's hope for transformation was even more impossible than forming a pair-bond with a human, and sharing it might be a violation of his privacy.

"Of course he does." Coquina began working on her other hand. "How can we make that happen?"

"'We'?"

Coquina shot her a sharp glance. "Of course 'we.' You think any of us want you to be miserable? You were transformed by Evart—that transformation must be possible again."

The warm feeling threatened to overwhelm her. She wished she were human to cry tears of relief and happiness. "I thought you'd think I was strange. Or aberrant."

"Well, I'm not saying I wasn't surprised," Coquina said, "but you can't believe any of us would think anything but the best of you."

Lamprophyre stared at Coquina, speechless. Finally, she said, "Have I told you before how sorry I am we were enemies for so long?"

Coquina hugged her. "We'll figure this out. All of us together," she whispered.

Lamprophyre hugged her back. "If we were humans, we'd be crying," she said.

"Thank the Stones we're not gushy humans," Coquina said with a laugh.

"Crying is surprisingly satisfying," Lamprophyre replied.

The rush of many wings filled the air, and dragons dropped down to surround the two. "Oh, you're hugging," Dolomite said. "Does that mean we can stop pretending not to know about Lamprophyre and Rokshan?"

Orthoclase laughed at Lamprophyre's stunned expression. "We've been around humans too long if we can pretend that well," he said. "You didn't think we'd disapprove, did you?"

"She did, and that's natural," said Flint. "Imagine what old Scoria will say. Or even Chrysoprase. I swear she's secretly three hundred the way she acts like she has a stick up her rear end."

"But we know you and Rokshan both, and we'll back you up," Bromargyrite said. "It's not so strange if you know Rokshan. He's practically a dragon in human form."

"That's what Coquina said," Lamprophyre said with a laugh.

"Well, she *is* female, and you know how smart all you females are," Porphyry said, jogging Lamprophyre in the side with an elbow. "Seriously, you shouldn't worry."

"I won't," Lamprophyre said. "I really won't. Thank you."

"Then let's try to enjoy this ceremony," Flint said. "It's either going to be fascinating or mind-numbingly boring."

"Humans don't pair-bond, so they have to dress up their marriage ceremonies to satisfy everyone that they're real," Lamprophyre said. "That ought to be interesting enough even for you."

The dragons spread out and settled in to wait. Aside from wanting a little time to herself, Lamprophyre had felt it would be better for the dragon guests to be in place before the humans arrived, so no one would feel in danger of being trampled or knocked over. She sat in peaceful quiet, enjoying the drifting, wordless thoughts of the clutch. They didn't hate her or think she was strange. They saw Rokshan as practically a dragon. For the first time in days, she felt everything would work out.

She heard the first humans approaching before they appeared, gathering at the far side of the parkland and proceeding on foot. They walked wide around the dragons, their thoughts full of wonder but not fear. How different from the first time Lamprophyre had set foot on the training grounds. Then, she'd been shot at. Now nobody pictured any of the dragons as a threat.

The roped-off space gradually filled with human guests. It looked as though they'd been herded, which amused Lamprophyre. All of them wore brightly colored clothing of a type she wasn't familiar with: long, billowing robes in deep, jewel-like colors with wide sleeves that revealed white underrobes. Their feet squelching in the mucky ground appeared to be bare, which Lamprophyre found unusual, given how humans loved sandals so much. She absently rubbed her foot in memory. That was something about a human body she didn't miss.

Then she felt Rokshan's presence, faint but still recognizable, and her heart beat faster. She hadn't seen him since yesterday before the storm, and it surprised her how much she missed him even for that short time. He was inside the palace, approaching the great front door, which was invisible from her position. She resolutely didn't look that way. She'd see him soon enough.

A deep, ringing tone filled the air, the sound of a brass disc like the one in the dining hall. Everyone in the roped-off area turned to look, so Lamprophyre did too. For a moment, nothing was visible. Then the brass disc sounded again, and in two beats it came around the corner of the palace. A couple of heavily muscled men carried its wooden frame, and a girl in yellow and green followed with the mallet. The disc swayed with the motion of its bearers, but that didn't affect its deep, rich sound when the girl struck it again.

Behind the disc walked King Ekanath, wearing a robe similar to everyone else's, but in the royal colors of green and yellow. Queen Satiya walked beside him, her hand resting lightly on his arm. Both were bareheaded, something Rokshan had said was symbolic of reverence before God. Following them in two snaking columns were the other members of the family, all Anchala's siblings except Khadar, the aunties, more distant relations—and there was Rokshan behind Tekentriya, robed to match his father.

Lamprophyre's breath caught in excitement. He didn't look her way, but she knew he was aware of her—couldn't help but be aware of her, since she was large and bright blue. She'd found herself still capable of seeing things from a human perspective, and she loved how handsome he was, as well as how attractive his spirit was to her dragon self.

The procession passed the pavilion and circled all the way around it until the brass disc reached the western side, where the dragons sat on either side of an imaginary hallway. Lamprophyre instinctively rose as the disc and the procession approached, prompting the other dragons to rise, too. The procession passed between them, and now Rokshan did catch Lamprophyre's eye. He smiled, the barest quirk of his lips, before going back to staring at the back of Tekentriya's head. Lamprophyre smiled too, enjoying his nearness, that warm feeling like a brand. She wished he was capable of feeling their bond, too.

The brass disc in its frame disappeared into the pavilion and passed beyond Lamprophyre's sight. Gradually, the rest of the procession joined it. Lamprophyre wanted to crouch so she could see everything, but it wasn't time for that, and Rokshan had explained it all to her anyway: the families arranged themselves by status and closeness of relation to the bride and groom and waited. There wasn't anything exciting about that.

Silence fell. Lamprophyre shifted her weight and coiled her tail more tightly around herself. Her body wasn't uncomfortable anymore, for the most part, but occasionally she had a moment where she remembered being human and felt out of place in her dragon body. That would pass. She wasn't sure if that was something she hoped for or not.

Another deep tone rang out, and everyone turned to watch a second brass disc in a wooden frame appear around the corner. This time, only two people followed it. Anchala and Torannum, their arms linked, paced slowly behind the disc, following the path the first procession had taken. They wore only white underrobes and looked ethereal, even strongly-built Torannum. They, too, passed between the dragons to enter the pavilion from the west.

As soon as they'd disappeared, music filtered toward them, growing louder until it was audible as pipes and voices singing a wordless song. Lamprophyre turned to watch the approach of a third procession, this one garbed almost entirely in yellow. Young men and women with the distinctive haircuts of the servants of the High Ecclesiasts carried the song with them as they walked between the dragons, followed by Khadar and the rest of the High Ecclesiasts in their assigned colors. The Archprelate brought up the rear, resplendent in a many-colored robe that echoed all five High Ecclesiasts. She didn't acknowledge the dragons, but her smile grew wider, as if she was happy to see them.

Once the Archprelate passed, Lamprophyre crouched low so she could see beneath the canvas. She heard the other dragons doing the same, as well as Orthoclase's silent irritation that he didn't have a very good view. Well, that couldn't be helped. There wasn't that much space.

Torannum and Anchala faced westward, so Lamprophyre had a good view of their faces before the Archprelate stepped in front of them. "Torannum and Anchala," she said in her sweet, high-pitched voice. "You come before Jiwanyil's representative in this place, at this time, to make oath of marriage to one another."

"We do," Torannum and Anchala said in unison.

"Kneel," the Archprelate said. Torannum and Anchala sank onto the padded stools.

"You kneel in acknowledgement of your respect for God. God accepts your reverence." She gestured for the two to stand. "You kneel again in acknowledgment of your respect for your ancestors."

Lamprophyre suppressed a yawn. If this was how it was going to go, with the two kneeling in respect to Stones knew how many things, it was no wonder they provided the bride and groom with stools.

Her mind wandered to Rokshan, standing behind his parents to the left of Anchala and Torannum. He was utterly convinced that it was possible to transform him into a dragon, and even though he'd stopped talking about it, she was sure it was still on his mind. Sometimes he even had her convinced. But in quiet moments, like now, she could give in to despair. Hyaloclast had restored her because she knew Lamprophyre's dragon body the way only a mother could, and because she had a dragon's memory to hold that form in thought long enough for the transformation to happen. Even if another dragon had that memory, Rokshan didn't have a dragon body to be restored to.

She realized she was tapping her fingers on the mushy ground and made herself stop. She would stop worrying about it. Worrying wouldn't solve the problem. And if Rokshan could be determined to make it happen, so could she.

"...and this you promise to hold dear until you pass into Jiwanyil's grace?" the Archprelate said. Lamprophyre had been half-listening, and that sounded like the Archprelate was coming to the end.

"We do," Anchala and Torannum said.

"As Jiwanyil's representative on earth, I name you husband and wife," the Archprelate said. "May your life together be long and fruitful." She laid her hands on their foreheads and bowed her head, and the families in the pavilion and the crowds surrounding it knelt with head bowed. It felt to Lamprophyre as if they were acknowledging the presence of deity, so she bowed her head even though Jiwanyil wasn't her God. He'd touched her life twice before, and she felt a connection to him regardless.

No one moved for a few beats. Then the Archprelate raised her head and lowered her arms, and said, "Go in peace, and may Jiwanyil's light shine on all present."

"Jiwanyil's light," the crowd repeated, and then Anchala and Torannum threw their arms around each other and kissed, prompting a cheer from the rising crowd. Lamprophyre rose and stretched stiff muscles. So that was a human wedding. If Hyaloclast hadn't returned, she would have had one of her own. She felt only a tiny pang of sadness at letting that go. Pair-bonded was so much better than married. She didn't think it was arrogant to believe that, not with how her connection to Rokshan felt.

The crowd was pressing forward to congratulate the bride and groom, but Lamprophyre felt Rokshan approaching her. Soon, he emerged from the crowd, looking disheveled from forcing his way through. "And now it's over," he said, "and there's a party, and I hope Manishi doesn't decide to remarry any time soon, because I don't think I could take it."

"It was lovely," Porphyry said. "Not at all like dragons do it."

Rokshan glanced at Lamprophyre. "I don't know how dragons pair-bond."

"You don't?" Dolomite said. "Then how did it happen for you and Lamprophyre?"

Rokshan's eyes went wide. "They guessed," Lamprophyre told him.

"They guessed," Rokshan repeated. He laughed and put a hand on Lamprophyre's flank. "Then I assume we're not outcast."

"Just different," Coquina said. "And we want to help you become a dragon."

Now Rokshan looked so astonished Lamprophyre thought he

might temporarily have been struck mute. "They say you're practically already a dragon," she told him. "So you have their blessing."

"I—" Rokshan's gaze swept over the clutch. "You know it's impossible," he said.

"Lamprophyre said you were determined," Flint said.

"Yes, but I only said that to keep her from falling into despair." Rokshan patted Lamprophyre's flank. "Sorry."

"It happened before, so it can happen again," Coquina said, "and we will figure it out. So don't either of you fall into despair. Now, does the party include us? Because I've been sitting for a thousand beats and I'm starving."

"It does," Rokshan said, "and I asked Akarshan to make something special for you dragons that I know Lamprophyre loves. I hope it's successful."

Lamprophyre lingered behind the others with Rokshan, wishing she were small enough to hold his hand. "What did you tell everyone about Lelitha?"

Rokshan sighed. "That she went back to Adakavi. I didn't give details. But Anchala and Sanyot and practically everyone else I know think I'm pining over Lelitha having rejected me. On the other hand, it gives me an excuse to spend all my time with you, getting over my heartbreak."

"I'm sorry. That must be uncomfortable."

"It will pass. It helps that my heart isn't actually broken." He brushed his hand over the scales of her leg. "I hope you don't mind that I keep doing this. I missed the way your scales feel."

Lamprophyre blushed. That touch felt so much more intimate now that she knew he loved her. "Dragons aren't as sensitive as humans, but it feels nice," she said. That reminded her of something else, something Hyaloclast had explained a few days before. She'd been uncertain of whether to tell Rokshan, since it didn't really matter to him, but... "Hyaloclast told me about the sensitive spot at the back of my head."

Rokshan raised his eyebrows. "Really? I thought nobody knew what that was for."

"Um, well, it turns out they do, it's just not something we learn about until our parents explain it. Explain sex. The spot is for getting ready for sex. It's not indecent or anything," she went on in a rush when Rokshan's face went red, "it's not like human breasts or something humans would keep covered up, it's just that when two dragons —oh, please don't look like that! I didn't want to embarrass you!"

"I can't stop thinking about how often I've leaned against that spot," Rokshan managed.

"*No*, it's not like that at all, I promise! It doesn't mean anything for a human to touch it, just another dragon. Like how a male dragon wouldn't be aroused by seeing a human female's breasts. And you're my mate, so it really isn't inappropriate at all."

Rokshan was still so red she was afraid he might forget to breathe. "I'll take your word for it," he finally said. "And it's a good thing we're pair-bonded, because I don't think I could bring myself to fly with you again if we weren't."

"Rokshan—"

"Lamprophyre," said a new voice.

Lamprophyre, startled, looked away from Rokshan to see Manishi standing before her. The adept held her maimed arm across her chest as if her right breast needed supporting, but otherwise didn't look as if it bothered her. "I want to speak with you," she said.

"I—at the wedding? Can it wait?" Lamprophyre said. She didn't actually care about discussing business, which was almost certainly what Manishi had in mind, at a wedding. She just didn't feel like talking to Manishi right then, or ever. She still felt inappropriate guilt when she looked at the adept's arm.

Manishi shrugged. "This won't take long. When can I expect delivery?"

"Um, delivery? Of what?"

Manishi gave her a long, considering look. "Of my eggshell, obviously. You said every three to five years—how far along on your cycle are you?"

"It—that's not exactly how it works," Lamprophyre said. "You didn't transform me. You don't get anything."

"The agreement was that I would *perform* the magic, not that it had to succeed," Manishi said. "You have that prodigious memory—tell me I'm wrong."

"You can't possibly expect her to deliver on that promise when you failed," Rokshan said.

Lamprophyre reviewed her conversation with Manishi in her head. Her heart sank. That *was* what she'd agreed to, wasn't it? "You're going to wait a long while," she said. "I'm not pair-bonded to anyone I can have an egg with."

Now Manishi turned her look on Rokshan. "Not yet," she said. "But I'm sure you'll find a mate eventually. I can wait. Just remember, you promised." She poked Lamprophyre in the stomach for emphasis —Lamprophyre guessed she'd wanted to poke her chest, but couldn't reach—and walked away, letting her maimed arm fall to swing by her side.

Rokshan and Lamprophyre stared at each other. "She's not going to give up nagging me until she gets what she wants," Lamprophyre said.

"You don't think she suspects about us, do you?" Rokshan said.

"I doubt it. Why would anyone not a dragon suspect? But maybe—"

Rokshan shook his head. "I considered that. But she failed once to transform you and it nearly killed her. Permanently injured her. I don't like her, and I think she might be slightly evil, but I don't think I can ask her to figure out how to transform me at that cost."

Lamprophyre resumed walking toward where the crowd and the dragons had gathered, at the far side of the training grounds. "I agree. The thing is, we have the serpentine artifact now. It shouldn't be impossible to find someone who can figure out how to make it work."

"Except that the person who makes it work has to have a draconic memory," Rokshan pointed out.

Lamprophyre prodded his shoulder, making him stagger. "Now who's giving in to despair?"

"Sorry." Rokshan sighed. "Look, let's have a nice meal, and go flying, and forget about this for a while, all right?"

The smell of lamb in a delicious sauce wafted to Lamprophyre's nostrils. "All right. Is that what I think it is?"

Tables with chairs had been set up for the guests, who were serving themselves from communal dishes. Off to one side stood an enormous cauldron presided over by Akarshan himself, chief cook at the palace and an old friend of Lamprophyre's. Lamprophyre peered over the edge and saw chunks of lamb floating in a pale yellow soup.

"Prince Rokshan wanted to see if you dragons would enjoy this," Akarshan said. "Normally the broth is thicker than this, but we use wheat or rice flour to thicken it and you wouldn't be able to digest that. But the spices should make up for it." He ladled the delicious-smelling soup into a dragon-sized bowl and handed it to her.

Lamprophyre tipped the bowl to her lips and drank. It wasn't as good as it was with rice and bread, but the flavor was every bit as wonderful and the lamb chunks were tender and delicious. "Oh, that is so good," she breathed. Akarshan beamed with pleasure.

She took her bowl to sit with the rest of her clutch and made room for Rokshan, who had a more conventional form of the meal. "This is my favorite human food," she said.

"It's wonderful," Orthoclase said. "And it would be even more wonderful with a sprinkling of granite and some crushed beryl."

"I was thinking of beryl myself," Porphyry said. "Your influence must be rubbing off on me."

"Waves of the sea," Orthoclase said. "It's the briny tang that does it."

"What does that mean, 'waves of the sea'?" Dolomite asked.

Orthoclase shrugged. "Some stones have old names like that. Poetic names that fit with a stone's appearance. Beryl is most commonly that sort of blue-tinged green color, and that's supposed to be like the waves of the sea. Though I've never seen the sea, so who knows?" He took another bite.

"There's a poem about lace agate that calls it the crystal forest," Lamprophyre said, "and—"

Memory struck. "The banded desert," she said. "I remember now. It's a stone."

"That was the destruction of Hamadri," Rokshan said. "If banded desert is a stone, and dragons are named for stones—"

"Then Hamadri really was destroyed by a dragon," Lamprophyre said.

The others watched her curiously. "What's Hamadri?" Coquina asked.

"What stone?" Rokshan said.

Lamprophyre felt chilled despite the warmth of the day. "Sardonyx," she said. "The banded desert is the stone sardonyx."

Rokshan looked as stunned as she felt. "You mean a dragon named Sardonyx," he said.

For just a moment, Lamprophyre thought she heard a distant, evil laugh.

SNEAK PEEK: SKIES WILL BURN

Lamprophyre sat back on her haunches and restlessly flexed her wings, sending a cooling draft over her body. At nearly noon on the first day of winter, the sun's rays weren't as punishingly hot as they would be in a few twelvedays—a few *months*—but the day was still unusually warm, warmer than was comfortable for a dragon. It hadn't rained in several days, and the dragon embassy courtyard smelled of dust and, faintly, the roast pig Lamprophyre had had for breakfast. It also smelled, closer to hand, of leather and the oily tang of warm metal. Such ordinary smells with such extraordinary meaning.

She lifted the tangle of leather straps and metal buckles in one hand and eyed it narrowly. Wide leather bands connected to an oddly shaped piece of leather, stitched to curve up on both long sides in an oblong cupped shape. Thinner bands hung off the tapering ends of the oblong, attached to fat metal triangles barely big enough to fit all her fingers through. Buckles swung and tapped against each other, making little *tink* sounds that contrasted with the soft purr of leather rubbing against leather.

"I don't know about this," she said.

"It was your idea, Lamprophyre," Rokshan said.

"Yes, but I didn't know it would look like this. And *this*—" She tapped a finger against the leather oblong. "Did it have to look so much like a saddle?"

"It's the only way to connect all the harness straps and keep them from crippling me," Rokshan reminded her. "Look. If you don't want—"

"I do. I'm sorry. It's just, now it's ready, I feel so foolish putting it on. Dragons aren't draft animals."

"You could think of it as a kind of clothing," her clutchmate Flint offered. "Utilitarian clothing."

"Dragons don't wear clothes, either." Lamprophyre sighed. "All right. Help me get it settled."

The...saddle...went first, fitted snugly into the notch above her shoulders by Flint. It was heavy and awkward enough it took a dragon to manage it. Then the straps under her arms that buckled securely across her chest. The iron buckle rubbed uncomfortably across her scales, but it wasn't painful, so she didn't say anything. Next, the straps above her arms that crossed over the base of her throat. Those were more comfortable, though they would have choked a human; dragon hide was stronger than that.

She cinched the buckles tight and twisted her torso to make sure the straps were secure. The metal triangles, the stirrups, bounced lightly off her sides. The harness actually wasn't that awkward, no worse than human sandals had been, and she'd endured those.

"All right, climb up," she said to Rokshan, crouching so the left-hand stirrup scraped the hard-packed earth of the courtyard.

Rokshan settled himself in his accustomed seat. "Oh," he said in a breathless voice. "That's...very snug now."

"Does it hurt?" Flint asked.

"Not hurt so much as...compress. I think the saddle needs to be of thinner leather."

Lamprophyre twisted to look at him, but as usual saw only her own shoulder. "Should we have them make a different one?"

"I've waited two weeks to race with you, Lamprophyre. I'm not putting it off because of a little discomfort." Rokshan fitted his feet into the stirrups. She felt the brush of leather against her skin as he fastened the hip straps. "They can make another one after we try this out. There might be other adjustments to make."

Lamprophyre shifted the buckle of the chest band. "Good point. Are you ready?"

Rokshan patted her neck. "Ready."

Lamprophyre nodded at Flint, who launched himself into the sky and winged his way southward toward the warehouses where the rest of the clutch lived. She drew in as deep a breath as she could manage against the chest band and followed Flint.

Flying wearing the harness didn't feel any different than it usually did, except for how the buckles pressed against her scales, rubbing lightly. On anyone but a dragon, that would result in painful sores over time, but no dragon's hide could be damaged by something as soft as iron. It was annoying, but no more than that, and Lamprophyre could bear a little annoyance.

They flew in silence across Tanajital, not needing to speak. Rokshan's presence on her shoulders was a pleasantly warm ember, constantly reminding her he was there. Occasionally the reality of it struck her: she, a dragon, was pair-bonded to a human she loved more than anything, and then she felt warm all over and not just from her mate's presence. Their bond had continued to strengthen over the last two twelvedays until now she could tell where he was from halfway across Tanajital.

She felt him run his hand over the base of her neck, below the sensitive spot at the back of her head. They weren't the same species, and couldn't share physical intimacy, but his touch meant so much more now that she knew he loved her.

Dragons rose into the sky ahead, orange and red and green and silver, and came to meet them as Lamprophyre approached. "So it works," Coquina said. "It's surprisingly attractive."

"You think so?" Lamprophyre asked. She'd felt so awkward, feeling them all stare at her, that Coquina's response was a surprise.

The drifting surface thoughts of the clutch showed they were all in agreement with Coquina. "It looks like jewelry," Dolomite said. "Very plain jewelry. I realize that doesn't make sense."

"We could make them brighter," Bromargyrite said, himself a beacon of brilliant orange and yellow. "If it's a success."

"There aren't many people we'll want to have ride," Orthoclase pointed out. "Just Rokshan and Melika and maybe Lokun."

"And it's not as if you need riders," Rokshan said. "This is purely for humans' benefit."

"Then I suppose it's time to test it," Lamprophyre said.

They flew low across the city to give the residents of Tanajital something wonderful to look at. Lamprophyre loved how the city's voice, a low, rumbling hum, grew higher and more excited whenever the dragons appeared. People stopped in the street and pointed, held their children up for a better view, and a few of them even cheered. How different from the first days almost a year ago, when Lamprophyre's appearance had started more than a few riots. Rokshan had said, back then, that it was human nature to quickly grow accustomed to the strange until it became normal, and then normal became taken for granted. Now, she knew from talking to the people who came to the embassy for the free soup, most citizens saw the dragons as part of the city.

They crossed the Green River and flew on a few dozen dragonlengths to the tall wooden structures, red as the floor of the coliseum, that marked the racing course. If Lamprophyre had to attribute dragons' success at making Tanajital love them to anything, this would be it. Rokshan's idle thought that humans might enjoy watching dragons race had turned into this semi-permanent collection of obstacles and the two tall spectator stands on either side. A third stand, topped by a green and gold canopy, gave the royal family somewhere to sit when they attended.

The seven dragons of the clutch alit on the field. "How should we do this?" Rokshan asked. "Run the obstacle course?"

"I was thinking of a speed test first," Lamprophyre said. "Something straightforward."

"Then let's make it a true race," Coquina said. Her clutchmates groaned. "What?" she protested with a smile. "You might win."

"The odds are not in our favor, love," Flint said, elbowing his mate. "But it's still a good idea. We'll be there in case Rokshan falls off."

"Let's not use those words, all right?" Rokshan said. "I don't want the Immanence hearing and deciding to make my life short and exciting."

Lamprophyre pushed off and flapped until she was just above the spectator stands. "Everything will be fine. Tell me when you're ready."

Rokshan patted her neck again, then gripped her ruff firmly. "Ready."

Lamprophyre glanced to either side, where the other dragons had gathered. "Go!" she shouted, and seven dragons sent up a tremendous wind as they took off for the horizon.

Lamprophyre had never flown as fast as she could with Rokshan as a passenger. Now his knees gripped her shoulders firmly, his heels in the stirrups dug into her sides, and she gradually sped up until she had to close her nictitating membranes to protect her eyes from the wind.

Coquina was already well in the lead, with Porphyry close behind. Flint and Bromargyrite flanked Lamprophyre, and she had just realized they were doing it on purpose when Orthoclase pulled ahead and Dolomite dropped to fly beneath her. She loved how much care her clutchmates had for Rokshan, how he was one of them for all he was human.

Below Dolomite, the ground streamed past in streaks of green and brown and gray, with the Green River a glittering stripe to the left. The horizon lay low and steady in the distance, misty with an oncoming storm. Rain would be welcome after so many dry days. Ahead, Coquina and Porphyry had reached the lone tree that marked the end of their race course and were wheeling to return. Orthoclase had made up ground and was barely a dragonlength behind the leaders.

"Hold on!" Lamprophyre shouted to her rider. She thought about slowing to take the turn more gently, but what would be the point of the test if she didn't push her limits? So she sped up instead, aiming to the right of the tree, which was tall and slender like a giant finger pointing at the sky. Flint and Bromargyrite moved away, giving her room to make the turn—

—and she banked hard, wheeled on her left hind leg, and tilted nearly sideways as she circled the tree and headed back toward the obstacle course. Rokshan's grip on her shoulders and ruff tightened, and he shouted, a wordless cry of exhilaration that made Lamprophyre's heart leap. He hadn't shifted at all and the saddle hadn't slid. Lamprophyre shouted with him and sped faster.

There was no way she could catch Coquina or Porphyry, but she pushed herself as fast as she could go. Rokshan leaned closer, pressing against the sensitive spot and sending a pleasant tingle through her body. He'd finally gotten over his embarrassment at learning that spot was related to sex, at least when a dragon touched it, but he still avoided leaning against it. She wondered what had made him do it now.

She sped past the finish line, which was more a mutually-agreed upon spot near the spectator stands than an actual line, and shed momentum until she hovered over the royal stand. "It worked," she said, somewhat breathlessly.

"It did," Rokshan said. His voice was strained, and he continued to lean forward across her neck.

"Are you all right? You sound as if you'd done the racing."

"Wind...took my breath," Rokshan gasped. "And I think my eyeballs tried to escape my skull. We'll need to figure out a way to protect me from the wind if we're going to fly that fast."

"I hadn't thought of that. Sorry."

"Don't be. It was amazing. And you were right. That's something I want to share with you, now and always."

Lamprophyre blushed. "Until you can fly on your own."

"Until then." Rokshan leaned forward and hugged her neck. Neither of them said what Lamprophyre knew they were both thinking, even without listening to his thoughts: the chances of Rokshan being transformed into a dragon were not good. They'd searched for a solution for weeks and were no closer now than they'd been on the day Lamprophyre had been turned back into a dragon from the human form she'd had for a twelveday.

She wanted it as much as he did, but with so much time passing with no success, she was ready to give in to despair and admit defeat. She had to remind herself frequently that twenty-five days with no success wasn't all that long, but her impatient heart didn't want to be reminded.

The rest of the clutch gathered around them, hovering in midair. "It worked," Flint said. "I can't believe it worked."

"What, you didn't have faith in your own creation?" Lamprophyre teased.

"Faith is one thing. Testing an idea in the real world is something else." Flint lazily flapped his wings until he was next to Coquina. "Now let's have you run the obstacle course and give it a *real* test."

"Or...maybe not. Who's that?" Orthoclase asked. He sat up alertly, half-turned to look in the direction of the city. Lamprophyre followed his gaze. A small figure sped toward them, one Lamprophyre recognized after a closer look.

"It's Rassika," she said. Worry crept over her. Rassika often ran errands for her, but those were always things Lamprophyre requested. For Rassika to be here on her own, or sent by some other member of the embassy household, something had to be wrong.

She listened to Rassika's thoughts as the girl drew nearer and found them worryingly single-minded, suggesting Rassika was in some distress: *find Lamprophyre, ecclesiasts here, hope I don't have to run all over Tanajital.* Ecclesiasts? The representatives of the human religion weren't officially at odds with dragons anymore, but that didn't stop some ecclesiasts from preaching to the heathen dragons, trying to convince them to worship the made-up dragon god Katayan. Lamprophyre didn't like the thought of dealing with ecclesiasts, however innocent their intentions might be.

She put a hand out to catch Rassika as the girl stumbled to a halt before her. "Don't speak just yet," she said. "Catch your breath. Nothing's so urgent it can't wait a few beats."

Rassika shook her head, but she was bent over with her hands on her knees, sucking in air without speaking. *Hurry back Depik says, don't know what they want, nothing good,* she thought.

"Is everyone all right?" Lamprophyre said when Rassika's breathing had stilled somewhat. She knew no one of her household was hurt, but Rassika didn't know dragons could hear thoughts, and that wasn't a secret Lamprophyre felt inclined to share.

Rassika nodded. "'S not that," she said. "'S ecclesiasts at the embassy. Want to talk t' you, my lady."

Lamprophyre exchanged glances with her clutchmates. They looked as concerned as she felt. "About what?"

"Dunno. Wouldn't say. Just that they need to talk to the dragon ambassador and they'll wait 'til you're back." Rassika took one last deep breath and let it out slowly. "It was two of 'em, my lady, and they di'nt have those people with 'em, the ones with the ugly haircuts."

"That's unexpected," Lamprophyre said.

"You don't think they want us to leave Tanajital again, do you?" Bromargyrite said.

"Unlikely," Coquina said. "The Archprelate likes us, and she wouldn't allow anyone to persecute us even if we do follow a different religion. Though that doesn't mean this isn't a couple of ecclesiasts with their own agenda."

"We won't find out if we sit around here guessing," Lamprophyre said. "I suppose I can go see what they want. Rassika, do you want a ride back?"

Rassika hesitated before nodding. Lamprophyre heard the traces of fear in her thoughts, but the girl was trying hard to suppress them, so Lamprophyre decided not to say anything that might reinforce those fears.

"I'll take you," Porphyry said, bending low to give her a leg up. He was a good choice, Lamprophyre thought, because he was a frequent visitor to the embassy and Rassika's thoughts showed she felt more comfortable with him than with the other dragons.

Lamprophyre crouched to let Rokshan up. "Supper tonight at the warehouses?" she asked.

"We can make adjustments to the harness," Flint agreed. "You bring the cows."

Lamprophyre nodded and leaped into the air.

She decided not to hurry back. Not only was she slightly tired from the race, she didn't think it was a good idea to let the ecclesiasts think dragons would drop everything at their summons. So she flew at her usual pace and admired Tanajital's gleaming metal roofs. The smell of gold sharpened her appetite. Cow for supper would be especially delicious.

"I wonder if Dharan would be more willing to ride a dragon if he could be strapped in," she mused.

"Dharan would only agree to the harness if you promised not to fly anywhere," Rokshan said. "I don't think you appreciate his hatred and fear of heights."

"I actually do, because when I had a human body, heights scared me. It was knowing I couldn't save myself from a fall that made them terrifying. But I think I could have borne to ride if I'd had that harness." She banked left to avoid one of the looming towers. The hum of the city was quieter now, during what would in summer be a rest hour getting people away from the worst of the heat. At this season, it was just tradition to nap indoors. Lamprophyre thought humans ought to welcome the cooler weather and take advantage of it to be active, but humans didn't think like dragons did.

Ahead, the blue roof of the embassy came into view. It had been a customs house long before Lamprophyre had arrived in Tanajital, and now Lamprophyre thought of it as almost a second home. It was as cozy as her own cave in the mountains, spacious enough to fit two female dragons and always smelling of fresh air and the warm, musky scent of dragon skin.

Two yellow-curtained litters waited in the courtyard, bright blotches against the dark earth. Their bearers had set them down on the spindly legs attached to the four corners and stood stolidly beside each one, arms folded across their muscular bare chests. Lamprophyre had developed an understanding of human attractiveness while she was temporarily in a human body, but she still didn't see the appeal of humorously bulging muscles.

The ecclesiasts hadn't been smart enough, or foresighted enough, to leave room for a dragon to land in the courtyard, and Lamprophyre had to perch on the roof ridge beam so Porphyry and his small passenger could alight near the dining pavilion. Porphyry crouched very low to let Rassika climb down, which she did with alacrity, though Lamprophyre didn't hear any unusually frightened thoughts from her.

"I'll see you later," Porphyry said as he beat the air to rise even with her head. "I cannot wait to hear what all this is about."

Lamprophyre grimaced. To him, no matter what the ecclesiasts wanted, it would all be an amusing story to be told round a comfortable bonfire. To her, the ambassador, it would likely be an annoyance at best and an infuriating demand at worst. She flapped gracefully to the spot Porphyry had vacated and waited for Rokshan to climb down before unfastening the buckles and shrugging out of the harness.

The ecclesiasts had emerged from the litters the moment she set foot on earth and now stood watching her disentangle herself. Their attention made her uncomfortable, and she fumbled more awkwardly than she'd intended getting the saddle free of the notch. She finally dropped the harness on the ground and said, embarrassment sharpening her tone, "Yes? How can I help you?"

The ecclesiasts looked at each other. The man was thinking *Jiwanyil have mercy she's bigger than a house*, though his awed fear didn't show on his face. The woman's thoughts were less fearful: *convince her of Jiwanyil's cause, heard they were logical creatures.* That was interesting, and potentially bad. Lamprophyre was in no mood to debate religion with anyone.

"My lady ambassador, greetings from the Archprelate," the woman said. She didn't bow, but Lamprophyre already knew ecclesiasts didn't generally bow to anyone not another ecclesiast. "I am Ashta, and this is Nirav. We have an important matter to discuss with you."

"If it's about how dragons should worship Katayan, I've already heard that one," Lamprophyre said. Rokshan chuckled under his breath.

Ashta didn't react. "Dragons' relationship with the Lonely God is not, at present, our concern," she said. "I have been possessed of a prophecy relating to your people, however, and the Archprelate instructed me to bring it before you."

This news didn't make Lamprophyre feel better. "And what prophecy is that?" she asked, hoping she didn't sound as sarcastic as she felt.

Ashta tilted her head to look Lamprophyre in the eye. "Jiwanyil instructs me to climb the holy mountain Nirinatan," she said. "What dragons refer to as Mother Stone."

ABOUT THE AUTHOR

In addition to the Dragons of Mother Stone series, Melissa McShane is the author of many other fantasy novels, including the novels of Tremontane, the first of which is *Servant of the Crown;* the Extraordinaries series, beginning with *Burning Bright;* and *The Book of Secrets,* first book in The Last Oracle series.

She lives in the shelter of the mountains out West with her husband, three children and a niece, and three very needy cats. She wrote reviews and critical essays for many years before turning to fiction, which is much more fun than anyone ought to be allowed to have. You can visit her at her website **www.melissamc shanewrites.com** for more information on other books and upcoming releases.

For news on upcoming releases, bonus material, and other fun stuff, sign up for Melissa's newsletter **here**.

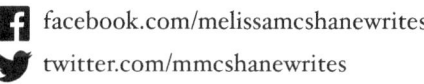

facebook.com/melissamcshanewrites

twitter.com/mmcshanewrites

ALSO BY MELISSA MCSHANE

Emissary

Warts and All: A Fairy Tale Collection

The View from Castle Always

www.ingramcontent.com/pod-product-compliance
Lightning Source LLC
Chambersburg PA
CBHW070752280626
47162CB00016B/167